STRAITS OF HELL

DESTROYERMEN

DESTROYERMEN

STRAITS
OF HELL

TAYLOR ANDERSON

A ROC BOOK

ROC
Published by the Penguin Group
Penguin Group (USA) LLC, 375 Hudson Street,
New York, New York 10014

USA | Canada | UK | Ireland | Australia | New Zealand | India | South Africa | China
penguin.com
A Penguin Random House Company

First published by Roc, an imprint of New American Library,
a division of Penguin Group (USA) LLC

First Printing, May 2015

LIBRARY OF CONGRESS CATALOGING-IN-PUBLICATION DATA:

Anderson, Taylor, 1963–
    Straits of hell / Taylor Anderson.
       pages cm.—(Destroyermen)
    "A ROC BOOK."
    ISBN 978-0-451-47061-4
    I. Title.
    PS3601.N5475S73 2015
    813'.6—dc23   2014043672

Printed in the United States of America
10   9   8   7   6   5   4   3   2   1

Set in Minion
Designed by Alissa Rose Theodor

To: Silvia—for everything.

For: "Taffy-3." Whenever anyone says something to the effect that "nobody would ever go up against odds that long," I just shake my head and say, "Taffy-3." If they know what I'm talking about, they say "Oh. Oh, yeah." If they don't, they should definitely educate themselves. When they do, they will know why no imaginary scenario I could ever conjure up can truly equal the "long odds" some very real young Americans once actually faced.

ACKNOWLEDGMENTS

Thanks again to Russell Galen, a great friend and the best agent anybody could ever have. Thanks particularly to Anne Sowards, who graciously agreed to jump into the middle of all this and become my new editor. I can't begin to say how great she's been or how much I appreciate her. Fred Feidler did the first read once (or twice or thrice) over again, and kept me from making more dopey mistakes than usual. Mark Wheeler and Col. Dave Leedom, USAFR, still help me "keep 'em flying." Electronic and comm tech advice still flows freely from my dad, Dr. Don Anderson. Dennis Petty, Mark Beck, Eric Holland, Gordon Frye, Lynn Kosminski, Kate Baker, Pete Hodges, Ron Harris, Robin Clay, and many more continue to support me with their friendship, contribute their time, or inspire me with memories and . . . anecdotes. (Jim Goodrich, in particular, keeps the amusing anecdotes coming. A certain "swarm" of wildly selfish little piggies that demonstrated amazingly Grik-like behavior springs to mind.) Matthieu Buisine has recently joined my "bullpen" of advisors, and his input, along with that of all the great folks who visit my Web site (taylorandersonauthor.com) will be increasingly crucial as the tale steams into even stranger waters. Last, but absolutely not least, I would also like to thank Jane Steele, who hands down is the best copy editor it has ever been my pleasure to work with.

CAST OF CHARACTERS

(The following does not necessarily reflect initial or even final deployments, but only those most pertinent to the events described.)

See index for details of ships and equipment specifications.

Note:

(L)—*Lemurians, or Mi-Anakka (People) are bipedal, somewhat felinoid folk with large eyes, fur, and expressive but nonprehensile tails. They are highly intelligent, social, and dexterous. It has been proposed that they are descended from the giant lemurs of Madagascar.*

(G)—*Grik, or Ghaarrichk'k, are bipedal reptilians reminiscent of various Mesozoic dromaeosaurids. Covered with fine downy fur, males develop bristly crests and tail plumage, and retain formidable teeth and claws. Grik society consists of two distinct classes, the ruling or industrious Hij, and the worker-warrior Uul. The basic Grik-like form is ubiquitous, and serves as a foundation for numerous unassociated races and species.*

x

At "Grik City" Madagascar

USS *Walker* (DD-163)

Lt. Cmdr. Matthew Patrick Reddy, USNR—Commanding. CINCAF—(Commander in Chief of All Allied Forces).

Cmdr. Brad "Spanky" McFarlane—Exec. Minister of Naval Engineering.

Cmdr. Bernard Sandison—Torpedo Officer and Minister of Experimental Ordnance.

Lt. Tab-At, "Tabby" (L)—Engineering Officer.

Lt. Sonny Campeti—Gunnery Officer.

Lt. Ed Palmer—Signals.

Surgeon Lieutenant Pam Cross

Cmdr. Simon Herring—Office of Strategic Intelligence (OSI).

Ensign Laar-Baa-Ra (L)—PB-1B "Nancy" pilot.

Chief Quartermaster Patrick "Paddy" Rosen—Acting First Officer.

Chief Boatswain's Mate Jeek (L)—Former Crew Chief, "Special Air Division."

Chief Engineer Isak Reuben—One of the "original" Mice.

Gunner's Mate Pak-Ras-Ar, "Pack Rat" (L)

Earl Lanier—Cook.

Johnny Parks—Machinist's Mate.

Juan Marcos—Officer's Steward.

Wallace Fairchild—Sonarman—Anti–Mountain Fish Countermeasures—(AMF-DIC).

Min-Sakir, "Minnie"(L)—Bridge Talker.

Leftenant Doocy Meek—British sailor and former POW (WWI). Now liaison for the Republic of Real People.

Corporal Neely—Imperial Marine Bugler.

Salissa Battle Group

USNRS *Salissa* "Big Sal" (CV-1)

Admiral Keje-Fris-Ar (L)

Atlaan-Fas (L)—Commanding.

Lt. Sandy Newman—Exec.

1st Naval Air Wing

Captain Jis-Tikkar, "Tikker" (L)—"COFO" (Commander of Flight Operations); 1st, 2nd, and 3rd Bomb Squadron, and 1st and 2nd Pursuit Squadrons aboard *Salissa* (CV-1).

Lt. Araa-Faan (L)—Tikker's Aryaalan Exec.

Frigates (DDs) attached: (Des-Ron 6)

USS *Haakar-Faask***

Lt. Cmdr. Niaal-Ras-Kavaat (L)—Commanding.
USS *Tassat***

Captain Jarrik-Fas (L)—Commanding.

Lt. Stanly Raj—"Impie" Exec.
USS *Scott****

Cmdr. Muraak-Saanga (L)—Commanding. (Former *Donaghey* Exec and sailing master).
USS *Nakja-Mur**

Lt. Naala-Araan [Cmdr. Cablaas-Rag-Laan (L) has been reassigned].

MTB-Ron-1 (Motor Torpedo Boat Squadron #1)—5xMTBs (#s 4, 7, 13, 15, 16).

Aef-M (Allied Expeditionary Force—Madagascar).

II Corps

General Queen Safir Maraan (L)—Commanding.

3rd Division

General Mersaak (L)—Commanding. "The 600" (B'mbaado Regiment composed of Silver and Black battalions), Exec 3rd Baalkpan, 3rd, 10th B'mbaado, 5th Sular, 1st Battalion, 2nd Marines, 1st Sular.

6th Division

General Grisa—Commanding.

5th, 6th B'mbaado, 1st, 2nd, 9th Aryaal, 3rd Sular

1st Allied Raider Brigade ("Chack's Raiders," or "Chack's Brigade")

Lt. Col Chack-Sab-At (L)—Commanding—bosun's mate (Marine Lt. Colonel).

21st (combined) Allied Regiment

Major Alistair Jindal—Commanding—Imperial Marine, and Chack's nominal Exec.

1st and 2nd battalions of the 9th Maa-Ni-Laa, 2nd Battalion of the 1st Respite

7th (combined) Allied Regiment

Captain Risa Sab-At (L)—Commanding—(Chack's sister).

2nd and 3rd battalions of the 19th Baalkpan, 1st Battalion of the 11th Imperial Marines

1st Cavalry Brigade

Lt. Colonel Saachic (L)—Commanding.

3rd and 6th Maa-ni-laa Cavalry

SMS *Amerika*

Kapitan Adler Von Melhausen—Commanding.

Kapitan Leutnant Becker Lange—Von Melhausen's Exec.

Adar (L)—Chairman of the Grand Alliance (COTGA), and High Chief and Sky Priest of Baalkpan.

Surgeon Commander Sandra Tucker Reddy—Minister of Medicine, and wife of Captain Reddy.

Diania—Steward's Assistant and Sandra's friend and bodyguard.

Gunnery Sergeant Arnold Horn—USMC—formerly of the 4th Marines (US).

Lieutenant Toryu Miyata—formerly of *Amagi*.

Mission to meet "Ancestral" Lemurians:

Ensign Nathaniel Hardee—Commanding PT-7.

Courtney Bradford—Australian naturalist and engineer. Minister of Science for the Grand Alliance and Plenipotentiary at Large.

Chief Gunner's Mate Dennis Silva

Lawrence "Larry the Lizard"—orange and brown tiger-striped Grik-like ex-Tagranesi (Sa'aaran).

Corporal Ian Miles—Formerly in 2nd of the 4th Marines.

The "Republic of Real People"

Caesar (Kaiser) Nig-Taak

General Marcus Kim—Military High Command.

TFG-2 (Task Force Garrett-2) (Long-Range Reconnaissance and Exploration)

USS *Donaghey* (DD-2)

Cmdr. Greg Garrett—Commanding.

Lt. Saama-Kera, "Sammy" (L)—Exec.

Lt. (jg) Wendel "Smitty" Smith—Gunnery Officer.

Captain Bekiaa-Sab-At—Commanding Marines.

Chief Bosun's Mate Jenaar-Laan

Inquisitor Kon-Choon—Director of Spies for the Republic of Real People.

In Indiaa
Allied Expeditionary Force (North)

General of the Army and Marines Pete Alden—Commanding. Former sergeant in USS *Houston* Marine contingent.

I Corps

General Lord Muln-Rolak (L)—Commanding.

Hij Geerki—Rolak's "pet" Grik, captured at Rangoon.

1st (Galla) Division

General Taa-leen (L)—Commanding.

Colonel Enaak (L) (5th Maa-ni-laa Cavalry)—Exec.

1st Marines, 5th, 6th, 7th, 10th Baalkpan

2nd Division

> **General Rin-Taaka-Ar (L)**—Commanding.
>
> **Major Simon "Simy" Gutfeld (3rd Marines)**—Exec.
>
> 1st, 2nd Maa-Ni-Laa, 4th, 6th, 7th Aryaal

III Corps

> **General Faan-Ma-Mar (L)**—Commanding.
>
> 9th & 11th Divisions composed of the 2nd, 3rd Maa-ni-laa, 8th Baalkpan, 7th & 8th Maa-ni-la, 10th Aryaal

VI Corps

> **General Linnaa-Fas-Ra**—Commanding.
>
> **The "Czech Legion"—Colonel Dalibor SVEC**—Commanding. A near-division-level "cavalry" force of aging Czechs and Slovaks, and their continental Lemurian allies. They are militarily, if not politically, bound to the Grand Alliance.
>
> **Flynn Field**—Primary Army/Navy air base in Indiaa, on the north shore of Lake Flynn, west of Madraas.
>
> **Colonel Ben Mallory**—Commanding.
>
> **Lt. Cmdr. Mark Leedom**—Exec.
>
> 4th 5th, 7th, 8th Bomb Squadrons (PB-1B Nancys), and 3rd, 4th, 5th, 6th Pursuit Squadrons (P-1C Mosquito Hawks "Fleashooters"). The 3rd Pursuit Squadron is composed of 9 Army Air Corps P-40Es.
>
> **Lt. Walt "Jumbo" Fisher**
>
> **Lt. (jg) Suaak-Pas-Ra "Soupy" (L)**
>
> **Lt. Conrad Diebel**
>
> **2nd Lt. Niaa-Saa "Shirley" (L)**
>
> **S. Sergeant Cecil Dixon**

At Madras (Indiaa)

First Fleet North

USS *Santa Catalina* (CAP-1)

> **Lt. Cmdr. Russ Chappelle**—Commanding.
>
> **Lt. Michael "Mikey" Monk**—Exec.

Lt. (jg) Dean Laney—Engineering Officer.

Surgeon Cmdr. Kathy McCoy

Stanley "Dobbin" Dobson—Chief Bosun's Mate.

USS *Mahan* (DD-102)

Cmdr. Perry Brister—Commanding. Minister of Defensive and Industrial Works.

Lt. (jg) Jeff Brooks—Sonarman—Anti–Mountain Fish Countermeasures—(AMF-DIC).

Lt. (jg) Rolando "Ronson" Rodriguez—Chief Electrician.

Taarba-Kaar, "Tabasco" (L)—Cook.

Chief Bosun's Mate Carl Bashear

Ensign Johnny Parks—Engineering Officer.

Ensign Paul Stites—Gunnery Officer.

Arracca Battle Group

USNRS *Arracca* (CV-3)

Tassanna-Ay-Arracca (L), High Chief—Commanding.

5th Naval Air Wing

Frigates (DDs) attached: (Des-Ron 9)

USS *Kas-Ra-Ar***—Captain Mescus-Ricum (L)— Commanding.

USS *Ramic*-Sa-Ar*

USS *Felts***

USS *Naga****

USS *Bowles****

USS *Saak-Fas****

USS *Clark***

At Baalkpan

Cmdr. Alan Letts—Chief of Staff, Minister of Industry and the Division of Strategic Logistics. Acting "Chairman" of the Grand Alliance.

Cmdr. Steve "Sparks" Riggs—Minister of Communications and Electrical Contrivances.

Lord Bolton Forester—Imperial Ambassador.

Lt. Bachman—Forester's aide.

Surgeon Cmdr. Karen Theimer Letts—Assistant Minister of Medicine.

"Pepper" (L)—Black-and-white Lemurian keeper of the "Castaway Cook," (Busted Screw).

Leading Seaman Henry Stokes, HMAS *Perth*—Assistant Director of Office of Strategic Intelligence—(OSI).

Among the Khonashi (North Borno)

"King" Tony Scott

"Captain" I'joorka—Respected warrior and Scott's friend.

Ensign Abel Cook—Commanding Allied Mission.

Imperial Midshipman Stuart Brassey

Moe the Hunter

Pokey—"Pet" Grik brass-picker.

Eastern Sea Campaign

High Admiral Harvey Jenks (CINCEAST)

Enchanted Isles

Sir Thomas Humphries—Imperial Governor at Albermarl.

Colonel Alexander—Garrison commander.

Second Fleet

USS *Maaka-Kakja* (CV-4)

Admiral Lelaa-Tal-Cleraan (L)—Commanding.

Lieutenant Tex Sheider (Sparks)—Exec.

Gilbert Yeager—Engineer; one of the "original" Mice.

3rd Naval Air Wing

(9th, 11th, 12th Bomb Squadrons & 7th, 10th Pursuit Squadrons.) (30 planes assembled, 30 unassembled)

2nd Lt. Orrin Reddy—COFO.

Sgt. Kuaar-Ran-Taak "Seepy" (L)—Reddy's "backseater."

Line of Battle

24 Imperial Ships of the Line Including:

HIMSs *Mars**, *Centurion**, *Mithra*

> *Attached to TF-11 commanded by Imperial **Admiral E. B. Hibbs**

DDs (of note)

USS *Mertz****

USS *Tindal****

USS *Finir-Pel****

> Lt. Haan-Sor Plaar (L)—Commanding.

HIMS *Achilles* Lt. Grimsley—Commanding.

HIMS *Icarus*

> Lt. Parr—Commanding.

USS *Simms****

> Lt. Ruik-Sor-Raa (L)—Commanding.

USS *Pinaa-Tubo* (Ammunition ship)

> Lt. Radaa-Nin (L)—Commanding.

USS *Pecos*—Fleet Oiler.

USS *Pucot*—Fleet Oiler.

Second Fleet Expeditionary Force: (X Corps)—4 regiments Lemurian Army and Marines, 2 regiments "Frontier" troops, 5 regiments Imperial Marines—(3 Divisions) w/artillery train.

General Tomatsu Shinya—Commanding.

Colonel James Blair—Exec.

Major Dao Iverson—Commanding Second Battalion, 6th Imperial Marines.

Nurse Cmdr. Selass-Fris-Ar (L)—"Doc'selass" Daughter of Keje-Fris-Ar.

Capt. Blas-Ma-Ar "Blossom" (L)—Commanding 2nd Battalion, 2nd Marines.

Spon-Ar-Aak "Spook" (L)—Gunner's Mate, and 1st Sgt. of "A" Company, 2nd Battalion, 2nd Marines.

Lt. Staas-Fin "Finny" (L)—"C" Company, 2nd Battalion, 8th Maa-ni-laa.

Lt. Faal-Pel "Stumpy" (L)—"A" Company, 1st Battalion, 8th Maa-ni-la. Former ordnance striker.

Lt. (jg) Fred Reynolds—Formerly Special Air Division—USS *Walker.*

Ensign Kari-Faask (L)—Reynolds's friend and "backseater."

Army of the Sisters

Saan-Kakja (L)—High Chief of Ma-ni-laa and all the Filpin Lands.

Governor-Empress Rebecca Anne McDonald

Sister Audry—Benedictine nun, and commander of El Vengadores de Dios, a regiment raised from penitent Dominion POWs on New Ireland.

Colonel Arano Garcia

Lt. Ezekial Krish

General Ansik-Talaa (L)—Filpin Scouts.

Sergeant "Lord" Koratin (L)—Marine protector and advisor to Sister Audry.

Attached DDs:

HIMS *Ulysses, Euripides, Tacitus*

Enemies

General of the Sea Hisashi Kurokawa—Formerly of Japanese Imperial Navy battle cruiser *Amagi.* Self-proclaimed "Regent" and "Sire" of all India, but currently confined to Zanzibar.

General Orochi Niwa—friend and advisor to General Halik.

"General of the Sky" Hideki Muriname

"Lieutenant of the Sky" Iguri—Muriname's Exec.

Signal Lt. Fukui

Cmdr. Riku—Ordnance.

Grik (Ghaarrichk'k)

Celestial Mother—Absolute, godlike ruler of all the Grik, regardless of the relationships between the various Regencies.

The Chooser—Highest member of his "order" at the court of
the Celestial Mother. Prior to current policy, "choosers" selected those destined for life—or the cook pots—as well as
those eligible for "elevation" to "Hij" status.

Ragak—Regent Consort of Sofesshk.

General Esshk—First General of all the Grik, and acting
Champion Consort to the new Celestial Mother.

General Ign—Commander of Esshk's "new" warriors.

General Halik—Elevated Uul sport fighter.

General Ugla, General Shlook—"Promising" Grik leaders under Halik's command.

Holy Dominion

**His Supreme Holiness, Messiah of Mexico, and by the Grace
of God, Emperor of the World**—"Dom Pope" and absolute
ruler.

Don Hernan DeDivino Dicha—"Blood Cardinal" and new
commander of the "Army of God."

General Ghanan Nerino

League of Tripoli
Representatives at Zanzibar:

(French) Capitaine de Fregate Victor Gravois

Aspirant Gilles Babin

(Spanish) Commandante Fidel Morrillo

(Italian) Maggiore Antonio Rizzo

Teniente Francisco de Luca

(German) Oberleutnant Walbert Fiedler

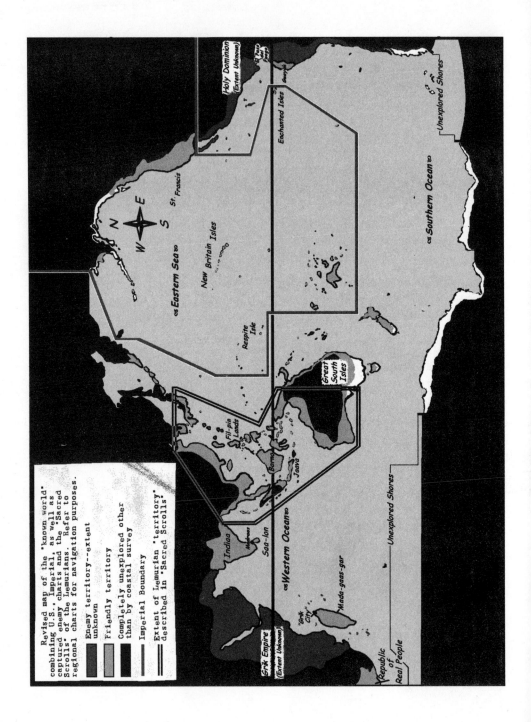

Revised map of the "known world"
combining U.S. Imperial, as well as
captured enemy charts and the "Sacred
Scrolls" of the Lemurians. Refer to
regional charts for navigation purposes.

Enemy territory--extent
unknown

Friendly territory

Completely unexplored other
than by coastal survey

Imperial Boundary

Extent of Lemurian "territory"
described in "Sacred Scrolls"

Grik Empire
(Extent Unknown)

Republic
of
Real People

Holy Dominion
(Extent Unknown)

Unexplored Shores

Enchanted Isles

St. Francis

Southern Ocean

New Britain Isles

Eastern Sea

Respite Isle

Great South Isles

Unexplored Shores

Fil-pin Lands

Borno

Jaava

Indiaa

Saa-lon

Western Ocean

Mada-gaas-gar

W N E S

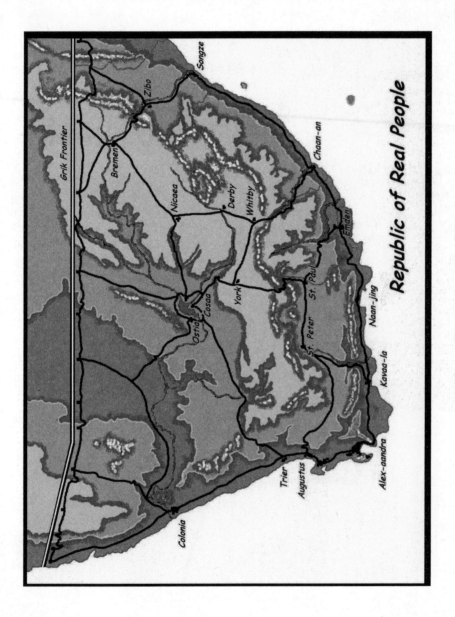

Republic of Real People

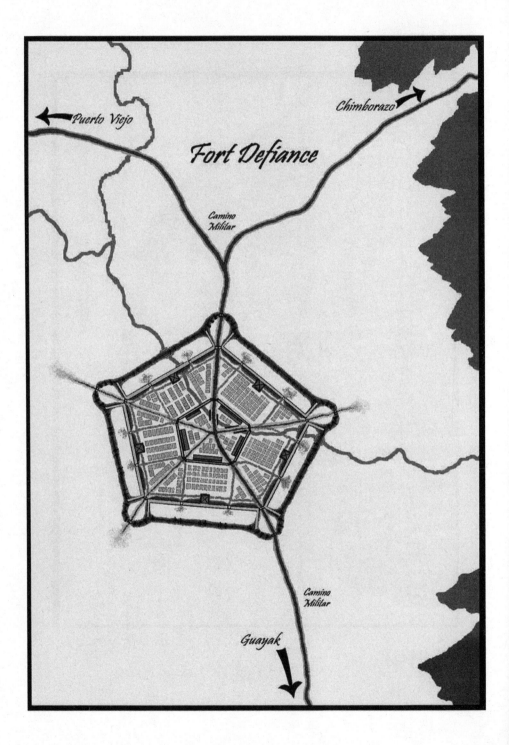

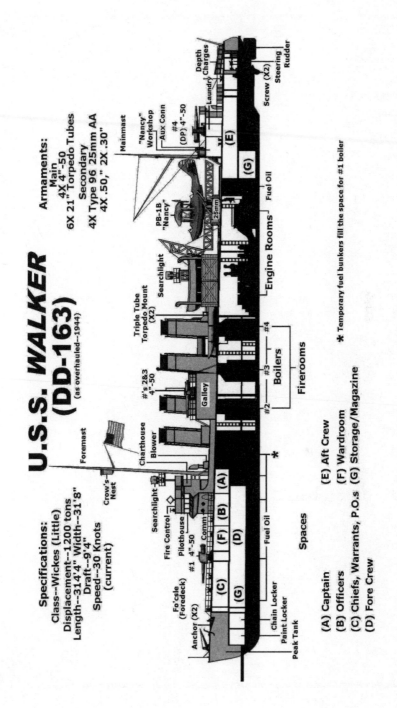

U.S.S. WALKER (DD-163)

(as overhauled--1944)

Specifications:
Class--Wickes (Little)
Displacement--1200 tons
Length--3144" Width--31'8"
Draft--9'4"
Speed--30 Knots
(current)

Armaments:
Main
4X 4"-50
6X 21" Torpedo Tubes
Secondary
4X Type 96 25mm AA
4X .50," 2X .30"

Foremast

Crow's Nest

Charthouse

Blower

Searchlight

Fire Control

Pilothouse

Comm

#1 4"-50

Fo'csle (Foredeck)

Chain Locker

Paint Locker

Peak Tank

Anchor (X2)

Fuel Oil

#'s 2&3 4"-50

Triple Tube Torpedo Mount (X2)

Searchlight

Galley

#2   #3   #4

Boilers

Firerooms

*

25mm

PB-1B "Nancy"

Engine Rooms

Mainmast

"Nancy" Workshop

Aux Conn

#4 (DP) 4"-50

Laundry

Fuel Oil

Depth Charges

Screw (X2)

Steering
Rudder

Spaces

(A) Captain
(B) Officers
(C) Chiefs, Warrants, P.O.s
(D) Fore Crew

(E) Aft Crew
(F) Wardroom
(G) Storage/Magazine

(A) (B) (C) (D) (E) (F) (G)

* Temporary fuel bunkers fill the space for #1 boiler

If I have discovered one genuinely profound truth in all my travels and adventures, it is this: mercy is a moral construct that does not exist in nature. No unthinking (as we would define it) creature possesses the merest notion of mercy. Raw nature quite literally subscribes only to the "law of the jungle" in which creatures kill, or are killed, for food, territory, breeding opportunities, and, yes, even pleasure. Those on the world from whence we came who naively maintained that Man is the only animal that kills for pleasure are fools—who have never seen their beloved, sated house cat torment its prey in the most horrid fashion. Their little monster is not hungry, nor does it fear for its life. Its prey, a small bird or mouse, for example, threatens no competition for territory or breeding opportunities. Their sweet pet tortures and kills without pity for amusement alone. Some may call this "instinct," but does that then mean that cruelty is "instinctive"?

Mercy is unknown in the animal kingdom, there or here. What predator will release its prey with a contrite countenance at the sound of a pitiful bleat or the panicked, hungry cries of its young that only it can tend? None whatsoever, for pity's sake, even when to make the slightest effort to slaughter the now-doomed offspring would be the greatest kindness it could do them. And when one mistakenly ascribes benevolent intent to some beast in its natural habitat, what one truly sees is complacency and satiation, even fear of personal injury. It is surely not a moral choice to do no harm.

The notion of "mercy" began simply enough among humans, on our "old world," and is perhaps best defined here as unexpectedly refraining from causing death or harm to another being that either "deserves" to die, or that it is in one's nature—or best interest—to slay. The earliest mention of the word "mercy," to my knowledge, comes to us from the Old Testament, when God spared Lot from the destruction he rained upon

Sodom and Gomorrah. That, however, might be cynically explained as the practice, common at the time, of allowing a few witnesses of a terrible act or massacre to go forth and spread the word of what will happen to others who do not submit to, or obey, a conquering king, warlord—or God. I strive to resist cynicism of that sort as best I can, though the struggle does grow tedious at times. Still, I endeavor to adhere to my own considered definition of mercy, which, simply put, is to avoid killing anything, either beast or sentient being, just because it appears menacing. Some may, on occasion, disagree with my personal judgment regarding whether certain creatures "need" killing, and I confess I may have been mistaken a time or two, but death is so amazingly permanent that I do prefer to "err" on the side of mercy when I can.

So. If mercy is not "natural," then the question would seem to be: from what does it spring? The Grik did not know mercy, as a race, though General Halik once demonstrated surprising restraint when he agreed to an exchange of prisoners. Clearly, that was in his interest at the time, and one might argue that true mercy was no part of his equation. Or was it? Subsequent behavior, addressed later, may pose that question to readers again, or to philosophers of another, gentler time.

Lemurians did not show mercy to their enemies until we taught it to them—but do most understand it even yet? I wonder. Some do. Chack-Sab-At showed it to the beaten Doms on New Ireland, for example, when he had to be tempted to slaughter them all. But Chack was ever remarkable in many ways—and Doms were not Grik. What if they had been? Would any have been spared? Is mercy so selective? Once the most peaceful of races—with some interesting exceptions—Chack's people embraced the warrior's path so quickly and firmly that I still remain at somewhat of a loss to explain it. No doubt they were strongly influenced by self-preservation, the most powerful instinct of all, but their apparently latent talent for war, which we encouraged, argues vigorously for the thesis that their passivity was never instinctual and they were not always as peaceful as when we met—and as their only relatively recent histories suggest. Lemurians are generally good people who understand compassion and friendship, and who are amazingly tolerant of other races with which they share basic values. But I personally witnessed some few displays of what I considered quite uncharacteristic . . . harshness at the time; more like the aforementioned house cat than any thinking being. Granted, they'd had little enough "mercy" shown them across the ages, so the concept must have been difficult for them to grasp. I suspect many showed restraint toward their enemies when occasionally asked, at least at first, only to please us.

Apparently only my human friends from Walker, and then the Empire of the New Britain Isles, fully understood the concept of mercy in those early years to the point that they not only desired it for themselves but were willing to grant it on occasion. Does that mean that humans in general are more devoted to mercy? No. The people of the evil Dominion were human, just like us, but on the whole the "true believers" of their twisted faith behaved just as cruelly as the Grik. If anything, they were worse. And those who did learn mercy—and appreciated it when it was shown them—as evidenced by Arano Garcia and his troops, who swore their oaths to Sister Audry and Governor-Empress Rebecca McDonald, had to throw off entire lifetimes of indoctrination to accept mercy and learn what it was.

Could that be the trick, then? I have no doubt that mercy is a gift from God. He has surely shown me enough of it in my life! But does the understanding of mercy spring forth, fully formed, within our infant hearts? I think not. I have come to believe that no being is born to mercy, but to know it and show it to others, one must first discover it. Perhaps the example must come as God once demonstrated it to Lot. Indeed, the Grand Alliance, which now includes the Union that sprang from a portion of it, has embraced that method a time or two. I would hope it is still possible that the lesson might come as my loving mother gently gifted it to me. But either way, if instruction truly is the key, it may be that one day we can teach it all across this new world of ours to any being capable of inspiration . . . unless, of course, perpetually assailed as we are by merciless foes, we ultimately forget all about mercy ourselves.

Courtney Bradford, *The Worlds I've Wondered*
University of New Glasgow Press, 1956

///// *Zanzibar*
Airfield #1
Near Menai Bay

"I am . . . uncomfortable with this meeting, my lord," General of the Sky Hideki Muriname cautiously admitted to Hisashi Kurokawa. The small, narrow-faced, balding officer had been *Amagi*'s last surviving pilot for her sole remaining Type 95 floatplane, and he'd since created an air fleet of dirigibles and helped train countless aircrews for their Grik allies. He'd also been responsible for creating an entirely different—secret—air force for Hisashi Kurokawa, and the stress of that might have contributed more to his baldness than anything else. He gauged the reaction of the brooding . . . madman who stood beside him (even Muriname no longer doubted Kurokawa was mad), who had become, for all intents and purposes, his emperor on this world. A furious grimace split Kurokawa's round face, and Muriname instinctively prepared for one of his leader's signature vitriolic rants. Instead, he watched with mounting relief as Kurokawa visibly controlled his rage and his expression changed to a rational frown. Lately, he'd been managing that more often than not. Muriname had to admit that his lord, mad or not, was a brilliant man—and an extraordinarily capable survivor. That their current situation was so much better than he could've dared hope just a few short months before—almost entirely due to Kurokawa's obsessive, manic determination—was conclusive proof of that. And for better or worse, Muriname knew his own destiny was irrevocably linked to Hisashi Kurokawa's.

Muriname glanced back at the cloudy sky they'd been staring at all morning while Kurokawa contemplated a measured reply, dabbing at the sweat on his forehead with a brilliant white pocket handkerchief. He almost snorted at the sight of it. The Grik had never denied even the most frivolous requests by their Japanese benefactors during their association, and he'd used that openhandedness to amass far more than handkerchiefs on his "Sovereign Nest" of Zanzibar.

"I confess that I am . . . less than enthusiastic myself, General of the Sky Muriname," Kurokawa finally said, affecting a mild tone. He'd continued using Muriname's Grik title, just as he had his own, "General of the Sea." He'd gotten used to it, and rather enjoyed it now. He still considered himself "Regent of All India" as well, but reasserting that—and more—would have to wait.

"We don't need these strangers!" Commander Riku, head of Ordnance, flared. "We have our own army and navy now"—he bowed to Muriname—"and our own air fleet as well. All better than anything the Americans and their ape-man lackeys—or even the Grik—can muster!"

That was more than likely true, Kurokawa mused, but they'd believed that before. The 354 Japanese survivors of the battle cruiser *Amagi* now gathered on the island had supervised the construction of the Grik war machine from scratch. Since the Grik weren't much interested in keeping records, all it had ever taken to shift untold tons of material, supplies, new machinery, and labor all over the place to build artillery, munitions, and mighty fleets of ships and dirigibles, was a Japanese project supervisor's word, or short note. That such a large percentage of all that—in addition to what the "Jaaphs" overtly asked for—had quietly gone from the very beginning to Zanzibar would've come as a great surprise to First General Esshk and the Celestial Mother. Of course, Kurokawa had added even more to their hoard by intercepting every Grik ship and warrior sent to Madras to aid General Halik for the past several months, and without long-range communications, the Grik had no idea. The convoys had finally stopped, however, just a few weeks before, and that left him wondering whether the Grik had finally figured out what was happening—or if something else had occurred.

"Our new equipment and weapons *should* be better," Lieutenant Iguri, Muriname's Exec, agreed tightly. "But *enough* better? And largely manned by Grik who still think we aid their vile Celestial Mother!" He looked imploringly at Muriname. "And our pilots . . . !"

Kurokawa kept a placid face as he tamed another inner spike of fury at these men's daring to question, or even discuss, his decisions. But he'd learned that the best way to keep and build their loyalty was to encourage them to invest themselves in his schemes. So long as they ultimately did what he wanted, he could control his anger and project an air of serene confidence. Let them dither and bicker all they wanted. He'd finally perfected the art of persuading men to believe he was wiser than they were yet truly respectful of their ideas. That way, even when he discarded their suggestions, they felt valued, as though they'd contributed and were involved.

"We must seek alliances," Kurokawa declared. "Our power is great, but Lieutenant Iguri is correct: that's largely due to the many Grik we control. The world is too large, and we are too few, to face it all alone," he added with great solemnity. "These strangers do not threaten us— they can't—but they might be of help." He snorted. "And frankly, they have taunted us long enough with their cryptic messages and solicitations. It's time we finally met."

The discussion ended, as it should with such an absolute pronouncement, and the men stood beneath the broad pavilion on the jungle-bordered airstrip, silently sipping refreshments brought by Grik servants. The strip was one of three in the vicinity of the growing installation around what they still called Menai Bay, on the southwest coast of Zanzibar. The island retained its brilliant white beaches, but was considerably larger on this world and the interior jungle was remarkably dense. The airstrips had been difficult to construct, taking tremendous effort to clear and prepare, but "their" Grik troops had provided all the labor required. Responsible for controlling that labor—and the warriors performing it—were other officers, all former members of *Amagi*'s crew, promoted to lofty ranks. Many were present now, quietly conversing nearby in their surprisingly fine Grik-made "temperate white" uniforms. *That was another excellent stroke,* Kurokawa reflected, watching them. *Nice new uniforms—except for the painted-on rank,* he reminded himself, with a splash of annoyance. *But Grik embroidery is deplorable, and it's the symbol that matters, after all. Even* Amagi's *lowliest seamen have some rank now, and it makes no difference if they only outrank Grik. A little power is enough to "invest" them too—and make them want more.* He smiled.

Turning to Muriname, he waved at the long row of aircraft lining the north side of the runway, their dull paint shiny with dew under a brief beam of sunlight. "They are wonderful, General of the Sky! I never tire of looking at them! The lovely green color and glorious, undefiled *hinomaru*! You have outdone yourself."

Muriname recognized the backhanded compliment. His first aircraft had been dirigibles—quite an achievement—but filled with hydrogen, they'd been very vulnerable in combat. He also knew Kurokawa hadn't been pleased when he added Grik swords to the otherwise Japanese insignia on the big airships. He'd done it to inspire his Grik crews to think it symbolized *them*—and it worked. Over time, the modified rising sun flag had been embraced by all the Grik at sea and in the sky, and Kurokawa had grudgingly accepted it. Now, however, even the simple red disk was recognized by the Grik as their own (red had always symbolized the Celestial Mother, after all), and Muriname had been more than happy to revert to it on his new aircraft.

"You have done well," Kurokawa decreed.

"Thank you, Lord. I apologize that they were not ready sooner. Perhaps they might have . . ." He stopped, preferring not to remind Kurokawa that they hadn't been available for the disastrous battles around Madras. A few had been complete, after more than a year of development, but large-scale production had been delayed by everything from problems with the radial engines, to the rubberlike material they needed for tires—from Madras. Commander Riku had certainly taken his time developing something to arm them with as well. "They're monoplanes, of course," Muriname continued, "but you can certainly see the fuselage shape of the Type Ninety-five floatplane we used as a pattern so extensively. I also incorporated many aspects of the Mitsubishi A Five M, Type Ninety-six, as best I could from memory, as I'm sure you've noticed. The elliptical wing and wheel pants, for instance. There is even a cowling for the engine, made of thinly rolled steel," he added proudly.

"Indeed," Kurokawa vaguely agreed. He cared little for the details of the planes, but was impressed by their existence—and Muriname's enthusiasm. And of course the last comment reminded him of how far their steel-rolling capabilities had advanced, and that had countless applications. The planes were mostly wood and fabric, and he doubted they'd ever have aluminum. But they were doing wonderful things with the hoard of reasonably good steel he'd secretly sent from Madras. "You know," he continued, "I had seen your sketches, and with their open cockpits and fixed landing gear, they look much like the new American planes. The first time I saw them, I thought you had surprised me with some of these!" His smile vanished. "Until they attacked."

"I had already left Madras, on your orders, when the new American planes came," Muriname reminded him. "I did not see them. From descriptions, however, I'm certain these will outperform them."

"Even with Grik at the controls?" Kurokawa probed, and Muriname hesitated, looking hard at Iguri. His executive officer had been against teaching Grik to fly anything but the suicide bombs they dropped from the dirigibles to an almost insubordinate degree, but they'd finally managed to contrive a seating arrangement adapted to Grik physiology. They *crouched* inside the fuselage, strapped to a saddlelike seat, and operated rudder controls in the *back* of the cockpit. The stick and other controls remained unchanged. It was awkward, and aircraft so configured couldn't be operated by humans, but it worked.

"The smarter ones fly well enough," Muriname defended with another glance at Iguri. "And we can't spare enough of our people from their industrial pursuits to form more than a core of pilots to build our squadrons around. I believe we have woefully misjudged the . . . intellectual potential of the Grik in the past. Only now, after the programs you initiated that allowed them to achieve mental as well as physical maturity, do we begin to see what they're capable of." He shrugged. "They make . . . adequate pilots, though they are, of course, difficult to train. And they have trouble with certain physical stresses of flight." He brightened. "I suggest they will make excellent pilots for the twin-engine bomber I have proposed."

"But you cannot assure me they will be a match for the enemy fighters in those." Kurokawa waved at the planes.

"With our better machines, they should do well," Muriname temporized, "and they will be more than a match for the enemy floatplanes that have plagued us so. And few as they are, our Japanese pilots will have no trouble with the American fighters, against human or Lemurian pilots." He looked at Kurokawa and the other officers. "I . . . doubt we can compete with the enemy's *modern* aircraft, their P-Forties, but they can't have many of those and they won't last long."

"Very interesting. An honest assessment, as usual," Kurokawa said, looking at the sky and calculating. "And I'm sure you're right, General of the Sky," he agreed, much to Muriname's surprise and relief. "We have little to fear from the P-Forties. They proved decisive at Madras, but I cannot imagine how the enemy could ever get them here. I doubt they can be configured to land on the enemy carriers, so they must operate from airfields like this—and there is no such thing even remotely nearby."

"How indeed." Muriname paused, glancing back over his own row of planes. "To slightly change the subject, my lord: clearly, I'm quite proud of them, but . . . are you sure we should display our latest aircraft to these strangers we wait to meet? I understand you want to impress them, but should we not conceal our strengths? I doubt they will be so open with us."

Kurokawa hesitated, absorbing the implied criticism with difficulty but granting Muriname's point. He took a breath. "We will not show them everything, General of the Sky, but since they are *flying* here to meet us, we must demonstrate we are their equals—not mere suppliants. If they can fly as far as it seems they have, then we must show ourselves equally capable. At no point can we let them sense that we actually *need* them, and we must stress always how much they need us."

Signal Lieutenant Fukui strode quickly under the pavilion from the radio shack nearby and braced to attention. "My lord!" he cried. "I received the expected request for a low-power, high-frequency transmission."

"You sent it?"

"Hai!"

"As we suspected, they obviously have sophisticated radio direction-finding capabilities," Muriname said. "And they must be quite close." Almost immediately, they began to hear a dull rumble, and everyone, including the "tame" Grik servants, craned their necks to the sky. Shortly, a large shape appeared, circling in from the southwest, and Kurokawa nodded in satisfaction. The strangers were approaching over the harbor where his impressive fleet lay at anchor. Some of the ships, his "dreadnaughts," had proven somewhat disappointing, but he'd been working hard to improve them and they were remarkably large; bigger than most "old world" battleships. The plane drew closer, and he recognized it as a three-engine transport of a style ubiquitous for a decade before the war back home. He couldn't tell if it was the German or Italian version, a J-U . . . something or other, or . . . whatever the other one was. They looked so much alike, and it didn't really matter. He'd find out soon, no doubt.

It began to drizzle as the big low-wing trimotor circled the airfield, then swept almost gracefully down toward the strip. Kurokawa saw the corrugated metal skin, and the designation "Ju-52" suddenly popped into his mind. *German, then,* he mused. The markings were Italian, though—at least he thought so—and other, unfamiliar markings had been added. The paint scheme was a brown-and-tan camouflage pattern, and he wondered if that was a clue to their source. *Impossible to say. If they are Italian, they could be from somewhere in Italian East Africa—or as far as Italy itself. A long distance, either way.* The latter was farther than the plane could fly without refueling, he realized, and the former was impossible—wasn't it? According to his understanding of Grik holdings in Africa, Arabia, and until recently, India, Italians *couldn't be* in East Africa without First General Esshk knowing about it . . . could they? And if Esshk had known . . . The trimotor touched down, bounced, then settled as it lost speed. Kurokawa hadn't allowed for an ostentatious greeting ceremony, but the pavilion full of officers had drawn the pilot's attention and the plane taxied back in its direction. He noted with annoyance that the plane, far heavier than anything the airstrip had been designed for, was leaving ruts that would have to be leveled.

The drizzle increased and became a typical afternoon deluge. For a while, the plane just sat there with muddy grass on its wheels, the engines winding down to a stop, and the exhaust stacks ticking and hissing, while the Japanese remained under cover. Kurokawa actually chuckled, a sound that drew several concerned looks. *Let them fret,* he thought. *It really is rather funny. Neither of us is willing to go to the other in the rain.*

Eventually the torrent eased, and a large cargo door opened in the plane's fuselage. A ladderlike step arrangement unfolded from inside, and four men stepped down on the wet, prickly grass. Kurokawa noted they all wore similar dress—rather faded, yellowish tan bush jackets and darker trousers—but a few differences were striking. Three of the men wore tall boots, but two wore brown and one wore black. The fourth man had scuffed shoes and puttees. All wore pistol belts, but these were different colors too. Most unusual of all, each man wore a distinctly different hat, from overseas caps to pith helmets—which also struck Kurokawa as rather amusing. His amusement didn't last, however, when he saw that the visitors were not gaping around with curiosity or interest; they were very calmly, intently, watching him. *Waiting.*

He glanced at the sky. The rain had passed, evolving into a heavy haze of moisture-laden air. "Well, let us see what we have here," he said, suddenly nervously furious enough to let his voice ring harshly. He stepped forward, followed by his immediate staff. Only then did the visitors move forward as well. Two other men, apparently pilots, appeared in the door of the plane but didn't step down. Instead, they merely sat, their feet dangling in the air. *Even they wear different hats!* Kurokawa told himself, attempting to lighten his mood. It didn't work. When they drew within a few feet, the visitors finally saluted. With some hesitation, Kurokawa returned the gesture, followed by his officers.

"Ah," said the tallest of the four strangers. He wore a round-topped hat with a patent leather brim and displayed a thin mustache. "You must be Monsieur Kuro. . . ." He paused and smiled apologetically. "Monsieur 'General of the Sea' Kurokawa! It is an honor to meet you in person at last. It is I, Capitaine de Fregate Victor Gravois, who has been responsible for contacting you in the past!"

"I am he," Kurokawa answered in the same English the visitor used. *They already know so much about us, including who—and where!—we are, which is disconcerting enough, but how does he know my name, my title, and that I speak English?* His mind raced.

"Excellent! Then please allow me to present my colleagues." The man gestured at the thin, dark-haired man beside him. "This is Maggiore Antonio Rizzo, of the Italian Aeronautica Militaire. No doubt he will find your aircraft interesting, should you care to let him see them more closely."

"It would be my great pleasure to examine them," Rizzo said, also in English.

"I am Commandante Fidel Morrillo," said an equally thin man with blond hair, not waiting to be introduced, "and I have the honor to serve the Spanish Nationalist Army."

Kurokawa nodded at him, blinking surprise.

"And this," Gravois added smoothly, indicating the fourth and youngest man standing, "is Aspirant Gilles Babin, my aide. Maggiore Rizzo's aide, Teniente de Luca, is one of our pilots"—he frowned, glancing back—"as is the representative of our German allies, Oberleutnant Fiedler," he added almost dismissively.

Kurokawa's racing mind sped up. Here were Frenchmen, Italians, a Spaniard, and a German, who'd all arrived in a German-made plane, all together and apparently friendly despite the obvious undertones of tension. Additionally, the Frenchman seemed to lead the delegation; its German representative had merely waved, somewhat sullenly, when he was named. Most bizarre. "You are welcome, gentlemen," he managed, and named his staff. When that was complete, he invited them under the pavilion for refreshments, and to avoid the rain that had fitfully resumed. Kurokawa was interested to see that the strangers were not surprised, or even overly nervous about the Grik servants. Obviously, they not only knew about Grik, but they also knew they could be "domesticated." Conversation was light but increasingly frustrating. The flight had been "long and uncomfortable," but there was no mention of its origin. The climate was "wetter here" than what the visitors were accustomed to. The nectar the Grik servants brought had a most "vigorous" flavor.

Never one for small talk, or much of anyone's talk but his own, Kurokawa felt his neck grow increasingly hot. Finally, he could help himself no longer. "I've long been extremely curious," he said, "ever since we received your first transmission. . . ." He paused, clasping his hands behind his back, and then blurted, "Just who and what are you, Captain Gravois?"

Gravois dabbed at his mustache with one of the handkerchiefs that seemed to be in such abundance. "To business so soon? I had thought we might take a little longer to simply enjoy the wonder of meeting new friends on this outlandish, savage world. No?" He sighed. "Who I am, I have told you, General of the Sea Kurokawa. It is I with whom you have communicated. My duty for the service I represent is that of . . . let us say 'analysis.'" He smiled. "And now envoy as well!"

"But . . . you apparently know a great deal about us—about *me*," Kurokawa said, heroically masking his growing rage and frustration. "Yet we know virtually nothing about you!"

"All in good time! We will tell you everything you wish to know, within reason, of course. To exchange information and establish friendly relations is why we came, after all. At present, I will simply say that my colleagues and I represent several . . . powers that have joined together for our mutual benefit and protection. I won't go into the background of it all just now, as you may find it extraordinarily confusing, but you may call us the 'League of Tripoli.' From that you may even deduce our origins on this world. . . ." Gravois smiled engagingly. "Or perhaps not. It matters little to you now in any event, and no doubt you are familiar with the circumstances of our arrival, having endured the same yourself—as all *real* people have. But our time here has been somewhat longer than yours, and slightly less contentious in some respects, allowing greater leisure to consolidate, grow, and begin looking around for friends—and enemies."

"You have enemies?"

"Of course! As well as friends. We always seek new friends."

"You are obviously aware that I—that *we*—have enemies," Kurokawa ground out. "Perhaps you have also seen how well I have prepared to face them again?"

"Impressive ships," Rizzo said, addressing Kurokawa for the first time since their initial exchange. "But how capable? Capitaine Gravois is a better judge of that than I, no doubt. Your new aircraft, on the other hand, appear a great improvement over your last attempts—though even dirigibles have their place." His last words sounded speculative.

Kurokawa could no longer hide his fury. "How *can* you know so much! How can you be so dismissive of my power, through a few short transmissions—and perhaps what you might have monitored. You cannot have known the things—the dirigibles, where we are, my *name*"—he stopped, staring directly at Gravois—"unless you have *spied* on us!"

"*I* have not spied, General of the Sea," the Frenchman stated soothingly, "but the League has eyes in as many places as it can put them. We must protect ourselves, as I have said. I merely analyze the information brought to me, about you, the Grik, others you do not know, and your primary enemies, of course. It is they and the Grik that make us most interested in you, as it turns out." He looked around, finding a chair. "May I sit?" Kurokawa nodded sharply and found a seat himself. Gravois sighed when he was settled. "Allow me to briefly summarize your situation, as I see it. Feel free to correct me at any point if I am mistaken. When I am done, I will go into more detail about the League."

"Very well."

Gravois sipped his nectar and smiled. "*Bon.* Now, where to begin? Ah. Your Imperial Japan was principally at war with the British, American, and Russian empires—"

"Not the Soviets!" Kurokawa pounced.

"Soviets?"

"The Russians, as you call them."

Gravois glanced at his colleagues, but the smile never left his face. "Indeed," he said, "such a major difference so quickly," he added cryptically.

"And proof you do not know everything!" Kurokawa almost gloated.

"And perhaps proof that there is a great deal about the nature of the event that brought us all here that *you* do not yet know, Monsieur Kurokawa," Gravois countered. "May I continue?"

Angry, but confused, Kurokawa nodded.

"You were at war with . . . some of the same powers that we were in conflict with," Gravois stressed. "And when you arrived here with your mighty battle cruiser, you allied yourself with the reptile folk. Entirely understandable, in your situation." He waved expansively. "And you have done amazingly well, considering what you had to start with. I commend you! The League commends you! Unfortunately, you have suffered a series of . . . misfortunes, that not only cost you your excellent ship and a majority of your crew, but a rather impressive fleet—and several armies of reptiles as well." He gestured around again. "You have rebuilt with astonishing speed and resourcefulness but have apparently withdrawn from your alliance with the reptiles and contracted into what is, of necessity, a principally defensive posture. What is more, your primary enemy, this 'American'-led alliance—of more powers than you might perhaps be aware—not only remains on the march, but has likely conquered the very capital of your former reptilian allies on Madagascar by now!"

"That's impossible!" Iguri blurted, and Kurokawa glared at him.

"Quite possible, I assure you," Gravois countered. "Even probable, given the transmissions we have monitored and certain . . . observations that were made, regarding the course of one of their fleets." He arched his eyebrows. "That, and the fact that apparently a major battle was fought, and we are still intercepting transmissions from that direction. Most are in code, of course," he said, waving the fact aside, "but we can deduce enough to be relatively sure that the action was at least partially successful for your enemies."

"Observations? Deductions?" Kurokawa demanded.

Gravois shrugged. "We were . . . observing with a submarine," he confessed, "that we have since lost contact with. I fear it may have run afoul of one of the monstrous fishes in this terrible sea." He cocked his head and smiled. "I don't suppose it has turned up here?"

They lost a submarine and treat it like a minor inconvenience—or is that just what they want me to think? "It did not. And if it was tracking a fleet under his protection, I consider it most likely of all that Captain Reddy sank it with his tiny destroyer!" Kurokawa almost gloated again. *What's the matter with me? Why should I antagonize these people? And I certainly should not relish any success achieved by my most mortal foe!*

Gravois glanced at Rizzo, then back. "That is a distinct possibility. The commander of the submarine had orders not to interfere with the Allied fleet unless he was certain it was in a position to threaten the reptile capital directly, and even then he was only authorized to . . . discourage it. Perhaps sink something important." He sighed. "The 'little destroyer,' as you call it, may indeed have destroyed our vessel. My analysis of Captain Reddy has painted him—and his people—as disconcertingly capable, and his ship *was* reported to be the primary escort of the Allied fleet." He sipped again.

"But . . . why should you want to 'discourage' Captain Reddy and protect the Grik capital? Are you allied with them?" Kurokawa demanded at last, voicing his chief concern that had been building as the discussion progressed. These people *could* have come from Italian East Africa, and General Esshk probably *would* have kept them secret from him if he could, particularly after their falling-out over Kurokawa's insistence that Regent Tsalka be destroyed. . . .

Gravois and Rizzo both laughed, and even Commandante Morrillo managed a sour smile.

"No, not at all. But . . . they have been allies of *yours*, have they not?" Gravois finally frowned. "The reptiles, the 'Grik' as you call them, are savages. You have done well to arm them enough to assist you, but not well enough to surpass you. With additional sophistication added to their numbers, they could become a threat even to the League." Rizzo leaned forward. "As could the Americans and their strange allies," he assured fervently, "perhaps even more quickly."

Kurokawa shook his head. "This is maddening. You contacted *me* with an offer of 'assistance,' yet the greatest assistance you could've given would have been to destroy Captain Reddy and his ship. You did not. You lost a valuable submarine 'protecting' the Grik—whom you do not want to win this war—from a 'more dangerous power,' which you do not want to attack unless they threaten the Grik! It makes no sense!"

"It makes perfect sense from our perspective, señor," Morrillo said, as impatient with Gravois as Kurokawa. "From all we've learned, the League of Tripoli is the greatest single power on this planet. And we have . . . considerable forces at our disposal. We even have aircraft, as you can see. We have been here longer than you, but what we still need most of all is time—time to build a lasting civilization of not only people, but the *right kind* of people, on this world. We cannot get directly involved here at present because we have other commitments—and frankly it is quite far. What we do *not* want is for the Americans and their . . . animal minions to gain supremacy in this part of the world. Nor do we want the reptiles to do so. That is in our own self-interest."

"What is also in our interest, is your survival, General of the Sea Kurokawa," Rizzo assured. "That you and your people not only survive, but thrive—and ultimately dominate this region—the entire world!— hand in hand with the League of Tripoli!" Rizzo glanced at Gravois, then leaned forward again, earnest. "There are . . . differences you will learn about, between the worlds we came from, your people and ours, but most of us were fighting the same war, for the same reasons. We were on the same side there, and should be here. We do not want the Americans or the Grik to win out here. We want *you* to win, and we will do what we can to help!"

"Different worlds?" Kurokawa almost shrilled. He wasn't keeping up with this well at all, and he was furious to see Muriname nodding slightly as if he understood every word. He shook his head. "But if the enemy has taken Madagascar, he has won the war! Not only that, he is within striking distance of *me*!"

"Your enemy has *not* won the war, General of the Sea Kurokawa," Gravois insisted. "And even if he's taken Madagascar, he will be amazingly lucky to keep it. Believe me, sir, we cannot possibly explain everything you want to know in one sitting—our greatest help to you for now will be information, after all—so may we adjourn to a more comfortable setting? Once there—and as your guests for some time, I should hope—we will address every question we are authorized to answer. During that time you will learn why it is in the League's interest to aid you—in what small ways you might require—against our common foes."

////// *"Grik City" Madagascar*
USS **Walker**
August 22, 1944

*T*he dreams were back. New ones. Bad ones. They differed from the ones that used to leave him anxious and sweating when he awoke, but those, in retrospect, weren't quite as painful. They'd been less frequent and faded quickly from his mind. Moreover, he generally recovered from the . . . sense of them as the day wore on. These were worse, as far as Matthew Reddy was concerned, because they stayed with him even when he woke—and they were so real! It was as if his eyes had been motion-picture cameras at the time, and he saw the awful images again and again, projected on his closed lids when he slept—and in his mind's eye just as clearly when he didn't. He didn't *dread* sleep; he had to have it and nobody got enough these days, but he'd quit sacking out on the cot in the charthouse behind the bridge. He didn't know if the dreams made him shout. It would be bad enough if his officers heard him but possibly catastrophic if the replacement enlisted hands did. That left only the short, sweaty naps he managed in his cramped, sweltering stateroom, where he could relive alone that terrible day when they, or rather *he*, nearly lost it all—and he'd still lost a lot.

He slept soundly on the rare occasions he joined his wife, Sandra, aboard *Big Sal*; the dreams weren't quite as bad then. Perhaps her touch, her mere proximity, took him to a more relaxed, less anxious state. He recognized that a recurring theme in the dreams was a sense of isolation, even abandonment. That was understandable. His old Asiatic Fleet "four-stacker" destroyer, USS *Walker* (DD-163), hadn't just been separated from the rest of a reeling navy after Pearl Harbor, the Philippines, and the disastrous battle of the Java Sea; she'd been swept to an entirely different world. That was bad enough, but he'd come to grips with it. They'd made friends, forged alliances, and helped create the means to resist multiple foes even more implacable than the Japanese. But USS *Walker*, beat-up and rebuilt again and again, always found herself in the thick of the action—too often by herself. That was getting old, particularly after the last time, when she grounded on a sandbar in the harbor of the principal city of her most ferocious foe, the Grik. All alone she'd fought, the tide going out and wave upon wave of furry/feathery, reptilian Grik swarming against her side and eventually across her deck. That was what he dreamed about—the terrible, lonely, bloody chaos of it all.

By itself, that shouldn't have really bothered him either, he thought. He was used to the sights, sounds, smells, and terror of desperate combat. What he wasn't accustomed to was the utmost anguish and mounting horror of complete and final failure. Miraculously, they *hadn't* failed, and in spite of everything, they'd clawed yet another victory from the literal jaws of defeat. But he couldn't shake the *sense* of it—that their victory was only transitory. That anxious urgency, that . . . doubt . . . as well as a harsh, fresh grief over a very personal loss—was what nagged him now.

Sandra helped. Being with her and enjoying the wonder of the new life stirring in her womb distracted him. But in the aftermath of the battle for Grik City, those visits were rare. There was too much to do, to prepare for, and Sandra was just as busy with all the wounded that the battle had provided her medical corps. He sighed, shifting on his grass-stuffed mattress in the boxy bed frame in the dark. Soon, he'd lose even the relief Sandra gave him if all went right in the morning staff meeting, and he dreaded the argument to come. He wanted her gone to protect her, of course, her and the child she carried. But he really had to get the wounded out of Grik City as well. They were too vulnerable and too many. He'd shamelessly appeal to her duty to them and their child, if he had to, and doubted even her legendary stubborn streak could overcome that combination. There'd be a fight, though . . . and he already missed her.

"Damn it," he muttered, sitting up and flinging the damp pillow away. The dream had killed his sleep, and his racing mind had left him too restless to even allow his tired muscles the recovery they deserved. He leaned forward so the meager circulation of the clattering fan could play across his sweaty face and neck. "I need a shrink," he snorted aloud.

Probably every ship's captain since the beginning of ships with crews has had to be an amateur shrink of some kind, he told himself. *Making people do dangerous things or go places they'd never go if given an honest choice has probably always taken a lot of psychology. Particularly if the voyage ends in fighting a battle that nobody in his right mind would want any part of.* He sighed again. *And we've been in the middle of a fight we never wanted, right up to our necks, for two and a half years. No leave, no downtime, hardly any real liberty . . . It's a wonder any of us is sane.*

He brushed back greasy hair with his fingers, doubting he'd ever deliberately engaged in manipulative shrinkery beyond what was required of any ship's captain in his situation. "Like that's ever happened," he snorted aloud, but quickly grew angry at his own self-pity. *Enough of that! What good does it do for the shrink to shrink his own head?*

He rubbed his eyes and looked around in the gloom. All he'd done was his duty, as he saw it, and that was all he expected of others. But he knew the main reason he felt abandoned and isolated. They, all of First Fleet South and its expeditionary force, were on the creaking end of a very long limb, surrounded by enemies and ridiculously outnumbered. Common sense declared they ought to pull out and regroup. The problem was, if they did that—simply surrendered Madagascar back to the Grik—everybody they'd lost taking the damn place would've died for nothing. Even worse, Matt honestly didn't believe they'd ever quit running once they started. His . . . analysis told him they'd reached a psychological, if not numerical tipping point in the war, at least against the Grik. They'd hammered them like they'd never been hammered before, and he knew in his gut that if they just kept slugging, kept smashing whatever the Grik sent at them here in their own backyard, they had to break eventually. Madagascar was only a tiny part of the Grik Empire, but it was the capital, as they reckoned such things. And after all the reversals the "invincible" Grik had suffered, even before they lost this place and their "Celestial Mother," they *had* to be getting brittle . . . didn't they? He closed his eyes. *As a nutty Captain Shrink, I know* we're *getting brittle. It's the tipping point, all right, and it can go either way.*

Flipping the light switch, he stood to face himself in the little mirror above the sink. He saw the stubble on his face and premature (he thought) silver spreading from his temples to infest the rest of his brown hair. Red rims around his green eyes bore eloquent testimony to his exhaustion. *Barely thirty-five, and I look* old, he lamented, preparing for the day. He knew instinctively that morning GQ was only moments away. His internal clock had become very precise over the last few years. He wet his face, lathered up with the odd-smelling Lemurian soap, and poised his razor. After all this time, he remained one of only a very few of his "original" destroyermen to stay clean shaven. The precedent was so well established by now that if he didn't shave himself, Juan Marcos, Matt's self-proclaimed "personal" steward, would clomp up to the bridge on his wooden leg and do it for him in his very own chair before the end of the watch. He didn't want that. Juan was still hurting after the fight— they all were—and he actually preferred shaving himself. He'd always believed he did it for the men, to show them that no matter how bad or downright weird things got, some things would remain unchanged. That continuity spanned all they'd been through, and in some ways even carried them back to the world they'd left and many loved on the China Station, in the "old navy" before the war. Staring at his reflection and suddenly contemplating "shrinkery" once again, he wondered how long he'd been doing it more for himself than for anyone else.

The squalling, tortured goose of the general alarm sounded as he finished dressing and adjusting his hat on his head. He gritted his teeth. The alarm had been going downhill for a long time, having even been sunk once, after all, but now . . . it was becoming unbearable. He was going to have to talk to Spanky or Tabby, or *anybody* who could come up with a replacement. Honestly, with all the technical miracles they'd cooked up over the last few years, how hard could it be? He sincerely hoped the alarm wasn't being retained for nostalgia or somebody's amusement, because it really wasn't funny anymore. He'd held off personally requesting that something be done, particularly with all the repairs *Walker* had needed after her latest fight, but he was just about ready to take that step.

With a final, skeptical glance in the mirror, he parted the green curtain and stepped quickly into the passageway leading to the companionway, aft. Mounting the steps, he emerged behind the bridge, near the main blower, and stopped before he was trampled by Lemurians—"'Cats"—and men trotting past as they headed for their stations. Some of the replacements from other ships, still amazed they'd been chosen for *Walker*, saluted as they passed. Matt shook his head with a sad, hidden smile. It was rightly considered an honor to serve aboard his ship, but it had proven a death sentence for far too many. He paused at the base of the stairs to the bridge and gazed at the predawn spectacle surrounding the old destroyer.

Fires burned everywhere on land, flickering as thick as the sparks that rose above them. They were cookfires for the army, mostly, stirring to the sounds of urgent whistles and drums. A few pyres still burned for the grievously wounded who fell away each day, but those had fortunately diminished. The combined human-Lemurian army occupying Grik City was camped under tents despite the practical shelter that already existed. None could bear to occupy the filthy abodes of their enemy, and they'd been razing the whole place to the ground in any event, using the material it provided to further fortify the city. The only structures left alone were the docks and adjacent warehouses—and the enormous Celestial Palace itself, of course.

The palace was stunning in size, if not architecture. It really did look like a "giant cowflop," as Dennis Silva had described it, though others had said it resembled a "squashed pyramid," since it did kind of have four rather rounded and indistinct corners. Courtney Bradford said it was as big as the Great Pyramid at Giza—even if it did indeed appear a "trifle compressed from the top." It was just as durably built as the Great Pyramids too, constructed of enormous blue-black granite stones that Courtney insisted were indigenous to the island, though they hadn't seen any nearby. Like the massive, ancient wall of rot-resistant Galla trees that stretched for miles and ringed the city like a sharp-peaked range of mountains to keep the wilds of Madagascar at bay, the palace, however hideous, had not been easy to build. Cleaned and brightened inside by knocking out sufficient blocks to provide light and ventilation, the various levels had become a hospital—and might serve fairly well as a fortress once they emplaced sufficient numbers of the big Grik guns (disconcertingly better than they'd seen before) that they'd found in the warehouses.

Matt looked out at the harbor beyond where his ship was docked and saw the dark shapes of First Fleet South moored beyond the protruding wreckage of Grik "dreadnaughts." USNRS *Salissa* (CV-1), was closest, and the largest ship in view. Once a vast, seagoing, sail-driven "Home" for thousands of Lemurians, she'd been converted to the first steam-powered aircraft carrier/tender this world had ever seen. Others followed, and there was a whole new class of purpose-built carriers entering the war. But their deployment was slowed by the necessary training of pilots for their planes at the Army and Naval Air Corps Training Center at Kaufman Field in Baalkpan. Other pilots were trained in Maa-ni-la, but they were all sent east to fight the so-called Holy Dominion.

Beyond *Big Sal* was SMS *Amerika*, a large ocean liner turned auxiliary cruiser from a very slightly different world than even *Walker* left behind. There were still a lot of theories flying around about that, but it was mostly just an intellectual exercise at this point. Where exactly all the various allies who'd joined together on this world came from didn't much matter anymore—or yet—to anyone but Courtney Bradford, who was the source of most of the theories in the first place. Other ships, still darkened for the night, lay at anchor; they were troopships, supply ships, oilers, all both wind and steam powered, as were the frigates (DDs) of Des-Ron 6, patrolling beyond the harbor. Closer in, the four operable PT boats that remained of MTB-Ron 1 took turns scouting the harbor mouth itself, and particularly the deep-water channel. One mystery submarine had cost them the self-propelled dry dock (SPD) *Respite Island*, and they'd remain on the alert for more, however unlikely more might be.

To the northwest, on a narrow finger of land, more fires burned.

Matt shuddered at the thought of their purpose. After the battle, all the Grik that fled the city had wound up there, cut off, and unable or unwilling to continue the fight. Very un-Grik-like behavior. It was possible they'd "fallen prey," after experiencing a condition Bradford referred to as "Grik Rout," but if that was the case, they'd all be dead by now, after an orgy of mindless slaughter. That hadn't happened. They were trapped, and a good-size chunk of II Corps was keeping them that way, but they didn't madly attack, slay one another, or simply leap into the sea. They just sat there. They were *eating* one another, to be sure. That alone was "normal" for starving Grik, but otherwise they seemed prepared to simply . . . wait.

Matt grimaced and stepped into the pilothouse.

"Cap-i-taan on the bridge!" "Minnie" the talker cried in her squeaky voice.

"As you were," Matt said as 'Cats slammed to attention. The only other human there was his exec, Brad "Spanky" McFarlane. He was a short, skinny guy who kept his reddish hair and beard close-cropped. He had a big personality, though, and everyone who met him always remembered him bigger as well. He alone remained relaxed, sitting in Matt's chair, certain Matt would wave him down if he tried to stand. He would have too; Spanky was still on crutches.

"All stations manned and ready, Skipper," Spanky reported. "Extra lookouts are posted, steam's up in numbers three and four, secondary batteries and the dual-purpose four-inch-fifty aft are standing by for air action."

"Very well, Mr. McFarlane."

A few Grik zeppelins had been spotted over the last several days, obviously scouting the situation in the fallen capital. The first came as a big surprise and got away scot-free. The others were quickly shot down by P-1 Mosquito Hawks (better known as "Fleashooters") from *Big Sal*'s 1st Air Wing. The pursuit squadrons of the wing were all flying out of a Grik airship base east of the Celestial Palace, and that was where Captain Jis-Tikkar (Tikker), who was *Big Sal*'s Commander of Flight Operations, or "COFO," kept his HQ. Tikker's pilots made short work of the zeps he'd been warned about by the screening DDs, but based on how many dirigibles the Grik had thrown at them during the campaign for Indiaa, they all expected there'd be a *lot* more around here.

"All hands will remain at battle stations until the forenoon watch, then set condition three." Matt looked at his watch, again thankful the poor thing had survived so much. "I've got time for coffee, but then I've got an early staff meeting aboard *Big Sal*."

Spanky turned in the chair. "Pass the word for coffee." He grinned. "But tell Juan to *send* it up. We ain't got all day."

A bosun's pipe squealed down on the fo'c'sle, calling the boatswain's mates to report, and Matt stiffened.

"Chief Jeek," Spanky explained softly. Already a bosun's mate, Jeek had been chief of *Walker*'s Special Air Division, handling the lone PB-1B "Nancy" observation floatplane she carried. Now he was chief of the starboard division and in line to succeed Chief Bosun Fitzhugh Gray. Nobody, Jeek in particular, thought he could ever *replace* Gray. The Chief Bosun of the Navy, or "Super Bosun" as he'd been called, had been a font of wisdom and an irresistible force of nature. Now he was dead, and his loss left far more than an empty slot that needed filling. He'd been like a father to Matt and many others in various important ways, and his death had torn a hole in Captain Reddy's—and by extension, *Walker*'s—heart. "Only the second or third 'Cat I ever heard learn to blow one o' those things," Spanky continued mildly. "Don't know how he does it, with his lips split like that." He paused, gauging Matt's reaction. "He'll make a good bosun."

"Sure."

Spanky nodded uncomfortably, then snorted. "Gives me the creeps, though. There's no doubt who his role model was, and I nearly jumped outta my skin the first time I heard him!"

"Best role model in the Navy," Matt said simply, and Spanky nodded.

"You said it, Skipper."

Lieutenant Tab-At, *Walker*'s engineering officer, chose that moment to storm into the pilothouse. She'd clearly been aiming for Spanky but hesitated when she saw Matt. He waved her forward. "Beg to report," she practically hissed behind sharp, clenched teeth. Her gray-furred ears were back, and her eyes flashed behind furiously blinking lids like an enraged Morse lamp. Her tail swished so rapidly from side to side beneath her kilt that it was almost a blur.

"Spit it out, Tabby," Spanky invited gruffly, hoping her anger wasn't directed at him. He loved Tabby like a daughter—mostly—but her feelings for him were more . . . straightforward. That could be a strain on both of them at times.

"That . . . idiot *mouse* is still not reported aboard!" she seethed. Matt saw Spanky's relief and knew what he was thinking: *All is well. Tabby's mad at Isak Reuben, not me.*

"Chief Reuben was wounded in the fighting for the Celestial Palace," Matt pointed out. He didn't add that the squirrely little guy was a genuine hero—again—having actually killed the Grik Celestial Mother himself. Granted, he'd done it by default, being the last one able after the rest of the party had fallen wounded or dead along the way. Even the mighty Dennis Silva had lost too much blood to reach the objective. Of the three who did, Irvin Laumer had been killed, and Lawrence, Silva's Grik-like Sa'aaran friend, had been too hurt to raise a weapon. That left Isak.

"He ain't hurt," Tabby countered, slipping further from the English-Lemurian patois that had evolved in the Navy, and much of the Allied military in general. That happened to a lot of 'Cats when they were mad. "Just little skaatches," she continued darkly. "He been m'lingerin' all this time, while there so much repairs!"

Matt did find it odd that Isak hadn't returned to his precious boilers as fast as he could. Maybe he was using his new hero status to push more of the vile cigarettes he and his half brother, Gilbert Yeager, (and a Baalkpan 'Cat named Pepper) had "perfected" from the awful tobacco indigenous to Java. He'd met only limited success with that, since the things were still pretty revolting, and most who used the waxy, yellowish weed—human or Lemurian—preferred to chew it, flavored with a kind of molasses. "What repairs are left, before the ship's ready to get underway?" Matt asked. Tabby looked at him and blinked, distracted from her rant.

"We get underway immediately, Cap-i-taan," she assured him. "The holes are patched, and the ship's not leaking much more than usual. EMs're still wiring in the new main junction box in the aft engine room, but the generator overhaul's done." She made a very human shrug. "There's still a lotta topside damage, and Mr. Saan-di-son says the port torpedo mount might not get fixed. It's shot full'a holes. Maybe we get tubes four an' six working, but number two's a sieve."

"If everything's shipshape, what do you need that little creep Isak for?" Spanky asked, genuinely curious.

"Cause he *b'longs* here," Tabby stated simply, as if that explained everything. Spanky looked at Matt and arched his eyebrows.

"Okay," Matt told Tabby. "Give Bernie all the help on the tubes you can spare. I really *like* having torpedoes." He paused, considering. "And go ahead and round up anybody in the hospital that the docs will cut loose, including Chief Reuben." He looked at Spanky. "*Walker* may need to get underway soon, and you might have to take her out—if you feel up to it."

Spanky nodded. "Just say the word. I'm a little gimpy, but how much running do I need to do?" He smiled strangely. "I kind of saw this coming, you know. After you came down on Adar about our little fiasco"—he waved at the brightening bay—"and how he needs to stick to the big picture. I figured you'd have to take more of the planning load on land as well as sea." He grinned. "Put some of that Academy history degree to work!"

Matt smiled self-consciously. "I hope not, Spanky. I think I proved at Aryaal that I'm not much good at planning big battles on land. But just as I reminded Adar that he's chairman of the Grand Alliance—and this new nation they've cooked up—I'm still commander of all Allied forces, not just the Navy. General Safir Maraan's a great leader and a wildcat in a fight, but she's also proven she can be a bit . . . impulsive." He considered. "She's had time to think about things, and I'll see how she is at the meeting. Worst case, I'll hang around to keep an eye on things until Generals Alden and Rolak get here from Madras." Both of them knew he'd hate that, and they hoped it wouldn't be necessary.

A Lemurian mess attendant finally arrived with the coffeepot, but Matt waved it away. "I'd better get going," he said, glancing at his watch again. "Better coffee on *Big Sal* anyway," he added softly, for Spanky alone.

Chief Jeek and a hastily assembled side party piped Matt over the side, bringing Chief Gray—and the dream he died in—firmly back to mind, and Matt strode quickly down the dock to the waiting motor launch with a grim expression on his face. The morning sky was bright and clear, but a stiff breeze had sprung up, making him clutch his hat to his head. The launch took him, swaying and burbling on the choppy water, out to *Big Sal*. Ordinary whistles piped him aboard after he ascended the long stairway up the great ship's side to the hangar deck above.

"Captain Reddy, good morning, sir!" greeted Commander "Sandy" Newman, *Salissa*'s executive officer. Matt managed a smile. Newman had been a Seaman 2nd on *Walker* when he came to this world, but was assigned here because he'd spent the better part of an enlistment aboard the *Lexington*. That made him one of their few "experts" on carriers. *The few who've survived, from* Walker, Mahan, *and* S-19, *have done okay for themselves,* Matt told himself with a jolt of bitter sarcasm he immediately regretted.

"Morning, Commander. Is the gang all here?"

"Mostly, sir. If you'll follow me?"

There was quite a spread laid out for breakfast in "Ahd-mi-raal" Keje-Fris-Ar's expansive quarters. The space wasn't nearly as large as his old "Great Hall," which would've been sufficient for a basketball game, but it was still bigger than any flag officer's quarters Matt had ever seen. The common area alone was bigger than the wardroom on a battleship. Back when the bear-shaped, rust-furred Lemurian shared simple breakfasts of akka egg with Adar and USNRS *Salissa* (CV-1) had been merely one of many monstrous "Homes" that remained almost perpetually at sea, they'd usually eaten alone at a small rickety table. Now nearly every meal was an event, accompanied by a strategy session around a massive, ornately carved table that would comfortably seat two dozen. And the gray-furred Adar was no longer High Sky Priest for *Salissa* alone, but of Baalkpan as well. Even more important to most individuals other than himself, he was also chairman of the Grand Alliance—or whatever the Alliance was becoming in his absence—and High Chief of Baalkpan itself.

Adar sat at the head of the table, and Matt was ushered to a seat across from Keje. The two exchanged grins, but Matt's was a little forced. He was disappointed that Sandra wasn't there. He understood her absence, but he missed her very much. Soon, he'd miss her even more if he got his way, he realized once again. *Probably just as well she's not here to argue,* he thought with a twinge of shame. He glanced at Adar and noted the chairman's reserved blinking. Adar was still uncomfortable about the . . . discussion they'd had after the battle for Grik City, when Matt pointedly accused that Adar's operational meddling had probably cost a lot of extra lives. Matt still wasn't entirely sure, but he believed Adar had taken the criticism to heart in a healthy way. He'd definitely taken great pains to make sure they were "all on the same page," ever since, and that was something.

The same 'Cat steward who took Matt's hat returned immediately with a cup of coffee. It still wasn't "right," but it was infinitely better than what Juan brewed. Other stewards brought food, and conversation dwindled as they ate. It was the Lemurian way not to discuss serious matters over a meal, and Matt heartily approved. Instead of talking, he concentrated on eating—and observing his companions. Lieutenant Colonel Chack-Sab-At sat with his betrothed, General Queen Safir Maraan. *Still betrothed?* Matt wondered, *or have they finally tied the knot?* Lemurian mating customs remained mysterious to him and varied considerably from one clan or Home to another. Chack, his blue Marine tunic and kilt over brindled fur contrasting with the white of most of the naval officers, was originally from *Big Sal* herself, though he considered *Walker* his true home now. He'd grown up in a society where mating was highly structured as to who could mate with whom, but otherwise amazingly informal. Essentially, weddings were consummated by . . . being consummated, as far as Matt could tell. Safir, with her black fur and silver eyes—and silver-washed cuirass—was from B'mbaado, where things were different. There'd been a genuine aristocracy there, and while the actual ceremony remained quite simple, her wedding would traditionally have been accompanied by a significant celebration.

Matt shook his head and smiled when he caught their eyes. They'd both been through so much, changed so much—as had all Lemurians everywhere in the course of this terrible war. Age-old customs and beliefs had been subverted or outright destroyed by the breakneck industrialization and mobilization of massive armies from previously isolated, insular Homes—and even species! The unavoidable comingling of cultures that accompanied it all had begun the process of creating a new, blended culture, just as surely as Commander Alan Letts was overseeing the creation of a new united nation at his "constitutional congress" in Baalkpan. Who knew how it would all sort out? Everyone, likely including Chack and Safir, was making it up as he went. In spite of everything, Matt had a growing confidence that, with people like Chack and

Safir as role models, whatever society emerged from the war—if they could only win it—would make the nation Alan was building a *good* place to live.

Matt's gaze swept other faces. There was Major Jindal of the 1st "Chack's" Raider Brigade, substituting for Chack's Exec (and sister), Risa. He often unofficially represented the human troops of the Empire of the New Britain Isles at these meetings. (Brevet) Lieutenant Colonel Saachic, from the Filpin Lands, was seated beyond Safir. He commanded the me-naak mounted cavalry in her II Corps, and had come as her aide. Down the table, COFO Jis-Tikkar (Tikker) ate heartily. The highly polished 7.7-millimeter cartridge case thrust through a hole in his sable-furred ear glinted under the "wondrous" incandescent bulbs dangling in their fixtures overhead. Matt caught Captain Jarrik-Fas, of USS *Tassat*, looking at him, blinking amusement, while he spoke to an Imperial Marine leaning near. He wondered what that was about. Jarrik was one of Keje's many cousins and looked a lot like him. He had a broader mischievous streak, however, and when Matt blinked questioningly back in the Lemurian fashion, Jarrik merely grinned toothily and the Marine stepped back. At the far end of the table was Kapitan Leutnant Becher Lange of SMS *Amerika*. His superior, Kapitan Von Melhausen, had no desire to leave his ship. He was an old man whose mind tended to wander at the worst possible times. He'd come to realize this himself and had made Lange master of *Amerika*, for all intents and purposes. Across from him sat Commander Simon Herring, the head of Strategic Intelligence. Of all those present, Matt still had the most difficulty figuring him out. Like a number of others now linked to the Allied cause, Herring had come to this world aboard a Japanese prison ship, and if he hadn't already been paranoid, his experiences at the hands of the Japanese had made him so. He'd made great strides since his bombastic, even somewhat subversive arrival and had since become a "real" Navy man. He'd also acquitted himself well in the fighting for the palace. After a bumpy start, he seemed to have come around to Matt's way of thinking in many ways, and had become a true believer in the cause of defeating the Grik. The paranoia—and a few secrets, Matt was sure—still lurked, but that was probably normal and appropriate for a snoop.

There were other officers—the table was full—but Matt caught himself staring at Ensign Nathaniel Hardee. He was a young man—a teenager, really—who ate woodenly and had the uncomfortable look of someone with no idea why he was there. Matt *thought* the young Englishman, "evacuated" to this world from Java aboard the now permanently lost *S-19*, had achieved the advanced age of sixteen. Like the slightly older Abel Cook, who'd arrived the same way, Hardee had grown up fast. He'd actually succeeded Lieutenant Irvin Laumer in command of PT-7, after that fine but troubled officer was killed trying to reach the Grik Celestial Mother. Hardee probably didn't expect to keep the "Seven boat," and even if he did, he had to be wondering why the master of one of the smallest craft the Alliance considered a warship had been summoned here.

The meal was winding down when a steward opened the door and Courtney Bradford swept in. Courtney, an Australian, had been a petroleum engineer and self-proclaimed "naturalist." He remained a very strange but often extremely valuable man. His eccentricities were—usually—more than matched by his insights and other contributions. Named Minister of Science for the Alliance, he'd been busier in his other role of "plenipotentiary at large" of late, but now seemed determined to make up for lost time. Following him through the doorway was a long-haired, black-bearded man whom Matt had never seen. The stranger was dressed in the same long, belted, tie-dyed camouflage frock now standard battle dress for all members of the Allied armies and Marines, but his nervously darting eyes and intent expression made it clear he was in unfamiliar surroundings. Suddenly, Matt knew who he was; he had been hoping for this meeting for some time, in fact. *Trust Mr. Bradford to surprise us—but maybe it's for the best?*

"Oh dear," Courtney exclaimed, worriedly wiping his balding pate. "You started without us!" he accused.

Keje stood. "You are late, Mr. Braad-furd!" he rumbled good-naturedly.

"Nonsense!" Courtney denied, groping for the large Imperial watch that would've rested in his weskit pocket—if he'd been wearing his weskit. His face went blank, then clouded. "If some . . . nautical gentlemen would summon the courtesy to contrive some alarm—fire a gun, perhaps, like civilized folk—to announce that something as momentous as breakfast was about to commence, we shouldn't all dash about in wild, anticipatory confusion!"

Matt joined the laughter, and stood as well. Courtney frowned and peered over the other diners at the table. "Might there be anything left at all? The merest morsel? I don't ask for myself, of course"—he glared at Keje, then motioned at his companion—"but Commander . . . um, 'Will,' I suppose must suffice, is quite famished, I'm sure!"

Chack and Major Jindal came around the table, extending their hands in the human fashion. "Will" recognized them, and his expression calmed as they shook.

"My friends," Chack announced, "this man and his people led my command through the jungle to the Wall of Trees. It is apparent now that had they not done so, the Celestial Palace might not have fallen."

And as goofed-up as everything else was, we'd have lost the whole battle, most likely, Matt agreed to himself. He stepped forward, offering his hand as well. "We're in your debt, Commander."

Will looked down. "Nay. It's we as awes ye. Ye's came an run aff the Garieks, an we did little enaw ta halp." He straightened and looked Matt in the eye. "Mr. Bradford says the Garieks'll be back, an' ya're army's hartin.' Gi us—me paple—maskits, an' we's'll halp as we can. He looked around the table. "We's nae want the Garieks back," he said with flashing eyes.

"We'll help each other keep them away, Commander," Matt promised.

Will grimaced. "Aym nae C'mandar. Jas Will. Anly the cap'n 'as a title." He cocked his head at Matt. "Ya're a cap'n tae, ain't ya? Cap'n Reddy, as ya've been dascrabbed."

"I'm Captain Reddy." Matt turned and introduced the others in the space, ending with Keje and Adar.

"But *ya're* Cap'n Reddy," Will persisted. "Ya're the man me cap'n wants ta jayn." He looked at Chack and Jindal. "An thams."

Matt glanced at Adar, who'd risen and was speaking softly to Keje. Keje nodded. "Please join us for breakfast, Will," Keje invited. "And Mr. Braad-furd as well, of course. Please forgive us if we begin our discussion before you finish, but we will return to your case in due time. Meanwhile, enjoy your meal."

A couple of junior officers vacated their stools so Courtney and "Will" could be served at the table. While that happened, the others returned to their seats.

"I suppose we may as well get started," Matt suggested to Adar. Adar glanced down the table at their visitor and nodded. "Very well," he said. "Commander Herring will no doubt complain that we reveal too many plans to the ears of strangers, but Will's folk cannot possibly want to betray us to the Grik!"

Herring sat back from the table, wiping his lips. "On the contrary, Mr. Chairman. I've already spoken with Mr. Bradford about the . . ." He paused and frowned apologetically. "They don't really have a name for their people other than 'people,' which seems fairly universal. Most claim British descent, but that might grow confusing with the Imperial presence here. . . ."

"Call us 'Maroons,' if ye mast name us," Will said around a mouthful of eggs. " 'Tis what we are."

Herring nodded thoughtfully. "In any event, I've interviewed Mr. . . . Will, and a number of his associates, and fully endorse his presence here. As Colonel Chack stated, the Maroons have already done us a number of services, not the least of which was the expulsion of the Grik from a couple of smaller settlements down the coast. This was done without the aid of modern weapons, I might add. I suggest they be incorporated into our land forces in some capacity without delay. Scouts and coast watchers, at least." He blinked. "I'm sure we all agree that our most pressing need is troops, after all."

Adar nodded. "Indeed. COFO Jis-Tikkar's limited reconnaissance flights in the P-Forty floatplane have confirmed that the enemy is massing an . . . intimidating force across the strait on the continent, though how they mean to get it here is not apparent. We have yet to determine where the enemy's primary naval bases are."

"We *must* get more eyes on what the Grik are up to," Herring stated unhappily. "One plane cannot scout sufficiently and with other unknown participants possibly in the game, I dislike continuing to risk our only modern aircraft." He looked at Tikker. "The Nancys do have the range."

"Barely," Tikker conceded reluctantly. "But they're our only real strike aircraft. An' we've lost so many to combat and fatigue—most fought in the battles around Madras, after all—that I can't like spending them or their pilots on reconnaissance flights. We'll quickly wear them out. They're also, well, kinda slow compared to the Pee Forty, an' the Grik have gotten better at hittin' 'em with their caanister mortars." He blinked a warning at Herring. "And don't forget the new weapon we found."

Near the airship field in Grik City, they'd discovered what amounted to a massed battery of hundreds of *rockets*. They were ridiculously simple—just large signal rockets—like they'd seen during the battle— but with small charges in their noses detonated by a contact fuse. Bernie Sandison had been amazed by their ingenuity and confessed he'd considered something like them for engaging Grik zeppelins from the ground, but the deployment of the P-1 Mosquito Hawks, or "Fleashooters," had made him abandon the scheme as too wasteful in time and materials. But like all Grik weapons, how wasteful they were didn't seem a concern, and he was worried about their potential. It was probably very fortunate that the field had been overrun before any aircraft flew over.

"In any event," Adar continued, redirecting the discussion, "it's clear that the Grik will come, and rather soon, I should think. It must be difficult for them to feed even the masses of warriors we *have* seen." He cleared his throat. "Our forces, on the other hand, are . . . limited. Some reinforcements have arrived; the two Austraalan regiments that were staging at La-laanti—or 'Diego Garciaa'—have brought General Maraan's Second Corps back near full strength, and the oilers and supply ships that accompanied them were welcome. Our ammunition and fuel reserves were grievously low. Other troops and replacement ships and aircraft are on their way directly from Baalkpan, but . . ." He paused, refusing to meet Matt's eyes. "Since it was not originally contemplated that we attempt to *take* this place so soon, it may be some time before further replenishments of any sort arrive." Matt nodded. He'd already said all he intended to on that subject. Belaboring it now was pointless.

"What about General Alden and General Rolak?" Safir asked. "With the Grik General Halik expelled from Indiaa, First and Third Corps should be free to come here."

"They are, and will," Adar assured, "but Third Corps is strung out between Lake Flynn, the Rocky Gap, and the low-tide crossing between Indiaa and Say-lon. General Alden has left all his cavalry, including Colonel Dalibor Svec's 'Czech Legion,' to guard against Halik's return, but First Corps must still march across half of Indiaa before it can embark. General Linaa-Fas-Ra's Sixth Corps might be brought more quickly, but it consists mostly of green recruits, still in training." He looked at Matt and Keje. "We have decided that it should remain behind to replace First and Third Corps when they come."

There was murmuring over that. They needed troops *now*, green or not. Most rightly suspected that General Linaa, a representative of Sular on the Island of "Saa-leebs" and a powerful opponent of uniting the various land and sea Homes into a single nation, had "objected" to a more active role for his corps. *Politics already,* Matt thought with a grimace.

"What help can we expect from First Fleet?" Jarrik-Fas asked.

"*Arracca*'s battle group, escorted by *Saanta Caata-lina*, has been ordered to join us, but repairs to both larger vessels will require perhaps another week," Keje replied.

"So a month or more, at *Arracca*'s best speed, to arrive," someone murmured.

"Furthermore," Adar added sadly, "it has been determined that *Mahaan* cannot be sufficiently repaired at Madraas for combat, or to endure the long voyage here. Nor can an SPD be spared to carry her to Baalkpan. Cap-i-taan Reddy has ordered that she be maintained at Madraas until she can be properly repaired or moved." Everyone looked at Matt, knowing how hard it must've been for him to order work suspended on *Walker*'s mangled sister, particularly since it had been one of *Walker*'s own errant torpedoes that nearly sank her. "The advantage to this arrangement, however, is that *Mahaan*'s entire experienced crew will transfer to one of the new-construction destroyers about to join First Fleet. That ship's current crew will be disappointed, no doubt, to transfer to one of the captured Grik dreadnaughts, but I think their disappointment will fade when they discover the interesting . . . improvements our people are making to them." He sighed, and looked at Jarrik. "To fully answer your question, however, it is my order—after consultation—that all elements of First Fleet now marshaling at Madraas, besides *Saanta Caata-lina* and *Arracca*'s battle group, must wait to escort First and Third Corps to us. The sea between there and here is too terrible to risk so many troops upon without powerful protection." He bowed his head to Herring. "And we still do not know the motives of the 'unknown participants' who attacked us with the strange sub-maarine, or if they have more."

"So . . . what does this mean?" Becher Lange asked, stirring on his stool. "How long before we can expect *significant* aid?" Everyone knew Lange was no coward, but as time passed with no response from his own Republic of Real People in southern Africa, he grew increasingly nervous. The Republic had agreed to join the war against the Grik by attacking from what the enemy considered a relatively safe direction, the "frigid" wasteland to the south. The Allied forces had initially conceived the attack as a mere demonstration to distract the Grik from an eventual attempt to seize Madagascar, but now the Allied forces needed the attack to prevent the Grik from focusing all their power against the island. The Republic had maintained wireless silence for a very long time to avoid unwanted attention, but when they struck, there'd be no reason to continue that policy. The lingering silence meant not only had they not yet attacked, but they might not have even received the news that they needed to.

"A month for *Arracca* and her battle group, as has been observed. Perhaps another for the rest," Adar replied. "I'm afraid that, for now, we will have to make do with what we have."

"We *will* make do, Mr. Chairman," Matt said, then added, "Somehow," with a wry smile. "And on paper, it doesn't look so bad. With Second Corps back to strength and everything else ashore, we have close to thirty thousand troops. That's as many as we defended Baalkpan with. And these are mostly veterans with way better weapons. We've got more ships, artillery, mortars, and air power than we had then—and the supply ships brought up some of the stuff we'd wanted to take this place: more Blitzerbugs, shotguns—and the first *good* copies of a Browning thirty cal." He grinned. "You all know what a chore it's been to perfect those!"

There'd been those who wanted to make Gatling guns all along, in the same .50-80 caliber as the "Allin-Silva" conversion muskets, but though they'd had the ability to do that for some time, Silva himself had suggested to Bernie that they concentrate all such efforts on making the far less complicated Brownings. The only thing holding them back had been good barrel steel to cope with jacketed bullets, and they'd accomplished that at last. They'd even provided a water jacket for good measure. Silva, Bernie, and eventually Matt had resisted Gatlings because, as Silva put it in a nutshell, "They're five times as heavy, six times more complicated, and with black powder loads at the ranges we been fighting, the smoke they make means you're done aiming as soon as you turn the crank. They'd still need gun carriages and at least one paalka each for the heavy damn things, so I say stick with twelve-pounders and canister—that you can aim between shots!"

Matt's announcement was greeted with pleasure, but he continued. "In reality, as you all know, things aren't so rosy. The Grik have better weapons too, and they don't always just run right into the meat grinder anymore. Worse, this time it's us that's overextended, and we have to expect them to try to make the most of it. That means a fairly rapid counterattack in my opinion as well. The ideal thing would be to stop them in the channel, the 'Go Away Strait' as they call it—for whatever reason—before they land. But with just *Walker*, the sail/steam DDs of Des-Ron Six, and *Big Sal*'s planes, we can't stop 'em if they mob us with transports, escorted by a really big mob of heavies we *know* they still have. If that happens before we get help, they *will* get ashore, so we have to prepare for it. General Queen Protector, if you would?"

Safir Maraan stood, shrugging off the revelation that they were on their own. She'd been on her own before. She stepped to a large painted-fabric map displayed on the wall opposite Adar that depicted northern Madagascar. It had been rendered as carefully as possible from captured Grik charts and aerial observations. Hopefully, the Maroons would help fill in what lay beyond the wall of trees. Safir drew her sword and pointed at the bay. "Assuming the enemy gets past the navy, we may also make a few other assumptions. They know this harbor even better than we, and I doubt they'd be foolish enough to attempt an attack through its mouth. The channel is too narrow, as we discovered to our pain. Sink one large ship there and no others could pass it by. We will mass captured guns—there are hundreds in the warehouses—at the eastern approaches, in any event."

"Why not the west side as well?" Jarrik asked.

Safir looked at him and blinked. "The eastern guns will range across, but mainly because all the Grik we ran from the city are there. They are rapidly eating one another up and I do not want to waste troops to kill them, but I doubt they will let us emplace guns in their midst."

"A shame we can't talk to them," Courtney Bradford said. "Perhaps we could have Rolak fly his pet Grik, Hij Geerki, down to have a chat. He may even get them to surrender."

"It could be done with one of the big 'Clippers,' if it carried enough fuel," Herring speculated thoughtfully.

"Why?" Adar asked, suddenly interested.

"They appear to be predominately *civilian* Grik, Mr. Chairman," Herring replied. "The first large group of such we have ever encountered. In the past, at Colombo for instance, the warriors slew them all, most likely to prevent their capture. Hij Geerki is living proof that civilian Grik *will* surrender," he added, "and just think what we might learn from them."

"There must be forty thousand of them!" Keje declared. "We could not feed so many!"

Herring shrugged. "Then we wait. There won't be so many for long."

Adar blinked disgust at the notion but bowed his head to Herring again. "The idea is worth considering. I will do so." He added a blink that amounted to wry amusement. "And, of course, if we *kept* the Clipper that brought Geerki, we'd have another long-range reconnaissance aircraft. . . ."

Herring acknowledged the point with a nod.

"But doesn't such a large number of Grik, right on the shore and virtually in our midst, provide the perfect place for the enemy to land?" Jarrik prodded.

"I would be more concerned about that if the enemy had any way to know they were there," Safir replied, "but it *is* one of the better places the Grik may attack. We already have a large percentage of my corps entrenched between the wall of trees and the harbor to keep the refugees where they are. That force is equally well situated to prevent a landing. But that brings up the pertinent point. The biggest problem we face on land is the scope of the perimeter we must defend around Grik City. We simply don't have enough troops to be strong in more than a few places at once. The western shore where we landed would be just as suitable for the enemy. We have improved the existing fortifications and made many more, but we cannot fill them all. We have even begun moving Grik guns to emplacements excavated in the wall of trees itself, though an attack from the jungle is my least concern. Even if the enemy attempted it, they could not move swiftly enough or maintain the necessary cohesion to storm the wall before we discovered their plan"—she nodded at Will—"and massed to meet them."

"We did it," Chack reminded her.

"They weren't looking." She grinned at him, then faced the others, the grin fading away. "To hold the city, we must keep looking all the time, and we *must* have early warning where the Grik will strike."

"Me paple'll halp wi' that," Will assured, "but let us fight! We want tae fight!" he urged.

"The Maroons shall fight," Adar decreed. "Bring your people in, and we will train them, even arm them if we can." He looked questioningly at Keje, and his friend nodded.

"We have many of the old muzzle-loading muskets aboard all the ships. As production of the newer ones improved, it was easier for the arsenal to ship finished arms wherever they were needed than to keep track of where—and to whom—the conversion barrels and hammers had and hadn't gone." Keje blinked irony at Matt. "No sense throwing away perfectly good weapons—and you never know when they might come in handy!"

"Well. That's settled, then," Courtney declared happily. "Muskets for the Maroons! But might I suggest we're overlooking yet another source of the scarcer commodity: troops!" All the Lemurians blinked questioningly at him. "Oh, come now! Haven't we been told that a large population of *Lemurians* still exists in the southern reaches of the island? Your very own ancestors! How can you stand not to meet them? How can we afford not to *recruit* them?"

"They willnae fight with us," Will declared, glancing around.

"How do you know?" Adar asked, and Will shrugged uncomfortably. "Me paple've . . . skarmished 'em, fram time ta' time. Thay're nae lak . . ." He shrugged again and looked at his plate. "Thay're . . . daffrant fram ye hare. Wild mankeys is all thay are. Thay run away."

Bradford goggled at him. "You said nothing of this before!" He looked at the others. "But it makes no difference!" he insisted. "Let us ask them," he pleaded to Adar. "Let *me*!"

"I will go with him," Chack promptly declared. "Risa and Major Jindal can lead the First Raider Brigade as ably as I, and in any defensive stance they will be under General Maraan's direct command in any event." He looked intently at Adar. "I myself was once . . . unhappy with fighting. Perhaps I can persuade them with the same arguments that once persuaded me."

"If you can even talk to them!" Keje snorted. "The La-lantis were difficult enough to understand."

"You may go, and may the Heavens aid you," Adar said, "once our situation here is more secure." Courtney's face fell. "Do we even know where these people are?" he asked Will.

"Nay. Not surely. Jas sout, alang tha mantains, east an' west, in tha jangle an' tha barren lands both. Different tribes."

"So they would have to be found before we could even contact them," Keje muttered, and looked at Adar. "I must counsel against it at present. We cannot spare officers such as Chack and the necessary security he and Mr. Braad-furd would require on such an indefinite mission."

"If they are as shy as Will suggests, a large force would only frighten them," Chack countered. "A smaller group might fare better; only Mr. Braad-furd, myself, and perhaps a few others." The last was directed at Captain Reddy as a question, and Matt almost groaned, but then reconsidered. *Why not?*

"*If* you go, and if Silva's fit, he can go with you," Matt agreed. "But if he causes any trouble, shoot him." He suddenly had an inspiration. He'd asked that Ensign Hardee be summoned to the meeting so he could get a feel for him. All reports said the kid had picked up PT tactics from Winny Rominger and then Irvin Laumer better than anyone. Maybe an independent command would be a good test—before giving him the whole MTB squadron, as he'd been contemplating. "Mr. Hardee?"

The kid had been watching the proceedings with wide eyes. If possible, they got even wider and he bolted to his feet. "Sir?" he squeaked.

"You take them, if Adar agrees to the mission. Draw one of the new Brownings for the Seven boat too. It's time all the PTs had something to defend themselves with."

Adar nodded, blinking a combination of yearning and concern. "Of course I agree, but the mission must be brief. As my brother says, we cannot spare Col-nol Chack, Mr. Braad-furd, and even a wounded Dennis Sil-vaa for very long." He sighed. "I only wish that I could go."

"Uh . . . Aye, aye, sir!" Hardee managed with a firmer voice, then sat, blinking as well.

In the silence that followed, Matt gazed around the table, preparing himself. Could he really do this without causing a rift that might wreck his marriage—and conceivably even the Alliance? He had to try. "Okay," he said. "As I understand it, our bigger mission is to hold what we've got until we can take the fight to the Grik." He nodded at Adar. "*My* orders as commander in chief are to accomplish that *by* taking the fight to the Grik however we can." He looked at Tikker, then Keje. "General Maraan covered the imperatives. She has to know when the Grik are coming, and we can't tell her if we just sit on our butts and wait. We have to scout, and scout *deep*—not just watch the approaches and send a few planes to look around now and then." He nodded at Tikker. "At the same time, we need to keep the wear and tear on our aircraft to a minimum, while maintaining the ability to concentrate them on tempting targets. If we do this right, we can make life a living hell for the Grik and maybe even prevent any 'mob' of transports or heavies from forming in the first place." He looked at Jarrik. "Des-Ron Six is yours, and can outrun anything the Grik have that we know of, under sail or steam. Take all but two of your DDs hunting up and down the continental coast. Don't tangle with any dreadnaughts, but thrash anything that looks like it can carry Grik." He looked at Keje. "As I see it, we need to shorten the trip for our planes. Escorted by the other two DDs of Des-Ron Six, *Big Sal* will take her Nancys and one squadron of pursuit ships, and park her big butt in the strait. Her planes'll pound troop concentrations on shore, ships, or anything they find at anchor in Grik ports." He looked back at Tikker. "The other pursuit squadrons will stay behind as air cover for the city."

"What about the DDs that escorted the supply ships—and *Walker*?" Herring asked.

Matt considered. "The new arrivals will provide security here. *Walker* will . . . kind of go with *Big Sal* too." He rubbed his nose. "Honestly, I'd thought I'd better stay here at first," he admitted, "but I think any misunderstandings we once had have been cleared up pretty well. I believe I'll take *Walker* out myself after all, as a quick responder to anything that breaks, good or bad." He grinned. "And who knows? We might do a little hunting of our own." He paused. "Mr. Chairman? I recommend that you remain in Grik City . . . for the time being."

Adar blinked, grateful for the renewed trust Matt was showing Safir Maraan—and him. "I will," he said, "but let us not call it 'Grik City' anymore. I think 'Liberty City' sounds much better."

"Liberty City sounds . . . swell," Matt said neutrally.

"What will *Amerika* do during all this?" Becher Lange asked. Matt tensed. He'd been expecting the question.

"Keep trying to raise your kaiser, and get him to hit the Grik," Matt said simply. "We *need* him to move. But while you do that, I want you to keep your bunkers full." *Amerika* was the only coal burner in the fleet, but the Grik had kept large quantities of coal in the city for their warships. "And start loading the nonwalking wounded immediately. They'll be more comfortable in a liner than in a pile of rocks. When that's done, load any other wounded who can't fight, walking or not." He looked at Adar before continuing. "In two weeks, whether or not the Grik come, or you raise your kaiser, you'll take all the rest of the wounded, the senior medical staff, Mr. Herring, Courtney if he's back, and"—he took a breath—"Chairman Adar, and get them the hell away from this island." Adar began to sputter, but Matt continued. "Your Lieutenant Meek can remain to continue attempts to communicate using your codes. Once clear of here, don't head for Madras. Steer east by way of Diego, and make a high-speed run straight through the Sunda Strait. Don't stop until you drop anchor in Baalkpan Bay."

Lange looked unhappy, but nodded. "In spite of her few guns, *Amerika* is not really a warship. But she can carry many people and she is fast. Your orders make sense—but would we not risk the same dangers that prevent our reinforcement? That require your other warships to protect your First and Third Corps? The sea between here and Diego Garcia is where the undersea boat was, after all."

"We sank it," Matt reminded, "and it didn't live there. It followed us down from Madras." He shrugged. "Zigzag the whole way if you want— you should have the fuel for it. How long it takes is not as critical as getting our people out of here."

"I will not go!" Adar almost shouted, seething. Matt turned to him.

"You *have* to, Mr. Chairman, and despite what you may think, this has nothing to do with what happened before. Look, you did what you came for; you took your ancient homeland back from the Grik. You should be proud of that, however it happened, and proud of the Alliance that made it possible. But you don't belong here now. Mr. Letts and a bunch of other folks've worked damn hard to turn part of that alliance into a nation—and they don't even know what to call it! It's time for you to go back and do your real job. It's time for you to lead where you're needed!" He gestured at Keje, Chack, and Safir, then down the table. "This is *our* job."

Adar looked stung, but Matt thankfully recognized from the 'Cat's hesitant blinking that Adar also knew he was right. He was glad. He'd meant every word he said and wanted Adar and the wounded safe. But on a purely selfish note, he also knew Sandra would go—easier at least—if Adar told her to.

"Very well," Adar said stiffly.

Matt took another deep breath and slowly let it out. "Thanks, Mr. Chairman."

///// *Sofesshk*
Grik East Africa

irst General Esshk and the Chooser rode alone in a large, garishly appointed coach drawn by a hundred harnessed warriors. They were traveling up an ancient baked-brick thoroughfare bordering the north bank of the river called "Zambezi" in the scientific tongue that stretched uninterrupted from one end of the prehistoric city of Sofesshk to the other. Marching behind them was an honor guard of a thousand warriors, Esshk's very finest, but many more thousands lined the road on either side, emitting a rumbling hiss that struck Esshk with an odd sense of irony. The sound was one of contentment, similar to the sound Uul warriors made when fed to satiation, but in these circumstances Esshk recognized it as the clamor of satisfied acclaim. He considered that ironic since he was triumphantly entering the cherished, timeless district of "old" Sofesshk, where the elite of the Empire abided beneath the daily shadow of the

Palace of Vanished Gods. This, after losing Madagascar, the Celestial City, and the great palace there, and even the Giver of Life herself to an invading host of prey! Fortunately for him, it was not *his* army that was defeated, and only chance had placed him there at the time. He'd done his best to salvage the situation, of course, and that was well-known here. But the fact remained that, however peripherally, he'd been beaten.

Several things had saved him. First, though he'd lost the Mother, he'd carried away her most promising candidates for succession. Second, he was First General, and a carrier of the Celestial Blood himself. That had inspired the Chooser to proclaim him "Regent Champion" until a new Giver of Life could be elevated from among the candidates he preserved. Third, he personally commanded the greatest, best equipped host in all the Empire; an army raised by and instilled with the principles of absolute loyalty and obedience to the authority of the Celestial Mother—embodied by the person of First General Esshk. Finally, that army, just now reaching its most lethal maturity at last, had *not* been defeated. All things considered, Esshk had escaped the disaster on Madagascar fairly well.

He contemplated his sole companion. Not a warrior, the Chooser was obese for a Grik, with a calculating, manipulative mind—exactly what Esshk was in need of—but he was prone to fits of panic that undermined his bold schemes. His dress was as garish as the carriage, with a gray cloak covered with tiny bones fastened about his neck, and the tiny teeth of hatchlings clinking in the brush of his crest. He'd taken to wearing a sword, unheard of for a Chooser, but he excused it with the explanation that all the Grik had to come to terms with total war having reached their shores. Esshk suspected he wore the somewhat delicate thing for far more personal reasons, but made no comment. He sighed. The little sword was finely made, and reminded him of Regent Tsalka. It might have even once been his. Tsalka had been a . . . troublesome creature at times, but Esshk certainly approved of his sense of taste. His palaces at Colombo and Madras had been things of beauty, decorated with fine, not-so-garish masonry, and flowing ivies reminiscent of Sofesshk itself, and not the more . . . utilitarian architecture that prevailed elsewhere in the Empire. He glanced to the south, across the mighty river. The "new" districts of the city were dedicated to commerce and industry. Warships and cargo hulls huddled along the shoreline, and crude buildings and countless squalid dwellings sprawled for miles beyond view. *Little different from the Celestial City on Madagascar,* he thought, wondering how long ago the Grik, even the Hij, had lost all sense of taste except when it came to personal adornment. In contrast, "old" Sofesshk was downright colorful, even if Imperial red predominated, and the dwellings reminded him of the more . . . imaginative structures he'd seen in the Lemurian city of Aryaal. It was strange. Had there once been a time among his race when they focused more on creating than expanding—and merely existing?

He stuck his snout outside the window to view their destination. Even that was different. Though the shape and stone construction of the unimaginably older Palace of Vanished Gods had clearly inspired the far more massive structure on Madagascar, it possessed a simple elegance despite its time-worn features. Perhaps that . . . rounding, that air of the ancient, was what the builders of the Celestial Palace had hoped to replicate? Esshk considered it likely, and that evoked a sudden suspicion that the austere approach embodied by the newer palace had adversely affected Grik architecture ever since. He snorted and shook his head, wondering why such things now cluttered his mind when he had far more important thoughts to consider.

He glanced at the palace again before leaning back into the carriage. The legends that had served the Grik as true history until just the last few hundred years were adamant that the Palace of Vanished Gods had been the very first capital of the united Grik race before the Celestial Mother crossed the Go Away Strait to establish a new palace. There, separate from the various tribal territories or "regencies," she could rule, impartial to all. But Sofesshk had remained the most sacred of cities and the Palace of Vanished Gods the holiest of shrines. If the Chooser and First General Esshk got their way, it wouldn't be merely a shrine much longer, but would shortly revert to its original purpose.

The Chooser growled at something he saw beyond the warriors lining the road. "Not all are here to welcome us," he warned. "The warriors of Regent Consort Ragak do not sound content, and they are thickest here, closer to the palace!" He turned to look at Esshk, his red eyes narrowed in calculation. "I dislike all this delay. A quicker counterattack in the immediate aftermath of our arrival, while the Regents were united in their outrage and bereavement . . . They were *eager* to cooperate however they could to avenge our Giver of Life and the defeat at the Celestial Palace!" He slumped back, shifting his tail aside. "And each day that passes, the prey—the *enemy*—grows stronger and more difficult to drive back into the sea!" the Chooser hissed.

"Regent Consort Ragak undermines us," Esshk observed mildly.

"You should slay him!" the Chooser snarled, but Esshk hissed amusement.

"If you are so confident of our position, why not simply choose him for the cook pots, as is your right? No?" Esshk hissed again. "I dislike the delay as well, but you yourself said that this elevation must proceed! You proclaimed me Regent Champion of all Ghaarrichk'k, and most other regents agreed to support us since I carry the Celestial Blood. But Ragak is Regent Consort of Sofesshk itself. If I slew him in his own regency simply because he called for the elevation of a new Mother before he and his armies join the swarm to rescue the Celestial Palace from the beasts that infest it, I could lose the support of other regents who might fear a similar fate." Esshk jerked his head to the side in negation. "That must not be. As you—and Ragak—have said, we must have a Mother!"

"Of course, and we will!" the Chooser insisted. "But like this? So . . . publicly?"

"It is the traditional way."

"There *is* no traditional way to fully elevate a new Celestial Mother without her own mother present! And as we discussed, I had . . . hoped to control the process to our benefit—and the benefit of our race!" the Chooser quickly added. "If the process is thrown out for all to see, how can we ensure that we—that *you* will remain Champion Regent, or even First General? Particularly without the final rite, whoever rises cannot truly rule until she achieves the age of wisdom!"

"In which case she must confirm her Champion," Esshk pointed out patiently. "You worry too much, Chooser," Esshk scolded. "If you will recall, we saved all of those who might rise. All. They remain silly little things, but they will remember. Do not fear that we won't be chosen by whichever one is elevated." Esshk paused. "And even though we have not yet struck back at the foe in a meaningful way, I have been making plans and gathering great strength. Forget Regent Consort Ragak. I will deal with him. And after today, we shall be free to press our attack with numbers and power never seen before!"

"Oh, very well, but forgive me if I chafe and continue to contemplate the consequences of disaster. For example, even if all proceeds as you say, will not Ragak and others attempt to exert unwholesome influences over our new Giver of Life while you are away at battle? I shudder to think what mischief he may cause in your absence."

"Rest easy, Chooser. Do not chafe. Do not shudder. In addition to my greater plans, I have commenced more modest preparations. I have said I will deal with Ragak, and I shall. You must concentrate on the duties appropriate to your position this day—but rest assured, life will soon grow most unpleasant for Regent Consort Ragak, and our proper enemies across the strait in the Celestial City as well." He was quiet a long moment while the procession neared the greenish lawn surrounding the Palace of Vanished Gods, and took in the substantial gathering. All the ruling Hij were present, arranged on the flanks of the palace or on raised benches erected around a central space at the western foot of the structure. Ragak was there, brightly adorned in the robes of his regency, and surrounded by his staff and other creatures who served him. Despite the exalted rank proclaimed for him, Esshk wore only his finest armor and a scarlet cape. He realized Ragak was watching him step down from the coach and ascend to the elevated pavilion that would've been reserved for a visiting Celestial Mother with select members of his staff. One of those was General Ign, commander of the "new" warriors there that day. The Chooser left to prepare for his own role in the drama to come, and Esshk made himself comfortable before glancing back at Ragak. To his surprise, his rival was still staring, eyes and jaws finally revealing the true depth of animosity he harbored. *Of course Ragak is bitter,* Esshk realized. *This is his regency, his city. If anyone must be Regent Champion here, in this very palace, it is only natural he would desire it himself.* Esshk bowed to Ragak, and the regent quickly looked away.

"He is impertinent, Lord!" General Ign hissed. "He *stares* at you, the greatest general of our race, as if you were his prey!" He huffed. "Allow me to slay him, Lord!"

Esshk repressed a snort of exasperation. While no doubt entertaining, Ign would start a full-scale battle between his and Ragak's warriors if he did that, regardless of the occasion.

"Do not trouble yourself, General," Esshk murmured in the growing roar of the gathering crowd. "I have faced combat on the battlefield and even survived the intrigues of court—and Hisashi Kurokawa! Mere stares are beneath my notice. But rest assured; I shall take *good* care of Regent Consort Ragak."

The Gathering Horns sounded deeply, and the crowd shifted expectantly. The elevation of a new Celestial Mother was about to begin. Thousands had joined the mob encircling the space at the foot of the palace. There were warriors, certainly, both Esshk's "new" ones and what he considered Ragak's "ordinary" Uul—but many Hij had joined as well, the highly placed mixing and jostling with those of more humble pursuits. In this one instance, perhaps, a shade of egalitarianism had colored a disparate mass gathering of Grik. All were there to see who would rise to rule them, but some were just genuinely curious. And most of the Uul had never even seen a female before.

When the hubbub reached its peak and it grew increasingly difficult for the cordon of Hij warriors to hold back the mob, the Chooser finally strode into the clearing, accompanied by a chorus of Attention Horns. Almost instantly, the crowd grew silent, the "civilian" Hij taking the longest. The Chooser gestured impatiently at one of Esshk's own officers who'd accompanied him, and the commander of ten hundreds raised a trumpet to the Chooser's face. With only the slightest hesitation, and with somber, rasping tones, he began an ancient chant. Esshk's thoughts wandered. He'd heard the elevation rites many times and knew the words by heart—and ultimately, the words themselves mattered very little since only the Hij understood them and the vast majority of Uul would never hear them again. A total of nine, the oldest of the thirty-two females he'd saved, would participate in the rite, and all would be elevated before their final test. Esshk wanted this settled quickly and hoped that one of the first group would rise above the others. The chances were good, since they were the best prepared in most respects— but sometimes that could be problematic as well, and the more often they had to perform the rite, the more . . . tedious things could become. If the first group failed, they had only enough females to perform the rite twice more if they meant to preserve the bloodline—which they must—and it would be *six years* before the offspring of the remaining females were old enough to try again. Ironically, that had been the ideal scenario Esshk and the Chooser originally contemplated, doubting anyone would oppose a First General's appointment as Regent Champion by the Chooser himself. But Regent Consort Ragak's self-interested ob-structionism had made the installation of a new Celestial Mother utterly imperative, to have any hope of a rapid, meaningful counter-offensive against the invaders.

At a command from the Chooser, a gap formed in the encircling crowd, and the nine candidates entered the ring. All were young and more slightly framed than the average male, but most had already begun to pack on the extra weight of fat that distinguished females of breeding age. One by one they entered the circle, entirely naked except for their painted claws, and took their places around the Chooser, standing demurely, eyes cast down. They all looked so vulnerable, so . . . alluring. Nothing like this could ever occur during the last quarter es-trus! Even so, Esshk was gratified to see that all bore the slightly cop-pery plumage, to varying degrees, of their exalted Mother. It was a good sign, he thought, and fitting that she be replaced by one who mirrored her beauty.

The Chooser's chant resumed, repetitively droning the phrases of el-evation at each contestant. None replied; there was no need. It was not as if any of them had a choice. The Chooser then addressed the crowd and encircling warriors, describing by rote their part in the drama. They were the living limits to the power of the Celestial Mother Becom-ing. Their meager lives were hers to use and take, but she must use them wisely because no Uul—or Hij—had more than one life to give. In the moments to come, they must stand impassive, be the limit, the wall of flesh that bound the Celestial Mother to her duty to all her people. His voice grew louder, more insistent, and Esshk leaned forward in antici-pation. With a sudden flourish of his cape, the Chooser dashed through the Hij warriors, and they raised their shields in unison. What hap-pened next, historically, was often most noteworthy for its brevity. This occasion was no exception. In an instant, the nine apparently shy, retir-ing creatures within the circle sprang indiscriminately at one another with a ferocity that was stunning even to such as Esshk. And what they lacked in training and technique, they more than made up for with wild, merciless savagery. Long claws slashed in a blur of motion and fountaining blood. Teeth ripped and gnawed, and tore away bleeding hunks of flesh. There were a few panting shrieks, but for the most part the battle progressed with almost no sound; everything happened so incredibly fast that it was impossible to focus on more than fleeting images of the slaughter.

In less than thirty heartbeats it was over, and nine bloody bodies lay on the ground beneath a drifting, swirling cloud of downy fur. There was feeble movement amid the tangle of twisted limbs, but Esshk's tongue flicked between his jaws in a gesture of disapproval. Then, in the near silence that still reigned, a blood-spattered figure shifted a limp corpse from across her legs and rose to her feet. She stood there, legs shaking, but triumphantly glaring at her dead and dying sisters, then at the crowd around her. Esshk leaned forward again as the Chooser rushed to examine the victor. She bore wounds, some serious, but apparently not sufficient to disqualify her, and with his jaws wide in celebration, the Chooser made cursory gestures at the other wounded females, who were quickly dispatched by plunging spears. Then he turned back to the last one standing, lowered his crest in submission, and cast himself upon the bloody ground at her feet. Thousands instantly followed. Only Esshk remained standing. There was no doubt he was the guardian and at that moment he symbolized the Mother as well.

"You have passed your test," Esshk said forcefully, and a roar of acclimation rose and fell. "The Chooser will lead you from this place to another, within the Palace of Vanished Gods, where your wounds will be bound and you will begin to receive instruction in the mysteries of elevated beings and the wisdoms of other Givers of Life who have gone before." His crest fluttered with feigned uncertainty, and he spread his arms. "I stand here as the Mother should, but I am not the Mother. I cannot complete the rite. In addition, you remain too young and unformed as yet to rule. That will quickly change, but in the meantime you must choose a champion to rule in your stead. Is it your desire, as it was the Mother's, that I should bear that burden?"

No doubt confused, and eyes beginning to glaze with shock, the new Celestial Mother Becoming merely jerked a hesitant diagonal nod, and without further ceremony, the Chooser and the Hij warriors swept her away toward the palace. Another roar of acclimation thundered behind her, and First General Esshk turned to descend from the elevated pavilion.

"A moment!" came a muted roar that Esshk barely heard, but it was taken up by other voices—surrounding Regent Consort Ragak. Esshk stopped and turned to face his rival, his eyes wide in apparent surprise.

"You wish to speak? Here? *Now?*" Esshk demanded, glancing in the direction the Chooser had herded the victor of the rite, then gazing around at the gathered thousands. The royal entourage had vanished into the palace, but few others had left.

"I wish to speak," Ragak replied, his voice ringing in the stunned murmuring that followed his outburst. "I wish to *challenge!*"

General Ign's crest sprang up and he grasped his sword with a snarl, but Esshk held out a restraining hand. "You would challenge the elevation?" he roared in disbelief. "It was clear-cut; of that there can be no doubt, and there were no irregularities or alterations of ancient custom."

"None but one," Ragak snarled. "You." He looked around. "I do not question the elevation, or even your posing as guardian. But I must question the propriety of one such as you, who lost the Celestial Palace, who *lost our former Giver of Life,* being named Champion of the Empire—all while you should be writhing in the agonies of the traitor's death!"

"You consider me a traitor?" a strangely quiet Esshk asked, brusquely restraining General Ign once more. "On what grounds? The Chooser does not think that—nor did the Giver of Life when she commanded me to evacuate her successors. Why should you?"

"Because your treasonous leadership has cost us many battles and much territory. You have been swayed by other hunters who do not think as we do, and largely because of that you have allowed the unnatural creation"—he stabbed a claw at Ign, then gestured at all Esshk's warriors—"of an army that does not *know how to fight!*" He stood as tall as he could, waving again. "And the Chooser shares the blame! He has stopped culling the weakest, less aggressive hatchlings as unsuited for the hunt, and that has wrought defeat after defeat—and the death of our Celestial Mother herself! No, only your treason—and his—can account for the ruin of our armies, our *swarms,* at the hands of meager, cowardly prey you grace with the title of enemy!"

"You spew nonsense like wind from your arse!" Esshk dismissed to a roar of amused approval. Even Uul understood phrases such as that. "And the creatures that slew the Celestial Mother *are* our enemy; mortal to our very race!" Esshk paused and gazed at Ign's warriors. "And as for my 'army that cannot fight,' few of its members were at the Celestial

City—and only those that were there allowed the fight to continue long enough for the bloodline to escape!"

"The Celestial City is the greatest, best defended city in all the Empire," Ragak scoffed. "Any fool should have had no difficulty holding it, and protecting the bloodline there!"

Esshk looked strangely at Ragak. "*Any* fool?" he asked mildly.

"Of course! And retaking it as well—with fewer warriors than lost it, I am sure, against the contemptible prey animals that infest it now!"

"Could *you* retake the Celestial City?" Esshk pressed, his tone thick with sarcastic admiration, and Ragak suddenly caught himself as thousands of slit-pupiled eyes turned to him. "I was not formed as a general," he demurred, suddenly cautious.

"But I was, and clearly failed to a treasonous degree in your vastly more sagacious estimation. You said 'any fool,' and you are not a fool—so a Hij who is not a fool should find the task almost effortless . . . should he not?"

Only then, glancing down at the sea of faces, both Hij and Uul, did Ragak realize he was caught. He'd known Esshk since they were hatchlings and had long envied his influence at court, but having known him so well—he thought—and technically outranking him as a regent, he'd never fully credited how cunning Esshk had become, or the accounts of his greatest strategies: goading his prey into lunging to its own destruction.

Esshk looked back at the crowd that Ragak had been so foolish to invite to this confrontation. Its presence probably made no difference, but it did make things simpler. "I have been named Champion of the Empire by the Celestial Mother Becoming," he stated. "As such, I now commission Regent Consort Ragak, as general." He looked back at Ragak. "You will take your army, untainted by the 'unnatural' trainings I have devised, and liberate the Celestial City at once!" He cocked his head. "Should you succeed, I will happily relinquish my duties as First General and Regent Champion to you, and destroy myself however you see fit." His crest rose. "If, however, you should fail, I will not punish your courage. You will remain a general under my command, and all your armies shall belong to me."

He turned back to the crowd. "In the meantime, while General Ragak prosecutes his mission, we will continue the utter and complete mobilization I deem required to defeat our existential foe. I will lend General Ragak what support I may, from the air at least, and release what transports he requires to move his army. But the rest of us will build the greatest swarm that ever was, and finish this threat forever!" He paused and bowed to Ragak. "Unless our newest general does it for us."

Ign bowed to Esshk in admiration, as underofficers shouted his warriors back into ranks—which further exemplified the differences between them and Ragak's warriors, who had begun drifting away as a mob. Ragak himself had quickly vanished.

"How much will you give him?" asked General Ign with a hint of concern. "Our greatest shortage at present is in transports, as you know. Can we spare any for Ragak?"

"We shall give him what I said," Esshk replied grandly. "He will have as many of the old transports as he needs—to carry himself and his army of mindless Uul to their doom." He was a complete convert to Kurokawa's principles, which had created the new army, and he had little desire to employ simple massed mobs of warriors again. He'd tried that before. Suddenly, he actually caught himself wishing he knew where the loathsome, ingenious "Jaaph" was now. He assumed Zanzibar, but there'd been no reports. It was time to find out. "Ragak may even prevail," he admitted, returning to the subject. "The enemy was sorely hurt. But at the least, he should make our return less difficult. We will, regrettably, have to keep the new transports that are under construction for our more considered effort." More irony. The design for the "new" transports was actually quite ancient, predating the "old" design by hundreds, perhaps thousands, of years. But they were perfect for what Esshk now had in mind, and could quickly be assembled in huge numbers. "Otherwise, we shall finally use the greater portion of the airship fleet we have amassed. Granted, they have fared poorly against the more capable flying machines of the enemy," Esshk confessed, "but we have so very *many* now—and I have seen for myself that the enemy's machines are vulnerable to massed fire. Besides, they cannot have too many of them. One of the reasons we always considered the Celestial City secure was that Kurokawa assured me that flying enemies could not reach so far." That was apparently true. But ships that carried flying machines could go wherever they liked.

He snorted, watching the last of the crowd disperse while Ign's warriors—his troops—marched back down the thoroughfare. Then he looked at the Palace of Vanished Gods. "That shall be our plan," he said. "We shall support Ragak—to a point. We shall bomb the Celestial City nightly, without pause, from the air." He caught Ign's expression and coughed a chuckle. "Never fear! Mere fire could never harm the Celestial Palace!"

"Then, Lord?" Ign asked.

"Then, General Ign, we shall arm ourselves with the latest marvels the Jaaphs left us making, and take the greatest swarm ever seen across the Go Away Strait. I . . . sense that all is upon the scale and the heart of our foe is finally in our reach. Kurokawa always said their heart was their iron ship he hated so, but ships do not take timid prey and teach them to build fleets and flying machines—and frightfully capable armies. No, I think we shall find our enemy's heart in the Celestial City when we return at last, and when I have devoured it, the scale will more than tip."

////// *Indus River Valley*

eneral Halik knelt and lapped cloudy water from the Indus River with feigned unconcern, but his eyes were fastened roughly two hundred yards away on the opposite, eastern bank—and on the regiment of me-naak mounted cavalry at the water's edge. They were expressionless, as all Lemurians tended to be, but appeared to be watching him just as intently. He rose, shaking droplets from his snout, and ostentatiously turned his back on the enemy to gaze upon his army. It was a ragged, beaten force, encamped almost where it dropped, but through the exhaustion and resultant disability, there remained the discipline, order—the *pride*, that so distinguished it, even in defeat. No other Grik army had ever achieved so much.

"That cavalry are 'regulars,' from a place called Maa-ni-la," General Shlook murmured, his snout also dripping after following Halik's example. "I have learned to distinguish the pennants they fly."

"They have formidable weapons," Orochi Niwa reminded, still staring at the Lemurians astride what might be best described as long-legged crocodiles. "Shorter versions of the new breechloaders we began to see even before the battles in the Rocky Gap. Carbines, but fully capable of reaching us here." He glanced at Halik, his expression slightly amused. Halik's disdainful gesture had clearly been meant to impress his watching army. "I would not recommend you turn your back on Colonel Dalibor Svec's cavalry, his 'Czech Legion,'" he suggested wryly. "They hate us even more than most." Niwa's use of the word "we" was not lost on the officers around him, and Halik in particular felt genuine pleasure that his Japanese—*human*—friend had fully returned to them. He'd been badly wounded and given to the Allies to cure. That they'd not only cured him, but returned him, demonstrated a measure of sincerity from General Alden that Halik would never have expected. It also allowed him to pursue independent confirmation of much that Alden had told him. "The Czechs—human and Lemurian—are primarily equipped only with shortened smoothbores such as the Allies used on Ceylon, but inaccurate as they are at this distance, they *would* strike us down if the entire regiment unleashed a volley," Niwa continued.

Halik glanced at his Japanese friend, pleased even more by the man's renewed mental vigor. "As we learned west of the Rocky Gap, General Alden has far greater control of the 'Czechs' than he once implied," Halik agreed. "And he gave his word that as long as our army continued its retreat toward, then across the Indus River, he would not molest us further." For reasons Halik could only barely articulate, even to himself, he'd grown to trust his most formidable foe. *Of course* Alden would attempt to deceive him in battle; that was how it worked. But they weren't fighting anymore, and with Orochi Niwa's . . . interesting counsel, Halik truly believed that Alden would keep his word.

"You agreed to retreat 'without delay,'" Niwa reminded. "When I last met with Colonel Svec, he seemed inclined to consider our occasional . . . delays to be in violation of that agreement." Since rejoining the Grik, Niwa had served as an emissary between the two forces.

Halik produced a Grik shrug as he gazed at his assembled warriors, still affecting disdain. He had to appear unconcerned no matter who was watching, *because* of who was watching. His army—all the Grik—had just been expelled from Ceylon, and then from India itself; land that had been considered sacred ancestral territory for hundreds, perhaps thousands, of years. That had never happened before. "General Alden wanted all the Grik out of India. We had to stop and wait now and then while other groups moved to join us." He waved around. "We could not bring all our people, but our army, which had dwindled to barely thirty thousand, has swelled to twice that number."

"One of the reasons Svec voiced concern," Niwa stated pedantically, but Halik's eyes became intent.

"We had no choice. We cannot know how things stand beyond those mountains to the west. How has the Grik Empire reacted to the loss of Madagascar—and the Celestial Mother herself? Is there war between the regencies? Have our whole people turned prey? We may be all that remains!" He sighed. "Alden has pulled the bulk of his army back, to reinforce the Allied effort against our homeland. Now would be an excellent time to retake a portion of what we lost—but what could be the point? Suicidal revenge?" he spat bitterly. "The enemy still has complete control of the air, and"—he gestured at the cavalry across the river—"a mobility we cannot match. We might even make it all the way back to the Rocky Gap, bleeding ourselves to death, before the enemy consolidated sufficiently to annihilate us completely." He shook his head. "No. We have no master, unless First General Esshk has somehow survived, and even he cannot help us here. I must cling to the belief that his priority for this . . . increasingly extraordinary army we have made, would coincide with mine: survival." He glared at Generals Shlook and Ugla, and each of his other officers, sparing only Niwa. He knew that *he* understood. "This army that you and I have grown to cherish above all things *must* survive, if only as a core for our shattered people to build around. *It* is now our people, our cause, our nation. And to it, as a whole, we must devote our utmost loyalty." He paused. "Yet we remain its masters. We are our *own* masters, from this point on, until relieved by First General Esshk—or he himself instructs us to destroy ourselves! I see no other way."

"So . . . what shall we do?" General Ugla asked. "We have indeed gathered many warriors, but few are what we have . . . grown to rely on. And there are a number of unwarlike Hij—and even a sprinkling of lower-caste females!"

Halik waved at the fertile, wooded valley. "For now, we remain here—a short distance farther from the river," he added with a touch of genuine humor. "We shall regain our strength and heal from our battles and the long, hungry march. There are food beasts in abundance and the climate is agreeable." He looked at Ugla. "We shall turn the new warriors into what we want them to be, and let the worker Hij help re-arm and equip us."

"Then?" General Shlook asked. "We still cannot strike east. Only one ten thousand—one 'division'"—he nodded at Niwa—"has muskets, and we have barely three tens of artillery pieces. Little enough ammunition for either."

"No," Halik agreed. "We cannot strike east. And I desire no further conflict with General Alden, or any of the Allied powers, in fact." He looked searchingly at Niwa. "Can you convince them of that?"

"If you speak the truth, I will try," Niwa promised, then frowned. "In spite of everything, they treated me well when I was their captive, and even released me back to you. I will not lie to them."

"I speak the truth," Halik assured.

"But they will ask why we tarry here, and prepare as for a fight." Niwa speculated. "Where shall I tell them we mean to go?"

"Tell them that when my army is rested and whole again, I shall march west toward the regencies of Persia and Arabia, to rejoin our race. If the Allies leave us in peace for that, I shall . . . give my word that if any force does one day return this way from that direction, this army will not join it."

Even Niwa, who knew Halik better than any being alive, was stunned by such a promise, and he stared at his Grik friend with wide eyes. "They will not believe that!" he finally managed. "If another Grik army comes this way, how can you *not* join with it?"

"I remain under the orders of General Esshk, First General of All the Grik. At present, I have no communication with him and must proceed based upon my understanding of his original intent. If you will recall, he never expected us to hold Ceylon, or even India. That was Kuroka-wa's dream." He hesitated. "It became mine for a time as well, as you know, but that doesn't matter now. Our primary task, yours and mine, was to build and blood a new army that would be capable of defending the Sacred Lands. We have accomplished that task and must now pre-serve that army for its greater mission. Allowing it to be swept along with another host, under the command of another general who does not know our enemy would only waste all that we have accomplished." He paused, thoughtful. "Just as when we first came to India, I am not subject to the command of any regent. If one attempts to exercise command over me or my army, I shall . . . decline."

"And what if such a regent will not take no for an answer?"

Halik stared intently at Niwa, then Ugla and Shlook, fully conscious of the implications of what he'd decided. Warfare between Grik regencies was common; often arranged between the regents themselves as much for entertainment as for population control. Such wars of sport had been halted during the current emergency, but even if they hadn't, it had never been the place of a "mere" general to instigate such a thing. Halik had been a "sport fighter" himself, before his elevation, but he'd never fought for his own entertainment and never intended to do so for others again. If he defied a Grik regent, it would be with all the skill and ruthlessness he'd honed against the Allies.

"Then I shall decline more vigorously," Halik simply said.

Colonel Enaak of the 5th Ma-ni-laa Cavalry lounged casually atop his vicious, crocodilian me-naak and stared thoughtfully at the departing delegation from Halik's army. Colonel Dalibor Svec of the "Brotherhood of Volunteers," or the "Czech Legion" as they'd come to be called here just as universally as they had on the earth they came from, even though his ranks held more Lemurians than humans, was not so relaxed. His mount, called a kravaa, reflected his mood. It was as formidable looking as a me-naak, complete with a bony, horny head, but it was a herbivore, after all, and the me-naak kept it wary. *Not afraid,* Enaak suspected. The beasts were well matched in strength and temperament, and if kravaas was afraid of me-naaks, the carnivores would know it, and his and Svec's cavalry could never operate together. *Not afraid,* he decided, *but always . . . ready.* He looked at Svec, the wild beard and long hair flowing in the breeze. *He's not afraid of anything— except maybe that we'll make peace with Halik.* His people had suffered a long time, forced to live in the cold, desolate mountains to the north while their enemy ruled this fertile, temperate land. But now that they had it, and Halik was leaving, he just couldn't bring himself to accept that *his* war, at least, might be over at last. *No,* Enaak realized. *His discomfort stems from his desire to chase Niwa and his party down to the riverbank and slaughter them all in plain sight of the Grik on the other side.* If he did, there wasn't a lot Enaak could do to stop him. Enaak was in nominal command of the five thousand cavalry tasked with "watching" Halik, but four thousand of those men and 'Cats belonged to Svec.

"I do not believe it!" Svec growled at last. He looked at Enaak. "*You* do not believe it! We should never have allowed them to escape, but should have destroyed them completely when we had the power to do so!"

Enaak nodded with some relief. At least Svec realized that five thousand cavalry weren't sufficient to take on sixty thousand Grik by themselves. "There is a broader war, Col-nol Svec," Enaak reminded. "It has grown cold here. Generals Aalden and Rolak must go where it still burns bright."

"We have been abandoned by our friends before, when the Russians made peace with the Germans—and then turned on us! I have an all-too-familiar feeling—"

Enaak whirled to face him. "That is enough! I will not hear such mutterings from you again! We have not stopped our war with the Grik, and never will! We have certainly not abandoned you in their midst; we have helped you gain the land you craved so long and won't turn against you—unless you turn against us first!" He continued glaring at the much larger man with his wide, amber eyes, his tail swishing in fury. When he spoke again, his tone was ice. "It is well-known that Imperials often settle disputes with a sword or pistol, on their dueling grounds. What is less known is that my people have a similar, if more infrequently invoked tradition of deadly challenge."

Svec stared back. Enaak had grown good at reading human face moving, but Svec's expression remained hidden behind his monstrous beard. Suddenly the man exploded into laughter. More furious now, Enaak whirled his me-naak to his company commanders still gathered behind him. "Fetch me a spear—anything, that I might use to challenge!" His cutlass would probably have worked as well as anything, but a spear was the traditional weapon and he was focused on proprieties just then. Svec held out a hand, trying to calm himself.

"No, no! Make no challenge! If you do, I shall not accept since I am in the wrong!"

Enaak looked back in consternation, and Svec visibly controlled his laughter and tried to explain. "I do not laugh at you, my friend. I laugh at myself, I think. I do not know. I laugh with relief perhaps?" He shook his head, growing serious. "My people have been twenty years fighting for this day, after the terror that brought us here." He pointed at the Lemurian "Czechs" behind him. "My other people have been fighting even longer. They once had a civilization here unlike any other of your race, and it was destroyed by the Grik. It is understandable that our purposes and our fears have grown so intertwined." He gestured at Niwa and his party who were climbing aboard the barge that would take them back across the river. "I don't believe the Grik can change as much as that man has said. To give and keep a pledge? My heart will not let me imagine such a thing. Yet my *mind* has seen how these Grik have changed how they fight, how they behave, and I have met this Halik myself. He is very dangerous, but yes, different as well. They have stopped eating prisoners and have left India as they agreed. I do not understand how that can be after all this time, but it is clearly so. I do not see how Halik can resist coming back with others of his kind, but we are rid of him for the time, and this land is rid of Grik. That is more than I ever expected to live to see." He looked wistfully at his troopers. "It is . . . hard to stop fighting. Sometimes, the harder a thing has been to achieve, the harder it is to stop striving for it, even when you have it in your hand." He looked back at Enaak. "The Brotherhood of Volunteers will start no fights with you—or Halik, as long as he does as he promised. But how will we be sure? If he does join another army and turn on us, or even if he does not, but another army comes, we must have warning!"

Enaak managed a grin. "We follow him, of course. We will take my Fifth and one of your regiments, and we will watch him until he is far from this land. General Aalden told him to expect that, after all, so we would break no pledge of our own. We'll merely ride along and see the sights and ensure that he does not turn back. He can't object to that! The rest of our force will wait for us here—and the garrison that was promised. Only when that is in place might we turn back, but we will always scout these approaches." He looked squarely at Svec. "*Keeping* what we have achieved is something else to strive for."

North Borno

Ensign Abel Cook and Imperial Midshipman Stuart Brassey sat in the shade of the shoreside trees with "King" Tony Scott and Captain I'joorka of the Khonashis, watching the ongoing effort to break up the shattered Japanese destroyer *Hidoiame*. The forward half of the ship still lay on its side up on the beach where it had been pushed after *Fristar* Home, her cables cut, had drifted ashore and smashed her like a bug. Salvage on that section had proceeded rapidly, and it now looked like a great, rusty carcass that had been picked over by iron hungry carrion eaters. Less had been done with the stern, still submerged a short distance away, although the "reserve" US Navy ship *Salaama-Na* had finally arrived from the East and would attempt to lift the wreck. *Salaama-Na* was a heavily armed, but otherwise unaltered Home. She and her High Chief, "Commodore" Sor-Lomaak, were ardent members of the Alliance and had fought valiantly to crush the invading Doms on New Ireland. *Salaama-Na* dominated the modest natural harbor, but many other ships were anchored there now, and an entire squadron of Nancys operated from hastily constructed facilities as well.

The city that had sprung up around the salvage project and the oil wells the Japanese had started by using slave labor from *Fristar* Home was clearly there to stay. It already had the largest concentration of people in all North Borno, boasting as many as eight or nine thousand, and it didn't even have a name yet. King Scott's people, a fascinating mix of Grik-like folk similar to Lawrence's Sa'aarans and human descendants of Malay fishermen, had been joined by a growing collection of other clans of the seminomadic Khonashi tribe. Members of other tribes, even ancestral enemies such as the Akichi, had begun to appear, tentatively testing the promise of friendship and prosperity, but none had a tradition for naming the places they lived. Interestingly, however, there was a general impatience for a name to be announced for the new "Union" centered at Baalkpan that they'd proudly joined, and they didn't understand the holdup.

Tony Scott sipped his fine Baalkpan beer and gestured past the labor on the beach and in the water nearby where his people were taking *Hidoiame* apart a piece at a time. All knew he was pointing at the long gallows erected in the space where Fristar's people had been corralled.

"A fine hangin, I'joorka," he said to his Grik-like Khonashi war captain with satisfaction. "I think ever'body enjoyed it."

"'Ould'a enjoyed it greater i' us hanged *all* the Jaaphs!" I'joorka grumbled. He'd also made it clear that he thought hanging was too good for them and the prisoners should have received a more . . . imaginative execution.

Abel grimaced, looking at the six corpses still dangling several days after the event. Captain Kurita and his senior officers had earned their fate. They'd murdered prisoners of war, massacred a Lemurian village near what should've been Yokohama, and generally caused all kinds of havoc. But their atrocities here had been very immediate, and it had been all he could do, as Baalkpan's representative, to keep the people from slaughtering all the Japanese survivors after the battle that destroyed their ship. Most had been moved to Baalkpan as prisoners of war, but the Khonashi had demanded justice. *They had it coming,* Abel acknowledged, *but I didn't enjoy it.* Glancing at Stuart Brassey, he was pretty sure his friend felt the same.

"How was your meeting with Mr. Letts?" Abel asked, changing the subject, and Tony gave him a rueful look. His wife, a tiny dark-skinned woman with sharpened teeth and a severe expression that somehow remained beautiful, stepped close with her own mug of beer and sat beside him. As usual, she wore only a leather skirt.

"Scary," he said with a glance at the woman. "I swear, I really did expect him to arrest my ass an' carry me back to Baalkpan as a deserter."

"Stupid," the woman said, and Tony could only nod. He'd gone missing two years before on the Baalkpan pipeline cut, and it had been assumed that *Walker*'s coxswain, who'd suddenly developed an absolute terror of the water, had been eaten by a "super lizard."

"I told you he wouldn't do that," Abel said, trying to ignore the naked breasts across from him. He'd gotten a lot better at that. "Silva did too. It's not like you could've made it back on your own after I'joorka rescued you." He gestured at Tony's withered leg. "In the meantime, you did great work here. If it hadn't been for you, we wouldn't have all these new friends!"

Tony nodded again. He'd begun to look as if the weight of the world had been lifted from his shoulders after a very long time. "That's what

Mr. Letts said. I swear. I'd've hated to leave my new people here, not to mention my wife." He straightened. "But I was ready to face the music. Just couldn't keep hidin' from my old pals anymore." He looked down. "What few of 'em is left."

"Well, you don't have to hide anymore," Stuart said firmly. "And now you're 'High Chief' of the North Borno Home—or whatever you wind up calling it—and entitled to representatives at the congress in Baalkpan."

"That's so weird," Tony said, and paused. "Mr. Letts says they're leaning toward calling the Union the 'United Homes,' or something like that, but they're gonna wait for Adar to get back before they take the vote. Everybody figures he ought'a be there."

Brassy frowned. "He should have been there all along, if what I hear is true."

Abel frowned too. "Maybe so," he temporized, reluctant to criticize, "but he'll be back soon enough on *Amerika*, with the wounded from Madagascar." He looked wistful. "I can't condemn him for being there when I wish I had been myself."

"You may get your chance," Tony speculated.

Abel shook his head, then smiled at I'joorka. "No, my next assignment— ours," he stressed, including Stuart, "is to serve as liaison for the regiment I'joorka has raised when it moves to India. We'll be watching General Halik. Not much chance for action there, I'm afraid."

"I know where he'd rather we were sent!" Stuart prodded playfully, and Abel flushed. It was no secret he was sweet on Rebecca Anne McDonald, the Governor-Empress of the New Britain Isles. "Do you blame me for wanting to fight the Doms?" he demanded.

"Not at all—or for trying to remind the Governor-Empress you exist!"

Abel flushed even deeper. He doubted Rebecca needed any reminders; he wrote her often enough even if it probably took a month or more for his letters to arrive. Sometimes she even wrote back—but she hadn't for a while now.

I'joorka grunted, licking his wicked teeth. "Us raise our regi'ent to aid our new country against the Griks. I don't know the reason us is getting sent to not kill Griks. Us ought'a go to 'adagascar!"

"There is plenty of work to do in India," Stuart said. "And surely you can imagine why we are reluctant to put you in direct contact with the Grik. Some of you do resemble them. Think how difficult it would be for supporting units, particularly aircraft, to tell friend from foe. It might be very risky."

"Then let us kill the Dons," I'joorka said simply. "None that look like us is killing they."

"That actually makes a lot of sense," Abel agreed, his eyes going wide. Then he grinned. "And I'll bet you'd scare the hell out of them! I'll mention it to Mr. Letts and see what he says." He turned to Tony. "In the meantime, you're one of the newest Homes to join the Alliance, but with all the good steel you're salvaging and the oil wells the Japs started, you'll soon be one of the richest. What will you do with all your new wealth?"

Tony scratched his head. "Derned if I know. Khonashis don't need much. No point in us tryin' to build ships an' add to the navy. From what I hear, there's more ships bein' built through the Alliance than they can easily crew." He shrugged. "An' folks here ain't sailors." He nodded at I'joorka. "They're damn fine fighters, though. Even before them 'Cat drill instructors came up from Baalkpan to standardize our training, I'da stacked 'em up against any infantry there is, without firearms."

Abel nodded. He'd seen their disciplined tactics firsthand. Tony's help had a lot to do with that, but Abel was sure the Khonashi had already been a cut above and were, hands down, the most "civilized" Grik-like beings they'd ever met, including Lawrence's Sa'aarans. He wondered if their long association with humans, as actual members of their tribe, had anything to do with that.

"I wish I could outfit I'joorka's troops with better weapons, like the new breechloaders," Tony said a bit wistfully. "Can all our new money help with that?" A couple hundred Japanese weapons had been captured, and some of *Hidoiame*'s big guns were salvageable as well, but they had very little ammunition for the small arms. Worse, it would be a long time, if ever, before more would be made. The Allies had never had enough of the Japanese Arisaka rifles to justify tooling up to feed them. After the Battle of Baalkpan, most of the Arisakas aboard *Amagi* had been taken by her evacuating crew, who had probably feared the Grik at that point, and those that remained on the gutted battle cruiser were too few and too badly corroded by fire and seawater by the time they were found to be of any use. Ammo *could* be made for Scott's rifles, but production of the standard calibers already in use was at capacity. For the present, the only ammunition for the Arisakas was what they'd taken from the Japanese, and those weapons had been issued to Scott's home guard.

"Money can't buy Allin-Silvas or Blitzerbugs; there just aren't enough," Stuart said. "All our production is going to the fronts, and we still haven't got a meaningful number of breechloaders in the hands of our troops in the East. That's the current push, though, now that Maa-ni-la and New Scotland are finally tooled up to make them, but that leaves almost nothing but the old muzzle-loading smoothbores for any new unit working up here. Please believe it has nothing to do with the quality of your troops or any notion whatsoever that they won't use the new weapons effectively. As I said, most Allied troops in the West are still using the same arms you've received."

"You'll get the new guns," Abel predicted. "Everybody will, eventually." He grinned. "And hopefully you'll even get them before you need them!"

"I had'ta ask, y'know?" Scott muttered, frowning. I'joorka just tilted his head in a Khonashi shrug.

They sat silently for a while, enjoying the shade and watching arcs of molten steel spew from the wrecked destroyer as Khonashis, human and reptilian, and a large number of 'Cats from Baalkpan torched the ship apart.

"Talk to 'ister Letts," I'joorka finally urged. "Let us kill Dons. You, the Alliance, hel' us kill Jaaphs. Let us *really* hel' the Alliance!"

The "Cowflop"

iberty City! That's a laugh!" Chief Gunner's Mate Dennis Silva hooted, staring down with his good eye on the harbor below. Smoke still rose from several places, a result of the little air raid the previous night. One enemy airship had fallen right between the Celestial Palace and the docks, and had burned satisfactorily for most of the night. He remembered fighting his way right through that spot not long ago, but the warren of filthy adobe structures was already largely gone. The zep had taken care of the rest. He had a fine, reclining perch on the northern flank entrance to the palace, and awnings had been rigged above all four entrances to the enormous structure, making shade for the ambulatory wounded who chose to spend their days where they could view preparations for the inevitable Grik counterattack. Many preferred not to look, with the scars of battle so fresh on their bodies and souls, and what remained of the city wasn't very inspiring anyway.

The palace was like an ant mound, or better, as Silva had said before, a giant stone cowflop on the denuded ground around a red ant bed. *Except ants are tidy critters compared to Griks,* he added to himself. He shrugged his mighty shoulders with less pain than he'd felt even the day before. *And with all the vents they've opened in this dump, it's cool enough to be sorta comfortable, even inside,* he mused. The whole level of the palace, about a hundred and fifty feet above the stinking ground below, had been scoured as clean as possible for a hospital to the seventeen hundred or so humans and Lemurians who'd take longer to heal from the battle to seize the city—or would never recover at all. *No reason for 'em to gawk around out here,* he reasoned. *Let 'em dream they're wallowin' in a bed o' daisies. That dern seep an' polta paste they been smearin' on me, an' pourin' down my gullet's had me seein' weirder things.*

"Polta paste" was an analgesic, antibacterial salve made from the ubiquitous polta fruit, a fruit that could also be eaten, drunk straight, or fermented into a beverage called "seep." Along with a number of other Lemurian foods, polta fruit obviously provided many of the nutrients humans and Lemurians required, but the medicinal (and recreational) side effects could be disconcerting to some. Like most human destroyermen, Silva had grown to prefer the excellent Lemurian beer for his "drinkin'."

He glanced back at the dim entrance to the palace. *Personally, I'd sooner be out here. I got all cut up scamperin' around on the inside o' this stupid joint. I seen enough of it.*

"Li'erty City is not a good thing to call it?" Lawrence asked. The orange and brown tiger-striped Grik-like Sa'aaran understood English and Lemurian perfectly, and spoke it just as well—as long as he could avoid words that needed lips. He was also one of Silva's best friends, after an interesting start, and now stuck to him like a loyal dog. A lot of that at present was self-preservation. He was utterly loyal, but in the land of the Grik he was also the only furry, toothy, semireptilian creature that *wasn't* Grik. He was a genuine hero, having helped kill the Celestial Mother. But in addition to the thousands of Grik bottled up northwest of the city, rumors had a few still running loose. Lawrence wasn't taking any chances that bad lighting would hide his distinctly different color, or that some of the "Impies"—from Chack's Brigade in particular, who'd never seen him before—would take him for a Grik. He'd be better to stick by Silva.

"No. 'Liberty City's' a stupid name. I know why Adar wants to change it—makes it less Grik soundin' than . . . Grik City, well, obviously. But the sad, sorry truth of it is, to ever'body who fought for this place, it'll always *be* 'Grik City.' Hell, 'Grik City' has already been stitched on *Walker*'s battle flag!"

"Can't polish a turd," agreed the dark-bearded man reclining next to Dennis. Silva looked at him. Gunnery Sergeant Arnold Horn had been chewed up in the fighting even worse than he. Both dismissed their wounds as "bites and scratches," and that was technically true. Most *had* been inflicted by claws and teeth. But Grik were equipped from birth with claws and teeth sufficient to eviscerate prey (and opponents), and both men had been extremely lucky to survive. On top of that, their very worst "scratches" came from Grik swords and spears—and Arnie Horn had taken a particularly nasty jab.

"I thought you were sleepin'," Dennis accused, "leavin' me here with nobody to talk to but a buncha' halfwit 'Cats"—he glared at several Lemurians nearby who blinked back good-naturedly—"an' this puffed-up gecko who thinks he did somethin' special by helpin' kill that bloated lizard lady on the top floor!"

Lawrence huffed, and the 'Cats made their funny, snorting snickers.

"You're just angry *you* didn't get to kill her," Lawrence defended sourly, but he knew one of the reasons Silva kept griping about Lawrence's deed was to remind people of it. Silva was funny like that.

"Sure I am," Dennis confessed. "Even madder it was that creepy twerp Isak who was with you. Gonna be hell in the firerooms."

"If he ever goes back," Horn said.

"Why? What's he up to? Hey! He's supposed to be *here* someplace, and I ain't seen him!"

"Tabby came around looking for him this morning, before you got back." Horn nodded at the wreckage of the zeppelin. "She can't find him and says he's AWOL."

"He's likely hiding so not to see Dennis," Lawrence stated.

"Naw, he ain't scared o' me no more. Shouldn't be scared o' nothin', now. I bet he's slinkin' around down in the basement of this joint lookin' for that giant poodledragon critter that got away. Gonna feed it another grenade! *That* was a hoot to see!"

Lawrence shook his head. "Scuttle'ut says it got out through a tunnel—there's a tunnel they say so' high-rank Griks get out."

"Is that so? Well, the big fat lizard lady didn't get out," Silva said with satisfaction. "But if that's the case, an' he ain't back in his firerooms or huntin' poodledragons with hand grenades, he's bound to be up to somethin' weird," Silva declared airily. He pointed out at *Walker*. "Whatever it is, the bosun'll . . ." Silva stopped, and clamped his mouth shut. Chief Bosun Fitzhugh Gray had been the closest thing he ever had to an honest-to-God, kick-hell-out-of-him-for-doing-wrong father figure in his life. He'd died defending the ship and his skipper, just like he always did, while Silva went haring off on a lark—like he always did. It didn't really matter just then *why* Dennis wasn't on *Walker* when his mentor needed him most, or that he'd been going for the throat of *all* the Grik. It only mattered that he wasn't where he felt he should've been, and that . . . ached. And then not to even finish what he started, and lose so many others—like Irvin Laumer—on the way . . .

For the first time in his life, Dennis Silva had been stopped cold. Thwarted. *Shut out.* Sure, he'd helped accomplish the mission; he and Arnie—and Lawrence too—probably made it possible. But he hadn't made it to the end—and then really almost didn't *make* it. That was an eye-opener. *If a man as indestructible as the bosun could die . . .* He shook his head, unwilling to finish the thought, and grunted. *That's the way he would'a wanted it, though,* he realized. *On his ship, by Cap'n Reddy's side. But he went down in the same big fight that took this shitty place called Grik City. The hell with Adar's stupid name.* "The bosun would'a scared it outa him," he finally said.

"There you are!" came a scolding Brooklyn accent from behind. Silva's scowl instantly changed to a beatific smile as he turned to face petite, dark-haired Nurse Lieutenant Pam Cross. They'd . . . endured an on-again, off-again, maybe back-on-again (Dennis was never entirely sure) relationship for quite some time, in which she engaged in complex rituals of deep understanding, wild confusion, adoration, and volcanic fury. All the while, Silva remained Silva—likely the cause of much of her erratic behavior—and imagined he was as close to "in love" with her as his imperfect understanding of the concept would allow.

"Right where I always am, my little honeydew!" he crooned. She rolled her eyes and snorted.

"You weren't here last night," she accused.

He waved vaguely down at the wreckage below. "Was too," he defended. "Most'a the night. Then I hobbled down yonder, careful as a crippled fawn," he added piously, "'cause I seen some fellas pokin' around that busted zep. Had to have a look at some little swivel guns they found. Kinda weird."

"You ain't supposed to go runnin' around!" Pam brayed. "You spring another leak, an' I'll just stand by and let you drain out! See if I don't!"

"Clearly, Chief Silva is ready for more than merely sitting about," came another voice, and Dennis craned around again, wincing a little this time. The Lemurians stirred, trying to rise.

"Why, Chackie!" he said, then frowned. "You ain't gonna make me call you 'Colonel,' are ya?"

Chack snorted a chuckle, waving at the 'Cats to remain comfortable, and moved around to squat beside his friend. "I'm still just a second-class bosun's mate on *Walker*, our Home. You outrank *me* there. Just call me 'Colonel' when it seems appropriate to do so"—he blinked amusement—"if you ever recognize such an occasion."

Dennis grinned. "So whatcha got?" He nodded toward Pam. "You gonna spring me from the torments of Torky-mada . . . ett, here?"

"Torky who?" Horn asked.

"Never mind." Silva looked expectantly at Chack.

"Are you up to accompanying me on a trip?"

"Back to the ship?"

"No, to meet some . . . other people. Cap-i-taan Reddy said I can have you if you're fit."

Silva leaned back on his cushion, resting his wrist on his brow. "Oh, I don't know. Done a lotta meetin' folks, an' I am feelin' kinda poorly. An' it seems all I do is go trambleatin' to an' fro of late."

"He's not going anywhere!" Pam decreed. "He's wounded—again! He needs to heal properly this time!"

Pam's outburst stirred Silva forward, and he eyed Chack more seriously. "Scuttlebutt's got you goin' south, lookin' for the great-grand'Cats of all the 'Cats. You really are?" He frowned, remembering when he'd briefly gone ashore with Chack and his brigade. "I recall there's some mighty interestin' boogers roamin' around down there. Might gimme a chance to do a little huntin'. . . ."

"Some *very* interesting creatures," Chack assured.

Silva's lips split into a particular gap-toothed grin that even Lemurians had learned to approach with caution. "Well, hell. Sounds like a hoot. Can't be as rough as our little hike to North Borno to meet Tony. . . ." He caught himself. "I mean, I'joorka's Malay an' lizard folks." He gestured at Horn. "*He* let a whole damn ship fall on him!"

"It was just half a ship," Horn denied. "What about me?"

Chack blinked regret. "I'm informed that your injuries will require a bit more time to heal," he said, "and you are scheduled to sail for Baalkpan aboard *Amerika* with the other wounded."

Horn looked down.

"Hey, tough luck," Silva said, uncharacteristically soft.

"That's okay. I need a rest from you anyway, you big jerk."

"You're a pal." Silva shrugged. "I hear that little Jap, Toryu Miyata, will be on *Amerika* too. And maybe Herring. So at least you'll have fellas to reminisce and jabber with."

"And *I*?" Lawrence demanded.

"Hey, his flipper's a lot better," Silva said. "Flap yer arm, Larry! Show him."

Chack was thoughtful. "I do not know. The People in the south would only see Laaw-rence as a Grik, I fear, but . . ." He looked searchingly at the Sa'aaran. "You have often proven remarkably useful. I am in command of the expedition and I know your value in . . . unusual circumstances, but that decision might best be left to Mr. Braad-furd. He is responsible for the diplomatic aspects of the mission."

"So you're goin'?" Pam demanded.

"You betcha!" Silva laughed.

"We'll see about that!" Pam stated harshly, and stormed back through the entrance. Silva watched her go.

"Say, she can't queer the deal, can she?"

"Lady Sandra has cleared you," Chack replied, contemplating that conversation. It had been much like a similar one he'd once had with General Shinya in which Shinya described Silva as an amazingly useful but dangerous man. Chack had to agree with that—and Sandra's assessment that it was always best to keep Dennis busy—and focused on being usefully dangerous in the right direction. Unconsciously, he blinked vague speculation, glancing after Pam. He knew she and Silva were sweet on each other, and he no longer—really—thought there'd ever been anything physical between the big destroyerman and Risa, his sister. But Risa would be remaining behind, and he was just as glad to keep them apart. As for Pam . . . "But Lady Sandra, even Cap-i-taan Reddy, will not *order* you to go. Paam has a point. While your wounds were not as deep or dangerous as Gunny Horn's, or as crippling as Lieuten-aant Mi-yaa-ta's, they were many. If you would rather . . ."

"No, no! I'll go. It's been too long since we went adventurin' together, just you an' me!"

Chack stood. "Very well. Much remains to prepare, and there are always delays." Chack waved out at the devastation. "But we must leave as soon as possible." He grinned. "I shall leave you to sort out your own, uh, preparations." With that, he turned and left, following Pam into the palace.

"Pam's gonna hate your guts—again," Horn warned.

"Maybe. But she'll be outa here, back on *Walker* when they go chasin' Grik in the strait, anyway."

"Wouldn't you rather be on *Walker*?"

Dennis considered, and his thoughts veered suddenly back to the bosun. "Not just yet," he answered quietly.

Suddenly, a small, colorful reptile with furry membranes stretched between its limbs scrambled up and leaped on Silva's chest with a "Grawwk!" of greeting. Not capable of actual flight, the creature was more of a tree-glider from Yap Island, where Silva, Lawrence, Sandra, and a number of others had been marooned for a while. Originally the pet of then Princess, now Governor-Empress Rebecca Anne McDonald of the Empire of the New Britain Isles, he'd been sent away purportedly due to his somewhat inappropriate behavior.

"Goddammit, Petey!" Silva snarled. "Get off! Go back to the Skipper's lady where you belong!" Petey promptly arched his back and heaved like a cat with a hairball, and before Silva could fling him away, he regurgitated a bolus of . . . something, on Silva's clean shirt. "Eat!" he cawed triumphantly, beaming up at Dennis with large, adoring eyes. "Eat, goddammit!"

"You might lose Pam for good this time," Horn deadpanned, "but at least *somebody* still loves ya."

///// *Second Fleet*
Off the coast of New Granada (Ecuador)
USS Maaka-Kakja *(CV-4)*

"With all respect, Your Highness, I do not care if you are my Governor-Empress," High Admiral Harvey Jenks declared, his carefully controlled patience beginning to crack. "We simply cannot risk the reinforcements you've brought by putting them ashore just yet, and I certainly cannot—*will not*—risk *you!*" Despite her small stature and normally almost-elfin face, a lesser man would've dissolved under the withering glare the young empress bestowed on Jenks. Admiral Lelaa-Tal-Cleraan, commander of *Maaka-Kakja*, still the sole aircraft carrier/tender with Second Fleet, was a personal friend of Rebecca Anne McDonald, and even she almost took a step back. Jenks held his ground, but began absently

twisting his long, braided mustaches with his fingers. The others gathered on the great ship's broad bridgewing reacted in various ways. High
Chief Saan-Kakja, Rebecca's Lemurian "sister" ruler of all the Filpin
Lands, stood beside her, but blinked her mesmerizing black and golden
eyes with a thoughtfulness that Rebecca's temper had abandoned. Sister
Audry, the young, straw-haired Benedictine nun, appeared slightly em-
barrassed, as did "Tex" Sheider, Lelaa's Exec. Sergeant "Lord" Koratin,
Audry's scarred, wizened, Lemurian Marine bodyguard and advisor
from Aryaal, stood at parade rest. His face didn't show it, of course, but
he had an air of boredom about him. Sister Audry's enlightened and
converted regiment of former Dom prisoners of war, her "Regimento de
Redentores," had a new colonel. Former Teniente of Dominion "Salva-
dores," Colonel Arano Garcia had an anxious expression on his dark,
handsome face. Surgeon Commander Selaas-Fris-Ar, Keje's daughter
and chief medical officer for all of Second Fleet, blinked consternation.
Matt's cousin, Orrin Reddy, *Maaka-Kakja's* Commander of Flight Operations (COFO), looked on with guarded amusement. A pair of Nancy
floatplanes, their blue paint now salt streaked and weathered, roared off
the flight deck and into the sky, bound for Guayakwil Bay to support
General Shinya's expeditionary force in the East.

Rebecca waited for the noise to subside, then continued her argument. "I regret that we were unable to bring the new carriers completing
in Maa-ni-la. There have been delays. But my sister and I did not come
all this way, bringing troops and weapons so sorely needed on this front,
merely to bob about aboard the most powerful element of an inactive
fleet!"

Jenks winced at that, but held his tongue. Lelaa didn't. "That's unfair, Your Highness," she scolded, relying on their friendship and her
status as the most senior representative of the "Amer-i-caan Navy Clan"
in the hemisphere. "Most unfair indeed. This fleet has not been 'inactive.' Far from it. And we have not sought a decisive fleet action with the
Doms at the Pass of Fire simply because we do not know what is there!"
She nodded at Orrin. "We have tried to scout the strange strait between
the continents and the enemy fleet gathered there, but there are too
many Grikbirds—'dragons'—for our planes to penetrate far enough to
see anything worth the terrible losses in aircraft and crews we have sustained in previous attempts."

"We brought more planes and pilots," Rebecca shot back.

"Which will allow us to try again," Lelaa agreed resignedly, "with further dreadful losses, no doubt."

"And as for going ashore," Selass interjected, "High Ahd-mi-raal Jenks seeks only to protect you and the troops you bring. As he has informed you, there is a terrible illness ashore that the locals call 'El Vómito Rojo.'" She shook her head. "So far it has not affected Mi-Anakka—Lemurian—troops, but it has been devastating to the human forces." She sighed. "Perhaps half of them are sick. Even General Shinya has fallen ill. And though the seep and polta paste seem to help prevent the secondary, more fatal symptoms, there have been several hundred deaths within the army. The civilian population of Guayak has been even harder hit." She blinked incredulity. "Some appear to be immune, having never had the disease, but many seem to accept it as merely a seasonal part of life. I cannot imagine why they don't simply move away. Through my correspondence with Karen Letts at Baalkpan, I am convinced the swarming mosquitoes on the coastal plain are to blame. They are not as bad at higher elevations."

"Where the Dom 'Army of God' gathers under that hideous fiend Don Hernan!" Rebecca snapped. Scouts of the enemy position and preparations had secured enough prisoners to confirm that.

"Yes, but they do not have polta paste to alleviate much of the suffering. If they come down and attack now, they would be even more devastated by the disease than our people are."

"Then we must hope they are as sensitive to losses as we," Koratin said dryly. Everyone knew that they were not.

"If I may?" Colonel Garcia asked quietly. Jenks looked at him, unable to hide the skeptical arch his eyebrow made. He remained unconvinced that Doms could be torn away from their fanatical adherence to their twisted faith, even though they now knew not all "Doms," the Guayakans for example, shared that faith in the first place. He'd talked with their spokesman, Suares, and through him to their alcalde, and they'd struck him as normal, if rather odd, people, just like any in the Empire. But Garcia had been a Dom officer, and his regiment was composed of men who'd fought fanatically *against* the Empire on the island of New Ireland. He found it hard to believe they'd just . . . stopped being what they were. Sister Audry and even Governor-Empress Rebecca were insistent, however, and he too had to admit that Garcia seemed devoted to them. "Please do," he finally said.

"If Don Hernan senses weakness in your army, he will attack regardless of losses," he said. "He may even calculate that he could march down from the mountains and destroy General Shinya before El Vómito could weaken his own force enough to stop it. I think it more likely, however, that he will wait until the worst of the season has passed, then strike with a healthy force while he believes yours remains weak."

"How long?" Jenks demanded.

"Another week. Perhaps two," Selass said. "According to Suares."

"Can you at least wait that long, Your Majesty?" Jenks pleaded. "We will commence transferring supplies immediately, and we can set the reinforcements ashore quite rapidly when the time comes, I assure you."

Rebecca hesitated, then nodded. "Very well. But in the meantime, we must discover what we face at sea. We all know Don Hernan, and I do not think he will be content to merely wait for his opportunity. I suspect he will move against the fleet in some fashion in conjunction with his land assault. We mustn't let him have his way in *all* things, in respect to his schedule." She looked at Jenks. "You say our aircraft cannot penetrate to the Pass of Fire without prohibitive losses to the dragons, but there is little they can do against well-prepared ships. I am directing you to dispatch a sizable portion of the fleet to investigate the pass at once!"

Jenks frowned. "I respectfully suggest that such a move would be extremely risky. We have no idea how large the Dom fleet is, and we risk losing that 'sizable portion' if it runs into something substantial. We should wait a bit longer. Perhaps we may even receive word from the strange 'other Americans' Lieutenant Reynolds and Ensign Faask encountered during their escape from the Doms."

"But you said such a communication would likely only come after we have dealt the Doms a harsh blow at sea."

"That's true. But I still counsel against it—and if we must move against the pass, we should do it with all our might or none."

"That is unacceptable," Rebecca stated. "The larger portion of the fleet must remain here to cover General Shinya—and land the reinforcements when the time comes. You will send a heavy scout to discover what it may, at long last, about the enemy fleet. Our ships are faster than theirs. The squadron can always retire if it runs into more than it can handle. Perhaps that move alone will prompt the other Americans to signal us in some way?" Her tone hardened. "I have acquiesced on all other points. Do not fight me on this, High Admiral Jenks!"

Jenks nodded reluctantly. "Very well, Your Highness." Rebecca turned to Orrin Reddy. "Is there no way that we can fly to meet these strangers? Circumventing the Pass of Fire, of course."

Orrin looked doubtful. "Fred Reynolds and Kari Faask suggested that themselves," he admitted. "Even volunteered. Nutty damn kids, after what they went through. But it's just too dangerous. There're the Doms and their Grikbirds to consider, sure. But we don't even know where the hell to send 'em. They got the impression these other Americans have a fleet in the Gulf of Mexico—a, ah, body of water on the other side of the Pass of Fire. Full of fuel and nothing else, a Nancy might make it that far, but what then? Even if there is a fleet, it'd be dumb-ass luck for one plane to find it. I'm afraid we'd just be wasting anybody we sent."

"The only other option is a land expedition from the Imperial colonies around Saint Francis," Jenks said, "but again, they don't really know where to go, and such a trip might take months." He shrugged. "They know where we are, Your Majesty, and said they would contact us when the time was right for them. I see no feasible way to contact them for the foreseeable future."

"Without a fleet action," Rebecca prodded.

"That was mentioned as a means of getting their attention," Jenks confessed reluctantly.

"All the more reason to send the heavy scouting force," Rebecca stressed. "As I said, perhaps they will consider that enough."

Orrin trotted down the steps from the bridgewing, heading for his office near the ready room. At the base of the ladder, as expected, he ran into Fred Reynolds and Kari Faask. He paused, shaking his head. "No go," he said. "I pitched your case, like I agreed, but they didn't go for it." He didn't mention how strongly he'd *objected* to their case. Fred and Kari both took deep breaths and then looked at the deck.

"Thanks anyway, Mr. Reddy," Fred mumbled.

"Hey, at least you're back flying," Orrin consoled.

"Sure. That's something. But we're not doing much. Most of the combat ops sortie out of Guayakwil Bay. We're just flying around, knocking holes in the sky and watching for Dom ships."

"Somebody's got to do it—and damn it, folks are sick on shore! You guys are still weak from what you went through. You want to get sick and finish yourselves off?"

"*I* not get sick," Kari countered.

"You want another pilot, then?" Orrin demanded. "Because Fred probably *will*. Him and me are still the only human pilots in this fleet, and will be until the Impies finally get some fliers out here. You don't see *me* clamoring to go ashore, do you? Let this bug run its course, and we'll all get plenty busy."

"Okay. Afternoon, Mr. Reddy. And thanks."

When Orrin was gone, Fred sighed at his Lemurian friend. "Would've been easier with his help, not to mention feeling less like running off. Nothing for it, though, I guess."

"Nope."

///// *Chimborazo*
New Granada Province
Holy Dominion

G eneral Ghanan Nerino, former commander of His Supreme Holiness's Army of the South, approached Don Hernan de Devina Dicha with a familiar sense of dread. Even when he didn't bear news he was sure the unpredictably capricious Blood Cardinal would dislike, he was uncomfortable in his presence. Bringing . . . disappointing information, Nerino had no idea how Don Hernan would react. Sitting on a padded wicker chair on the porch of the residence of the alcalde of Chimborazo, the Blood Cardinal sipped from a steaming mug in the cool, late-morning air. Seeing him gaze about with such a benevolent expression behind his immaculately trimmed mustache and goatee, Nerino would have found it easy to imagine that Don Hernan was not really a maniac after all, if he hadn't seen such ample proof to the contrary.

He *was* a maniac, to be generous, and a singularly dangerous one. Since he was second in authority only to His Supreme Holiness himself, Don Hernan's power was unchecked, and he practically ruled the Holy Dominion in the name of the Messiah of Mexico who was, even Nerino believed, Emperor of the World by the grace of God. But even by the standards of God's harsh laws, interpreted and set forth in holy tracts by His beloved priests, Don Hernan's rule was peculiarly frightful. As prescribed, he ruled through terror, but he took his responsibility to an extreme unremembered in Nerino's lifetime. Pain was the gateway to grace, and blood was the price of God's love and favor; that was the way of things. The effusion of both was celebrated and ritualized throughout the Dominion, but neither was to be wantonly wasted. That Don Hernan could so casually and often arbitrarily command the deliberate squandering of so much blood from behind such a pleasant demeanor of gentle piety inspired equal measures of horror and amazement in Ghanan Nerino, and convinced him that Don Hernan was mad.

Nerino moved through the priests gathered behind Don Hernan, standing in silence. Their lord had decided that morning that he didn't want to see any people, only the unspoiled beauty of the mountain village and God's creation surrounding it. Therefore, all the troops encamped east of town had been forced to move with fanatical urgency in the predawn dark, and every villager had been warned to stay out of sight until midday. It hadn't been necessary to remind them what would happen to them if they were seen. No doubt, Don Hernan would watch their execution with the same expression he now wore. This was yet another example of how erratic, impulsive, and stunningly profligate in time and resources his whims had become, even as he constantly urged haste in preparing the Army of God to expel the invaders infesting the coastal lowland.

Ghanan Nerino had tried that once already, and had lost an army in the attempt. He was fortunate, he supposed, that he'd been so painfully wounded by the flaming bombs dropped by the invader's flying machines. That had isolated him from blame for the debacle, and doubtless granted him some grace in Don Hernan's eyes. The filmy bandages still covering his face and hands were a constant reminder of his suffering— his "grace"—and had probably allowed him to speak more freely to Don Hernan than he would otherwise have dared, but grace was transient, he knew quite well, and he always wondered when his would finally run out.

He still wasn't sure precisely what his status was. Don Hernan still called him "general," even though he led no troops; Don Hernan himself was in sole command of the Army of God. Nerino assumed the Blood Cardinal had, initially at least, suffered his presence as an advisor because he actually did know more about the heretic army than anyone else. He'd since taken upon himself the task of coordinating the gathering of even more information about the enemy since, to his surprise, no one else was doing it. To be fair, he hadn't expected much intelligence from his own staff before the Battle of Guayak, but he knew better now. His rank remained good for something. He started appropriating and evaluating the reports of spies, and passing what he learned to Don Hernan during their increasingly frequent meetings. "Spymaster" was his new "status," he supposed.

A musical chime within the residence proclaimed noon, and Don Hernan started as if released from a trance. "Ah, General Nerino!" he said without turning. "You continue to improve, I trust? Surely God has sped your recovery for the task ahead!" Nerino was taken aback by the address. He'd approached so quietly, there was no way Don Hernan could have known he was there. But then again, he *would* have known, because he'd commanded Nerino's presence, and of course his general would be waiting upon him at the appointed time.

"Thank you, Your Holiness. I am sure of it," Nerino respectfully replied.

"Join me, General," Don Hernan invited, gesturing grandly at a chair across the small table beside him. "Have refreshment!"

"Thank you, Your Holiness," Nerino said, stepping forward and easing into the chair. His burns were healing well, and even his chin whiskers were beginning to return, but he'd lost a great deal of weight during his recovery, much of it muscle. He'd once been somewhat round; the result of a soft, well-fed life, but now he was almost thin and felt weak and sore.

After the usual pleasantries that prefaced any conversation with Don Hernan, even a sentence of death, the Blood Cardinal leaned back in apparent satisfaction before gazing intently at Nerino. "And what have you heard from our spies? Most particularly, what is the state of the heretics' army, now that El Vómito Rojo is upon them?" Don Hernan's voice had a sudden predatory tone.

Nerino nodded, but cringed inwardly. The Army of God had mustered almost a hundred and ten thousand men, composed of what remained of Nerino's Army of the South, more troops originally intended for the conquest of the Galápagos, and still other forces hastily gathered from all over the Nuevo Granada Province. A division of the elite Blood Drinker infantry was even rushing southwestward from as far away as the Templo de los Papas, in Nuevo Granada City itself. It was scheduled to bring a "special gift" from His Supreme Holiness, from the mountain village of Popayan several hundred miles to the north, but they'd received no word as yet whether the division had even arrived at that remote place, much less resumed its difficult march. *The "gift" will make its journey even more arduous*, Nerino reflected, *but might prove decisive if it comes in time.* The Army of God was already larger than the one the heretics had destroyed around Nerino, but the heretics had also been reinforced—within a strategically dangerous fortification. Don Hernan didn't want to wait for the Blood Drinkers to arrive, despite his excitement over the special gift, but he had been willing to delay his final assault long enough for El Vómito Rojo to decimate the enemy. El Vómito was a seasonal, often deadly, lowland fever. On this coast it was associated with rotten air rising from stagnant pools created by spring melt and late-summer rains, but was much less prevalent in the more wholesome air of the higher, cooler clime the Army of God now occupied. Unfortunately, Nerino's spies had reported that while the fever *was* upon the heretics, it had not had the expected effect.

"The position the heretic general has taken—Shinya is his name, you may recall—is most formidable, and . . . awkward for us, as you know," Nerino generalized. "It is supported by sea from both Guayak, and now Puerto Viejo as well." He nodded grimly. "Indeed, it is confirmed. The people there, culturally related to the Guayakans, did not, ah, 'successfully resist' the heretics that landed there to cut that narrow segment of the Camino Militar."

"As I told His Supreme Holiness!" Don Hernan brooded. "Heretics on every hand! And the ones within our midst are at least as dangerous as those from across the sea! None can be trusted; all must be cleansed!"

Nerino hesitated in confusion over what Don Hernan meant by

"all." "Of course," he said neutrally, before continuing. "The enemy now commands all junctions of the Camino Militar, from every direction but the south, beyond Guayak"—he frowned and spread his hands—"which does not signify. After the . . . indisposition of my army, there are few troops left to draw from the south—and no way to communicate our need in any event, since the heretics control the sea as well." He paused, realizing he'd just reminded Don Hernan of his own failure once again. He hadn't been blamed, but quite a few fine officers under his command had been, to their pain. He hurried on. "Our first objective remains, as I see it, the destruction of this 'Fort Defiance' as they style it, that they have erected. It *is* quite impressive," he stressed again. "Once that has been achieved, we can move to expel the heretics from Guayak and Puerto Viejo."

"Not 'expel,' General Nerino," Don Hernan objected coldly. "Exterminate."

"Of course, Your Holiness."

Don Hernan eyed him thoughtfully. "But what of El Vómito? I asked you before. Surely it has weakened the heretic army by now? The sickness should have reached its peak and done half our work for us."

"The sickness *has* reached its peak," Nerino carefully confirmed.

"But why did you not say so to begin with?" Don Hernan scolded gently, a soft smile on his face. "The time has come for the Army of God to march into the valley and across the plain to slay the few survivors, still sick and weak! When that is done, we will raze Guayak and Puerto Viejo to the ground before we move to take the Galápagos." He smiled more broadly. "The final conquest of the world is finally at hand, my dear general! Rejoice!"

Nerino shifted uncomfortably on his chair. Don Hernan studied his expression, and his own smile began to fade. "What have you not yet revealed?" he demanded.

Nerino took a breath. "There appear to be more than a, ah, 'few' heretic survivors. It seems that the sickness has already peaked—and begun to fade, Your Holiness. Our spies say there was much fever among the human heretics, but they use medicines we do not know, that relieve and shorten the symptoms of the ill and even save many of the most grievously afflicted. It is said that they may even be able to *prevent* the disease in some cases!"

"Impossible!" Don Hernan proclaimed. "No medicine can do that! It must be sorcery of the darkest sort! All the more reason to destroy the heretics without delay!"

"But they have not been weakened as much as we hoped, and the animal warriors—the 'Lemurians' that constitute fully half their force—did not take sick at all." Nerino braced himself. "I most humbly suggest that we not underestimate the animal warriors again, Your Holiness. I did, once. Why should I not? But having done so, I learned what a terrible mistake it was. They *are* demons," he said almost wonderingly, as if realizing it for the first time himself. Perhaps he was. "Most unnatural demons. And I do not know, honestly, if they are in the power of the Imperials, or the other way around!"

"They *are* demons," Don Hernan somberly confirmed. "And your confusion is well founded because even I cannot enlighten you. I have known one," he added bitterly, "and thought it just a pet. But whether its . . . human companion was truly that devoted to it, or it had some power over him, I cannot say. Either way, I shall certainly not underestimate the creatures, and will not rest until all are swept from the face of the world." Nerino said nothing, stunned by Don Hernan's admission that seemed to imply the recognition that *he* had once made a mistake. Nerino was tempted, but finally didn't mention that he too had met a Lemurian; a most intimidating female captain named Blas-Ma-Ar, if he remembered correctly. It was just as well that he said nothing.

"Too many of your former troops who fought them insist they are Jaguar demons," Don Hernan continued darkly, "or some such creatures whose coming was foretold by the Jaguarista bandits that style themselves rebels against the temple!" He glanced at Nerino with a frown of regret. "We cannot silence them all, you know. The army needs every man—for now. A few examples should be made so the rest will at least keep their filthy thoughts to themselves. But ultimately, the only way to end this evil is to destroy it."

"And we shall prevail, of course," Nerino quickly assured him. "But the Army of God will suffer no matter what we do. That may delay further campaigns for a time. Perhaps . . . we should delay *this* one just slightly longer. At least until the reinforcements—and the gift—arrive."

"That may be," Don Hernan reluctantly acknowledged, to Nerino's relief. "And I will send courier dragons to find the column of Blood

Drinkers. Try to hurry them along. But if what your spies report is true, the heretics *are* at least somewhat weakened just now. They will only get stronger the longer we wait. It therefore remains that the time to strike—both at this 'Shinya' and against the enemy fleet as well—is upon us regardless." He reflected a moment, gazing at the villagers beginning to emerge from their homes. "I had hoped to delay our naval attack a short while longer. You could not know the details, but it had to be clear to you that our Western Fleet met great . . . difficulty against the Heretic Navy. Otherwise, they would not have been able to land an army here. New weapons and strategies have been devised for use by the elements of our Eastern Fleet gathered at El Paso del Fuego, and I am confident we have both a qualitative and vast numerical advantage now at sea." He paused, frowning. "But new things of any sort are always so troublesome to predict," he confessed with a frankness that again surprised Nerino.

"In addition," he continued, "other things are in motion, beyond what is seen, that cause me some concern. . . . You know that the heretics have other enemies in Africa?" Nerino nodded, even though Don Hernan had only recently informed him of that. "I dispatched a mission across the Atlantic to contact them, but nothing has been heard," Don Hernan admitted. "Perhaps it was lost. It is a dreadful voyage. Or perhaps *our* other enemies, Los Diablos del Norte, have interfered. Even in the face of our withdrawal of so many assets in the Caribbean, Los Diablos have done remarkably little—that we have seen." He shook his head. "Far too much is unknown to me in these strange times, and that only makes it more imperative that we eliminate the most pressing, apparent threats as quickly as we can. To completely destroy Shinya and his fort, we must deprive him of all support, so we *must* release our own fleet at El Paso del Fuego to accomplish that task. I have sent courier dragons there as well, bearing the appropriate commands. It is time that General Shinya, his 'Second Fleet,' and all who aid them on land and sea were erased."

Nerino must not have hidden his expression well enough, because Don Hernan regarded him with a softly quizzical look. "You are concerned that we move precipitously?"

Nerino quickly shook his head. "Not with you to lead the army, Your Holiness. I do . . . fret very slightly that with no senior officers in your army who have faced the heretics before, there may arise similar, ah, confusions such as those that plagued my army when first we met the foe." He didn't remind Don Hernan that he'd pleaded with him not to execute the very officers he'd soon need so badly, but feared he'd already gone too far.

Don Hernan appeared to shake off his introspective mood and smiled indulgently. "Do not 'fret,' my dear General Nerino! Our fleet has been poised to move for some time, but it will take a little more, certainly, before it can sail and meet the enemy. This shall be a coordinated attack, and you will necessarily have *some* time to familiarize your officers with what they will face, and what is expected of them. If the Blood Drinkers arrive in time, all the better, but we must march within a week of receiving word that the Eastern Fleet has put to sea! It will take another week for the Army of God to reach the enemy, so I would estimate that you might expect as many as three to prepare.

Nerino was stunned, as much by what Don Hernan had implied as by how little time he'd have to take the reins. "You . . . You're giving me command?"

"Of course! *I* am no general, and who better than you? You shall command the army in the field, and I command you. You will provide the example the army needs to fight, and I have—and will—provide examples of the price of failure! How could either of us hope for a better arrangement than that?"

////// *Fort Defiance*
North of Guayak

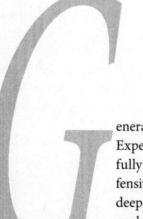eneral Tomatsu Shinya, commander of the Allied Expeditionary Force in the East, stepped carefully to the top of the northernmost section of defensive works closest to his quarters and took a deep breath. The air was full of woodsmoke from cookfires inside the fort, but it still tasted cool and clean compared to the stale, unmoving air he'd been breathing in his buttoned-up bunker. It was good to be out and about after being laid up so long, but he still felt like hell. His fever was gone at last, as was the bloody vomiting that was the most frightening symptom of the sickness, but he was still dizzy and had terrible headaches. He ached all over as a matter of fact, and the very thought of food left him nauseated. He'd turned the corner, though; that was clear. That he could move around at all was proof of that. Unlike malaria, this disease offered no temporary respite. One either got better or died. Too

many, almost a thousand now, hadn't improved, and they'd been carried outside the high earthen outer wall of Fort Defiance and buried along the road back to Guayak. Shinya gazed in that direction for a time, past the interior of the great fort, which bustled with activity and continuous improvement. The thick, earthen outer ramparts were arranged in the shape of a rough pentagon (which Orrin Reddy had described as a smushed starfish when seen from the air), and they bristled with heavy guns, particularly the bastions, or "lunettes" as Shinya called them, that rounded the points of the pentagon. Many of the heaviest guns had been captured from the Doms at Guayak; others had been brought ashore from Imperial ships of the line at Puerto Viejo and trundled here on their naval trucks with backbreaking effort. All were supported by firing steps and had thick overhead protection, as did the various magazines scattered strategically around the enclosure. Traps and barbed-wire entanglements laced the broad killing ground beyond, making the defenses even more formidable. Inside was a second wall: a sheer, earth-reinforced palisade even higher than the surrounding ramparts, with observation towers strategically placed. Within that was a compound the size of a small city, complete with covered sewers washed clean by water diverted from a stream. Despite the sickness and the concentration of nearly sixty thousand troops, Lemurian, Imperial, Guayakan, and recruits from the now desperately committed port city of Puerto Viejo, Shinya supposed it was the "healthiest" fortification ever devised on this world.

"Should you be up and about so soon?" Colonel James Blair of the Empire of the New Britain Isles inquired in a mildly scolding tone, stepping up behind him. Blair was one of the few Imperials who hadn't shown any symptoms of El Vómito Rojo. At least not yet. Did that mean he was immune, perhaps bolstered by liberal doses of Lemurian medicines, or still susceptible? There was no telling.

"I've been away from my duties too long," Shinya replied, "not even able to take a proper report." He rubbed his forehead. "Or in truth, understand one." He straightened, looking up at the high mountains to the east. Low clouds hid the peaks from view. "I must know the enemy's current dispositions."

"You've been ill," Blair countered with a smile, "and your duties *have* been performed regardless. You have a capable executive officer, after all, who has not been sick."

Shinya managed a pained smile at Blair. "Of course, Colonel. You're quite capable, and no offense was meant." He frowned. "And still just a colonel," he mused. "I should've done something about that long ago. How you've dealt with all the posturing Imperial *generals* lavished upon us during my incapacity remains a mystery."

Blair grinned. "As your executive officer and empowered with your mystical authority, I immediately turned them back into colonels as soon as they arrived. A few were quite indignant."

Shinya snorted a laugh. "You've become a most resourceful officer, my friend. But that does not lessen my frustration at having been so long indisposed. Please, as our American friends would say; what have I missed?"

Blair nodded at two Lemurians climbing the berm to join them. One was female and the other was missing most of his tail. Shinya got the distinct impression all had been waiting to talk to him—as soon as he was well enough to know what they were saying. "Here are Captain Blas-Ma-Ar and Leftenant Faal-Pel of the Eighth Maa-ni-laa," Blair said. "They can help me brief you more completely. I know you're acquainted with Captain Blas, but I believe Leftenant Faal-Pel is more commonly known as 'Stumpy.'"

Shinya's smile grew more genuine. "Of course I know Lieutenant Stumpy," he said as the pair drew near. "He was a destroyerman aboard USS *Walker* long before he took up a rifle. Good afternoon, Captain, Lieutenant," he said louder. "I trust you're well?"

Blas and Stumpy saluted smartly, and Shinya and Blair returned it. "We're fine, Gener-aal," Blas replied. "You doin' better?"

"I am indeed," Shinya assured her. Blas nodded almost imperceptibly at Blair. The two had been *very* worried about Tomatsu Shinya, and what his loss might mean for the entire war effort in the East. "You two have been largely responsible for the creation of these works," Shinya continued. "Tell me what you think of them."

Blas glanced at Stumpy, who fidgeted slightly, then looked back at Shinya. "Well, none of us were real happy about buildin' 'em in the first place, but I guess you knew that." Shinya nodded, and Blas continued. "Pretty much everybody was for stayin' after the Doms. That said, we know we couldn't'a done that until the supply train caught up." Blas performed a very human shrug. "Then everybody got sick—at least the

Impies and locals did. I hate to think what would'a happened if the Doms hit us on the march, with everybody strung out an' pukin' theirselves ta' death. Stoppin' here made good sense from a supply standpoint, but even more sense now." She looked at Shinya, who was still nodding. He well knew that whenever someone asked Blas what she thought about anything, they'd get the whole truth, complete with her unvarnished opinion. "But that's not what you asked," Blas said, almost reminding herself. She gestured around. "We've built a helluva good fort here, Gener-aal. Way better than the defenses we threw up around Guayak, and they weren't nothin' to flip yer tail at. It was a close call, but we walloped the Doms well enough in front of them. Here? It'd take a lot more Doms to come near as close to breakin' through as they did at Guayak. As long as we have ammo and air support, I think we could stay here forever."

Shinya looked at Blair. "And what of the Doms?"

"Our scouts report that they stopped their retreat in the mountains, near the town of Chimborazo. There was confusion for a time, before that wicked Don Hernan himself arrived with a sizable force, presumably from the north where they'd been gathering their Enchanted Isles invasion force. So whatever we've accomplished, it seems we did manage to delay that operation, at least." He snorted. "But Don Hernan's not been content to merely halt their retreat. He's put a spine back in his army—I shudder to think how he did that—and is obviously gathering his forces to attack us here."

"How many?"

"That's difficult to say, General Shinya." Blair actually chuckled. "Our scouts and theirs are almost all locals who know one another. Ours are invested in defeating the Doms—and survival, of course— whereas theirs are only interested in saving themselves and their families. Sometimes they skirmish when they meet, but there's considerable fraternization as well. I suspect the scouts on both sides wind up telling their counterparts a great deal of what they have been sent to discover. I'm sure it's safer for all concerned," he added wryly. "But it's made learning the exact number of enemy troops somewhat inconvenient. I think that would be the case in any event since it's always difficult to estimate the size of an army from within it. At the same time, we have, I think, successfully misled the enemy into believing the sickness that struck us was not as severe as he obviously hoped. That there is some truth in that has no doubt made the larger fiction that we're quite ready for them a bit easier to accept. But our latest reports imply they're preparing to strike regardless, fearing that any advantage El Vómito might give them will be lost."

"So *they* didn't catch it after all?"

"Not to any large extent. It appears that Surgeon Commander Selass was right about that as well."

"Did you *know* about the Bloody Spews?" Blas suddenly blurted, and Shinya looked at her, surprised.

"The Bloody Spews?" he asked.

"That's what the sickness is called in the ranks," Blair told him.

"Oh. Of course." He looked back at Blas and sighed. "Yes. The vice alcalde, Señor Suares, told me to expect it, and that was largely why I chose to halt our advance. We might've finished the Doms before they could reconsolidate, but at some point we would've been stopped by the sickness. Better here, behind well-situated defenses, than on the march."

"That's what I thought," Blas said, glaring now at Stumpy. "Lots'a stuff makes more sense now."

"The fever is passing from all our troops?" Shinya asked Blair. "Those who did not succumb?"

"Slowly, General, and some new cases are still reported every day, but I think the worst is behind us. Our current strength is about forty thousand, fit for duty. Mostly Lemurians, of course. Another ten thousand or so are recovering and should be fit before too much longer, but the rest remain gravely ill."

"So many still sick?"

"I'm afraid so." Blair hesitated. "On that note, we do have significant reinforcements prepared to join us. Saan-Kakja and the Governor-Empress have arrived at last, but High Admiral Jenks refuses to allow them to land until the fever season has passed entirely."

"Quite right," Shinya murmured. "We can't risk a resurgence of the disease, and Selass is sure that the fever is spread by mosquitoes. As long as any of our people still carry the sickness and mosquitoes remain abundant, the infection could be transferred to any who joined us." He brooded in silence for a moment. "But how many Doms *are* there?" he demanded.

Blair spread his hands. "We don't know. Chimborazo rests at an altitude nearly high enough for our pilots to require oxygen—which we cannot provide. And there are enough dragons, ah, 'Grikbirds,' to further discourage adequate reconnaissance from the air. I understand our planes and pilots can both fly somewhat higher, but the performance of both—and particularly the machines—degrade enough to make them easy prey for the enemy air . . . creatures."

"I've talked to some of the scouts myself," Blas said, "and some flyboys too, who got as close as they could. We've lost a good many planes, General," she interjected. "The only thing that all sources seem convinced of is that the Doms are coming soon, and there'll be a lot of 'em." She shrugged again. "All we can do is be as ready as we can, however many there are."

"And hope the fever passes sufficiently to allow our reinforcements to come ashore—if there are too many of them for us to handle," Blair added. Blas and Stumpy both looked at him, then turned their gazes to Shinya. "That seems to be about the size of it," he agreed.

///// *TFG-2*
USS Donaghey
August 30, 1944

rums thundered and the alarm bell rang as USS *Donaghey* went to general quarters just as she did every dawn since she'd dropped anchor at the southern African port of Alexaandra, capital of the Republic of Real People. Bekiaa-Sab-At's Marines climbed to the fighting tops with their rifles or aided the gun's crews in running out their eighteen-pounders, while youngling powder monkeys stampeded from below with pass boxes. Shot garlands near the guns stood full of stacked canister rounds, on the off chance some attempt was made to board the ship. Keeping solid or even exploding shot at hand was pointless. They'd have little effect against the monstrous and mysterious dreadnaught *Savoie* that also lay at anchor a quarter of a mile away and had kept *Donaghey* effectively imprisoned for the last weeks.

Commander Greg Garrett paced his quarterdeck, watching with a sense of profound pride the precision with which his ship prepared to fight. He knew his crew was slowly going nuts with frustration—he was himself—and there was little he could do about it. The exercises and drills they performed—particularly running out the guns—had started out almost as a dare, to see how *Savoie* would respond. He *had* to do something to keep his crew on their toes and remind them—and their captors—that they were destroyermen. Maybe it helped. His crew remained professional and defiant, and the apparently French officer who "visited" from *Savoie* every other day behaved with a measure of respect, even if he was somewhat grudging and condescending. Otherwise, except for watching closely with their binoculars—as he watched them—the enigmatic strangers hadn't further threatened them. They obviously felt immune to *Donaghey*'s twenty-four 18-pounders, believing that continuously pointing two of their ten 13.5-inch guns at Garrett's 168-foot wooden sailing frigate was sufficient warning not to do any of the things they'd expressly forbidden, such as attempt to leave, land, signal the city in any way, or transmit a wireless message. Those acts would "regrettably" result in *Donaghey*'s immediate destruction.

"Good morning, Cap-i-taan Gaar-ett," greeted Inquisitor Kon-Choon, his large blue eyes looking about. He, at least, was always impressed by Allied military drills of any sort. He was a Republic citizen, its chief of intelligence in fact, but had also very specifically been forbidden to go ashore. Whoever these strangers were, they knew an awful lot.

"Morning, Inquisitor Choon," Greg answered sourly. Choon loved to keep him guessing about things; his was a secretive nature. But Greg believed the strange 'Cat had been straight about not knowing any more about this situation than he did. That didn't stop him from feeling occasional flares of resentment that the Republic snoop hadn't figured out *some* way to communicate with his people on shore to find out just what the hell was going on. "They'll be coming over shortly," Greg added unnecessarily. Choon nodded.

"Perhaps Lieutenant Morrisette will let something else, ah, 'slip,' I think you say?"

"Maybe," Greg agreed. They'd learned a *few* things from the Frenchman's visits. The first had been *Savoie*'s name, from which Lieutenant Wendel "Smitty" Smith, *Donaghey*'s gunnery officer, had remembered some of the ship's specs—such as the size of her guns—and pedigree. Built by the French just before the Great War (back home), she was about 540 feet long and displaced close to 24,000 tons. An oil burner, she was capable of around twenty knots. In addition to her main battery, she carried quite a few respectable secondaries as well, which they could see. Smitty didn't remember what they were, but Greg supposed they were 5.4 inchers—enough alone to slaughter a fleet of *Donagheys*.

The second significant thing they'd picked up was that *Savoie* and her crew were members of something Morrisette had offhandedly and possibly accidentally referred to simply as "the League." It was something, but still infuriating in its meagerness. They hadn't gotten an explanation for the large goofy flag the dreadnaught flew, in addition to a smaller tricolor. But it was the same as the markings on the huge submarine *Walker* sank. Courtney Bradford had expressed his view at the time that the emblem was that of a French fascist party of some sort that might've grown in conjunction (or to supplant) the Vichy government, but that was just a guess. They had gotten the distinct impression from Morrisette that, whoever and wherever his people were, they were well established, and not alone. That was about it. What they were doing here, and why they were interfering remained a mystery.

Greg raised his binoculars and watched a heavily laden barge set out from the docks and row out to *Savoie*. At least the strangers had allowed the kaiser, Nig-Taak, to keep *Donaghey* well supplied with fresh food, and those supply runs, every other day, were the purpose for the "visits" and probably the only reason they had any contact with their captors at all. Three men, probably Morrisette and his usual guards, left the dreadnaught and boarded the boat before it turned toward *Donaghey*. Greg watched the men waving and shouting at the . . . beings at the oars.

"Why do they put up with that?" Bekiaa-Sab-At asked, joining them with Lieutenant Saama-Kera (Sammy), Greg's Exec. "The mixed folk," she added. A race of supposed human-Lemurian hybrids called Gentaa, possibly descended from ancient Chinese explorers, had sprouted in the Republic. They were taller than Lemurians with generally pale-colored fur. They still had tails, but their faces had more human characteristics. Contrary to the Allies' first impression of their condition, Choon had explained that the Gentaa were fiercely insular and had established *themselves* as a kind of exclusive labor class, concentrating on controlling virtually all dockyard activity and exerting political power in much the same fashion as labor unions. It was a pretty strange setup, but Greg had seen similar arrangements in China.

Choon blinked curiosity. "I honestly do not know. If anyone else treated them as we have seen these strangers do—practically as animals—they would have thrown them to the fish." He looked at Greg. "Understand, the 'hybrids' as you call them look after themselves and are not much interested in business of the Republic that does not directly affect them. They are loyal to the kaiser, but would probably not much care whether these strangers were here or not as long as they were paid for their work." He looked back at the approaching barge. "But such . . . subservience is not their, um, 'style.' I suspect, perhaps, they understand the gravity of the situation and have decided to 'play along.' For now. What that means, I cannot say."

The boat came alongside and the officer in charge—it was Morrisette again—left instructions to his men, both armed with bolt action rifles. Promptly, he climbed the side of the ship and stepped aboard. Greg met him with his officers, but didn't pipe him aboard. For his part, as usual, Morrisette saluted them, but not the Stars and Stripes fluttering in the morning breeze, aft. Loud voices rose from the boat as the guards directed the Gentaa to begin taking the supplies aboard.

"Good morning, my friends!" Morrisette exclaimed, a false smile on his narrow face.

"We're obviously not friends, or your ship wouldn't keep pointing guns at us, preventing us from moving, or talking to our real friends here," Greg replied, tightly controlling his voice.

Morrisette pouted. "But of course we are friends! Look." He pointed below. "I even left my guards in the boat! I will continue to do so from now on, as long as you do not threaten me, or attempt to talk with the monkey men who bring your supplies." He smiled. "Not that you could learn much from *them*!"

Suddenly Greg understood, remembering previous visits. Even Choon had been surprised by the hybrids' total lack of any effort to communicate with them. They'd thought they were truly that intimidated at first, but when they kept acting dumb, even when briefly alone with one of *Donaghey*'s crew, they'd begun to wonder what else was at play. Now, clearly, the hybrids had been deliberately playing the brutish laborers all along. Greg saw Bekiaa stiffen with realization as well, but Choon made no reaction.

"We're no threat to you or your ship," Greg quickly replied, hoping Morrisette didn't notice their surprised realization. He doubted he would. He couldn't know Lemurian body language well—could he? And Smitty's face hadn't revealed any more than Choon's.

"Of course not," Morrisette said with a touch of condescension. "So why not enjoy each other's company?"

"Hard to 'enjoy' being held hostage. You realize what you're doing, to us and this city, is an act of war?"

"Oh no! Not war at all! You misunderstand entirely. It is merely our intention here to *prevent* war. The last thing we want is war, particularly with your mighty Alliance!" Greg detected sarcasm in the statement, but also an element of truth. That didn't make any more sense than anything else.

"You'll have a war soon enough, no matter what you want, if you don't let us go."

Morrisette looked reflective. "Perhaps we will have war one day, but not soon. Your forces are far too busy to worry about you for a great while yet."

"How do you know that?" Bekiaa demanded, and Morrisette's expression darkened.

"I have said too much," he murmured to himself as if no one were around, then plastered the smile back on his face. "Suffice it to say that we desire peace, and are only here to keep it."

"That's the biggest load of horseshit I ever heard," Smitty muttered. Morrisette's smile cracked. Instead of responding, however, he snapped at one of the Gentaa with a pack basket full of vegetables. "Hurry up!"

"If all you want is peace, then why keep us from seeing our friends and going about our business?" Greg demanded.

"Because your business is war! And your business here is to embroil these people in your war!" Morrisette caught himself and took a breath. "Come up here," he called to his guards, "and hurry these monkey men along. They dawdle, and I have more important duties today!" One of the Gentaa suddenly tripped and sprawled on the deck, crashing into Inquisitor Choon and spilling a load of something that looked like polta fruit to roll across the deck. Choon was almost knocked down as well.

"Idiot! Imbecilic animal!" Morrisette ranted. "No, don't pick it up. Just leave it and get off the ship!" He whirled to Choon. "You! *Spy!* Stand still! Guard, ensure that that animal passed nothing to this one!" Everyone bristled at that.

"Now wait just a damn minute," Greg growled, but Choon quickly stepped forward. "It is nothing," he said. "After so much time among your people, I've grown accustomed to going naked." Greg knew that wasn't true. Many of his Lemurian crew wore as little as they could get away with, but Choon was always well dressed. Still, something made him keep his mouth shut when Choon simply stripped. He did note how his icy blue eyes remained intently upon Morrisette the entire time, however. "The poor creature merely tripped, and almost tripped me," Choon explained conversationally. "We never touched otherwise. How could he possibly have passed me anything? But please, poke about among my clothes if it will entertain you."

Morrisette glared at him, but he waited while one of his guards went through the clothing. Apparently sensing the tension, the Gentaa quickly finished the transfer of supplies and left the ship. When the guard gestured helplessly, Morrisette nodded for him to search Choon as well. Greg Garrett took a step forward, crowding the Frenchman. "You can look at him. He volunteered that, for Christ's sake." His expression turned hard. "But if your man touches him, you'll never leave this ship."

"You would take *me* hostage?" Morrisette demanded, incredulous.

"No more than you've done to us. But you will *not* come aboard my ship and molest any member of her company. Is that perfectly clear?"

"He is a spy, and not part of your crew," Morrisette protested, but backed away a step.

"He's no spy. He *is* a high official in the government of this republic you're holding hostage as well. You say you want peace. How does abusing him further that aim?" Greg shook his head. "I don't even want to hear your explanation. You wouldn't give me a straight answer anyway." He gestured at the dreadnaught. "This whole thing is an abusive farce, and there'll be a reckoning. In the meantime, you can easily see that no message was passed to Inquisitor Choon, so get the hell off my ship."

Morrisette hesitated, then straightened. "You may come to regret your tantrum when I do not allow the supply barges to approach your ship for a while. Good day."

"That could've gone better," Greg muttered when the barge pulled away, the Frenchman pointedly not looking at them.

"Not much better," Choon disagreed, adjusting his kilt and reaching for his coat. When they looked at him questioningly, he merely walked casually over to one of the guns in the waist, knelt, and retrieved a purple fruit from under the carriage. "The scattered fruit, the fall—particularly when it involved me, whom they already suspect—was a simple distraction from the one fruit the operative deliberately tossed where I retrieved it." He looked at Garrett. "You played your part quite well, by the way, adding even further to the distraction, and focusing it entirely on me."

"Well, thanks. I guess."

"Operative?" Smitty asked.

"Yes," Choon acknowledged. "He was one of mine. As soon as I recognized him, I expected something like this." He'd grasped the stem of the fruit while he spoke and slowly drew it out, pulling with it a small glass vial. Inside was a note. "You will excuse me, I'm sure, while I retire to my quarters to decode this."

Almost all of *Donaghey*'s officers lingered on the quarterdeck for more than an hour, waiting impatiently for Choon to reappear. When he did, they crowded around him. "It seems there will be an effort to carry several of us ashore to meet with the kaiser, under the cover of darkness," Choon announced.

"How?" Greg demanded, pointing at *Savoie*. "That thing keeps arc lights on us all night long to stop us from doing any such thing."

Choon spread his hands, blinking. "I do not know how, only that it will be. Never fear. This has clearly taken considerable time to organize, and I doubt the kaiser would have ordered the plan to move forward if there was not an excellent chance of success."

"Or unless something's spooked him," Bekiaa suggested.

Choon blinked at her. "There is that possibility, I suppose."

CHAPTER 10

///// *USS* **Walker**
Grik City Dock
September 4, 1944

"Y ou'll shove off at dawn?" Sandra asked. Her tone was matter-of-fact, but her expression betrayed her unhappiness. Matt looked at her, and his heart seemed to crack. He loved her so much and despite her evident fatigue and disappointment, the setting sun washed her upturned face with an extra touch of that angelic . . . something that only pregnant women possessed. To Matt's surprise, she'd accepted her orders to accompany Adar and the wounded back to Baalkpan. She *had* argued, bitterly and intensely, but not for nearly as long as he'd expected. It was as if that something, whatever it was, (conspicuously absent during the fight to take the city), had finally asserted itself with a pragmatic protectiveness for the life she carried that trumped her conscious desire to share his fate, no matter what. Matt was profoundly grateful, but as she looked up at him, absently sweeping away loose strands of sandy brown hair, her eyes were like little pools of life for his thirsty soul. Not trusting his words, he merely nodded.

All around them on the dock, preparations continued. *Salissa* was already in the strait, still escorted by DES-Ron 6. Soon, her planes would start scouting the Grik coast more closely, and the DDs would split up and go hunting. It was time for *Walker,* already fueled and provisioned, to join them. The old destroyer's crew was completing the transfer of ammunition from the nearest warehouse, so recently offloaded from a pair of "fast freighters" docked nearby. They were strange ships, captured Grik "Indiamen" as so many Allied auxiliaries were, but these had been razeed to corvettes, or "DEs," and then converted to steamers. They retained a vestigial sailing ability, with two masts rigged fore and aft, and their engineering plant took up a lot of cargo space. But they were quick and dependable—and relatively expendable—for long-range supply runs across a hostile sea. Matt knew that captured Dom ships were being similarly refitted in the Empire of the New Britain Isles to help the lagging supply effort in the East. He was suddenly struck by the irony of the ships. No longer fit for frontline combat operations even as the swift-sailing DEs they'd originally become, but too numerous and useful to retire, they'd been converted into everything from freighters such as these, to small unit transports and Nancy seaplane tenders. In the same way, so many aging four-stacker destroyers—like *Walker*—had been converted before the "Old War."

He looked back at Sandra. "Yes," he said at last, managing a smile even though this would be the last time he saw her before *Amerika* sailed for Baalkpan in a couple of days.

"You'll be careful?" she demanded doubtfully, adjusting the collar of his shirt.

"Sure. *You* be careful," he urged, glancing significantly downward. "For both of you."

She frowned. "It's not fair, you know."

He nodded again. "I know."

Their tender moment was interrupted by a roar on deck, and they looked up at the ship. She'd changed a little since the fight. Attached to the boat davits aft of the torpedo mounts were large wooden rafts, fi-

nally replacing her old, mesh-bottomed ones with something more useful in this ferocious sea. They wouldn't be much good for a lengthy
stranding, but they might protect a few people long enough for them to
be picked up by another ship or boat. Also, and just as important to
Matt, they provided at least some barrier against boarders. With them,
the new extra machine guns, and the Nancy seaplane supported on its
catapult aft, *Walker* was more top-heavy than she'd ever been, but Matt
intended to stick fairly close to *Big Sal* and keep his fuel bunkers topped
off, using the underway refueling procedures they'd practiced so carefully. He didn't expect she'd roll much more excessively than normal.
They quickly located the source of their distraction. Chief Jeek was
overseeing the last torpedo going aboard, to be stored in the inoperative
number two tube. *Walker* ordinarily had no space for spare torpedoes,
but even if the tube wouldn't work, it was silly not to fill it. The hoist
lifting the heavy weapon had gotten tangled with one of the wireless
aerial supports, causing the torpedo to spin, fouling the support, and
jerking the 'Cats on the taglines to the deck.

"What's wrong with you idiot monkeyheads!" Jeek bellowed, throwing a 'Cat at a snaking tagline. "That fish gots a *warhead* on it! You
wanna blow up the ship? *Goddaam it!*" he practically shrieked when the
support pulled the aerial too taut and it snapped at the foremast like a
pistol shot, falling across the funnels and the amidships deckhouse like
a high-tension spring. "Secure! Secure!" He grabbed a tagline himself
just as several other Lemurians got a grip on the others, and with supreme effort, they managed to stall the spinning weapon. Matt closed
his eyes and rubbed his forehead with a groan. Jeek must've seen him,
because he launched into a tirade reminiscent of Chief Gray's finest, except for the number of Lemurian words mixed in. "Set it down—on the
truck, not the veg'taable locker! You not tell the difference?" Jeek demanded of the hoist operator. "*Easy*, don't just drop it! Is you brains
turned to shit? Is you too stupid to know which end to *eat* with! There,
cut that wire—watch out, it gonna snap back! You! Outa the way! You
want it to cut you stupid head off?"

Just as Jeek seemed to be getting things under control, there came
another threatening shout just above Matt and Sandra, on the gangway
forward. "What the hell's *in* there, Isak?"

Isak Reuben had finally returned to the ship with a light wooden crate about three feet square that he'd apparently cobbled together out of scrap wood. Dragging the crate with a rope, he'd nearly made it past Sonny Campeti, *Walker*'s gunnery officer, who had the deck, but who'd been distracted by the commotion aft.

"Nuttin'," Isak proclaimed in his reedy voice.

"There's *something* in there, damn your lyin' ass!" Campeti denounced. "It's moving—and making noises!"

Matt and Sandra exchanged glances. A little "normal" chaos after all they'd been through might be refreshing. Both knew this episode would unfold "naturally" only if they stayed apart from it, so together, hand in hand in the gathering twilight, they prepared to watch the show.

Spanky had hobbled up from aft, past the still-ranting Jeek, and turned his attention to the crate. Isak seemed to wilt at the sight of him, but then straightened, possibly emboldened by the Exec's amused expression.

"It's about time you came back, Chief Reuben," Spanky said. "Did you know Tabby wants you on report?"

"I'm wounded," Isak defended, displaying a bandaged arm. "An' was excyooged."

"That's why you're *not* on report. But you will be if you don't answer Lieutenant Campeti's question."

Isak shrugged, and Matt was intrigued by the "mouse's" sudden attitude. There'd been a time when Isak and his half brother, Gilbert, would've walked a mile out of their way to avoid even talking to an officer. Matt suspected that Isak's part in slaying the Celestial Mother had instilled a greater confidence in him when it came to such encounters.

"It's a pet," Isak finally confessed. "Always wanted one. Deck apes always get the pets, an' us snipes never do. Why, the first 'Cats that came aboard went to the deck division. Then Silva got to keep Larry the Lizard, an'"—he seemed to remember Sandra might be watching—"Miz Tucker—I mean, Mrs. Minister Reddy—got to keep Petey when he showed back up from the east." His expression turned even more sour than usual. "An' when me an' Gilbert finally did get us a pet, when Tabby came down to the firerooms, she went an' *took charge*! It ain't fair!" His voice had gone from almost confrontational to plaintive. The box rumbled and Campeti took a step back.

"What *kind* of pet, Chief Reuben?" Spanky asked patiently.

"Just a little one."

"What *kind*?"

Isak looked around. With the turmoil aft under control, they were drawing attention. Earl Lanier, the ship's bloated cook, had approached with his arms crossed over this grungy T-shirt, and even Tabby was watching now, blinking angrily. Jeek trotted up and saluted, blinking embarrassment. "Sorry XO. The fish is stowed—but the aerial's down. EMs'll get right on it."

"That's okay, Chief." Spanky nodded at the cobbled-together hoist. "You and the fellas have done well under the circumstances. I guess we'll get proper yard facilities built someday, but in the meantime we have to make do. Have Mr. Palmer let me know as soon as communications are restored."

"Ay, ay, sur."

Spanky turned back to Isak. "What kind?" he demanded more forcefully.

"Here, I'll show ya," Isak replied, patting the box and unhooking the top. Before he could even raise the lid, a dark form banged it open and jumped into view, teetering on the side of the crate. Everyone drew back because even in the deepening gloom it was obvious that Isak's new pet was a Griklet.

"Griklets" were baby Grik, and not only had no one ever made a "pet" of one; no one had ever even managed to capture one alive. They were savage little things, with no more apparent sense than an alligator— with the agility of a monkey. Even the young of Lawrence's comparatively civilized Sa'aarans weren't considered "people" by their elders until they more or less reached maturity—of action and thought. The things had given them all kinds of grief when they first discovered them on Ceylon, their holding pens opened by retreating Grik. They ran in packs, attacking whatever they thought they could catch and eat, and every attempt to deal with them in a nonlethal way had failed. Ultimately, the Allies resorted to shooting them on sight. It had been much the same in Indiaa, to a lesser degree, because many "civilian" Grik had been evacuated before the fighting and not simply slain by their warriors. The same must've been the case here, since almost no Griklets had been seen in the city. Of course, no one doubted that the Grik cooped up west of the harbor had eaten their Griklets first. . . .

"Wait just a damn minute!" Campeti said, drawing his .45. "We've had enough Grik on this ship lately!"

Matt was inclined to agree, but he didn't interfere. He was amazed by how calm the thing seemed to be. It just stood there, glaring around, its nearly plumage-free tail swishing and its crestless head bobbing as it sniffed.

"Yeah!" Earl agreed, stepping forward. "You want a pet, get a puppy! Give it here and I'll cook it!"

"Like hell!" Isak growled. "He's mine! You got any idea how hard he was to catch? That's what I been up to," Isak told Spanky. "I caught him, an' I been trainin' him. Why, he's tame as a duck."

Spanky frowned, and Campeti took that as his cue.

"No Grik of any size is getting on this ship again," he said. "Shut that lid and get him ashore. Mr. Bradford can cut him up—or teach him to play Chinese checkers for all I care."

"That ain't fair!" Isak practically wailed. "You leave him be, you ever want any more o' my PIG-cigs!"

"I don't smoke 'em," Campeti growled. "Box him up!"

"Wait . . . ," Spanky began, but Earl lumbered forward.

"I'll get him!" Earl said.

At the sight of the mountain of flesh, the Griklet squealed and bolted. Perhaps instinctively going for height, it skittered up the stairs to the amidships deckhouse. Dashing between the legs of surprised 'Cats trying to clear the aerial, it finally reached the top of the number two 4"-50, where it paused, looking frantically about.

"No!" Isak screeched. "Lemme get him!" He snatched a crumbling cracker from his pocket and trotted up the stairs after his little friend.

"Get that thing!" Campeti shouted.

"Belay that!" Spanky countered. "Let the mouse do it."

Campeti, Tabby, and Earl crept slowly up the stairs, and then eased closer. Isak was standing on the gun's "bicycle seat," holding the cracker made of the somewhat pumpkiny-tasting Lemurian flour. "Here's a cracker, Grikky," Isak crooned in what he probably thought was an entreating croak. Lanier snorted. The Griklet hissed, but stretched its snout toward the cracker.

"I'll be damned," Spanky murmured from below, having limped to a point he could watch better. Perhaps emboldened, Isak wheedled, "here Grikky, Grikky!" Earl, unable to contain himself, guffawed.

Terrified by the horrible sound from the bloated monster, "Grikky" leaped over Isak, bounced off the ready lockers, and used the number three gun as a springboard to launch himself over the starboard side of the ship—to splash with a shriek in the water of the harbor below.

"Noooo!" Isak wailed, lunging for the opposite rail. There was no hope. Even several weeks after the battle, particularly so close to the dock where they'd dumped thousands of Grik, the harbor was still full of flasher fish torpidly nibbling the last morsels from a vast submerged bed of bones. And, of course, Grik didn't swim. Lanier exploded in laughter, and Isak rounded on him with flashing eyes. Almost as quick as his lost pet, the wiry human jumped on Earl, climbing around and up on the cook's back, wrapping his legs around his chest, and began raining blows on Lanier's head, screeching "murderer" at the top of his lungs. Quite a crowd had gathered on the main deck below, and general laughter erupted as Lanier waddled in circles, roaring like a bull, trying to peel the enraged fireman off his back. Surprised by Isak's uncharacteristically strong reaction to . . . anything, Tabby and Campeti's first reaction was to step back. Now they rushed forward to drag Isak down.

"What the hell's the matter with you, you little twerp?" Earl gasped, fingering his ear. "You bit me, goddamn it!"

"Murderer!" Isak seethed, going almost limp in Tabby's arms. "I'm gonna get you for this!"

"I didn't touch the little shit!" Earl defended, looking around. "Anybody see me touch it?" The laughter had subsided to a thoughtful silence. "And even if I had, killin' Griks ain't murder. It's what we do."

"Grikky was different! I spent weeks gettin' eem ta trust me, an' you scared eem ta death as quick as that!" Isak snapped.

Earl started to say something more, but Campeti shoved him back. "Just shut up. Get the hell back to your galley and stay there!" He turned to Tabby. "C'mon. Let's get him down the stairs. Let Spanky sort this out."

A few minutes later, Tabby and Campeti were supporting Isak in front of the Exec. The onlookers remained, but the silence had turned respectful, and Spanky realized that, Griklet or not, the crew was on Isak's side. He leaned heavily on his crutch and sighed. "Listen to me, you nut," he began gruffly. "You leave Earl alone. He didn't murder your pet. He's a turd, but he was just doin' what comes naturally to him—just like your . . . Grikky, flippin' his lid and jumpin' over the side. We've seen Grik do that over and over when they're scared. Anything could've set him off eventually; blow tubes, or fire the main battery, and over he'd go. So even if he was tame as a bunny, you never could've kept him on the ship. We might've turned him over to Courtney to study"—he glared at Campeti—"but not to cut up. I mean, why would he, when he's done it a hundred times? But whatever we came up with, he'd've had to go. That said, you did good work with that thing, good enough that I won't report you attacking Earl to the Skipper as long as you write up how you managed to actually tame a Griklet. Hell, I don't think Larry's people even know how to tame their own kids!" Everyone knew that the captain had seen everything from the dock but would ignore it without an official report. It was always better for things like this to be handled by subordinates whenever possible.

"Okay," Isak mumbled halfheartedly, "but that fat bastard Earl has to pay."

"You leave him alone! You mess with him anymore and I *will* report you to the Skipper—with the recommendation that he not only bust you, but take you out of your firerooms and assign you to Earl as a mess attendant. You hear me?"

"Yah. I hear."

Spanky looked at Tabby, and some kind of understanding passed between them, because she nodded and poked Isak in the ribs. "C'mon, you. You got work to do."

Spanky looked meaningfully at Chief Jeek, who also nodded. "Right! Break it up!" he shouted to the onlookers. "We all got work!"

On the pier, Matt chuckled when Spanky caught his eye, making tearing motions at his hair.

"That was . . . different," Sandra said, and Matt looked at her. Her expression was unclear in the falling darkness.

"What? The aerial casualty shipping the torpedo? Nah. Stuff goes haywire all the time. You know that. And taking torpedoes aboard is always ticklish. I'm actually encouraged that Jeek got it straightened out so fast."

"That's not what I mean. I'm talking about the incident with Isak and his pet Griklet."

"What about it? It was funny. And in all honesty, a Griklet's not much weirder than some of the critters the guys used to try to bring aboard in the old days, in the Philippines."

"I'm talking about Isak himself. We've all been through a lot, but him going from a virtual cave dweller in the firerooms to, well, the slayer of the Grik empress, or whatever she is, has done something to him." She shook her head. "Maybe it'll pass. Probably will. But right now I'm not sure whether he's finally starting to join the human, or human-Lemurian, race"—she made a throwing-away gesture—"or if, after everything, he's beginning to crack up."

Matt snorted, but then considered. "You know, I've been thinking how ships' captains have to be kind of amateur shrinks. I guess doctors do too." He smiled. "But I think Isak was always cracked. What does your shrinkery tell you about me?"

Sandra started to answer, hesitated, began again, then shook her head. Matt started to prod her, when her face lit up with a sickly green light. He looked up at the Celestial Palace and saw a flare beginning to fall—just as others went up near the airfield. He looked out to sea, beyond the harbor mouth, and saw more flares illuminating the DD on picket duty.

"Captain Reddy!" Signal Lieutenant Palmer cried from the top of the gangway. "I guess they tried to reach us"—he gestured at the fallen aerial—"but *Amerika's* Morse lamp sends that *Big Sal* spotted Grik zeps out in the strait, coming in from the northwest! Lots of them!"

"How many is 'lots,' Ed? And can *Big Sal's* planes intercept them?"

"There must've still been sunlight up that high because they said, well, *hundreds*, Skipper! And Keje says they're high enough that they'll *be* here before any of his planes can catch 'em!"

Matt grabbed Sandra by the wrist and started dragging her up the gangway. "Take in all lines!" he shouted. "We're getting underway! Signal *Amerika* to get underway immediately as well, and pass the word!" Gaining the deck, he and Sandra automatically saluted the flag aft, and then Campeti, but Matt didn't ask permission to board.

"What about your regulations—that keep me off your ship?" Sandra asked ironically as bosun's pipes and whistles shrieked.

"I doubt Grik bombing practice has improved that much, but they're about to drop a lot of 'em—and the docks have to be their primary target. No way I'm leaving you standing there. I'll bring you back when it's over."

////// *Grik City Airship Field*

rik zeps!" came the cry from the hastily built comm shack, loud enough
that Captain Tikker heard it in the HQ
tent nearby. A little groggy, he jumped
up from the dingy cushion he'd flopped
down on seemingly moments before,
exhausted after a day of shifting the 1st
Pursuit Squadron back out to *Salissa* and organizing the command and
support structure of the other squadrons to operate independently.
"His" P-40 floatplane had been the first ship sent across, along with the
pitiful few spares remaining to keep it in the air. All that was left on the
field—they hadn't even named it yet—were the nineteen P-1 Mosquito
Hawks, or "Fleashooters," of the 1st Naval Air Wing's 2nd and 3rd Pursuit Squadrons. Tikker ran outside the tent, pulling on the peacoat that
would cook him now, but that he'd need at altitude, along with a flight
helmet and goggles.

"How many, an' how far out?" he demanded of the comm-'Cat emerging from the shack, who immediately fired a flare in the air from his copy of a Remington flare gun. NCOs began blowing whistles. The 'Cat looked at him, blinking rapidly, evidently nervous. "The picket ship report a hundred plus, jus' ten miles out, bear-een tree two seero!"

"Confirm receipt," Tikker ordered, blinking as well, as much in consternation as to clear the brief nap from his eyes, "and inform *Salissa* we're goin' up."

"*You* goin' up, sur?" the comm-'Cat asked. Tikker had placed his new Aryaalan Exec, Lieutenant Araa-Faan, in charge of the pursuit squadrons remaining at Grik City.

"I'm here," he said simply, trotting away toward the flight line, where ground crews were turning the props on the little ships to push oil out of the lower "jugs" on the five-cylinder radials. "Araa will get plenty experience commanding when I'm gone," he muttered to himself. Armorers were carefully inserting the long, strange-looking magazines down through the tops of the wings to feed the .45 ACP "Blitzerbug" submachine guns in the wheel pants. These magazines were new, and had just arrived at the field from the fast little freighters. As always, Tikker was pleased by the ingenuity of his people. They'd taken the simple "stick" magazines that Bernie Sandison had designed and added a pair of drums at the top. The drums were even streamlined, to reduce drag. Tikker was concerned about how reliable they'd be; too much spring tension when fully loaded and not enough when they were low might cause jams, but if they worked as advertised, they'd effectively double his ships' meager ammunition load. He knew a bigger, better Fleashooter was in the works, designed to carry the new Browning machine guns in the wings, but it made him glad that somebody back home still thought in terms of upgrading what they already had, instead of just waiting for the new stuff to ship.

Ground crews were already helping other pilots into their "chutes," and up on the wings of their planes when Tikker supplanted the pilot gearing up to take the ship beside Araa's. "You sit this one out, Ensign," he said gently. The younger pilot handed over his parachute and backed away with wide eyes Araa saw.

"You goin' up?" she demanded, blinking a combination of surprise, anger, and belated respect. Tikker almost chuckled at her eagerness, remembering how excited he'd once been to leap into an aircraft—any aircraft—and have at the Grik. Had it really been so short a time since Colonel Mallory fearfully refused to let him take the controls of the old PBY that they'd literally flown to pieces?

"Is everyone going to ask me that?" He eyed her while the crew-'Cat helped him into the chute. He remained ambivalent about the things and would never open one over the water, but over land was a different story—and sitting on it provided some protection from ground fire. "I could ask you the same, but I won't. Like you, I bet, I gotta see with my own eyes what the Grik are bringing us this time. The pilots who intercepted the first zeps the other day said they're some different from the ones we fought at Madraas. I gotta know if those differences make them more dangerous before I head back out to *Salissa*." He shook his head. "Never like bein' surprised when *Salissa*'s at stake." He grinned. "I bet you'll get more chances than me to look at 'em even better before much longer, but I applaud your desire to do so quickly. I won't interfere with your squadron leaders," he assured, "any more than you should, beyond general orders we might decide are pertinent."

Araa blinked acceptance—and consternation. *Her eyes really are quite eloquent,* Tikker thought. *And attractive.* He pushed that realization aside. "Would you fly on my wing?" he asked, blinking innocently.

Perhaps three minutes had passed since the first alarm, and rockets and flares were going up all over the city. As he strapped himself into the open cockpit of the little monoplane, he made a note to himself to point out that the display was very pretty—and doubtless highly visible to the enemy, who might otherwise have had some difficulty with their dark target. Word had it that this was a very big raid, and he supposed it was understandable that people would get excited. *He* was excited. But they had to do away with the rockets. At least the ships were dark, he noted, glancing out at the harbor. Their horns were sounding the alarm, but there were no lights. "Contact!" he shouted. A ground crew-'Cat propped his motor, and it coughed to life, joining others already running up. He adjusted the throttle until the engine settled down, then pressed the Push to Talk button beside it. They had "raa-dio" in the pursuit ships now, literally manufactured in *Salissa*'s shops. They were basically the same as the Talk Between Ships (TBS) sets on the ships, only miniaturized as much as humanly—or Lemurianly—possible. The new sets, mounted behind the seats, were still so big and heavy that they af-fected the Fleashooters' already meager payload and there flat-out wasn't room for a battery. They'd only operate with the engine running. "All stations, all stations!" Tikker said urgently. "This is COFO Jis-Tikkar. Lay off the daamn fireworks! You're showin' the enemy right where to bomb!" He cleared his throat. "Second and Third Pursuit, let's go get 'em!"

Except for the light show, it was almost completely dark now, but the airship field was big enough for four pairs of planes to take off at a time, guiding off one another's blue exhaust flares to prevent collisions. Tik-ker pushed his throttle lever forward, glad all "new" aircraft controls were more like those on P-40s than Nancys. Pulling back to advance a Nancy throttle always struck him as odd. *Everybody ought to make knobs go the direction you want to go!* He'd decided this sometime back. His engine roared, and the little plane darted forward, tail rising imme-diately. The strip was bumpy despite all the work they'd done, but like all of Grik City, mere weeks after its capture, a strange ferny grass had begun to grow. He wondered about that, but at present it was enough for him that it shouldn't be too dusty for the next flight taking off. And it wasn't bumpy long. P-1s took to the air like startled lizardbirds. He loved them.

Tikker hadn't trained in the precious P-40s they'd rescued from the swamps around Chill-Chaap, and the pilot of the one they'd brought along wearing a pair of salvaged Japanese floats after another trainee ruined its landing gear had been lost when the SPD *Respite Island* went down. He and a couple other 1st Naval Air Wing aviators had very care-fully figured out how to fly it from the exhaustive manual prepared at the Army and Naval Air Corps Training Center at Kaufman Field in Baalkpan. Their first flights had been hair-raising, but they and the plane had survived. Tikker knew "his" P-40 was a slug compared to Ben Mallory's "clean" 3rd (Air Corps) Pursuit Warhawks, but it was faster than anything else he'd ever flown and he worshipped the raw power of its mighty twelve-cylinder "Aall-i-son" engine. He'd always love Nancys too, both for what they could do, and for the simple fact that they'd have lost the war a long time ago without them. But for sheer flying delight, fast and agile, he'd take a Fleashooter any day.

There was no question that one rode inside the relatively massive P-

40, and even in a Nancy, but one almost literally *wore* the little P-1. He'd heard its Baalkpan bamboo and fabric lines were inspired by something called a "P-26," then scaled down to match the 220 "horses" its five-cylinder radial generated, but its performance hadn't been scaled down at all. Weighing barely nine hundred pounds empty, the little ship could match the reported 230 mph speed of a P-26, and Tikker was sure it was much more maneuverable. Its limitations were its short, four-hundred-mile combat radius and meager payload. Most frustrating of all, even its relatively pitiful—compared to a P-40—armament and a full load of fuel and ammo were about all it could bear. Tests had determined that it *could* take off loaded with up to two hundred pounds of bombs, but only from a carrier steaming into the wind. Tikker thought he could do it off a strip—if it was long enough—but so far, the only P-1s to carry bombs from a shore base had done so with its guns removed. None of that mattered tonight, because P-1 Fleashooters with their pairs of Blitzers had proven to be utterly murderous weapons against Grik zeppelins over Madraas. Tikker had no doubt that he and his veteran squadrons would reap a heavy harvest against the incoming raid, but with so many enemies coming, he feared it wouldn't be heavy enough.

High-powered arc lights, similar to *Walker*'s, had been scattered strategically around the city, away from important targets (*someone* had been thinking about such things), and now their bright beams rose high in the sky, searching for the invaders. It wasn't long before the first ones appeared, transfixed by the roving lights. *This is new,* Tikker thought with growing surprise. "Does ever'body see this?" he asked, speaking into his mic. In the past, regardless of the size of the raid, Grik airships had always attacked as a mob, much like all their warriors once had. He immediately heard a number of nervous confirmations. "Looks like they're in some kind'a stacked formation, staggered from about five thousand feet. . . ." He paused, straining his eyes upward, but the beams only revealed the upper craft periodically. "To who knows how high," he added, for the benefit of his pilots and those listening on the ground. "They must be guiding off exhaust flares too—or something else." He paused. This changed things. "Lieutenant Araa, take the Second in against the lower ships. Watch for fire from above. We know they have defensive weapons! I'll take the Third and try to find the top of the formation and hammer them from above." It was immediately clear to him that the Grik had figured out that they were most vulnerable from high attacks and had stacked their raid—how high?—to guard against them. He suspected the 2nd had the most dangerous job, but he needed to see for himself what the Grik were up to, and, he hoped, show them that it wouldn't work.

"Ay, ay, Cap-i-taan!" Araa's voice crackled back. "Second Pursuit, taallyho! Make your shots count! They a lot of these buggers!"

"Third Pursuit, follow me," Tikker ordered, pulling back on his stick. He knew that "following" anybody would soon be problematic, and he could only pray to the Heavens that his fliers could avoid colliding with one another—or the enemy—in the dark. Things were about to get very exciting. Up he went, still leading his squadron, he hoped, and skirting the enemy formation with his curving climb to starboard. He nearly slammed into a wayward zep, passing it before he could possibly take a shot. "Heads up!" he said. "I barely missed one! Somebody knock it down!" At ten thousand feet, he banked back to the left and looked down—just as excited voices filled his headset:

"I got one! It burning down!"

"I got one too! Look at that! Is bigger than I ever seen before, but burn bigger too! How-waa!"

"Watch yursefs!" Araa's voice broke in. "They shootin' back!"

"They's droppin' bombs! Hit 'em!"

"*I* hit!" came a startled cry. "They shootin' back a *lot*! I losin' power!"

Far below, Tikker began seeing Grik firebombs erupt across the northwest side of the harbor—right where the starving Grik were camped—but the pattern was widely dispersed and some had to be falling on Safir's troops as well. Even as he watched, the flaring detonations sprawled across the harbor itself. "Grik fire" would burn on water as readily as fuel oil. "The docks are the target!" he cried in his mic, hoping *Amerika*, *Walker*, and the rest of their ships had made it out. Some couldn't possibly have, he realized at once. A lot of the captured Grik ships were dedicated sailors, and many others would've been forced to hunker down and take what was coming, unable to clear the sunken Grik fleet in the dark that blocked a long stretch of the dock. He prayed for them. Even so, his force had apparently gotten above the highest Grik zeps. The growing conflagration below, the searchlights, and the flaming airships falling to the ground finally revealed the bulk of the

raiders. He'd been right! They'd managed—and somehow maintained—
an amazingly tight formation, stacked at least three levels high. The 2nd
was slashing through it, dim white tracers spraying in among the enemy. Blue and yellow hydrogen-fueled flames licked skyward from their
victims, but an utterly unprecedented number of bright orange flashes
spat back at his darting ships!

"I hit! I hit!" came another cry, and another.

"You on *fire*, fifteen! Get out!"

"You nuts? I still over the wa—" A small flare far below scattered
into falling, sparkling fragments.

Another P-1 just exploded, right in the middle of the Grik formation—and Tikker hadn't even seen any fire aimed at it. *What?* The
plane's fiery chunks slammed into a zep, causing a spectacular aerial
mushroom of fire, but it was small consolation.

"Shaat!" Araa shouted in what sounded like a mix of terror and rage.
"I hit some-ting! It nearly take my staar-board wing! I gotta get down!"
There was a brief silence while both squadrons swallowed that, then: "I
think I make it," she continued. "Wing's cut half in two, but the aal-
eron's okay. I got control, an' the bracing wires is holding. Be aad-vised:
I think maybe one in tree of these buggers not carry bombs, but is
loaded wit extra swivel guns—that shoot faster than we seen. Also, I
think I hit some kinda cable strung between two of 'em!"

Of course! Tikker realized. *That's how they're doing it! Every airship
on each "level" must be attached to the ones around it!* Not only did that
keep them together, but it provided a spiderweb of protection from attackers darting between them! And there'd been word about some new
swivel Silva had found, poking around in some wreckage. . . .

"Get on the ground, Lieutenaant Araa," Tikker ordered. "Second
Squadron, concentrate on the zeps on the outside of the formation. We
get them, maybe they'll drag more down before they cut their cables!"
They wouldn't be able to break the bulk of the enemy formation that way,
Tikker realized, and suspected those outside zeps would be the most
heavily armed, but that was all he could think of at present. "Third Squadron! We'll attack the top formation in the center from above, but do *not*
pass between them! Maybe we can drop a spiderweb of burnin' Grik
down on top of the rest! Make your shots count. They'll burn everything
on the ground before we can land and rearm for another round!"

A chorus of "Ay, ays" answered him, and Tikker bored down on the—hopefully—still most vulnerable tops of the highest formation. Even as he did so, he saw the firebombs below begin smearing flame across the dockyard where at least some ships doubtless remained—and most of the warehouses stood. He found a dark shape in the vicinity of his invisible sights. *Gotta get some light on those somehow,* he thought absently, and pushed the spring-loaded lever at his side. Cables drew back around a series of pulleys, pulling the Blitzer triggers in the wheel pants. He barely heard or felt them fire—they were a far cry from the nose-mounted .50 cal he'd had rigged in a Nancy that nearly shook the plane apart—but the burning white phosphorus in the hollow bases of his bullets arced lazily into his target as he swept past barely thirty yards above and lined up on another. The rest of the 3rd did the same. When he banked back around, he saw they had indeed lit up perhaps a dozen zeps, their burning carcasses beginning to tumble down toward those below amid rushing gouts of flame and fireflies of burning fabric. His tactic seemed to have worked. The bad thing was, he'd run out of ammo once before in a very dire situation and had learned to carefully husband ammunition, probably better than anybody in the 1st Naval Air Wing, so he knew he only had enough left for maybe two more runs despite the increased capacity of the new magazines. The survivors of 2nd Squadron were likely already empty. There simply was no way they could get all of what looked like eighty or more Grik zeppelins still relentlessly dropping firebombs across Grik City. They'd land, rearm, and have at them again as they retired, burning many more, no doubt, but his people on the ground were going to have a very rough night and there was little he could do about it. How many irreplaceable planes had he lost so far? Five? Six? How many more would be too damaged to fly again? Somehow, he didn't think this raid was even close to everything the Grik would be sending across that cursed strait.

"Burn 'em down," he practically hissed in his mic, his voice harsher than anyone had ever heard. "As quick as you're empty, get on the ground and load up again. We can't get 'em all," he admitted, "but every one we do is one that won't be back!"

USS Donaghey
Alex-aandra Harbor
September 4, 1944

USS *Donaghey*'s officers had carefully watched the mighty dreadnaught for any reaction to the confrontation with Morrisette for several days now, but as far as they could tell, there'd been no response—other than that Morrisette hadn't returned. He or his superiors probably considered that a punishment of sorts; depriving the Allied ship of fresh provisions from shore. But the embargo would have to last a very long time before it really hurt, and Greg Garrett didn't intend to remain under *Savoie*'s guns that long, one way or another.

They'd also watched the now-familiar city of Alex-aandra for any developments. Even after they had stared at it day after day, the city, sprawling at the base of the high mountains surrounding it, stirred their interest. It was old, for one thing, but not in a dilapidated way. It was obviously prosperous and well kept, but it had the air of the comfortably long established, if not the ancient about it. The architecture was a bizarre but somehow harmonious mix of the classical and the Eastern, with columns and pagodas and even domes. Greg Garrett hadn't been to the Empire of the New Britain Isles, but he'd heard its principal city of New London had architectural aspects that would be comforting to someone with European sensibilities—in a forest-island setting. But the closest thing he'd seen on this world to the "familiar" had been the South Jaava city of Aryaal, with its stone walls and structures. Alexaandra was by far the most "advanced" and "civilized" city he'd seen, but it was just weird enough, plainly reflecting the many cultures from the likely . . . different . . . histories that influenced it, to make it the most peculiar city he'd seen as well. Maybe a bit like Istanbul with an Asian twist?

Except for a little excitement on the docks among the Gentaa when the barge returned there after its last visit, there'd been no unusual activity ashore either. Fishing boats still put out to sea before dawn, where they'd remain until after dark. As always, a pair of Republic harbor monitors with their flimsy superstructures and twin armored turrets steamed vigilantly near the harbor mouth. Choon had admitted that there were a dozen of the things, but Greg had only ever seen two at a time. All together, they might be a handful for *Savoie*, but they were slow, and could likely never get close enough for their own guns to seriously harm the dreadnaught. They'd been forbidden from closing with *Donaghey* as well. So in most respects, in spite of the cryptic message Choon decoded, each day continued to pass just like any other they'd seen since first dropping anchor under *Savoie*'s guns. Greg drilled his crew, and he and Sammy inspected the latest repairs made to correct the damage the ship sustained rounding the stormy cape. Most had been made right, but they were still short on canvas, spars, and cordage that they hadn't been allowed to acquire. Smitty exercised his gun's crews, and Bekiaa drilled her Marines. Choon, as usual, paid particular attention to that—or was it her?

Finally, another day began to dwindle and with the coming of darkness, two arc lights aboard the battleship speared *Donaghey* in their rude, blinding glare. All was in accordance with what had become their grindingly frustrating routine with one exception: without revealing how he knew, Choon had stated that *that* night might offer a "charming diversion" from the monotony they'd all endured.

Greg and his officers had assembled at the quarterdeck rail, shielding their eyes from the painful light. "What do you think will happen, Inquisitor Choon?" Bekiaa asked.

"I do not know, my dear cap-i-taan. I know what *I* would do, but I cannot be sure some circumstance of which I am not aware has made them prepare another scheme."

"Well, what would you have done?"

Choon smiled. "I'd rather not say, lest it cause you to mentally prepare for something that will not happen."

Bekiaa snorted frustration. "Must you always be so secretive? Even with your friends?"

"I cannot help it," Choon confessed. "It is the way I am made." He hesitated. "I will say that, whatever happens, I would expect it to coincide with the return of the fishing fleet, so we don't have much longer to wait."

An hour or so after full dark, the colorful lanterns of returning fishing boats began to dot the harbor. They'd been told to steer clear of *Donaghey* as well and most did, but as usual, several seemed intent on "pushing" it. In the past, Greg had assumed it was their way of showing defiance to *Savoie*'s decrees, but now he wasn't so sure. One of the boats, a broad-beamed little schooner with a bright array of lanterns rigged out on booms, was coming in fairly erratically, under full sail, and Greg watched with alarm as it grew closer.

"Are those guys drunk? They'll foul our bowsprit! Stand by to fend off!" he yelled forward.

"They do seem drunk," Choon lamented. "The boredom of a long, hard day at sea, heaving nets and cleaning fish. Such a life is often alleviated with drink. I believe they will miss us."

He was right. Cries of alarm echoed across the water, and the boat veered away—only to be caught with her fore and aft rigged sails rattling and flapping in the offshore breeze. "That's done it," Sammy said with some amusement. "That bunch of drunks will never make their proper berth now." One of the searchlights shifted slightly to glare at the troubled boat, and her people, scurrying in confusion, froze under the blinding beam and covered their eyes. The bow began to come around and with a loud *boom*, the foresail filled and yanked the head around—just before the boom snapped like a cannon shot and the sail plunged into the sea.

"That's *really* done it!" Sammy said as the mainsail filled and the boat heeled over, dragging the wreckage in the water. All was confusion aboard the fishing boat as it began a sickening pirouette downwind—toward *Savoie*.

"Most unfortunate," Choon agreed. "That poor crew is liable to hear some very stern words when they are pushed against *Savoie*." He nodded at the battleship. The light on the crippled schooner had continued to follow it. "And the visitors seem quite distracted by the spectacle as well." He looked at Greg. "I would not be surprised if someone took advantage of that."

"You mean this was all an act?" Bekiaa demanded. Then she blinked amusement. "They are quite good actors—and excellent sailors to pretend to be so bad!"

"Indeed."

"Cap-i-taan," hissed a lookout on the starboard rail. "A boat approaches in the shadow!" Greg nodded. He'd actually expected that, and had even considered using the long dark shadow cast by the arc lights on his ship to steal ashore. The problem was, *Savoie* would doubtless see them put the motor launch in the water. They could slip the smaller whaleboat over the side, but they'd have to row so far out against the prevailing wind before they turned toward shore that the trip would take hours. And without someone waiting for them—which they couldn't coordinate—to bring them back to a point they could row back in, there was little chance they could be back aboard by dawn. And if Morrisette chose that dawn to inspect the ship . . .

"Is this what you would've planned, after all?" Bekiaa asked Choon.

"Almost exactly."

Greg looked at him. "Okay. Inquisitor, Bekiaa." He considered, then nodded at Chief Bosun's Mate Jenaar-Laan, a dark brown 'Cat with a bristly white beardlike mane. "You too, Boats. The four of us will go." He looked at Sammy. "You have the ship. If the frogs get wise and try to board tonight, just act like we're still mad about the other day. Morrisette said he wasn't coming for a while, and we've decided not to let him. Same thing in the morning if we're not back by then."

"What if they, ah, insist?"

"The boat is alongside," the 'Cat lookout said. "Is a long, skinny thing with lots'a oars. Looks faast. They ask for Inquisitor Choon and representatives of the Alliaance. They gonna take you out where a steamer's waitin' for you!"

"Tell 'em we're coming." Greg looked back at Sammy. "If they come aboard anyway, don't fire unless you have to. Take 'em 'hostage.' Maybe *Savoie* won't blast you immediately then, but I have a feeling, one way or another, things are finally about to get interesting."

The boat looked a lot like a large "shell," much like those used in racing at the Naval Academy, but it was beamier and had a higher freeboard. The oars—ten to a side—were manned by powerful specimens of the hybrid Gentaa, but the coxswain at the tiller was a man. "Come along!" he whispered loudly. "Quickly now, if ye please!" To Greg, he sounded like a dark-haired version of Doocy Meek, but he looked Chinese once Greg, Bekiaa, Choon, and Chief Laan squeezed themselves into the cramped stern sheets and got a vague look at him in the shadow of the ship.

"Good evening, Corporal Meek," Choon greeted him, confirming Greg's suspicions. "How nice to see you. I'd like to have passed your father's good wishes under more relaxed circumstances, but perhaps there will be a better opportunity shortly."

"Inquisitor Choon," Meek said with a respectful nod. "Ready all!" he commanded in a low tone. "Row!" Simultaneously, twenty oars reached and grabbed for the water, and the long, narrow boat lurched away from *Donaghey*'s side. Greg was amazed by how quickly they accelerated across the windswept water—and how unerringly they remained in the darkest shadow of the ship as they sped directly away from her. Greg watched the Gentaa strain at the oars and was surprised by how effortless it seemed to them. As far as he could tell, even after a quarter hour passed and the "shell" must have achieved twelve knots or more, none of them was even breathing hard. He wondered how long they could keep it up.

"You've a lovely ship, Captain Garrett," Meek finally said, speaking normally and breaking the silence. He jerked his head behind them. "S'a great shame that monstrous iron bugger back there's kept her still so long." Greg started to ask how he knew his name but realized that, underestimated by Morrisette and the League, the Gentaa had probably reported a great deal about them.

"Thanks," he said, nodding forward. "Your vessel's pretty slick as well."

"Thank you, sir, but this ain't mine. We'll be joinin' my ship shortly." He looked at Choon. "How's me da?"

"Very well the last time I saw him," Choon replied. "We've received that there has since been a great battle at Mada-gaas-gar, however, and since we cannot transmit, I've been unable to inquire about him specifically."

"Aye, we received the same," Meek confirmed, "as well as the signal for us to attack the 'Grik' as ye call 'em, but"—he shrugged—"we're all in much the same situation, with that bloody great battleship pointin' her bloody great guns around."

"Actually, the situation is not the same at all," Choon murmured somewhat sharply. "And if Kaiser Nig-Taak has not yet realized that, perhaps we can now persuade him." Greg looked at the Lemurian snoop, surprised by his tone, but Choon said nothing more.

Much more quickly than Greg would've imagined, they reached the area patrolled by the Republic monitors, and with a word from Meek, the Gentaa shipped oars. Both monitors were visible some distance away to the southeast and northwest, their masthead lights glowing bright, but now that the oars were silent, they could hear the telltale machinery noises of another steamer close by.

"Ahoy there!" Meek called.

"Aa-hoy!" came the reply of a Lemurian voice, even as a third monitor began to resolve itself in the gloom.

"Careful as ye board," Meek cautioned. "I'm sure ye know it's none too wise to have a dip in these seas."

They remained on the armored deck of the monitor as it steamed eastward in a wide arc toward what Meek described as the "Navy docks." The chuffing rumble and groaning vibration of the double expansion engines were easily felt and heard—but not as far as *Savoie*. The Gentaa rowers of the interesting shell had simply picked it up out of the water and laid it on the monitor. Greg presumed they'd ride in with them and then carry them back to *Donaghey* when the time came. With Choon's help, Greg had spoken briefly with the monitor's Lemurian captain when he came aboard, ascending to the flying bridge. But the 'Cat's oddly Republic-accented Lemurian was further distorted by a German influence, and after Choon went back on deck, their further attempts at communication had been embarrassing for both of them. Greg had quickly rejoined his friends. The vessel's freeboard was very low, but the sea was light and at her poky speed of around five knots, water only occasionally sloshed across her deck. Bekiaa was talking with Inquisitor Choon in low tones, and Chief Laan was discussing the shell with Meek. Greg stood silent, gazing at the harbor and the city that encircled it.

Alex-aandra was brightly lit, and so was *Donaghey*, particularly now that she had the attention of both arc lights once again. *Savoie* was less distinct behind her glaring beams, inflicting her huge, dark, brooding presence upon what would otherwise have seemed a rather amiable harbor. The monitor reminded Greg of a ferry, not only because of its current purpose, but because it seemed to bull its way through the water in much the same way. *Walker* knifed through water with her sharp bow and narrow hull, and his *Donaghey* shouldered the sea aside, always with a buoyant feel beneath his feet. But the monitor didn't pitch or roll or do much of anything other than just bash its way along. *Fine for a harbor,* Greg realized, *and a good gun platform, nice and stable. But there's no way anything shaped like this could survive the perpetual storms off the cape, the "Dark," to join First Fleet in the Indian Ocean.* He looked at the armored turret behind him and frowned. Choon had told him that the two breech-loading bag guns in each turret were eight-inch rifles, capable of firing a shot weighing 150 pounds. They could've shredded *Donaghey* as far away as they could hit her, but they would have to get much closer to *Savoie* than anybody suspected the armored dreadnaught would let them in order to be of much use. And even *Savoie*'s numerous secondaries could sink them before they got within range. Greg had been disappointed and still was. Choon, Lange, Doocy Meek—all had hinted that one of the more important contributions the Republic could make to the war effort against the Grik was superior artillery to anything the Allies had yet deployed. Greg glanced at the guns again. *Yes, still impressive, and better than most of what we're using now. But we've got pretty much the same things in the pipeline. And our new four-inch-fifties are better.* He grunted. *But Choon's so damn secretive, they might have a lot of stuff he still hasn't blown about. Bekiaa thinks it's charming, but I'm getting sick of the game.* He knew he was growing impatient with the situation, and a great deal of his irritation was starting to wash off on Choon—and the Republic in general. It was just so frustrating to keep hearing calls from *Walker* and the rest of his friends for the Republic to attack the Grik. Not only could he not respond, but he didn't know if the Republic was even still preparing to join the fight. All he'd seen since he got here was a peaceful harbor bowing to the will of a big iron bully, and he'd had enough. *One way or another,* he determined, *I'm getting some answers tonight.* He looked at Choon and caught Bekiaa's eye, saw her slight nod. *"Charming" or not, I think she's ready to choke Choon herself. But what good would it do? He won't make a peep until he gets the okay from his kaiser. Well, he'd better get it tonight, or I'll let Bekiaa choke the kaiser too.*

*T*he monitor eventually neared a pier away from the city lights and as soon as it was secured, Corporal Meek ushered them ashore. Awaiting them was a small group of guards in Romanesque costumes—but with bolt action rifles on their shoulders. They surrounded a short fireplug of a man in somewhat similar dress except that his was both more ornate and yet more practical in appearance. His gave the impression that it had been more often worn in combat than in ceremony. "Welcome," he said. "At long last, welcome. I sincerely apologize for the sequestration you have endured, as well as the means by which we were forced to finally bring you ashore. I hope your ride was not overly unsettling?"

"It was fine," Greg stated. "Nothing compared to our voyage here in the first place."

The man grimaced, and his vaguely Asian eyes narrowed in the meager light. "Quite," he agreed. "Your treatment after that, since your arrival, is a personal humiliation to me, and I beg your forgiveness." He straightened. "I am General Marcus Kim, commander of the land forces of the Republic of Real People, at your service." He nodded at Choon. "I know the inquisitor, of course, and gather that you are Commander Greg Garrett, captain of the USS *Donaghey*? A fine ship indeed." He looked at the others.

"This is Captain Bekiaa-Sab-at, commanding *Donaghey*'s Marine contingent," Greg supplied, "and my other companion is Chief Bosun's Mate Jenaar-Laan. May I assume you brought us here to meet your kaiser—your 'Caes-aar'—at long last?"

"Indeed. I shall personally escort you to him. Hopefully, together, we might finally decide the best way to solve the . . . dilemma facing all our peoples, particularly as represented by that monster crouching in the harbor. If we can alleviate that distraction, perhaps we can proceed with our more important collaborations."

Greg took a breath, both encouraged that the locals understood the priorities and dismayed that, apparently, *Savoie*'s presence had so effectively prevented the Republic from focusing on the offensive deemed so critical by Captain Reddy.

"I sure hope so," he said.

Still guarded—or under guard? Greg wondered. Kim and Choon boarded them on a conveyance that resembled a small Pullman car more than anything else, drawn by large beasts that looked like a cross between a camel and a giraffe. He'd have to get a better look at them in the daylight, but apparently the Republic used the creatures much like the Allies employed the vaguely moose-shaped paalkas. They didn't travel far. Within half an hour, they stopped before a columned structure still outside the more congested sections of the city, and Kim led them inside. "This has been known as the 'Peace Palace,'" he explained ironically. "With the 'War Palace,' the, uh, *Amerika* abroad, the kaiser resides here. Ah, if you would, please leave any weapons you may have brought with the attendants there." He gestured. "I apologize again, and no offense is meant, but it is required. Even I may not go armed in the presence of the kaiser. It is the law." Reluctantly, Greg nodded, and he, Bekiaa, and Chief Laan unfastened their belts with their 1911 Colt copies, magazine pouches, and 1917 pattern cutlasses, and handed them over. Kim seemed to sigh with relief. "Thank you. Believe me, under the circumstances, I can understand your hesitation. But you really are entirely safe. No one here wishes you harm, and we truly are all on the same side. This way, if you please." Kim led them through an ornate hall and into a smaller chamber, just as opulent, with luxuriant blue tapestries embroidered with gold and silver thread hanging from the walls. Inside, there were a number of people of various species, including several Gentaa, waiting expectantly. In the center of the chamber was a wooden throne—there was no other word for the baroquely carved object—upon which sat a robust Lemurian draped in silklike robes that matched the tapestries. *He looks older than I expected,* Greg realized, *older than Toryu Miyata described him. I wonder if the emergency is responsible for the silver streaks in his fur.*

"His most Excellent Highness, Emperor Nig-Taak," General Kim announced, and he and Choon both bowed. Greg and his companions saluted. "May I present Captain Greg Garrett, Captain Bekiaa-Sab-At, and Chief Boatswain's Mate Jenaar-Laan of the United States Ship *Donaghey,* here on behalf of the powers allied against the dreadful Ghaarrichk'k," Kim said.

"The powers we have sworn to join," Inquisitor Choon pointedly reminded, surprising Greg again with his tone. Apparently, there'd been a different Choon hiding within the seemingly endlessly patient one they'd come to know.

"You are welcome! Welcome indeed," Nig-Taak said, his voice soft and controlled. He blinked amused . . . perhaps annoyance at Choon. "It is good to see you safe, my friend," he added, "and I have not forgotten our commitment to the Allied cause." He waved. "But as you know, there has been a complication." He looked at Greg. "And please, do not let the word 'emperor' mislead you. It is an ancient, honorary title—and implies perhaps that I have greater power than is the case."

"You retain the moral power to honor agreements and lead your people in war," Choon insisted. "The Senate can only advise on that subject. Please tell me that *some* preparations have been made to comply with Captain Reddy's request."

Nig-Taak blinked strong displeasure. "*Some* have, but as you know, the bulk of our armies are quartered here, as are most of our training facilities, factories, armories, transportation centers. . . . I can move *nothing* now without them detecting it! Sending spies ashore must have been the very first thing they did after they arrived. And with that . . . *thing* sitting out there in the harbor, threatening our city, I have been unable to send more troops and equipment to join those already deployed." He suddenly stood, blinking profound frustration. "Those people *know* things!" He pointed at Garrett. "Things they cannot know unless your codes have been compromised in some way! We have sent no transmissions, so they must be spying on you as well. They arrived here knowing exactly what we meant to do, and for reasons I cannot fathom, have threatened to bombard Alex-aandra with their great guns if we lift a finger against the Ghaarrichk'k!" He held every gaze, then looked back at Greg. "As soon as they submitted their demands, they staged a demonstration of their power. I'm sure you, at least, can appreciate that if they bombard this city, *thousands* could die!" He looked back at Choon. "And the Senate does fund my leadership, as well as the armed forces at my disposal. I can do nothing more without their agreement, which they will not give." He swished his tail. "Perhaps most mysterious to me is why on earth they would care if we attack the Ghaarrichk'k in the first place! It is maddening!"

"I don't know, Your—Your Majesty," Greg murmured. "But I can confirm, by their flag, that they're the same goons we've run into before. You received the reports of the submarine *Walker* sank?" Nig-Taak and General Kin both nodded. "So their actions here do seem consistent with the behavior of the sub—that only attacked when it became clear that Madagascar was the target of the task force that went there. These strangers seem more concerned with thwarting the Allies than aiding the Grik."

"But . . . why?" Kim demanded.

Greg shrugged. "I have no idea. Neither did anybody else. But that's really kinda irrelevant right now. The Allies have taken Madagascar, and there're millions of Grik frothing at the mouth to have it back. Captain Reddy's expecting—has to have—a Republic assault to distract the Grik, and he's going to need it quick. Why this is important to you, beyond the preservation of your honor, is that if he can't hold Madagascar, make it an impregnable bastion of supply for the war here in the West, he can't send forces to help the Republic—and everything will eventually fall apart."

"But what can I do?" Nig-Taak demanded. "I have told you what is at stake!"

"And Cap-i-taan Gaar-ett has just reminded you as well," Bekiaa said forcefully, speaking for the first time. "The Republic is already at war with the Grik. The presence of *Amerika* at the battle for Grik City has confirmed that, and if the Grik do not already know it, they soon will. If the Alliance loses, or even if it is forced back from Mada-gaasgar, the Republic will be left all alone." She shrugged. "Why not destroy *Savoie*, and then proceed as planned?" She looked oddly at Choon. "I know you must be able to, and we can help. We have two aircraft struck down in *Donaghey*'s hold, and a modest supply of our new armor-piercing bombs." She shrugged again. "Just sink the daamn thing and get on with it."

When no one responded immediately, Greg suddenly knew that Bekiaa's suggestion had already occurred to the people there at some point and been rejected, which meant they thought there was at least a chance it might succeed.

"Why not?" he asked. He looked at Choon. "You've been mum about an awful lot, particularly about your country's military capabilities. I get that—orders. But now it's down to it and we gotta move! If you—we—can get rid of that damn battleship and get on with the war, we *have to* do it!"

"I shall make this plain at last. Had we been able to communicate with you, I would have done so sooner," Kim replied slowly, looking at his kaiser. "We may have the *capability* to 'get rid' of it, as you say, but the consequences to our people—and in the Senate—remain the greatest barrier to our finding the will to try." When Nig-Taak said nothing, Kim continued. "As has been revealed—and is apparent," he added sourly, "we are weak at sea. We have no fleet that can steam to the aid of your friends. We never even contemplated the need, and we mistakenly believed that the monitors were sufficient protection against any enemy entering our harbors. As we traveled here from the dock, Inquisitor Choon informed me that you ask a great deal about our aerial capabilities. Sadly, though we gradually began developing air-craaft some years ago, we saw no pressing need for them and are not as far along as you in that respect." He stopped. "In any event, for the purposes of our alliance, we have a good army, well equipped. None of the members of our mission aboard *Amerika*, sent to find you, was told to conceal that the Republic is formidable on the ground, always on guard for threats from the north. *Savoie* does not bathe the city with light as she does your ship, and a boarding action under cover of darkness has been considered."

"And rejected as too costly," Nig-Taak interjected. "We have fast-firing weapons," he confessed, "based on the 'maaxims' *Amerika* brought, that might suppress some return fire, but *Savoie* also has large numbers of similar, better-protected weapons. To achieve surprise, we could not evacuate the portion of the city that would be subject to indiscriminate fire from her maachine guns and secondary baatteries. The toll in civilian lives, not to mention one of our most important industrial quarters, could be . . . extreme."

"A bombardment has been contemplated," Kim resumed. "We *do* have excellent artillery, as has been promised."

"I told him of your interest in the guns on the monitor," Choon confessed to Greg. "They are powerful, and sufficient—we thought—for their purpose, but they are old now." He flicked his tail. "We do have better."

"Better, larger, *and* smaller, more mobile." Kim paused. "Are you familiar with the 'French Seventy-five'? I suspected as much," he added, seeing Greg nod. "A variation of that weapon forms the backbone of our field artillery." He shook his head. "So yes, we have considered a bombardment. We probably do have sufficient coastal defenses, some rather ingeniously concealed, to destroy or disable *Savoie*—but again, at what cost? His Majesty is right. If we open fire, *Savoie* will respond and the city might be destroyed. Thousands could die. Then there is another unpleasant fact to consider. *Savoie*'s presence and behavior might certainly be considered an act of war, but she has not actually *harmed* anyone. If we fire on her, there is no question that the Republic would be at war with whoever sent her."

Choon took a breath, having apparently been waiting for this particular subject to arise. "I must submit, Your Majesty, that whoever sent *Savoie* to intimidate us into abandoning our allies—there can be no other explanation—has already committed a grievous act of war against the Alliance by sinking *Respite Island*. They are therefore already at war with the Republic of Real People, if we truly do wish to be a full member of the Alliance and worthy of its friendship, respect, and above all, assistance." He held up a hand. "The next question then would seem to be whether they do—or would—consider themselves at war with us whatever we do. Remember, for some reason it seems important to them that their war remain . . . indirect just now. Why would that be? Perhaps they are not as powerful as they seem?" Nig-Taak stroked the fur on his chin, deep in thought.

"If Choon's right, that would raise a couple of options in my mind," Greg said. "One, we attack without warning and sink *Savoie*. Your monitors converge under cover of a night bombardment from shore, maybe even giving me a chance to get my planes in the air. Then we hammer the hell out of the thing. We could do it. Maybe your city takes a beating, maybe not. If it does, that's too bad. All of our cities have taken a beating, but you know what? That's war, and you're in this one already up to your eyes whether it's touched you yet or not. The Grik will eventually see to that if we don't kick their asses, no matter what *Savoie* does. But if we take her out and beat the Grik, we can face whoever sent her together when the time comes. He paused and waved his hand. "Second option, we send for somebody from *Savoie* to come here and talk." He grimaced. "Anybody but that idiot Morrisette. Then we tell 'em to get the hell out or else. Call their bluff, if it is one. If it isn't, it might go harder on your city, harder on my ship, but we'd still hammer them. If you really do have enough shore batteries to deal with her, your monitors might even still get their licks in because *Savoie* just can't shoot at everything at once." He looked around. "I may be wrong, but my guess is, if they were here to start a 'real' war, there'd be one by now. If not . . . they'll go away."

He stared hard at Kaiser Nig-Taak. "Either way, this can't go on. We should either blow 'em out of the water, or tell 'em we will if they don't scram." He straightened. "I have . . . My ship has a mission, both to coordinate the war effort with you and to scout farther west." He shook his head. "This current situation is utterly unacceptable, and we have to do something to change it. At the same time, I must respectfully remind you that the Republic has a mission too."

Nig-Taak stared at Greg Garrett for a long time before he finally nodded. "Very well. It will be as you say. I shall summon the commander of *Savoie*, her 'Contre-Aamiraal Laborde.' It is early yet, and I expect he will come." He blinked irony. "The man has always been scrupulously polite. You shall remain," he told Greg, "but you must not be seen." He sighed. "The meeting will not be lengthy, and you should easily be able to return to your ship, fully aware of what the day will bring."

Garrett and his companions took refreshments and continued to discuss their plans with their hosts while they waited for a reply from *Savoie*. Sure enough, barely an hour passed before a delegation of officers arrived and was led into the "Peace Palace." Greg, Bekiaa, Laan, and Choon all concealed themselves behind a tapestry hiding an alcove that Greg assumed must've been intended for exactly what they were doing—listening to a conversation they shouldn't be present for. He grinned at the thought of the cliché. Sadly, they couldn't see what was happening, but they could hear.

"Good evening, Your Majesty," came a deep, pleasant voice with a French accent.

"I hope it might be, Contre-Aamiraal Laborde," Nig-Taak replied evenly. "Forgive me for asking you here at this hour, but I find it increasingly distressing that you have not yet informed me how much longer you desire to remain our guests. The harbormaster's complaints are growing quite tiresome."

"I regret that I am still not at liberty to say," Laborde replied. "As I have assured you many times, I am only here at the direction of my government, and must remain to enforce our . . . requests until I receive further orders."

"Sadly, that is precisely the answer I expected of you. Very well," Nig-Taak replied, his tone hardening. "Then I'm afraid the time has come for you to obey this order from *me*: your ship will be provided fuel, water, and provisions, beyond what you already daily demand," he inserted bitterly, "and make all appropriate preparations to leave this place immediately. I must insist that I see your fine ship steam out of this port and beyond the horizon by sunset tomorrow. Is that perfectly clear?"

A stunned silence ensued, broken by Morrisette's indignant voice. "You dare order us. . . ."

"Yes!" Nig-Taak interrupted. "I *do* dare. I am the leader, the kaiser of these people who, to a soul, are weary of your presence and the daily threat it implies." He leaned forward. "You have been here a great while, essentially enforcing our inactivity, but I shall tell you now that we have not been idle! Enough time has passed that we have been able to quietly, carefully, make certain preparations to counter your threats, and if you disregard my warning, we must proceed to do so."

"You threaten me?" Laborde demanded, his voice turning harsh.

"Warn. Consider it a warning from the harbormaster if you like, for reasons of state. You have overstayed your welcome, and it is time for you to go. If you do not?" There was the slightest pause. "I will have no choice but to enforce the civil laws against vessels loitering indefinitely in port, posing a menace to navigation, and monopolizing valuable space alongside a government and commercial pier. That is the warning I would give a friendly visitor. You, however, have behaved in a most unfriendly fashion, not only to this Republic, but to vessels calling at this city from other sovereign powers. One might even conclude that your actions are those of a belligerent nation and if you remain here beyond tomorrow, I will have no choice but to conclude that a state of war must exist between your people and mine, and act accordingly."

"What on earth could you do?" Laborde murmured curiously while Morrisette and another officer ranted in protest. "After all this time I do not think you would risk your city or its people to a conventional contest." He raised his voice over the others. "What if I tell you now that there is no possibility that I can accede to your demand?" he barked, apparently trying to rattle Nig-Taak, or make him reveal whether the timing of the demand might be critical to whatever the kaiser intended. "And I would feel compelled, if forced, to resist those sent to 'arrest' us on these ridiculous charges with every weapon at my disposal?"

Greg heard General Kim snort. "Then I must tell you, Contre Aamiraal, that the only difference it would make to *you* is that there would be fewer of your crew left for us to, um, take into custody."

"Those few, of course," Nig-Taak continued conversationally, "might then be subject to charges of murder—and death is the only possible sentence for that."

Morrisette actually shrieked in outrage, but Laborde shushed him harshly. After a moment of quiet murmuring with his other officers, Laborde spoke. "You will have my answer at dawn. One way or another." He turned on his heel and took several steps, but paused. Conveniently for Greg, it was in a place he could just glimpse through a slight gap between the tapestries. "All we have done since we arrived is try to save you from yourselves," Laborde said stiffly. "This mad dash you make to join a war that is not yours is not rational. The Grik pose no real threat to you at present. They do not like this land and are currently occupied elsewhere—as you know."

"The Grik are a threat to all beings, Contre Aamiraal Laborde, even you. And as you are clearly aware of the same reports as I, then you must know that this is the very first time, in all our history, that an opportunity has arisen to destroy that threat forever."

Laborde glanced back at Nig-Taak. "You have great faith in your new allies, represented by that quaint little ship out there," he said ironically, nodding in the general direction of the harbor. "You are aware that they have other enemies? A power called the 'Holy Dominion'?"

Nig-Taak said nothing.

"I should not tell you this, but my conscience demands that I inform you that the Dominion is aware of the Grik and has sent a delegation to meet with them and discuss, if not an alliance, then at least a cooperative strategy." He shrugged. "A League, ah, 'asset,' detained that delegation for the same reason that we have lingered here; to prevent a wider war. You realize that is our only aim?"

"That may be *one* of your aims, Contre Aamiraal, but I must suspect the strategy behind it. If your League was so benevolent, you would gladly join us against the Grik—and the loathsome Dominion—instead of trying to prevent us from confronting them."

Laborde's expression almost seemed to flutter between a wide range of emotions before it hardened again. "If you spurn our protection, I doubt I can further justify preventing the Dominion mission from continuing on its way to meet the Grik," he warned.

"Further proof that our well-being is not a priority of yours, Contre Aamiraal," Nig-Taak ground out, his tone scornful. Laborde's threat contained vital information, if that information was true, but he knew humans quite well and sensed the petulance, perhaps even desperation, behind it. "I am sure you will do what serves your interests best—as it most assuredly best serves *Savoie*'s interests to leave this place."

"I think it should be clear to all by now that *Savoie* is here to keep us out of the war in order to contain the greater conflict within parameters they believe they can control—for their own reasons," Inquisitor Choon said later, after the delegation had departed.

"And by so doing, they *do* protect Alex-aandraa, but why?" General Kim asked.

"Easy," Greg answered. "As an outpost for them."

Nig-Taak nodded slowly. "I must agree with Cap-i-taan Gaarrett. They have been free to come and go within the city and establish themselves in various ways, making us increasingly accustomed to their presence. I foresee now that eventually, another of their ships will arrive, and then another, bringing more and more of their people. At some point we will become completely powerless to evict them. All the more reason to do so now."

"But if they release these Doms to contact the Grik," Kim began.

"The Grik will likely eat them before they can make themselves understood." Nig-Taak scowled. "And even if they do not; if they become the closest of friends, the Allied cause will not be much worse off in the short term. They cannot possibly quickly combine their efforts. Under the circumstances, will the Grik send warriors to aid the Doms? Would the Doms send troops here? I think not. Both are quite thoroughly engaged." He looked around the room at the larger number of advisors who'd joined them. "But though we are technically at war with the Doms, by virtue of our alliance, we have not really considered ourselves so. We must consider what to do about that."

There were unhappy nods.

"Swell," Bekiaa grumped, returning to the present. "But that leaves *Saavoie*. What'll she do? Looks like we've left her no choice but to start fueling—or shelling the city. We should'a just kept our traps shut and blasted her."

"Perhaps," Nig-Taak conceded. "But I had to take the chance, to 'pull the bluff.' And if Cap-i-taan Gaarrett is right, that they want Alex-aandraa for themselves, one ship cannot take it outright, no matter how powerful." He swished his tail in thought. "So they still will not want open hostilities with us here. They know we can hurt them, even if they steam some distance away. Now they will wonder what else we might do, and why I am suddenly so confident."

"It's a good bluff, Your Majesty," Greg said, "and maybe the best thing you could've done. Not sure I'd've had the guts to try it," he added, considering all the civilians within range of *Savoie*'s guns. He wished he'd been able to see Nig-Taak's face during Laborde's initial response, but doubted he'd have given anything away; doubted the French admiral could've noticed even if he had. To those not used to Lemurians, their faces were inscrutable. *But what if this 'League' somehow knows 'Cats better than we think they do?* He shook his head. There were too many "what ifs," and he couldn't keep track of them all. He was a Destroyerman, pure and simple. *Let Nig-Taak, Adar, or Courtney Bradford figure that stuff out. Just point me where you want me to fight.* Suddenly, he knew he'd caught a tiny glimpse of some of the wild crap Captain Reddy had been forced to deal with ever since *Walker* first limped into this screwed-up world, and he didn't like it one bit.

"We will find out tomorrow if they 'bought it,' as your people say, Cap-i-taan Gaar-ett," Inquisitor Choon stated at last. "If they did, they will leave. If not, there will be great suffering in Alex-aandra, but in the end, *Savoie* will trouble us no more. I suggest we all prepare for the worst, of course, and it is high time we returned to *Donaghey.*"

"Agreed," Greg said, then looked at Nig-Taak. "But what if—" He caught himself and mentally cringed. "What if after all this, they don't leave, but don't open fire either. They just sit there like nothing ever happened and call your bluff. You're not really going to just start shooting at them, are you?"

"No, Cap-i-taan Gaarrett," Nig-Taak said. "We will not. We will do our best to convince them it *was* merely a bluff, resentfully resuming our normal contacts. Then, after the sun sets and their lights come on once more, we shall proceed with your 'first option' after all."

///// *USS* **Walker**
Grik City
September 5, 1944

I t was a bright dawn beyond the harbor mouth, but the pall of smoke ended that as soon as USS *Walker* crept inside. *Big Sal* followed close behind, having steamed all night to join her, and the first two ships of her remaining P-1 squadron were poised on the catapult, ready to fly. Matt had initially been against the huge ship's returning to the confining harbor—particularly after the damage reports started coming in. But Keje was right; the warehouses were hopelessly exposed to raids like the one the night before, and they had to transfer whatever naval ordnance had survived to her capacious storage. They had no choice. Nancys circled overhead, unseen through the smoke, but their engine sounds were clear as they kept watch to the west. Nobody really expected the Grik to return in daylight, but they had to be prepared.

Fires burned everywhere, most from the crumbling remains of

fallen zeppelins, all the way up to the base of the Celestial Palace itself, but the warehouses had been decimated as well. And the falling, burning zeppelins had probably caused at least as much damage as the bombs they'd dropped. The only good news was that relatively few of Safir's troops had been killed, dispersed as they'd been, but more than a hundred had been killed or wounded in the trenches in front of the Grik holdouts. Who knew how many of *them* had burned?

"Looks like Cavite after the Japs hit it," Spanky said softly, leaning against the starboard bridgewing rail with Matt and Sandra. Bernie Sandison had the conn and was peering anxiously through the bridge windows, trying to spot the numerous navigation hazards that had joined those already choking the inner harbor that night. Lookouts called out nearly constant sightings. No one knew how many zeppelins had fallen in the water, but it had been quite a few. Some remained exposed, their rigid bamboo frames smoldering and hissing steam. The PT squadron and dozens of motor launches plied back and forth as well, fruitlessly searching the water for survivors of several ships that had burned to their waterlines, or shifting work and firefighting parties where they were needed most. Matt already knew they'd have to dock in a different place than they'd left. The fast oiler had somehow survived, scorched and leaking, but her damage had been caused by the complete destruction of her sister. Most of its high explosive ordnance had been off-loaded at least, or the oiler wouldn't have made it. But enough black powder for the muzzle-loaders on the DDs had remained aboard for a just slightly less cataclysmic explosion that gutted her completely and hammered her closest neighbors with debris—not to mention killing most of her crew.

"Yeah, just like Cavite in a lot of ways. But this might be even worse," Matt practically whispered.

Sandra tore her horrified gaze from the destruction all around and looked at him in surprise, concerned by his tone. She hadn't been at Cavite, but she'd heard their descriptions. How could this be worse?

Spanky arched an eyebrow at him. "How do you figure, Skipper? Sure, it's bad; we lost most of our harbor facilities last night, not to mention precious ordnance. But Safir'd already dispersed most of *her* ordnance to magazine bunkers around the city."

"But even some of those went up, according to reports," Matt reminded. *Walker*'s aerial had been quickly repaired, and damage assessments had been streaming in all night. "Tikker lost five pilots and seven planes—more than a third of what he had to start with. And more'll be down for repairs." He waved around. "Tikker said they got forty zeps—about the same percentage as what he lost—but we can't replace his planes, and I bet the Grik have a lot more zeps where these came from." He rubbed his eyes.

"What did they learn about the new guns on the Grik airships?" Sandra asked quietly. Matt startled her with a chuckle, but there was no humor in it. "Somebody wasn't paying attention to Silva again. He found one after that first little raid and reported it, but apparently the word didn't get around. Anyway, they're not exactly new, but they're damn effective at close range," he said. "They load from the breech with a kind of preloaded jug, wedged in place. *Old* technology and pretty dangerous, but when they work, they do fire faster. Poking around the debris from last night, they found that a number of their gunships carried as many as a dozen of them."

He looked back at Spanky with a sad smile. "And despite the apparent similarities—the isolated, exposed nature of the position, the difficulty of resupply—this *is* worse than Cavite. Worse than the whole situation we left behind in the Philippines, because, unlike MacArthur, Safir is just going to have to sit and take it. She can't maneuver in the jungle to keep her troops safe, but has to stay here, under this," he said, waving around too, "maybe every night." He paused. "And from a purely selfish perspective, even as our air cover whittles away, *this* fleet isn't going to leave her to fend for herself!"

"What are we going to do?" Sandra asked, her tone frustrated.

Matt looked at her. "*You're* going to do what we agreed. *Amerika's* on her way back in. When she ties up, she'll take on the rest of the wounded, and you, Adar, and all the rest we discussed will get the hell out of here."

Sandra bit her lip but didn't argue. "Courtney will be delighted that he missed the boat," she pointed out instead. Bradford, Silva, Chack, and several others had left with Nat Hardee and the Seven boat only two days before to search for what they were calling the "Lost Lemurians."

"We still need him to find those people if he can," Matt grumbled. "And Herring doesn't want to go either."

"Why should he? He's becoming a fair destroyerman," Spanky pointed out, "and a decent navigator. We need more bridge officers."

Matt nodded. "I know, but I wanted him back in Baalkpan, running his snoop shop."

"You need 'snoops' out here too," Sandra suggested.

Matt rubbed his face. "Agreed. Okay. But there's still just something about the guy. I mean, sure, he's becoming a good officer and maybe it's just his way, but I never can shake the feeling that he's up to something." He managed a rueful smile and shrugged. "Probably doesn't matter as long as he's on our side." He frowned. "But that pal of his, that Corporal Miles. He's trouble, and I want him gone. Back to Baalkpan or in a rifle company where he belongs. Keeping Herring's probably the best way to separate them."

"Uh, Miles went with the Seven boat. Volunteered," Spanky said.

"Really?" Matt snorted. "Well, that long with Silva, he'll either come back a new man or a corpse."

Sandra pursed her lips, but she had to agree.

"Soo . . . ," Spanky drawled. "What're *we* gonna do?"

Matt shrugged. "Stick to the plan—with a couple of modifications." He glanced at the sky. "These new Grik bomber formations had mixed results, but the fact that any of their airships made it back at all will probably convince them to stick with them. Okay. It's gonna be tough around here, but all tied together, they can only hit fixed, preselected targets. No way they can chase one on the move." He sighed. "We'll put more of *Big Sal*'s pursuit ships ashore to defend this place, and I'll get Adar to order *Baalkpan Bay* to shift all her pursuit ships, crated if necessary, aboard *Arracca* when she and *Santy Cat* come down. Maybe they can get here faster than they think. Russ Chappelle and Tassanna will pull out all the stops, if I know them." Russ commanded *Santa Catalina*, and Tassanna was commander—and still "High Chief"—of the USNRS (CV-2) *Arracca*. Matt brightened slightly. "And they can at least keep a trickle of planes coming down on fast transports from Madras. *Baalkpan Bay* should get more P-Ones before she escorts First and Third Corps down, but even if she doesn't, the same thing that applies to *Big Sal* applies to her. The Grik have to know where she is to hit her from the air and her Nancys can handle any surface threat." He considered. "It's a long damn haul, but I think I'll endorse the plan to risk a Clipper coming down after all. We need the recon, and after the pasting they took last night, maybe Hij Geerki really can talk to those starving

Grik. We can't afford to keep so many troops concentrated watching them. And who knows? If we feed 'em, maybe we can at least keep 'em busy cleaning up after their buddies."

There *had* been limited success at Baalkpan in turning captured Grik into—something less dangerous—and a few had even accompanied Abel Cook as bearers during his adventurous survey of North Borno. That only seemed to work after they'd experienced "Grik Rout" and been on their own for a while, but if the trapped Grik weren't all warriors . . . Matt took off his hat and ran his fingers through sweaty hair. "I might ask Ben if he can spare Lieutenant Leedom down here too. *Big Sal* needs Tikker back, and his Exec, Lieutenant Faan, right? She got banged up pretty bad bringing in a crippled ship. Besides, we need somebody with plenty of experience fighting zeps in charge of our air defenses. Next to Tikker, I think Leedom's probably got the most."

Sandra snorted. "Ben Mallory will throw a fit! He's chomping at the bit to get back in action, and I think he's starting to wish he never recovered those P-Forties from that Tjilatjap swamp, thinking his precious squadron is keeping him out of the war!"

Matt sobered. "I know he'll hate it, but Ben stays with his planes. They turned the tide for us once, big-time, and I suspect we'll need them just as badly again someday." He shrugged. "Maybe here—but not yet. They'd be too vulnerable on the ground, and they're about the only ace we've got left up our sleeve," he added glumly.

Spanky grunted doubtfully, still contemplating Matt's notion about Hij Geerki talking to the Grik. "That all sounds swell, but we're still lookin' at a couple of weeks before even *Arracca* and *Santy Cat* get here. We still gonna chase Grik in the strait?"

Matt nodded firmly. "We have to. But we'll also concentrate more on finding and hitting Grik airfields. Another reason we need the Clipper. It can fly higher than anything they can hit it with, and has the range to really *search*. Don't you get it? The Grik *can't* tie their zeps together in the air! They've got to mass them somewhere, somewhere big and clear, to do it before they lift. We find where they're doing that, and we might burn the whole damn flock on the ground!"

Spanky smiled through his teeth. "That'd be swell!"

Jeek's pipe *screed*, calling the special sea and anchor detail as *Walker* edged toward a relatively undamaged portion of the dock. Deck apes scampered to secure lines to throw to waiting hands ashore amid the usual controlled bustle of any docking procedure. The sheer, mundane normalcy of it all seemed to soothe the spirit of everyone on the bridge. "All stop!" Bernie ordered, and the lee helm signaled the engine room. Just then, there came a great gust of steam from the tops of the aft two funnels, and a heavy cloud of black soot drifted forward—and largely down upon the party gathered on the fo'c'sle, amid a growing chorus of indignant cries. Campeti's outrage was audible as well, on the fire-control platform above the bridge. Some made it into the pilothouse. Sandra coughed delicately, and Spanky rolled his eyes before covering them with his hands. Matt actually laughed, amazed as always how in the face of everything, his people—human and Lemurian—could always manage to keep things . . . well, *real*.

"It seems Chief Reuben is intent on reminding everyone of his displeasure over the loss of his pet," he observed dryly. Blowing tubes was a time-honored way for the "snipes" in engineering to inconvenience the "deck apes."

"'Everyone' is right," Spanky grumbled, waving a hand in front of his face to hide a lopsided grin. "I taught him that, you know, but Isak's always been an artist at judging the wind just right to get the, um, best effect—but he never used to have the nerve to do it without . . ." He coughed and waved his hand again. "Well, I'm not sayin' *I'd* ever condone such a thing."

"I think our little mouse has finally discovered the nerve for a lot of things," Sandra reminded.

"You want me to jump on him?" Spanky asked doubtfully.

"No," Matt said. "I think he's earned the right to"—he smirked—"blow off a little steam." He turned. "Pass the word for Mr. Palmer," he called to his talker. "And signal Chairman Adar, at the new HQ in the Cowflop." (Hardly anyone could bring himself to call it a "palace," and another one of Silva's nicknames had stuck.) "I want him to start packing because I want him, the rest of the wounded"—he paused and looked at Sandra—"and *you* the hell out of here aboard *Amerika* before the sun sets and the Grik zeps come back."

///// USS **Donaghey**
Alex-aandra Harbor
September 6, 1944

"I still can't hardly believe they bought it," proclaimed Wendel "Smitty" Smith, staring at the mouth of the harbor over his shoulder; a harbor that had been finally, sullenly abandoned the evening before by the League's dreadnaught, *Savoie.* "Figured we were goners. Warm meat, just waitin' for the splash." He looked apologetically at Greg. "Sorry, Skipper, but those were awful big guns, and I guess they were pointed at us long enough to kinda give me the heebie-jeebies."

"You don't have to tell *me*, Smitty," Greg said. Implied was a reminder that as *Walker's* old gunnery officer, Greg knew perfectly well what *Savoie's* big rifles would've done to *Donaghey.*

Smitty brightened slightly. "Oh well, I suppose when push comes to shove, frogs're frogs wherever they are, an' they'll always run when it comes to a fight."

"That's bull and you know it," Greg muttered. "There was nothing wrong with French fighting men even where we came from; just stupid leaders—a lot like we had." He shook his head. "They didn't run away because they were scared," he considered. "And these aren't the same Frenchies we used to know either."

Donaghey was in the process of shifting over to the dock so recently occupied by the intruder. Greg had been mightily concerned that *Savoie* might send at least a few parting salvos from her big guns, possibly even targeting his ship. The League had sunk *Respite Island* after all. But Greg had never brought that up with Morrisette, content to let him think the Allies didn't know. Even if he'd raised a stink, Morrisette and his "League" would've probably disavowed the attack as the act of an isolated element, impossible to control, Greg reflected. Actually firing on Alex-aandra, or Greg's ship while anchored there, would've been impossible to disavow, and apparently they didn't want a "real" war after all. At least not yet.

"Me neither," Lieutenant Saama-Kera agreed. "I mean, I didn't think it would work. I got no opinion about 'frogs' other than them 'Frog-Grik' critters at Chill-Chaap—and I know *they'll* fight." He shuddered at a memory he shared only with Bekiaa, of all those present. "Why you call the League folks 'frogs'?"

"Just skip it," Greg said.

"'Kay," Saama-Kera replied, still confused, "but it *did* work, an' maybe we should'a pulled this stunt a long time ago."

"How, Sammy?" Greg asked. "No way to coordinate anything with Nig-Taak until the other night." He looked at Choon, who'd spent the night ashore in his own home for the first time in months, but had returned bright and early that morning. "That was good work, Inquisitor," he said with genuine respect.

Choon bowed. "I did nothing."

"But your organization did, and it was first rate. Maybe you ought to give pointers to Herring and our snoops."

"We have had much longer to establish our service, and intrigue comes naturally to us. It was like mother's milk to several of the cultures that settled here over time."

Sammy nodded curiously.

"In any event, *Savoie* is gone," Choon stated. "And we will immediately attempt to establish communications with your—our allies at Maada-gaascar." Greg had tried himself, free at last of *Savoie*'s threats, but apparently the ring of mountains around the city had prevented *Donaghey*'s transmissions from getting through. Now he waited expectantly, but in contrast to his encouraging announcement, Choon blinked discomfort.

"We are having some difficulty with that. As you know, our wireless equipment is situated in the mountains and can receive transmissions from vast distances, particularly when the conditions are right, but it has been a great while since we transmitted anything at all." He blinked again. "We can still receive, have never stopped, in fact. But there appears to be a minor problem with our transmitter. Fear not," he hurried to add. "We will soon sort it out. And the first thing we will do is inform the Grand Alliance, this 'Union' you serve, that you are here and safe, and explain why you were unable to report when you arrived. We will also describe *Savoie* and the people aboard her in great detail, as well as the bizarre circumstances that prevented us from launching the attack they desired. Assurances will be made that we will make up for lost time and you, Cap-i-taan Gaarrett, and your ship, will be commended for the part you played in expediting *Savoie*'s departure."

Greg shifted uncomfortably. He hadn't done anything but sit there. Maybe Nig-Taak and General Kim had appreciated his pep talk, but that was all he'd done.

Choon continued, still blinking. "We cannot transmit," he repeated, "but have received word that First Fleet South did indeed wrest the sacred isle from the Grik, though it is now somewhat awkwardly placed for the purposes of reinforcement and resupply. It also seems our enemy has begun his own counteroffensive with a damaging raid from the air. Cap-i-taan Reddy expects such raids to continue and must counter them while still preparing to defend against the seaborne threat." He took a breath. "My kaiser has already commanded that we resume moving troops and equipment to our northern frontier with the Grik, preparations that had been delayed by *Savoie*, and will extend his personal apology to Chairman Adar and Cap-i-taan Reddy that such were not as timely as we all had hoped."

"Great," Greg said, frowning. "But what about us? It seems to me we should turn around and head back. Try to help, if things are that strapped."

"No, Cap-i-taan Gaarrett," Choon said gently. "Your ship was sent here—and beyond—for a reason: to explore westward, with a particular eye toward discovering the extent of Dominion control of the Western Atlantic, if possible. We *will* soon be 'back on the air,' and will relay any messages you send for as long as we can receive them." He looked at all the surrounding officers. "Speaking for myself, I also hope that you might make contact with other potential allies during your travels, most specifically a particular power that your forces far to the east have made a brief acquaintance with."

Greg nodded, remembering the reports of the ordeal endured by Fred Reynolds and Kari Faask. "Okay," he agreed as *Donaghey* finally touched the pier and her crew began securing her. "That makes sense." He gestured around. "But I need supplies. Canvas, cordage . . . everything."

"Of course. Detail your needs and all will be met." Choon hesitated. "But my kaiser has requested that you leave one of your flying machines and it's aircrew behind so we might examine it and more quickly advance our own fledgling air service. As you may have gathered, we have the technology already and can quickly, ah, 'gear up' to build the machines, but it would help us immensely to study your proven, operational specimen—not to mention the professional techniques of your aviators."

"This better not be a bribe," Greg warned.

"Of course not! Merely a request."

Greg frowned. It was hard not to be skeptical after all the sneaking around everyone had been doing—and after dealing with the League! But his people had *Amerika*, after all, the Republic's biggest ship. He rubbed his eyes, wondering how many hours his most "professional" pilot had in Nancys. Green as they all were, not many.

"My kaiser will understand perfectly if you refuse," Choon assured him. "We all know such generosity would leave you, who are going beyond relief, without a spare aircraft."

Greg shrugged uncomfortably. "Sure, I guess. I'll have to ask the pilots and some of their wrenches to volunteer, but that shouldn't be a problem. They're all sick of being aboard here."

Choon flicked his eyes at Bekiaa, then continued. "Thank you. In that vein I have one further request. Kaiser Nig-Taak desires, at my suggestion, that some of your officers remain here as well, to liaise and advise. I understand that might present an even greater hardship than the loss of your aircraft," he said, then hastened to add, "But in exchange, we would like to send several of our officers along with you. All are fine soldiers and sailors, and some have even explored as far as some certain isles off the coast of the southern continent to the west." Choon blinked. "They may be of great help to you, with respect to currents in particular. It has also become important to the kaiser and me that should you encounter the Doms, at least a few of our people, regardless of how symbolic their number might be, accompany you to confront this other common enemy we must share if we are to be the allies you have proven you deserve."

Greg swallowed. *The Republic officially jumping in the war against the Doms? That could be huge. Granted, there's not a helluva lot they can do to help right now, but if we lick the Grik, or at least roll 'em back . . . Even* potential *help against the Doms might encourage High Chief Saan-Kakja and Governor-Empress Rebecca McDonald, who often seem to feel they're carrying too much of the load in the East—well, West from here.*

"That sounds great, Inquisitor. But who do you want? Or should I just ask for volunteers for that too?"

"I shall only ask for one person, specifically," Choon said, gazing directly at Bekiaa now.

"What?" she exclaimed, taken aback. "Why me? I can't stay here!"

"As I have explained before, many times, the training you give your Maa-reens is most impressive. The discipline and combat skills you teach are quite different from those our legions have learned. We always expected that we would have to face the Grik one day, but believed our better weapons would keep us from having to get, ah, 'in their faces,' be 'stuck in,' as you say, and fight with them hand to hand. Your experience proves that belief was . . . misguided. We do not know how to fight the Grik as you do, and our legions need your example." He blinked gentle entreaty, knowing how wounded her soul had been. "And besides, who among us has more experience fighting the Grik under so many different circumstances?"

"Cap-i-taan?" Bekiaa pleaded, but Greg just shook his head, still stunned by both the appropriateness—and sheer gall of the request. It made perfect sense, of course, but *damn* did he not want to lose Bekiaa!

"Captain Bekiaa-Sab-At, the decision is yours," Greg finally managed as formally as he could. "But I want you to think about it long and hard."

Later that evening, after going ashore in Alex-aandra for the first time in daylight and making the first necessary contacts he'd need to ensure that his ship was properly refitted, Greg Garrett returned aboard. Now he had to get as cleaned up as possible so he and his officers could join the kaiser, all his advisors, the Senate—and God knew who all, for a celebration to commemorate their joint "victory" over *Savoie*. Tomorrow, *Donaghey* would be shifted to a beach where she could be careened and her refit would begin. The early stages of that would be in the hands of the Gentaa. That was what they did, part of their "concession." Greg didn't mind. Most of his crew would then be released upon the exotic city of Alex-aandra for a long-deserved liberty, and his people and those that lived here would finally start getting to know one another properly. He grinned at that; it was his first real grin in a long time. He'd never been a prude, but he'd hadn't much approved of the . . . less genteel traditions many enlisted US Navy personnel engaged in ashore. Asiatic Fleet sailors, in particular, had taken those traditions to stunning heights—or lows, in his view. USS *Walker* had been his first overseas assignment, and to say he'd been amazed by the level of misbehavior in China and the Philippines was a vast understatement. With a lot more experience and a little more age, he'd come to recognize the . . . safety valve, the *breaker*, that such relatively innocent mischief helped to trip—as long as it remained ashore—and his stance had slowly moderated to a degree. Particularly as those ancient traditions had been handed down in the middle of a pressure-cooker war to this new "American Navy Clan." He suddenly caught himself almost amusedly eager to see how the locals would respond.

Staring out to sea, he wondered what Bekiaa would decide—and what awaited him and *Donaghey* when his beloved ship finally set sail to continue their mission. Something interesting, no doubt. But he also worried where *Savoie* had gone. General Kim said she'd arrived from the northeast, so it was likely she originated from somewhere in the Atlantic. But when she steamed away, she'd headed due south until she was completely out of sight. Greg had been tempted to send one of his planes after her, just to see which way she turned, but decided it would be too risky in the cold, damp skies off the coast. He was *very* worried what that monster might do if Laborde decided to take his frustrations out on First Fleet South. His country, government—whatever—had already attacked it before. Why not again, unless they intended to maintain the fiction of peace? "Where'd you go, you big fat bitch?" he whispered to himself. "Where the hell did you come from?"

It was starting to cool off as the sun set, a front arriving from the south that had most of his crew either miserable or delighted. He took a deep breath and went below to put on his finest uniform.

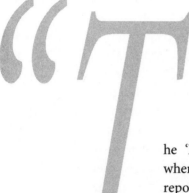

CHAPTER

16

///// *Zanzibar*

he 'League of Tripoli' is centered near where Tripoli should be!" Lieutenant Iguri reported, a bit smugly, Muriname thought, as the two toured the engine factory deep in the jungle of the island. The huge structure was very difficult to see from outside, even from the air. Kurokawa had always been paranoid that the Grik would begin spying on them with the very dirigibles they'd made for them, and discover what they'd been up to all along. In retrospect, Muriname thought, if the Americans truly were on Madagascar, his paranoia might have been a good thing after all. He looked at the glistening radials perched on wooden trucks and listened to the rumble of machinery. He was confident they wouldn't be overheard, and paused to look at Iguri. His executive officer had been hanging around the airfield where the Ju-52 was parked, spending time with Oberleutnant Fiedler. The young German pilot seemed friendly enough with his Italian copilot, but he always stayed with the plane as though afraid to leave it. He even slept inside. He'd seemed hungry for someone to talk to, however, when Iguri started dropping by.

"That much has already been revealed in discussions with the others," Muriname reminded impatiently. "What else have you learned—and does Fiedler know you are interrogating him?"

Iguri frowned. "Honestly, I think yes, but he doesn't seem to care. I don't believe he is very happy with the alliance his people are involved in, and particularly with their place as a, um, junior partner. He was sent here as an 'equal member' of the delegation in fact, but was then practically ordered to stay out of the discussions by the Frenchman."

"So it is true, then, that a fascist alliance, this 'Confédération des États Souverains' that wound up in North Africa, had France, Italy, and Spain as the dominant partners, and Germany and a few other countries were merely associated allies?"

"As was Japan, it would seem, sir," Iguri confirmed, "but we—*they*—were not involved in the campaign that brought them here. The Germans on the other hand had supplied aircraft, armor, and transports, and are now supposedly equal members of the League."

"A different world indeed," Muriname reflected, contemplating all he'd learned. Never had he even considered such a thing was possible, but it made perfect sense, he supposed. They were obviously on a different earth than the one they left, so why couldn't there be more than two? He'd tried to explain the situation, as he imperfectly saw it, to Kurokawa, but the General of the Sea *wouldn't* grasp it and had finally actually ranted that it made no difference at all. Perhaps he was right. He looked at Iguri. He already knew everything his exec had picked up from Fiedler, but the semi-independent confirmation was . . . interesting.

Apparently, the First World War had essentially restarted—over empires again—but the participants had shifted about a bit. Bolshevism had been stamped out, but fascism had run rampant in Europe to the extent that it gobbled up France (as a reaction to Bolshevism), and fascist Germany, still apparently "Nazi" Germany, had been too racked by internal conflict and even civil war to rise to the summit of power Muriname remembered. In fact, part of the original purpose of the "Confédération" had been to assist the struggling fascists in Germany!

Combined with Japan and half the rest of the world with a lust for expansion, the Confédération des États Souverains had hurled itself at the creaking empires of the British, Americans, Russians, and Chinese. That was the "different" history Muriname now contemplated. The pertinent part that he, and even Kurokawa, had to consider was that the Confédération and its allies had embarked on an invasion of British Egypt from Italian Libya in 1939! Muriname didn't know if the actual invasion had commenced before a substantial fraction of the ships, troops, and supplies had "gone missing" from their own Mediterranean Sea and wound up on this twisted world. That their history prior to that was so diverse just went to show how truly twisted it was after all. None of the emissaries would reveal the extent of the convoy that arrived at the different Tripoli of this world, but Muriname didn't think they were merely boasting when they said it was a "considerable" force.

"Keep talking to Oberleutnant Fiedler," Muriname ordered. "Try to discover as much from him as you can, including what are his true feelings about his associates, and his own people's participation in this 'League of Tripoli.' Most particularly, try to find out what he thinks about the League's strength and capabilities."

"Of course, General of the Sky!"

Muriname watched with a frown as Iguri exited the engine factory. Iguri was a capable officer and a good pilot. Muriname had trained him himself, in *Amagi*'s old Type 95 floatplane, which had been restored to a perfectly airworthy condition in spite of what they'd once told General Esshk. He was hardworking and honest, two traits Muriname prized, but just a bit . . . overzealous, and perhaps too worshipful of Kurokawa for comfort. For example, Muriname had actually gotten somewhat protective of his Grik airship crews over time, and made it a point to learn more about the creatures they relied so much upon. He had to guard against showing it, but it had disturbed him to see the airships and their pilots wasted so badly in combat. Iguri maintained a semblance of Kurokawa's disdain, even hatred toward the Grik, and had acquired a streak of arrogance and ambition from the example Kurokawa set that was out of proportion to his rank, skill, and experience. In spite of that, Muriname liked Iguri and hoped he wouldn't push the German pilot too far in their conversations, or himself too far in the air.

After going through the motions of inspecting the assembly line as he did nearly every day, Muriname left the factory and strolled the quarter mile down the white sand pathway through the overhanging trees to the signal tower on the edge of airfield number one. Taking the steps two at a time, he climbed to the high, camouflaged platform where he joined a Japanese officer and several Grik, waving signal flags at a pair of planes taxiing toward the downwind end of the strip. Even more than teaching Grik to fly real airplanes, Muriname was proud that he'd finally broken through whatever mental block the Grik had against grasping the concept of things as fundamental as signal flags. That they'd already used them to some extent, to coordinate attacks at sea, for example, should've made it easy for them to translate moving flags into more complex meanings—easier than teaching them to understand spoken Japanese, certainly—but that hadn't been the case. Then, one day, one of them grasped it—then another. Soon they all did, and Muriname was forced to conclude that the mental acuity of the Grik was even more linked to maturation than he'd ever imagined. He couldn't help being fascinated.

"General of the Sky!" the Japanese controller cried, saluting crisply. The Grik did as well, with their flags in their hands, and Muriname momentarily panicked that they'd inadvertently sent the two planes careening into the jungle. He sighed with relief when he realized the pilots were past, already nearing their takeoff positions, and wouldn't look at the signal flags again except as signals to take off—to "attack."

"As you were, ah . . ." He glanced at the painted rank patch on the sleeve of the man's dark khaki tunic. Enlisted and junior officers' fatigue uniforms were sensibly patterned after the Special Naval Landing Force. "Carry on, Ensign. I'm merely here to observe."

The ensign bowed and ordered his Grik to signal the planes. Engines roared, and the two craft began to move. They seemed ungainly at first, almost waddling through the thick, prickly grass, before they began to accelerate. Almost immediately, their tails came up and they gathered speed. He knew they weren't carrying any ordnance, or even very much fuel—aviation gasoline was still in extremely short supply—but Muriname was gratified to see how quickly the planes, his own creations to a large extent, took to the air. They thundered down the runway, already rising as they passed the signal tower at the halfway mark. Still in a gratifyingly tight formation, they pulled up and away, banking northward toward the harbor. Soon, though he still heard them, they were lost to view.

"Good planes," came an accented voice from the steps below. It was Oberleutnant Fiedler, venturing farther from his own plane than Muriname had ever seen him. "May I come up?" he asked.

"Please do." Muriname waited a moment while Fiedler joined him. "You approve of our new aircraft?" he asked conversationally.

"*Ja.* Amazing that you could make such things in the . . . conditions here. I have been watching them for a while now as your pilots practice, and I would say they are at least as good as the Arado Sixty-six I first trained in."

Muriname smiled. "Perhaps not as maneuverable, but faster, I believe. I was honored to fly the Arado Sixty-six on a visit to Hamburg in 'thirty-eight."

"Not a good time to be there," Fiedler said grimly. Muriname began to ask why. He remembered his visit with pleasure. "I was learning to fly the Yokosuka K Four Y, Type Ninety seaplane at the time," he said instead.

"I do not know it." Fiedler seemed distracted, as if watching for the planes to return, and Muriname paused. "Well," he said at last, "you at least are still able to fly. I am not able to as often as I would like." He gestured at the row of planes across the airstrip. "And these are very much like fighter aircraft. Smaller and slower than what we left behind, of course, but better than what our enemies have. And still quite exhilarating. Perhaps you'd like to try one?"

Fiedler looked tempted, but shook his head, curling his lip. "Gravois would object."

Muriname smiled again. "Surely not. If he is concerned about the safety of his pilot, he still has Lieutenant de Luca to fly him home. Use the excuse of 'learning more about our capabilities.'"

Fiedler looked at him strangely and started to say something before stopping himself. "De Luca is a pilot," he agreed, "but not the best. He is primarily our navigator and radio operator. You may have noted it is he who goes to our plane to send and receive reports." He smiled at Muriname. "And no, it would do you no good to 'detain' him. Only Kapitan Gravois has our codes."

Muriname chuckled, confirming that had indeed been his first impulsive thought. For some reason he found himself rather liking this German pilot. Fiedler took out a case and removed a hand-rolled cigarette. Muriname never smoked but wondered where the German got tobacco. Was it from this world or the last? Fiedler lit up.

"Besides, I doubt Gravois would be much interested in what I might learn," the German finally added, very carefully. "At least about what he would consider your 'primitive' aircraft."

Muriname bristled inwardly, but recognized that Fiedler had just told him a great deal. Clearly, the League of Tripoli possessed other modern planes in addition to the Ju-52. That should've been intuitively obvious, he supposed. They were cavalier about the loss of a submarine, and that they'd been willing to risk such a valuable aircraft on the dangerous flight here in the first place said a great deal about their material reserves. Muriname nodded slightly, acknowledging the gift of information. "Then fly one of these for the pleasure of it. One pilot to another, you spend a great deal of your time all alone. And to be honest, your friends appear to have more regard for your services than your insights. That would seem to me a perfectly good reason to enjoy yourself when you can." He gestured once more at the planes. "Fly one. Perhaps someday, if I visit your League, you might return the favor."

Fiedler studied Muriname while he took a long drag on his cigarette, then finally nodded. "I might arrange that one day, if our leaders are satisfied with the outcome of this mission." He nodded again decisively. "I will fly, with pleasure," he said. "And in return, I shall reveal one of my 'insights' to you. One pilot to another. As you have been told, we— the League, I mean—know a great deal about you and your enemies. How that came to be is a long story in itself, but it is true. In fact, as Gravois might already have said, information is the greatest aid we are prepared to give you at present. Beyond that, it is up to you to decide whether you are more or less likely to prosper by seeking any further assistance from the League of Tripoli. Like your mad Kurokawa, Gravois and his superiors have their own plans, *always*, that are rarely respectful of those they consider to be in their power."

///// *USS* **Walker**
August 9, 1944

*U*SS *Walker* was steaming north-northeast through the predawn sea south of where her charts showed the Seychelles ought to be. The islands were there, according to captured Grik charts, but so were quite a few others that shouldn't have been. *Walker* had steered that direction alone because she could inspect the area and return more quickly than any other ship, and not particularly because Matt had expected to discover a massive Grik fleet there, waiting to pounce on Madagascar from the north. Finding the Seychelles on Grik charts in the first place had been something of a surprise. The islands were relatively distant and isolated from Madagascar and the mainland of Africa, and the Grik weren't given much to exploration in the Indian, or "Western" Ocean. Too many mountain fish dwelt there, and they didn't have sonar pulses to frighten the leviathans away from their paths. There was growing evidence that *something* was going on out there, however, based on the thickening number of Grik "Indiamen" *Walker* encountered—and destroyed—on her way. Her scout plane would fly with the dawn to inspect farther afield.

Big Sal and her two escorts were parked just west of the Comoros Islands, near the middle of the "Go Away Strait," and had discovered many Grik dwelling in scattered villages, as well as a large force that had appeared to be assembling. She bombed the hell out of the apparent "combatants" remorselessly, losing a couple of planes to the dangerous new rocket batteries like those they'd discovered at Grik City. But most of her efforts were focused on destroying three- and six-ship convoys that came every few days, likely carrying more warriors and supplies to join those already gathered there. That *seemed* to be the main staging area for the expected Grik counterstrike, and if so, the Allies had them bottled up fairly tight. As always, without communications, the Grik were blissfully ignorant of the peril they sailed into, and their destruction was as simple as shooting fish in a barrel. Simple enough to inspire a growing concern in both Matt and Keje that the buildup in the Comoros might even be a diversion. They were pretty sure that General Esshk either hadn't been at Grik City, or he'd escaped. Everyone agreed that Esshk was no Halik, but he'd apparently picked Halik and given him his head, so he wasn't just an ordinary Grik either. . . .

Tentative, risky scouts over the African coast (in the face of even more antiair rocket batteries), continued to reveal larger concentrations of Grik and teeming cities reminiscent of Grik City itself, but there was no sign of the massive fleet that would be needed to move and protect a significant invasion of Madagascar. There were broad, navigable rivers, for example what should've been the Zambezi, that might serve as waterways for fleets hidden inland, but the Nancys didn't have the range to explore them, and the massed, nightly zeppelin raids kept *Big Sal* and the probing DDs from lingering too conveniently near the confining coast. Jarrik-Fas had proven that these raids need not be restricted to Grik City when he took his two DDs in close to launch their scouts. Only one returned, with little new information—and the DDs were chased off by twenty zeppelins and their "suicider bombs." The ships escaped serious damage, but the zeps had responded quickly enough that they had to be based nearby. Now, not only did they have no better idea than before where that base might be; they had to assume there was more than one. Altogether, despite the destruction of a couple dozen small Grik ships and the slaughter of some of their warriors on land, it had been a frustrating week in the "Go Away Strait."

Matt looked at his watch before staring back out at the darkness beyond the fo'c'sle. "Sound general quarters, if you please," he ordered, inwardly cringing in anticipation of the strangling goose. Instead, there was the slightest pause—and a *bugle* sounded over the ship-wide circuit. He whirled in the dark pilothouse as the familiar, urgent notes blared, and stared uncomprehendingly. *Walker* had *never* had a bugler since he'd joined her on another world in the Philippines, and no one had ever stepped forward with the skill. He waited until the man with the instrument—it *was* a man—finished, then stood at attention while the crew responded to the call with delighted confusion. Only then did he notice that Bernie Sandison, at the torpedo director, Sonny Campeti, Spanky, and Lieutenant Doocy Meek, the liaison of the Republic of Real People, were all grinning at him in the gloom. Matt stepped closer and saw that the bugler was the Imperial Marine he'd seen attending Jarrik-Fas on several occasions.

"Been practicin', Captain," the man apologized, "learnin' all the calls, down in the engine room. Just got the music before we sailed, from Commander McFarlane," he explained.

Matt looked at Spanky. "Gettin' sick of that damn duck call," Spanky groused. "Hope you don't mind."

Matt concealed a grin. "I doubt I'll miss it," he replied, then turned back to the bugler. "But who are you, and where'd you come from? You certainly didn't report to *me*."

"He's an 'exchange' Impie, assigned to Jarrik's Marine contingent on *Tassat*," Spanky explained airily, waving a hand. "I traded for him, when old Jarrik told me what he could do." Matt refrained from asking what Spanky had traded. "Glad to have you aboard, uh . . ."

"Corporal Neely, sir," the man said. "Glad to be aboard."

"Very well. Carry on."

"Aye, aye, sir."

"What does he do besides blow a bugle?" Matt quietly asked Spanky as the stations belatedly began reporting "manned and ready."

"Isn't that enough?" Spanky shrugged. "He's a Marine, and we've needed a few of those aboard from time to time."

Juan Marcos clomped up the stairs on his wooden leg, coffee cups clattering on his tray. Matt reluctantly took one and sipped the vile brew Juan poured. "We'll launch the Nancy as soon as it's light," he said. "If there's nothing worth serious attention in the Seychelles, we'll turn · back to rejoin *Big Sal* and have a look to the south."

Ed Palmer, *Walker*'s communications officer, mounted the steps and entered the pilothouse from the port side, aft. There was a worried expression on his youthful face. Matt liked Ed a lot, but always dreaded his appearance when he had that look. "Good morning, Skipper," he said. "Got some . . . interesting traffic."

" 'Interesting' usually means good news and bad news. Let's get the worst over with first," Matt said.

"Aye, aye, sir—but it's kind of mixed, for context?"

Matt made a "hand it over" gesture at the message form Ed held, then read it himself in the binnacle light. The sky was turning dirty yellow, but wasn't bright enough to see by yet. "Well," he said at last, eyebrows rising. "The good news first. *Donaghey* is safe, and will soon sail west from Alex-aandra. Had a"—he glanced at Palmer—" 'interesting' time of it too. The voyage was tough, as expected, but then Greg Garrett found our Republic friends bottled up by a curious French *battleship* named *Savoie*." He spent a moment describing her particulars, as they'd been reported, then glanced around and caught the surprise, especially on Meek's bearded face. "She flew the same flag as that big pigboat we sank, and belongs to something called the 'League of Tripoli.' Greg and Mr. Meek's people couldn't learn a lot about them except they really were French." He shook his head, mystified.

"Buncha Veeshy bastards," Spanky growled.

"Who knows," Matt said. "Inquisitor Choon's snoops thought there might be other folks with them, and in their 'League,' but couldn't figure out for sure. About all they did learn is that this League, whatever it , is, really doesn't want us to beat the Grik." He let that sink in. "That seems clear because they prevented the Republic from completing preparations for its attack in the south, or even communicating with us, by threatening to bombard the capital city. That kept things at a standstill for a while. Unlike the pigboat, though, they wouldn't risk a direct confrontation, because when Greg and your kaiser"—Matt nodded at Meek—"finally told them to 'leave or fight,' *Savoie* steamed away. Nobody knows where she went, but Greg fears she might've come this way for some reason and we should be on the lookout. Said they knew a hell of a lot about us and thinks we should change our codes too." He considered. "'League of Tripoli.' What the hell does that mean? Either way, unless they've got some secret base in the Indian Ocean . . ." He stopped. The *submarine* must have had such a base, he realized now, and it wasn't like there weren't plenty of places it could be. And General Pete Alden's conversations with the Grik General Halik in Indiaa left him sure that their old nemesis, Hisashi Kurokawa, had somehow survived. Could *he* be wrapped up in this? Wherever he was, on the outs with the Grik or not, he might be willing to provide a base for a rogue battleship no matter whom it belonged to if he thought it would benefit him.

He took a breath, noticing that the others must be thinking the same thing. "Chances are, *Savoie* steamed back into the Atlantic. That's where Choon's people think she came from. But we need to be watchful—and change our codes," he added to Ed.

"Aye, aye, sir."

"In the meantime, obviously, the Republic's offensive has been delayed. Maybe by months." He glanced at Meek.

"It's winter there, you know," he explained. "Some snow, high up, but cold an' wet. Especially on the escarpment. It'll be difficult to move men and guns."

"We'll make do," Matt said. "*Arracca* and *Santa Catalina* will be here soon, and much as it goes against my grain to trust to luck and think rosy thoughts, we really don't have any indication the Grik are ready to jump on Madagascar as soon as we'd feared. Now"—he waved the sheet—"the rest of this is mostly routine stuff, but I can confirm that *Santa Catalina* and *Arracca* and her battle group have sailed at last."

"Good. Will they hug the coast, looking for Grik on the way down?" Spanky asked.

"No. They can scout, sure, but I don't *want* them to run smack into any Grik until they get here!" Matt answered, and there were chuckles. "We'll look together when they do."

"Anything else, Skipper? Any other news?" Bernie asked.

"Another air raid on Grik City last night, mostly just tossing the rubble around and killing starving Grik. We lost another plane and pilot." He brightened. "But the Clipper came in this morning with Lieutenant Leedom to take over as COFO there, and he brought Rolak's pet Grik down with him. There can't be twenty thousand Grik left alive northeast of Grik City. Maybe Hij Geerki really can talk 'em out. Mr. Bradford's mission down the east coast of Madagascar in the Seven boat hasn't turned up anything yet, but they're fine. Otherwise, nothing new out here. Things are heating up in the East, though. Governor-Empress McDonald and Saan-Kakja have joined High Admiral Jenks." He frowned. "Rebecca has ordered Jenks to make a heavy probe toward the Pass of Fire, where Costa Rica ought to be. I sure hope they know what they're doing," he added softly. "But if they can figure out what the deal is, it may not be long before things start shaking loose in the East. Shinya's been sick, and so have a lot of his people. Something like malaria, Selass says. But they're getting over it. Maybe just in time, since it looks like Don Hernan is stirring."

"Too much war for us to fight all by ourselves anymore, Skipper," Spanky said with mock sadness, recognizing the frustration that had crept into his captain's tone.

"Lookout says 'laand,' Cap-i-taan, bear-een seero two seero, 'bout twenny miles," came "Minnie's" squeaky voice. She was the shortest adult Lemurian Matt ever knew, and though she was studying navigation and striking for quartermaster's mate, her occupation at battle stations was always bridge talker. She'd actually taken the ship's wheel in battle before, but she was too short to see out the windows without something to stand on.

"We've always got plenty of war wherever we are, Spanky," Matt replied without humor.

"I'll say," Bernie Sandison agreed with conviction. "And I'm glad *Amerika* is already on her way to Baalkpan," he blurted, then looked around self-consciously. "I mean, with the bombing raids on Grik City every night," he added.

"Yeah," Matt agreed softly. "And a probably hostile *battleship* on the loose. I'd really like to know more about those guys"—his expression hardened—"and why their sub attacked us. They may not want an 'open confrontation,' with the Republic, but sinking *Respite Island* sure kicked one off with *us*, as far as I'm concerned."

"Might've been an accident," Spanky muttered doubtfully. "Somebody misunderstood orders and got trigger-happy, or something."

"Either way, they'll have some explaining to do if we run into them here," Matt said, a little surprised by the hubris that a few primitive torpedoes and a sound powerplant inspired in him—and in everyone else, judging by the sounds of agreement he heard. *They feel it too,* he realized. *After all we've been through, what's an old French battleship to us?* He snorted and glanced at his watch again. The sky was much brighter now. "Call the special air detail, and stand by to launch our plane," he said. "Slow to one-third."

"Ay, ay, sur," Minnie cried.

"One-turd, aye!" answered the 'Cat called "Poot"—for other reasons—at the lee helm and bells clashed. Tabby returned the signal a moment later, and the roar of the blower aft of the bridge and the vibrating rumble of the engines and shafts began to fade. Chief Quartermaster "Paddy" Rosen, always at the big brass wheel when *Walker*'s crew was at GQ, muttered something about "turds in the pilothouse" to the 'Cat, whose tail went rigid with embarrassment—again. Regardless how he tried, he always had trouble with "th" sounds. He could do them; he simply forgot. A lot.

The catapult just forward of the aft deckhouse was rigged out thirty degrees to port, its forward section folded down and secured. The engine of the PB-1B Nancy floatplane perched atop it had already been run up—customary whenever GQ was sounded. Now, the observer propped it again, and it roared to life once more. Matt always liked to watch the plane take off, and now he stepped to the port bridgewing, staring aft. The little "Nancys," so reminiscent of the PBY Catalina that had inspired their lines, even down to the blue-and-white paint scheme and the white star in a darker blue roundel with a red dot in the center, had been the workhorses of the Allied air arm. And the single, four-cylinder, Wright-Gypsy–type engine mounted in a pusher configuration had been so successful that they used it for many other applications. Matt knew that Nancys were finally bordering on obsolescent, with all the rapid advances being made, but they remained the most ubiquitous aircraft in the Allied inventory, by far, and were likely to remain so for some time to come.

He saw Chief Jeek, no longer in direct charge of the Special Air Division, hovering behind its new chief and watching what he did. The new chief's tail occasionally swished fretfully under the scrutiny, despite all he could do to control it. Matt smiled nostalgically, remembering how Gray had so often "supervised" other chiefs in the past as he firmly formed them for their duties, his mere presence—and total silence, when possible—lending the authority the new petty officer would need to lead. Almost grudgingly, Matt decided that Jeek would make a fine bosun.

"En-sin Laar-Baa-Ra requests permission to launch," Minnie called.

"Very well," Matt replied. "Tell him to be careful and try not to be seen if he can help it."

In moments, the Nancy's engine revved up to full power, and the impulse charge in the catapult fired with a swirl of white smoke and flung the plane over the side and into the air. Matt watched a moment longer as it swept out over the water, gaining speed, and then clawed for altitude. Still smiling slightly, he stepped back into the pilothouse, unconsciously checking the compass binnacle in front of the big brass wheel. Paddy Rosen smiled back at him, probably relieved that his skipper's weeks-long sour mood seemed better that day.

"Secure from general quarters," Matt said. "All ahead . . . standard," he added instead of his customary "two-thirds," which would just earn Poot more ribbing later whether he said it right or not. "Set condition three." Condition III meant that half the crew would stay at their battle stations, and it had been *Walker*'s default steaming condition ever since she came to this strange world, except when she was secured to a dock.

"Captain Reddy," Doocy Meek said, approaching to stand beside him as Matt stared through binoculars, hoping for his first view of the Seychelles. They were supposed to be rocky, but that was all he knew. A broad cluster of tiny-to-intermediate islands scattered across a clear, brightening sea. But he didn't know what else to expect. Things were always different here, it seemed. The sea was clear enough that the lookout should quickly spot shoaling water, at least. Water depth was always in his mind, and it particularly haunted him now.

"Hmm?" he said. "Lieutenant Meek." He lowered his glasses. "What can I do for you?"

Meek took a deep breath. "Just glad we've finally heard from the Republic," the older man said. "From home."

"Me too. And not just because we need them in the fight, although it's a relief they're still with us, even with the delay." He shrugged. "And a delay now doesn't seem quite as frightening as it did."

"All the same," Meek assured, "our Caesar—kaiser—whichever you prefer, will not dawdle. He'll make every effort to get back on schedule as quickly as he can and perhaps, with communications established, his offensive can be better coordinated with your effort—when it comes."

"I was just thinking that."

"*I'm* thinkin' what it'll mean if we really do find a sizable collection of Griks in the Seychelles," Spanky interjected. "Their ships've been leadin' us here like bread crumbs."

"We'll see," Matt said. "They've had time to gather a lot, if they started quick enough, and they're getting better at the 'indirect approach' to things." He shook his head. "We'll see," he repeated. "Be nice to have 'em pinned down, though, one way or another."

They talked of various things as the watch progressed, drinking more of Juan's "coffee" and discussing what the Republic would bring to the war. Meek had never been comfortable holding back, but now he didn't have to anymore. An addendum to the message addressed to "all officers of the Republic in communication with officers of the Grand Alliance" finally gave him complete freedom to tell Captain Reddy whatever he wanted to know. Commander Simon Herring appeared on the bridge with Greg Garrett's full report, forwarded by Inquisitor Choon, and began pumping Meek for things of interest to him that Matt hadn't even thought of, such as the role of the Gentaa in Republic society. It was an interesting, diverting conversation that passed the time as the distant islands gradually came into view from the pilothouse. And all the while, whatever they did, everyone was anxiously waiting to hear what the scout plane would report. When it finally came, it was by voice in Lemurian, and Ed Palmer called the bridge. Minnie listened for a moment before turning to Matt with a grin. "We got 'em, sur. Ensign Laar sends that there's Grik Indiaa-men gathered 'round several islands, maybe a couple hundred of 'em. Plenty for a big army o' Griks!"

"Heavies?"

"He thinks twelve o' the big iron-claad baattle-waagons, an' as many o' their cruisers. Maybe more at farther islands."

Matt nodded. They'd discovered that the cruisers were probably even more dangerous than the battleships in a close surface action, but were more vulnerable to air attack. "Any idea how many warriors?" he asked. Counting Grik was extremely difficult from the air. They didn't use squad tents and shelter halves like the Allies. If they used shelters at all, they were often haphazardly rigged flies with as many Grik crammed under them as could squeeze in. Halik's army was an exception to that, but the only one they'd seen.

"Laar not get close enough for that without orders. You still want him to not get seen?"

Matt considered. They'd found a big force, plenty big enough to be a threat to Grik City, and with unimpeded access from the west and points north, it was liable to grow bigger. It was already much larger than he had any intention of tackling alone. This *had* to be the main Grik effort, building in a place that Esshk would think they'd consider an unlikely threat. *That* part of his plan had already worked, since they hadn't really expected to find anything in the Seychelles.

Now I'm trying to shrink Esshk's head, Matt realized wryly. *I guess I have to, but it's hard enough figuring out what makes* people *tick.* He cleared his throat. "Helm, left standard rudder. Make your course two eight zero. We won't get any closer just now. Have Ensign Laar probe northwest—carefully—and then return to the ship for recovery. This to Admiral Keje: We seem to have found where the Grik are staging their major effort. Leave Jarrik and two DDs to keep the Comoros Islands bottled up, and proceed north with your remaining battlegroup to rendezvous with us here. If the Grik don't move, we'll wait for *Santa Catalina* and *Arracca*'s battlegroup to arrive, and we'll destroy them together."

Even as he gave the order, something nagged at Matt. It seemed like a reasonable strategy, just as did the one he was already crediting to First General Esshk and hoping to thwart. To retake Madagascar, the enemy had to mass, and this was the first successful example of that they'd seen. But their reconnaissance was stretched very thin, and for the first time they were in the enemy's own backyard where he had an entire continent to draw on—and hide things. He rubbed his neck, deciding he'd gone from one extreme to the other—from giving the Grik too little to too much credit for imagination. *The Grik are assembling an invasion here, in a more thoughtful place than usual, and when it's ready, it'll attack—if we don't destroy it first. It's as simple as that.*

////// *Zanzibar*

atsuma has been sighted, Lord, approaching the harbor mouth under the flag of the
Celestial Mother," Signal Lieutenant Fukui
reported, his tone wary. Hisashi Kurokawa sat in his spacious, almost elegant
office in the headquarters complex that
had been erected, well concealed from the
air, near the harbor. He looked up at Fukui from behind a finely crafted
desk that had been fashioned by one of his men who'd apprenticed under a master cabinetmaker, and frowned. On the desk were the plans of
a new class of ship he desperately wanted to build, instead of merely
continuing to convert some of the crude Grik dreadnaughts for a more
pressing purpose. Some of those were already complete, but he still dis-
trusted their engineering plants—and the improvements they'd made
to their watertight integrity had been—he frowned deeper—"stopgap"
at best. Even so, his attention had not been as much on the plans as

upon the conversations Muriname reported having with the German pilot—and what they implied.

"You no longer salute me, Fukui?" he barked.

The lieutenant braced to attention and performed his most perfect salute. Kurokawa allowed him to stand rigid for a moment before touching his own brow and waving at the man. "Now," he said, "what was it you were gibbering about?"

"*Tatsuma*, Lord! She has been spotted approaching the harbor, flying the red banner!"

Another flare of irritation swept through Kurokawa, one born of indignation. *Tatsuma* was his own personal yacht, a double-ended sidewheel steamer he'd been forced to leave behind when he led the Grik Grand Fleet against Madras. He seethed to think the Grik now controlled her. Then he stood suddenly, his mind racing. *She must bear an emissary from General Esshk!* "Where are our visitors from the League?" he demanded.

"Most are still in the quarters we provided them. They sleep quite late. Some are inspecting our munitions factory, and the German pilot remains at the airfield."

"None are near the harbor?"

"No, Lord."

"Make sure that none approach it. Double their guards. If any question why, tell them a Grik worker has lost its mind." He waved in the air. "Say it violently attacked someone. They should believe that. And since we can't tell one Grik from another, we must protect them more carefully until the dangerous one is discovered. In the meantime, direct *Tatsuma* to dock beyond the shipyard where the conversions are underway. That should conceal her. What time was my meeting with Captain Gravois?"

"Fifteen hundred hours, Lord." It was 0900 now.

"Very well. I will meet *Tatsuma* myself, with a company of our most loyal guards. Tell them that we do not know whether *Tatsuma* brings loyal representatives or mutineers like General Halik. They must not hesitate if we tell them to kill everyone aboard!"

"Of course, Lord."

"I think I should like to hear what our old allies have to say before I meet with the new ones again," Kurokawa murmured.

*   *   *

"First General Esshk politely inquires whether we still live, and if so, are we yet prepared to resume the hunt against our common enemy," Kurokawa said wryly to Muriname as the two approached the conference room in the jungle near the barracks set aside for the visitors. As usual, a strong guard contingent accompanied them. "Madagascar *has* fallen, and the Celestial Mother *is* slain," he added almost wonderingly. "General Esshk has retreated to the continent and prepares to retake the island, but the Americans and their ape-man lackeys are on Madagascar in strength sufficient to concern him—and me. They may scout far enough northward to discover us here. That might be . . . inconvenient at present."

"Inconvenient, or an opportunity? Do not forget Fiedler's warning," Muriname replied.

"I see no 'opportunity,'" Kurokawa flashed back. "Only a more urgent need to seek support from that arrogant Frenchman. How can there be an opportunity?"

"The American position on Madagascar must be tenuous, their supply lines vulnerable, Lord. Taking the place must have shot their bolt, and seems to me an act of desperation. If General Esshk can destroy them or drive them away . . ."

"Their power to resist us might be broken at last, without selling ourselves to these strange foreigners," Kurokawa finished for him.

"That is what I was thinking. You . . . did not kill the Grik emissaries?"

"No. I merely confined them to *Tatsuma*—for now. Under guard."

"Good. It may benefit us to renew a dialogue with General Esshk."

Kurokawa glanced at Muriname, calculating. "You may be right about this 'opportunity' after all, General of the Sky. I appreciate your insights regarding this."

Muriname gulped, hoping Kurokawa wouldn't begin to consider him a threat. It was rarely wise to disagree with, or even reveal one's inner thoughts to Kurokawa.

"And the current situation is intolerable," Kurokawa continued. "The 'League' that professes such concern for our well-being tells us almost nothing. If not for your and Iguri's conversations with one discontented man . . . And even what we *do* know is maddeningly incomplete!"

"We can't press Fiedler too hard," Muriname stressed. "He wouldn't have told us as much as he has if he did not think that Gravois would surely have disclosed some of the most basic details by now. His relative isolation from his comrades has benefited us. How else would we know even what we do?"

Over time, Fiedler had revealed that the League controlled the Mediterranean, a fair percentage of North Africa, and had a toehold in Italy, France, and Spain. Incorporating people—and other "beings"—already present, they'd spent nearly six years consolidating their position and carefully, systematically, spying on potential rivals. Only now had they begun to take an active role in subverting those perceived rivals before they became more formidable. He'd confirmed that the Human-Lemurian Alliance in the Pacific and Indian oceans concerned them due to their rapid advancement, and they considered the Grik a potentially even greater threat due to their numbers, and frankly, their fearsome nature. From that, and the paucity of further information, Muriname had deduced that the League's primary strategy in the region was to keep the Grik and the Allies focused on each other for now. It followed that, though the strangers professed to want Kurokawa's people to "win," all they really wanted was to keep everybody fighting one another as long as possible so *no one* would gain the strength to challenge the League.

"On reflection, the German's 'isolation' and his willingness to speak now strikes me as somewhat too convenient," Kurokawa growled as they reached the conference room. "How do we know that he hasn't told us exactly what he was instructed to?" Muriname said nothing. That hadn't even occurred to him.

"The time has come, General of the Sky, to prod these fools into declaring their true intent, one way or another. With the Americans so close and the Grik on their heels, we must have the help this 'League' has promised, or be rid of them at once."

Two Japanese guards opened the doors to the heavy wooden structure. Long, gunportlike coverings had been left raised down the length of the building for ventilation, and other guards insured that no one approached close enough to hear the conversations inside. Muriname joined Gravois, Rizzo, and de Luca at the table, wondering where the Spanish officer was. Kurokawa strode to the end of the table, slapping his leg with the garish, Grik-made riding crop he so often carried—and that made his agitation so apparent when it came.

"I have had enough," he declared, softly at first, but his voice began to rise. "You have been here quite long enough to learn all you care to know about us, but still reveal precious little about yourselves. You speak of support, friendship, and common cause, but remain infuriatingly vague about what those things mean to you. You crow about how much you know about our enemies and say you want to 'help' us, but you do not tell us how or why." His face turned red. "I believe that is because you fear *us*, and do not mean to help at all! You fear us and our enemies, and would prefer that we destroy each other so you never have to face us, either one." He paused, taking in their astonished expressions, but saw nothing to make him think he was wrong. "I am not blind," he snarled. "I have sources of my own and know where you come from; what you are. I also know that though you may be strong at home, you are weak in this sea—a sea now infested with forces of the Americans and their ape-man lackeys not so very far from here. Madagascar *has* fallen, and the Americans *are* there! Surely you have confirmed that by now yourselves, yet you said nothing! I can only conclude that the endless, useless chatter that we engage in day after day is designed to distract us, and you only mean to support us with meaningless words, to keep us in a fight you are too weak to make!"

Gravois shifted in his chair and pinched his mustache between his thumb and forefinger. "Well," he said. "You are not altogether wrong," he confessed with a slight smile. Kurokawa was too stunned to speak at first. Before he could vent his mounting rage, however, Gravois continued. "We have been entirely honest with you. We *do* want you to win, and we desire only friendship between our peoples. But we also want you to continue your war against the various allies that oppose you— without becoming too powerful yourself."

"Gravois!" Rizzo hissed.

"Oh, be quiet, Maggiore Rizzo! We obviously cannot continue this charade!" He looked at Kurokawa. "What would you do in our position? We accept you as a friend, an ally, but our leaders will never accept you as their superior. If you grow too strong, you will try to take that place." He smiled and shrugged. "We know you *very* well. And we are relatively weak in this sea, as you say, and cannot afford a major war here now," he confessed. "In fact," he continued, "though we will help you, we cannot afford a major war against your enemies at present either. As I have alluded, they are much more widespread than you know." He sighed. "Not only have they conquered India and Madagascar from you and the Grik; their influence extends throughout the East Indies, Australia, and most of the Pacific. They even have a toehold in the Americas—not to mention small colonies in your own homeland of Japan. Indeed, were the . . . significant forces they have deployed against another enemy they confront in Central and South America free to join them here, I do not think any of us could prevail against them without a full commitment by the League."

"We know of this 'other enemy,'" Kurokawa stated, almost petulantly. "This 'Dominion.'"

"What do you know about it?" Gravois asked, genuinely curious. Kurokawa clouded. "Not much," he snapped. "Only that it exists."

Gravois massaged his mustache again. "We know little beyond that ourselves, but we are attempting to learn more, even as we speak." He shrugged again. *He does that a lot,* Kurokawa thought darkly. "As I have told you, our own resources are not unlimited and the world is vast." He grimaced. "But in addition to all that, the American-Lemurian Alliance has sent a mission to a small power called the Republic of Real People situated in the south of Africa."

Kurokawa's brows rose at that. "The 'other hunters'!" he exclaimed.

"You know of them?" Gravois asked, surprised himself.

"Yes," Kurokawa proclaimed with some satisfaction. "General Esshk of the Grik and I once attempted to enlist their aid. There was no response."

"Actually, there was," Rizzo said. "They have been preparing to join the war *against* you for some time, but we had . . . assets there to prevent that. Peacefully, of course," he added with a glance at Gravois.

"How could you accomplish that?" Muriname blurted.

"Suffice to say that we did—for a while. We have no direct contact with those assets. They must remain silent to avoid detection themselves. But it seems clear from reports we have received from Tripoli that the effort to dissuade the Republic has now ended and it will attack the Grik, though its offensive has been seriously delayed." He frowned. "I do not know which best serves our purposes." He looked steadily at Kurokawa. "*Either* of our purposes. Should you warn the Grik of this or not? Assuming, of course, that you have the means to do so . . ."

Gravois cleared his throat. "But the point we have been trying to make is that no matter how mighty the League might be, it must be subtle at times. It can't fight everywhere, or its power would become as diluted as the American-Lemurian Alliance. We must assume that the Alliance, at least, has finally discovered our existence through contact with the Republic, if no other way, and our leaders prefer to avoid overtly antagonizing it *or* the Grik, and that we maintain the appearance of official neutrality as long as possible. We *will* help you, discreetly for now, and primarily with information. For example, I will tell you that the Allies have sent part of their fleet at Madras to reinforce and resupply their forces on Madagascar. It is believed that this force may pass near enough to Zanzibar to discover your presence here. To avoid that, you should prepare to destroy, as suddenly and completely as possible, any snooping Allied ships or planes."

"Can you tell us the position of the enemy forces when they are near?" Muriname asked.

Gravois hesitated. "Possibly," he said.

"Then we should attack!" Kurokawa shouted triumphantly. "Our new weapons will take them completely by surprise, and we will scour them from the sea!"

"I would . . . counsel most ardently against that," Gravois said with a smile.

Kurokawa's eyes bulged in fury. "Are you mad? To have such an opportunity and not take it is abject cowardice!"

Rizzo bristled, but Gravois remained impassive. "I suggest that it would be *wise* to allow the first force to pass unmolested, if possible. It is of little consequence. You may only achieve the surprise you seek once, and if you desire the greatest return on your advantage, attack the *second* convoy from Madras. It will be much more important to your enemies."

Kurokawa stared. "How do you know all this? So far I have taken your word that you know all you say, but I must know how!" he demanded hotly. "Most of the enemy's wireless traffic has been in code, and their radio chatter is largely in the language of their lackeys! If you have broken their code, I demand access to it!"

"Demand?" Gravois replied with a slight frown. Then he shook his head. "We have not broken their code and it remains troublesome, but we can translate the Lemurian voice transmissions. An amazingly complete picture of Allied strategy can be assembled from loose, offhand chatter, and Lemurians are delightfully talkative creatures!"

"How do you understand them?" Muriname asked. Gravois seemed to consider, then glanced at Rizzo. The Italian officer nodded reluctantly. "I freely told you that we lost a submarine," Gravois said, "but what I did not say is that it—and other elements—have been deployed to observe your enemy for some time. For security reasons I cannot say how those elements are maintained, but it should suffice that the submarine once found itself in a position to capture a few Lemurians without risk of discovery. They'd been left to watch a destroyed Lemurian city on the coast of Java, near Tjilatjap, as a matter of fact." He spread his hands. "The prisoners were persuaded to be helpful. Sadly, they didn't know what they'd been left to guard, but were most cooperative in other respects. I believe some still survive as interpreters, though we now have others who understand the language."

"That is . . . amazing," Muriname murmured. He knew the Grik had captured Lemurians before, but they were always eaten, and few ever survived long enough to be questioned. Even then, little was ever learned from them. He wondered if the League had better methods of extracting information, or did its prisoners cooperate better simply because they weren't Grik?

"Most interesting," Kurokawa agreed, his tone surprisingly composed. "Almost as interesting as how you have, after so long, gone from revealing practically nothing to telling us more than I can believe." He waved away Rizzo's objection and nodded at Muriname. "I must consider this, and particularly how to respond to the enemy convoys you described. We can meet again tomorrow, if that is convenient for you. Perhaps I will have more questions, and a better sense of things then."

"At your service, General of the Sea Kurokawa," Gravois said as he, Rizzo, and de Luca stood. When it became clear that Kurokawa didn't mean to stomp out before them, as usual, they awkwardly took their leave. When they were gone, Kurokawa finally sat and exhaled heavily. Muriname stepped over to stand before him.

"Do you believe them?" Kurokawa asked.

"Yes, Lord."

Kurokawa nodded. "So frustrating! I wonder if we shouldn't have simply tortured all we wanted to know from them from the start." He smirked. "As passive as they claim to be, the League probably wouldn't want to 'antagonize' us either!"

"But Gravois seems to wield real power within it," Muriname said reflectively. "And after reporting that he arrived safely, which I'm sure he did as soon as he landed, I doubt we could hope for any assistance from the League if he suddenly stopped reporting."

"The League," Kurokawa hissed, "will 'assist' us in destroying every threat it fears, including ourselves! Gravois as much as admitted that! We will end up no better than the other, lesser members of their strange association, and likely much worse. No! I—*we*—have not worked so long and hard, and suffered so much to merely trade our old Grik masters for others that will use us the same! We have a *purpose* on this world, General of the Sky! Why else are we here? And it is not our destiny to be ruled by anyone, but to rule ourselves! To rule everyone!"

Muriname felt his heart sink. Kurokawa's madness was nothing if not consistent. The worst part was that Muriname agreed with most of what his leader said but was rational enough to understand that nobody could ever rule this entire, savage world. He would've been perfectly happy to cooperate with the League if he weren't so sure that Kurokawa was right about them as well, and they were just as mad as he.

"We are not in control of this situation," Kurokawa said, his voice coldly calm. "That has been the case for far too long, and we must do something about it." He turned his head to gaze at the jungle outside. The sky was darkening and storms would come. "For now, we shall remain the devoted friends of our new allies from the League of Tripoli. We will learn what we can from them and always push for greater commitments on their part. At the same time, we will release *Tatsuma* to carry a message back to General Esshk, informing him that we happily escaped the disaster at Madras with as much of the army and navy as we could save, in spite of the rebellion of his protégé, General Halik. It will go on to inform him of *everything* we know about the League—except where its members are, of course—and what we are trying to get out of our association with them. I don't believe I will mention what we learned of the Republic just now either. General Esshk is no fool, and I prefer him less focused on us. An attack from the south should keep him distracted." He smiled. "Like the League, it can only benefit us if our 'allies' remain confused." He returned to the subject of his message. "Finally, it will assure Esshk that we have never stopped the hunt against our mutual foes and are poised to demolish a great fleet on its way to reinforce the enemy now holding the Celestial City."

"We shall attack the *first* force Gravois described?" Muriname asked with concern.

"Not unless it discovers us," Kurokawa replied. "Gravois's point about achieving the maximum effect from our surprise was well taken." He smiled. "Esshk doesn't know the full extent of the force he faces. How can he? And even if he did, he can't expect us to stop everything that passes by. But we *will* destroy the second, more 'consequential' force Gravois described!" he growled, then chuckled, his mood whipsawing in that disconcerting way. "Our message to First General Esshk will end with my appropriate condolences on the loss of *our* Celestial Mother, and my concerned speculation that the treachery that lost my regency in India might have left me with insufficient authority to command the necessary obedience from the Grik forces we've assembled here. A suitably impressive appointment from him would go a long way toward ensuring our success. Another, more expansive regency, perhaps?"

Muriname barked a laugh in spite of himself.

"Hilarious, is it not?" Kurokawa said in the most genial tone Muriname had ever heard him use. "I will bribe him with his own ships and troops!"

"But what will Gravois say if he discovers what we do?" Muriname cautioned.

"What can he say? We only continue to fight as we have—which is what he says he wants, after all."

Fire in the East

////// USS *Simms*
Second Fleet Task Force 11
330 miles ESE Approximate Position "El Paso del Fuego"
(Costa Rica)
September 12, 1944

L ieutenant Ruik-Sor-Raa paced the damp, windswept quarterdeck of USS *Simms* as she bounded through cross-grained seas. The sea spray kept the nearly blond fur of his face and hands, not protected by the dark peacoat, a duskier shade than usual. The sky was a dull gray brown, but anything but lifeless, throwing a stiff northwesterly wind close enough that *Simms* had to rely on her staysails alone to keep her engine from working too hard. Not that *Simms*'s fine engine needed the help, Ruik reflected. It was still doing most of the work. But like every frigate, or "DD" skipper, he was ever mindful of his fuel state, and as the task force he was assigned to drew ever nearer the mysterious pass or strait where the Dom fleet was supposed to be gathering, thoughts of fuel—for combat speeds—plagued his thoughts more and more.

His Filpin Lands–built Scott Class sailing steamer had recently undergone an extensive and lengthy refit and repair at New Scotland, and she still showed every sign of being better than new. She was 210 feet long, with twenty 50-pounders, two Y guns, depth charges, and 260 officers and crewfolk. She was capable of more than seventeen knots with her engine at full speed and her sails drawing a kind wind, and, at 1,800 tons, was even heavier than USS *Walker*. Ruik loved her, even as he understood that she was already outdated and would be hopelessly outclassed in the armor-plated brawls that had most recently characterized the naval battles in the West. Out here, in the Eastern Sea Campaign, she was still somewhat better than "state of the art." At least against the Doms. He hoped.

He raised his glass and stared at HMIS *Icarus*, steaming some distance off *Simms's* starboard quarter. *Icarus* was old, one of the first Imperial ships the Allies ever encountered. She was a square rig steamer as well, but classed a "ship sloop" by her navy. She'd been "up-armed" with thirty-pounders, but retained her paddlewheels for steam propulsion and was having a lot harder time keeping station. Ruik snorted in sympathy. He considered Lieutenant Parr, *Icarus's* skipper, a very good friend, and though the man dearly loved his ship, he had to be at least a little frustrated at times like this, comparing her to Ruik's. And it wasn't just age. *Simms* was better in virtually every respect, having drawn on much more modern designs for, well, everything. Ruik snorted again and raised his glass. His and Parr's ships were screening Task Force 11's extreme left, and even with the tumultuous sea, the force arrayed to his southeast was a stirring sight. Nearly half of Second Fleet, minus *Maaka-Kakja* and her own battle group, of course, had been committed to the Governor-Empress's powerful probe of the Dom fleet. The force included two dozen steam frigates, or "DDs," though some of those were now designated destroyer seaplane tenders (AVDs), and were less heavily armed than their newer counterparts. Eight mighty ships of the line of seventy to one hundred heavy guns apiece constituted Imperial Admiral E. B. Hibbs's main battle line, and he flew his pennant from

HIMS *Mars*. There were oilers and colliers aplenty—the Empire's steamers still burned coal—and there was even a troopship packed with seven hundred men, sent along just in case an opportunity arose. Finally, the ships of the line, or "baatlewaagons," as the Lemurian sailors called them, as well as the other most vulnerable ships, were enclosed by an inner screen of dedicated anti-Grikbird auxiliaries. These were the equivalent of the fast transports in the West, but they were equipped with a variety of new weapons designed to deter attacks from the Grik-like flying "dragons." Saan-Kakja had surprised them all by arriving with enough of the new Browning copy machine guns to put two or more of them on each of the dedicated vessels.

Ruik was encouraged by that, and the overall power he beheld. This was the first time they'd ever gone after the Doms with more than a handful of determined ships. But he still remained unsure how he felt about the whole operation; he could see both sides of the argument. He liked and admired Governor-Empress Rebecca, and agreed with her desire to find out what they faced. If they couldn't do it by air, a strong surface force had to try. But High Admiral Jenks was right as well. Air power—of whatever sort—was far more important than Ruik thought Governor-Empress Rebecca fully grasped. If the Dom's "Grikbirds" could keep Second Fleet's air away from the region, there was a good chance the enemy had finally figured out how to make the things more effective against surface ships than they'd been off Saint Francis. . . .

"What do you think we're gonna run into, Skipper?" Ruik's Maa-ni-lo Exec, Gaal-Etkaa asked, mirroring his own thoughts.

"I don't know," Ruik answered honestly. "I wish I did. When it gets right down to it, as my Amer-i-caan friends say, nobody really knows what the daamn Doms have anymore; what they've apparently drawn here from their forces in the Aat-laantic. . . ." Ruik coughed a laugh. "Aat-laantic! Not so long ago, I didn't think anyone could sail so happily here as we do now, without falling off the world! Now I learn there is yet *another* vast sea beyond the land of the Doms! I can barely imagine it. I . . . begin to feel old, somehow."

Gaal-Etkaa blinked amusement, but then laid his ears back. "I'm twenty. Older than you. But I think I know how you feel. So much change, so fast. More in the last few years than our people have absorbed for . . ." He stopped, shrugging in the human way, and they both laughed. Gaal sobered. "But I cannot help wonder what we, our ship, might soon be forced to absorb," he said more quietly, glancing at the 'Cats nearby. Their laughter had established for the crew that they were unconcerned by the tangible worries that naturally filled the ship, but they knew each other well enough to share their candid, private thoughts.

"*Simms* is more than a match for even the heaviest Dom ship ever seen in the Pacific, or Eastern Sea," Ruik said without boasting. "And the consensus is that the fleet she helped destroy can't be of significantly inferior quality than the reserve the enemy has brought through the strait we've been sent to investigate. Why would it be? The Doms started the war with their attack on the Empire, and then Saint Francis. You'd think they would've sent their best." He paused and looked around again. "But I must confess that something naags me."

"Ah, the Diaablos del Norte? The 'other Amer-i-caans' the Doms confront in that other sea?"

"Indeed. Nobody has a clue what nature of fleet *they* have, only that they supposedly have one. That makes it impossible to say what the Doms had thought was sufficient to keep them in check." He swished his tail with the usual frustration. "I'm reminded of our own strategic deployment: First Fleet gets all the newer, better weapons to fight the Grik in the West, because that's who everyone considers the greater threat. Fine. I even agree, based on what we've seen. But what if the Doms always considered the Diaablos the greater threat, and kept their 'second string' fleet in this sea?"

Gaal thought about it a moment, then shook his head. "Naah. They had the numbers against the Impies before we jumped in, but they weren't good enough. I think the Impies'd've held their own, at least defending the Isles."

Ruik blinked disagreement. "Not as screwed up as Don Hernan, McClain, and that daamn Billingsly had things there. The Empire nearly lost it all, real fast, even with our help. They'd have lost all their colonies, and New Ireland too. I'm not saying there wouldn't have been a brisk fight for the rest of the New Britain Isles, but I think they would've lost. We, the Alliance, were the wild card that threw 'em off."

Gaal was silent. "You may be right, Skipper," he said at last. "The Heavens know ever'body says the Doms take the 'long view.' I guess if they thought they needed to keep their better stuff in the Aat-laantic, to keep the Diaablos off their back, but thought they still had the weight to knock out the Empire at their own pace, they'd'a done it."

"Especially if they thought that would eventually free them up out here to send stuff east through the strait, to gang up on the Diaablos."

Gaal looked at Ruik, troubled. Then he grinned. "Naah," he said again at last. "We're just a couple destroyer 'Cats, yarnin' at the rail. Don't you think Ahd-mi-raal Lela an' High Ahd-mi-raal Jenks would'a thought of that?"

"Yes," Ruik agreed, suddenly almost certain, "and I bet that's why they've kept us bunched up between the Enchanted Isles and Guayak so long. The same kind of worries. The thing is, I do know the Governor-Empress Rebecca McDonald fairly well, and she wants the Doms dead bad enough that I'm not sure she'd listen." Ruik gazed back out at the fleet, beyond the laboring *Icarus*. "Wish it wasn't so rough. It would be nice to have a few Nancys up, looking around ahead of us." Nearly every Allied ship now carried at least one spotting plane, but the sea and weather had to be calm enough to recover them, so none were flying at present.

Gaal looked at him more closely. "Hey, this really is naagging you, isn't it?"

"I guess," Ruik confessed.

"You think we're heading into a trap?"

Ruik shrugged. "Maybe. Once we get closer in. I'll want to double the lookouts starting tomorrow, especially if this overcast holds."

"Ay, ay, Skipper. Uh, Skipper? Have you talked about this with Ahd-mi-raal Hibbs?"

Ruik looked away. "No. Not that it would do any good. He's just following orders too. I have talked with Commaander Grimsley, Ahd-mi-raal Jenks's old XO in *Aa-chilles*. I think he feels the same way. I guess we'll just have to keep our eyes peeled."

"Yaah," Gaal said slowly, looking in the general direction they were headed, toward the invisible strait. "Oh well," he added, falsely cheerful. "We oughta know in a couple o' days, one way or another."

One of the speaking tubes arranged in an ordered cluster near the wheel squealed loudly. *Simms*'s first lieutenant, who had the watch, pulled the whistle plug on the one leading to the "comm shaack" almost

directly below. Second Fleet didn't have TBS equipment yet, but everything had CW capability now. "Conn, ay," he said, leaning forward to
listen. Ruik saw his ears flutter. "Grikbirds!" he cried at his captain.
"Mebbe five of 'em, bear-een seero four seero! *Finir-Pel* pick 'em up!"
USS *Finir-Pel* was another of the newer Scott Class DDs, as were most of
those that the "Union" had contributed to Second Fleet. They were one
example of how "better" actually had made it east. *But that brings us
back to how "better" is no longer "good enough" in the* West *anymore,*
Ruik considered again. He straightened. Lieutenant Haan-Sor-Plaar
didn't spook easy, and *Finir-Pel* and USS *Mertz* were screening northeast of the fleet—closest to the most likely contact point with the enemy.
"Sound general quarters," Ruik barked. "All hands to baattle stations;
prepare for flying taagits!" He looked at Gaal before extending his glass
and focusing it in the direction of the signal. "I'll have those extra lookouts in the tops now, if you please."

Simms rumbled with drums and the alarm gongs stationed around
the ship as the controlled chaos of clearing the ship for action ensued.
The great guns were not run out in preparation for an air assault, but
nets were rigged to catch falling debris—and to prevent Grikbirds from
gaining the deck. *Simms*'s meager antiair weapons were made ready,
and small arms issued.

"*Finir-Pel* says the Grikbirds go!" shouted the OOD, the tension in
his voice bleeding off a bit. "They head back nort'east!"

"Just a scout," Gaal said, scratching under his ear. "We had to expect
that. We already knew they keep Grikbirds on some o' their ships, like
we do Nancys." He scowled. "Feed 'em slaves, or whoever's handy. But
their 'air' is a little more 'all weather' than ours."

"A scout this far out?" Ruik murmured skeptically." Grikbirds only
had about a forty-mile combat range, and Allied efforts to observe the
pass of fire had always been able to get that close with minimal losses—
probably inflicted by Grikbirds flying off their own small squadrons of
picket ships. Only after that did they start hitting impenetrable *swarms*
of the damn things. But it had been a while since the Doms had sent any
ships much past a hundred miles. Why now?

"You want me to secure from gen'raal quarters?" Gaal asked.

"No. Not yet."

"Hey, it's no big deal," Gaal said, studying his skipper. "So they have a few ships pokin' around. Maybe their Grikbirds saw us, but they can't tell 'em *what* they saw. I don't know if they can tell 'em anything. Grunt an' point, maybe. That'll tell 'em we're out here, but not what we got. I think you worry too much."

"You could be right. But there's been too many times I—and others—haven't worried enough." He gestured around at the sky, the sea. "And what worries me now is we can't fly and Grikbirds can. And there's something *else* they can do. If the Dom fleet has come out after us, the Grikbirds that saw us can daamn sure lead it right to us."

"Well . . . good. Finally, we'll get to whip the whole Dom fleet, once an' for all, an' wrap this sideshow war up so we can go west an' kill real Grik with our brothers."

Ruik sighed. Gaal's attitude reflected that of many Lemurian sailors and Marines in the East, and it was always hard to keep them focused on the fact that this was "their" war too.

"Suddenly, I think I understand one of the strange phrases so often used by the human members of our Amer-i-caan Navy clan," Ruik said, blinking ruefully. " 'Be careful what you wish for.' " Gaal blinked back in utter confusion.

Task Force 11 continued pounding east-northeast in the face of the mounting gale as the day progressed, but the Lemurian Sky Priests aboard the flag were sure the wind and sea would moderate overnight. Ruik's sea sense agreed, and they were even beginning to catch occasional beams of light through the western overcast sky as the sun fell toward the sea. Nancys would lift with the dawn to make a definitive determination regarding what might be lurking over the horizon. Ruik suspected they'd find nothing, or at most the two or three ships that Gaal believed had sent the Grikbirds aloft. Still, Ruik remained uneasy, reminded of a peaceful morning stroll he once took with Governor-Empress Rebecca and her Prime Factor, Sean Bates. They'd gone sport shooting for a kind of upland birdlike thing on the slopes of the mountains beyond the New Scotland port of Scapa Flow. That pleasant diversion ended with a fight for their lives as a plot unfolded that almost destroyed the Empire.

It has become natural for me to 'worry too much,' Ruik decided. *But does that mean it is wrong for me to do so?* He glanced toward the line of battleships churning along in the distance. *Perhaps. Admiral Hibbs made himself a hero in the battle off New Dublin, yet does not seem much more concerned than Lieutenant Gaal.*

"Why don't you get som-teen to eat, sur?" asked his quartermaster at the wheel. "You been up here all day, wet through." She shivered exaggeratedly. "We ain't far enough north to be this cold!"

Ruik grinned. "Ah, but the air that is here has been up there and brings the cold down with it! We get little change where we are from, around Borno and the Filpin Lands, except when the strakkas come. But the warm world lies in a much narrower band, ah 'laat-i-tude' than I ever expected, and here it seems that the cold world can move against it quite easily from both the north and south! I do not understa . . ."

The voice tube from the comm shack screeched. Pulling the plug himself, he leaned over. "Cap-i-taan speaking!"

"*Mertz* sends more Grikbirds! *Hundreds* o' Grikbirds bear-een nor-nor'east!"

"Grikbirds!" came the cry from the foretop, and Ruik stared up and forward. Several 'Cats were pointing to the left. "Grikbirds!" the lookout called again. "West-nort'west! Bear-een, ah, tree fo seero! All the Grikbirds there is!"

"Silence there!" Ruik shouted at the rising panic in the sailor's voice, even as he raised his glass. The darkening sky was full of clotted formations of wiggling shapes, the motion resolving itself into the furious beats of hundreds of wings as he adjusted the telescope. The creatures were still too far away to reveal details, but he knew what he would see: Bright, feathery/furry bodies with slashing teeth and claws—essentially, colorful flying Grik. He had to assume they were carrying cannonballs, as usual, to fling down on the ships, but couldn't tell yet. Those weren't much of a threat to the ships themselves, but they'd kill anybody they fell on—and there'd be a *lot* of them this time!

He looked to starboard and caught *Icarus* flashing her Morse lamp, making sure they'd gotten the word. "Make smoke!" he ordered. Grikbirds necessarily had highly developed—and sensitive—respiratory systems and didn't like smoke at all, but Ruik already knew *Simms* would be hard-pressed to make enough to discourage the things in this wind. "Send to *Icarus* that we'll close with her; combine our defenses," he ordered. Gaal thundered up from below, surrounded by other 'Cats, and Ruik caught his stunned blinking. He almost laughed. "This is no

'scout,' Lieu-ten-aant! It would take a fleet, a big one, to carry so many
of the creatures! I believe your 'wish' is granted and the Doms are out.
Coming right at us!"

The sea strobed with flashes in the northeast, as Grikbirds fell on
Finir-Pel and *Mertz*. At first Ruik supposed the bursts of light came
from the defenses aboard the two DDs, but there were too many. Way
too many. Dozens of smoky sparkles twinkled across one of the ships
amid bursts of water alongside. Then, even as Ruik realized what was
happening, the distant ship simply exploded in a great, expanding ball
of orange fire and roiling smoke. Other sparkles lit the deck of the other
DD. She didn't explode, but did veer suddenly away, with flames rushing up her mizzen mast.

"They're not carrying solid shot this time!" Ruik shouted. "They've
got *bombs*!"

"How?" Gaal demanded. "Doms don't have percussion fuses, and
Grikbirds daamn sure ain't gonna light a bomb!"

"*I don't care how!*" Ruik roared. "All hands on deck! Everybody but
the comm division and a minimum watch in engineering! Anyone not
already assigned to antiair weapons will draw small arms and prepare
to defend the ship!"

A fair-size clump of Grikbirds broke away from the swarm bearing
down out of the Northwest and angled toward *Simms* and *Icarus*. Ruik
felt his spine turn to ice. "Staand by!" he cried, wishing his ship had
been equipped with at least a few of the new machine guns.

"Here they come!" someone squeaked.

Maybe two dozen Grikbirds suddenly tucked their wings and
stooped, plummeting down out of the sky at about forty-five degrees. A
few dropped their bombs almost immediately, but most bored in. *Simms*
could protect herself against Grikbirds attacking in the "same old way,"
dropping heavy rocks or roundshot and then going for her crew. The
flying monsters had no hands for weapons and had only those they were
born with in their jaws and on their feet. They were savage opponents
but quite vulnerable to gunfire and the bayonet. *Simms* had little defense against explosives dropped from the air, however. A large number
of swivel guns, loaded with tins full of musket balls, were mounted on
her rails, and the Allies had actually taken a page from the Grik and
employed what were essentially portable antiair, muzzle-loading mor-

tars that could spray heavy charges of shot. These were tried and relatively true, performing on the principle that if one put enough lead in the air at the critical instant, some was bound to hit. The problem was, even massed as they were, their effective range was only about three to five hundred feet—and they'd only get one barrage. After that, it would be down to small arms. All the Allin-Silva breechloaders to arrive in the theater had gone straight to Shinya, and he still didn't have enough. *Simms*'s crew had only Baalkpan and Maa-ni-laa Arsenal percussion-fired smoothbore muskets. All would be stuffed with "buck and ball" or heavy loads of "Grikshot." They'd be effective inside a hundred tails—and *very* effective at thirty or less, but were slow to load. That left only several "Blitzerbug" SMGs belonging to the pilots in *Simms*'s tiny air division, close-range weapons as well, and chances were the Grikbirds would already be dropping by the time they opened up.

Ruik wished he could maneuver, but *Simms* was already too close to *Icarus* now. The Impie ship had very similar armaments, and he hoped their combined fire would be enough. "Ready . . . ," he yelled, timing his command as closely as he dared, knowing all the shooting would be over in a matter of seconds. After that, his ship would be helpless.

"Fire!"

Ten swivels and eight mortars barked almost as one, their operators yanking lanyards that slammed brass hammers against musket caps. A cloud of white smoke enveloped the ship as a rain-dense rush of lead lifted to meet the attackers. As they'd drilled for conventional attacks of this sort, the rest of the crew now opened with their muskets. Several bombs detonated dully alongside, probably the early drops he'd seen, throwing desultory splashes as high as the rail. He strained his eyes to see the effect of their fire.

The wad—"formation" was an inappropriate term—of Grikbirds had been shattered, and quite a few were tumbling, broken, toward the sea. Others had dropped their bombs, hopefully short, and were clawing at the air with ragged wings. The rest—maybe half—came on, finally drawing the fire of the Blitzers and some of the more independent-minded crewfolk who wanted actual targets for their muskets. Some were hit, but it didn't much matter. At a little more than mast height, all the remaining attackers dropped.

Ruik watched the weapons fall. They *looked* like cannonballs, maybe a little bigger than usual, and they weren't smoking or anything like that. . . . Most landed in the water, jolting the ship with detonations on and under the water. Some didn't seem to go off. One hit the main top, bounced, and exploded in the air over the waist with a bright flash and screech of flying fragments. Three landed on the deck. One went off under the left wing of the Nancy, where it sat on its catapult over the main hold, shredding it and flipping the wreckage almost over the side. 'Cats went down, screaming or silent, and the plane, tangled in the foremast backstays, sagged almost to the water. Another bomb had landed on the fo'c'sle, and was rolling aft as the bow pitched up. Ruik, crouching now, saw that this one *was* smoking. When it suddenly burst, it didn't do so with the same force as the others, but with a much greater flash. Opening his eyes, Ruik saw flames spreading across the deck, toward the wrecked aircraft, and back forward toward the guns lashed there. More screaming 'Cats rolled on the deck, flailing at themselves, while others raced to help them or ran for hoses and buckets of sand. Ruik realized with pride that *Simms*'s crew was reacting with all the professionalism he could ever hope for, their damage-control instincts kicking in without thought. A few had even already reloaded their muskets and were chasing the rising Grikbirds with fire. Only then did he remember feeling the jar of a third bomb strike the deck, not far behind him on the quarterdeck. Subconsciously, he probably hadn't expected to live long enough to turn and see. Now he spun to the rising cries just as the thing rolled toward the wheel. 'Cats dove away from it, but the quartermaster watched it come, eyes widening as she still clung to her post. It wasn't smoking. It wasn't doing anything—yet. "Secure that, before it blows!" he roared.

"You . . . you think it ain't gonna?" Gaal asked nervously, but trotted forward, scooping up a coiled line. The bow pitched down and the bomb teetered, started to move, and Gaal gently dropped the rope down around it. After the slightest hesitation, he clenched his eyes shut and crouched down to grasp the bundle and hold it in place.

"I hope not," Ruik answered, his legs gone weak. He looked around, saw the shooting had stopped. The Nancy was on fire, but hoses were already on it and he doubted it would catch the tarred rigging aflame before it was jettisoned. Damp sand was still being thrown on the deck, but none of the flames from the "firebomb" had caught the wet wooden deck and whatever had been in it was quickly burning out. He glanced at *Icarus*, but couldn't tell if she'd been hit at all. She seemed undamaged. Far beyond, amid the rest of the fleet, the scene was less reassuring. The Grikbirds were leaving, their strike complete, and Ruik marveled that the Doms had trained them so well. Unable to match the Allied aircraft, they'd made do with what they had and somehow turned Grikbirds into something more like partners than mere tools, at least to the extent that they could make them perform more complicated, less instinctive tasks. *We've already been seeing that in the air,* Ruik sourly reminded himself. *Now, instead of continuing the attack with claws and teeth, they're heading back where they came from, to rearm, most likely.* The only good thing was that Grikbirds got tired, and the Doms couldn't possibly "turn them around" as fast as the Allies could their own air power. *That's something, at least.* He raised his glass. *And we must've gotten a lot of them,* he thought hopefully. *Not near as many are flying away as came in against us. But they hit us hard,* he realized, sobering. Columns of smoke rose from seven ships that he could see, and whichever DD hadn't been destroyed outright in the north was now fully aflame. *Probably really ganged up on them, since they were closest,* he thought grimly. *Finir-Pel and Mertz. Both gone.* He didn't have time to contemplate all the friends he'd just lost. He shifted his gaze. Admiral Hibbs's ships of the line had suffered too; a couple smoking, one afire and lagging now. . . . *Looks like one of the antiair DDs is dead in the water. . . .*

"Cap-i-taan," Gaal said, joining him now that others had taken charge of the unexploded bomb. His tone was more formal than Ruik had ever heard it sound. "From *Mars*, sur: 'Large Dom Fleet sighted, bearing zero two zero. No numbers, sur. Just 'large.'"

Ruik glanced up at his own lookouts. Most in the maintop were dead or wounded, just now being brought down. The lookouts in the foremast hadn't raised an alarm. He trained his glass on Gaal's bearing but couldn't see anything. Too dark now. *Mars* had much taller masts, however, and her lookouts would have the advantage. They might've even seen the enemy ships signaling one another—or their returning Grikbirds. "Our orders?" he asked.

"*Achilles* and *Tindal* are undamaged and now closest to the contact. They'll try to close with and shadow the enemy, discover its disposition, and pass their observations to the flag. We are to close with the battle line and prepare for a night fleet action."

Ruik nodded. Of course. How easy it had sounded when they set out: "Find out what the enemy is doing at El Paso del Fuego. If you run into more than you can handle, retire back to the rest of the fleet." But how many ships had been crippled in the Grikbird attack? How many *could* retire? He took a deep breath. "Aacknowledge." He gestured at the 'Cats gathered around the bomb, gently shifting it to a large, padded pass box. "And find out what makes that daamn thing tick. Take it apart in the launch, towing behind us if you have to, but I want to know if it represents as big a jump in Dom ordnance as I'm afraid it does, and if we'll be facing exploding shot from their great guns by morning."

"Ay, ay, Cap-i-taan."

////// *Second Fleet*
USS Maaka-Kakja

*T*he pounding she heard became part of her dream, something Governor-Empress Rebecca Anne McDonald knew often happened with any number of sounds and activities. It was something she'd grown accustomed to. But she'd also learned to tell when the influence was external, and whether it was something that required her waking attention. Oddly though, just then, she resisted leaving the pounding, pulsing fire dream that surrounded her younger self as she stood beside a bleeding Dennis Silva on USS *Walker*'s burning, sinking fo'c'sle. Around them, the night flashed and moaned with roaring projectiles and tortured machinery, the dark was laced with tracers, and an entire city burned against the backdrop of the black jungle isle beyond. Before them, shattered *Amagi* hissed and crackled as her broken, flaming corpse settled into the sea. Amazingly, in spite of the danger she was reliving, that had been unprecedented in her short life, and regardless of the gore-spattered face that stared down at her, a gap-toothed grin belying the obvious agony of a ruined left eye, "Princess Becky"—for that was all she'd been at the time—felt safe.

The pounding resumed, the *other* pounding, and Silva's grin turned mildly scolding. "Go on, li'l sis," he said gruffly. "You gotta git. You an' Larry brung me the shell that sank that damn thing"—he nodded at *Amagi*—"an' you got more t'do." He grinned again. "Me too. I'll be along d'rectly."

Rebecca murmured an objection, but finally stirred in her bed.

"Your Majesty! Your Excellency!" came the urgent and probably repeated call from the passageway beyond the door to the suite she shared with High Chief Saan-Kakja. Reluctantly, she opened her eyes. "I'm dreadfully sorry to disturb you," the voice continued insistently, "but Admiral Lelaa and High Admiral Jenks beg you to come at once! There has been a . . . development regarding Task Force Eleven!"

Saan-Kakja was already sitting up in the pile of embroidered cushions she slept among across the compartment, blinking irritation. "Oh, do stop braying in the passageway like a great pregnant paalka!" Saan-Kakja demanded. "We are awake! Send in our stewards to make us presentable and bring us to life, and we will join the Ahd-mi-raals as shortly as we can!"

"Of course, Your Excellency," came the muffled, apologetic reply, and Saan-Kakja blinked her mesmerizing eyes at Rebecca. "I do hope this 'development' is not too dire, Sister," she said, "but apparently, if our primary desire was to 'get a rise' out of the Doms, we might have succeeded."

"I think you just called High Admiral Jenks's assistant chief of staff a pregnant paalka," Rebecca scolded lightly, then lowered her voice. "But it is too soon for Task Force Eleven to have *provoked* a response from the Doms. I fear it may have encountered one they had already prepared."

"Very well," Rebecca granted icily, after hearing the initial confused reports flooding in from Task Force 11, mixed with the occasional exasperated sigh and resentful glare from High Admiral Jenks. It was well after midnight and apparently TF-11 was still closely engaged in a vicious running fight against a vastly superior force. She'd noticed as soon as she was fully awake that *Maaka-Kakja* was already underway and steaming at top speed. "If you must hear the words before you can bring yourself to propose a solution, High Admiral, you were right; I was wrong. Now what exactly is the state of our engaged task force, and what are we going to do to help?"

"The 'exact state' of the task force is 'desperate,' Your Highness. I can be little more specific than that, since Admiral Hibbs is unsure himself. He has no notion of how large the enemy fleet is, but is certain it is larger than his. We must assume the entire Dominion fleet has sortied. And there's cursed little we *can* do. At least until the dawn!" he added with mounting frustration, looking at Orrin Reddy who was reclining, grim faced, in a chair by the bulkhead. "No doubt you've noticed that the fleet is already moving toward the point of contact, but though that point is now moving in our direction, it remains over four hundred miles to the north! We will be closer at dawn, and can launch aircraft to support Task Force Eleven—or what's left of it by then," he added bitterly, "but they will be near the limit of their endurance, flying into the wind, and will not be able to linger long. Other than that . . . ?" Jenks twisted his braided mustaches and let out a long breath.

"Allow High Ahdmiraal Jenks a moment to refocus his anger back where it belongs; upon the enemy," Admiral Lelaa-Tal-Cleraan said softly, gently scolding her friend, then sipped monkey joe from a mug. Everyone else in the bustling "battle room" behind the bridge was drinking tea, even Lelaa's Exec, Tex Sheider, and she remained one of the few high-ranking Lemurians anyone had ever known who habitually drank the ersatz coffee of this world by choice. "The situation *is* confused," she continued. "There can be little doubt, however, that the Doms have sortied a large percentage of the fleet they have been gathering so long, and unleashed it in our direction." She glanced back at Jenks. "I consider it premature, perhaps even dangerous, to assume it is their *entire* fleet, but it is clearly substantial. It is . . . unfortunate that our own fleet was not consolidated to meet it, but it might be for the best. The damaging enemy air attack would've caught us equally unprepared and would probably have focused on *this* ship, had the fleet been together. Early reports on their new bombs are mixed regarding their effectiveness, but I find it likely that *Maaka-Kakja* could have been seriously damaged, at least. I do not need to tell anyone here how great a blow it would have been to our entire effort in the Eastern Sea if Second Fleet's only carrier was destroyed before the real battle even began."

"There is that," Jenks grudgingly agreed. "Air power is our single greatest advantage. Without it, things are far too evenly matched for my taste, particularly with our supply lines so long and tenuous. But with dragons dropping bombs now . . . Our advantage is already diminished."

"How dangerous are the bombs?" Saan-Kakja asked.

"There's two kinds of 'em, fragmentation and incendiary," Tex Sheider supplied. "Small and light enough for Grikbirds to carry, neither is very powerful, with the one having about the same effect as a twelve-pound case shot. Lieutenant Ruik on *Simms* actually took a dud that hit his ship apart, and we don't have to worry about the Doms using the same kind of things in their cannon, thank God. Said there's some kind of clunky, Rube Goldberg inertial detonator inside that would go off if they tried to shoot one out of a gun. It's not percussion, but it takes a pretty good jolt. The other one's got a small bursting charge that spreads something like naphtha around. They ain't like our incendiaries, and burn out pretty quick—but 'quick' can be plenty long enough on a ship. Those are the ones that did the most damage." His expression turned grim. "We lost a third of the DD squadron, including *Finir-Pel*, *Mertz*, and *Theseus*, in the opening round. Ship of the line *Poseidon* caught fire bad enough that she had to be abandoned. She blew up later. Nearly every other ship was hurt to some extent, mostly in their sailing gear, which means the whole task force is running only as fast as it can steam. . . ."

"*With* the wind," Lelaa added, "which gives the Doms the ability to control the engagement. Every one of their vessels seen is a sailing steamer, just like ours, which may finally answer a number of questions. . . . But the pertinent point at present is that with the wind in their favor, their ships are faster than ours. They've been lunging forward periodically and lashing at Hibbs's formation at will, all night. His gunnery remains superior and he's sure he has disabled a number of enemy capital ships, but his are suffering cruelly as well. Several can only barely keep up as it is, and if they fall out of formation . . ."

"They'll be mobbed under," Tex finished for her. It was a habit they had that many recognized. Having been friends and colleagues so long, they tended to think alike to the point that they often spoke for each other.

"How soon can we know the size of the enemy fleet?" Saan-Kakja asked, but Jenks shook his head.

"With the dawn, at best. Hibbs says his task force has precisely four undamaged aircraft available. If any remain by daylight, he will send them up to see. Obviously, even if the sea has moderated sufficiently by then, he can't recover them underway. Perhaps they can reach us."

Orrin grunted, making it clear what he thought the chances of that might be. The planes would have a tailwind, but after their scout and likely combat with Grikbirds and the enemy ships—he doubted any flier in Second Fleet could resist making an attack—they'd be low on fuel and probably damaged.

"And the Dragons?" Rebecca asked.

"They haven't rejoined the fight," Tex replied, "but we have to expect they will when the sun comes up." He shrugged. "They've got Task Force Eleven right where they want it, and they *will* try to wipe it out. Pull out all the stops."

"My God," Rebecca murmured.

Jenks stared hard at his Governor-Empress. "If the task force survives until dawn and Hibbs determines that the Dom fleet is insurmountable, you will be faced with a most dreadful decision, Your Highness."

Rebecca's heart seemed to crack in her chest. "I know."

"There is nothing to decide," Saan-Kakja interjected. "And I am surprised at you, High Ahd-mi-raal Jenks," she added. "This is a terrible thing. Another of many terrible things we have all faced in this war. Yet you allow your . . . aanoy-aance at my sister to focus your attention too closely on the immediate threat to Taask Force Eleven."

Jenks arched an eyebrow. "Isn't that enough?"

"No. You look only at the small picture. What happens in the larger one? Do you really believe the Doms finally come out on a whim?"

"She is right, Haarvey," Lelaa said gently. "We are sailors and spend all our time thinking about the sea and ships; fleets, and what they do. We sometimes forget to remember *why*."

"Shinya," Jenks said, realization dawning.

"Right," Tex agreed. "There are such things as coincidences. I've seen enough of 'em to believe. But *people* don't cook 'em up, not in wars, and I don't think this is one."

Saan-Kakja was blinking agreement. "Regardless how the fight began, or what kind of new weapons and Grikbird training the Doms now use, their fleet has come out. They did not come against Taask Force Eleven; they came against Second Fleet. And what is the *purpose* of this fleet? To support General Shinya's continent-aal campaign! The Doms would strike our fleet just now only to prevent it from that." She paused. "It is my belief and counsel that the evil Don Hernaan has ordered this attack now only because he is poised to strike our weakened force ashore." Her gold-and-black eyes narrowed. "And now that I have expressed my belief and rendered my counsel, I must insist that the time has come to reinforce General Shinya at last, with everything at our disposal, despite the illness that lingers in his camp. How many lives will we spare if his entire force and all our new friends at Guayak and Puerto Viejo are exterminated?"

"Nothing to decide, indeed," Rebecca agreed, her small voice like stone. She looked at Jenks. "I've made two terrible mistakes. First, when I ordered you to divide your fleet against your better judgment. That was a foolish usurpation of authority rightly earned by and vested in you, High Admiral. This last year's events in the Empire of the New Britain Isles have left me easily frustrated by delay when it comes to discovering and eliminating vipers. My second mistake, however, was allowing you to talk me out of taking our relief forces ashore in a timely manner. You only counseled prudence there as well, and my personal presence no doubt colored your judgment, but *that* was the debate I should have pressed." She took a long breath and clasped her hands behind her back. "You remain Commander in Chief East and must continue to look to the strategic situation, but these are my orders to you as your Governor-Empress, and there will be no debate. Every troop transport, cargo ship, and auxiliary of any sort that Second Fleet does not need for the battle to come will immediately turn for Puerto Viejo; there to off-load every soldier, Marine, every piece of remaining ordnance and equipment, and even their own armed crews to rush to the relief of Fort Defiance. God grant only that we are not too late. The remainder of Second Fleet will continue on to the rescue of Task Force Eleven, and the *defeat* of the Dominion fleet now at sea. I presume you will begin by sending as much air support as possible in the morning," she said, blinking encouragement at Orrin, "but how you do it is up to you with one exception, and the exception is in regard to the 'dreadful choice' you referenced earlier," she added bitterly. "Admiral Hibbs will not allow his force to be nibbled to death. No single capital ship will be left to be 'mobbed under' by the Doms. Instead, if such becomes necessary, he will deploy an adequate rear guard to engage his pursuers in sufficient force to allow his faster ships to continue on, and break contact if possible."

Jenks was taken aback, but nodded respectfully, knowing what that order had cost Rebecca inside, likely condemning so many to their doom. But he looked at Saan-Kakja, then back at Rebecca. "A number of those ships and crews belong to our allies from Baalkpan, the Filpin Lands, and the American Navy Clan. I remain unsure how this new union they are forming might apply, but I suspect that Saan-Kakja would be its most senior representative here."

"I am the senior representative of the youngling Union in the West," Saan-Kakja confirmed, "and I concur entirely with my sister's decision. And to further reassure you, no alteration in the domestic organization of the various powers that compose that new Union have any bearing on your authority here. You are *still* CINCEAST. But my sister is right. Shin-yaa needs our troops, and we must take them to him."

"Thank you, Your Excellency," Jenks said. "Puerto Viejo is roughly four hundred miles distant. A two-day voyage with this wind," he added, then frowned again. "But do I understand correctly that you both, personally, still intend to go ashore?" he asked sourly.

"Under the circumstances, do you still contend that we'll certainly be safer here than there?" Rebecca asked, her own tone softening. "My orders were clear, and I know I give them with the full concurrence of High Chief Saan-Kakja when I add that you *will* defeat the enemy fleet, even at the cost of this ship."

Jenks nodded. "Very well, Your Majesty." He straightened.

"What if we lose?" Tex asked. His tone was matter-of-fact, but it was the question in all their minds.

"Then the fleet will retire to the Enchanted Isles," Rebecca ordered. She didn't have to add "what's left of it."

"Leaving you and High Chief Saan-Kakja, two of our *heads of state*, trapped in enemy territory," Lelaa observed.

"No," Saan-Kakja denied. "We and Gen-er-aal Shinya's army will continue to occupy friendly territory in the enemy's land, and rely on Second Fleet and the Grand Alliance to find a way to support us." She looked at Jenks. "But that would be the case in any event . . . and Second Fleet will not lose."

///// *Fort Defiance*
September 13, 1944

squadron of lancers is in!" Major Dao Iverson of the 2nd Battalion, 6th (Imperial) Marines said urgently, when General Tomatsu Shinya glanced up at his hurried entrance to the reinforced comm shack where he'd only just arrived himself. "Through the northeast lunette," Iverson specified. Each rounded protuberance, or "lunette," of the pentagon-shaped fort had its own heavily fortified gate, complete with firing steps and embrasures for heavy guns all along their flanks that could pour enfilading fire on any force attacking between them. "Their lieutenant begs to report a matter of importance," Iverson explained.

"I imagine he does," Shinya replied, waving the message form he'd been scanning, already suspecting what the report would involve and knowing only something big would even bring the lancers in. They'd

been . . . avoiding him to a degree, and generally reported via sema-
phore, flashed Morse, or couriers. The Imperial Lancers with his army
hadn't been "real" lancers since their prewar career officers had led
them through a series of fairly senseless actions during the Battle of
Guayak, aimed more at amassing notoriety for themselves than actually
accomplishing anything. A lot of good troopers and precious horses
had been wasted. Shinya had broken most of the useless officers, done
away with the lances, and organized the units as dragoons and mounted
infantry scouts, each armed with cutlass, pistol, and a pair of shortened
muskets. A large number of captured horses had enabled him to expand
this force with locals born to ride any manner of creature, and they
were just as effective with the modern weapons he gave them. All this
had caused considerable friction, since the lancers had been drawn
largely from aristocratic families on New Britain Isle, supplying their
own expensive animals. Absorption of local troops had been resisted,
and accomplished only with the threat of further demotions. Some resentment still lingered toward him, even after the locals had been largely
accepted in the ranks.

Shinya didn't care, as long as they obeyed. He was used to resentment. He still didn't have what he'd call "good" cavalry, not like the
me-naak mounted 'cav in the West, from the Filpin Lands, but it was an
effective scouting force. The Doms still used lancers, and though they
were apparently similarly aristocratic here, and just as prone to impulsive charges, they were actually very good. Firepower evened things out.

"Send to High Admiral Jenks," Shinya told a harried comm-'Cat.
"'Message received and understood. Good luck. Will advise our situation soonest.'" He looked at Iverson. "Pass the word for my personal
staff to assemble at the northeast lunette immediately. No need to summon anyone else yet, but officer's call will be at my HQ at oh two thirty
hours. I'll see you at the lunette, Major."

"Aye, aye, sir," Iverson replied, turning. "Runners!" he cried.

Shinya shook his head, trying to clear a lingering spell of light-
headedness, then strode in the direction of the lunette. Colonel Blair
and Captain Blas-Ma-Ar joined him almost immediately as he walked.

"Things are poppin," Blas said. It wasn't a question.

"Yes. Task Force Eleven is heavily engaged with a large enemy fleet
carrying many Grikbirds. The flying beasts used explosive devices of a

sort to some effect, and the situation is in doubt. There's no way to know whether we will face similar weapons here," he added, "but we must be prepared. High Admiral Jenks is taking the rest of Second Fleet to rescue Task Force Eleven and destroy the Dom fleet. Needless to say, that means our own naval air cover will be diminished at a time we are likely to need it most. Our squadrons at Guayakwil Bay are down to the bare bones."

"Needless to say," Blair agreed wryly.

Many of Shinya's staff was already gathering at the lunette when they arrived, including Lieutenants "Finny" and "Stumpy," who were waiting for Blas. Gun's crews and infantry were watching the lancers tend their animals, pulling saddles, watering, and distributing feed bags. Except for their weapons, the troopers looked just like most other Allied troops now, with their tie-dyed camouflage frocks and trousers— which was yet another source of resentment. They'd been proud of their elaborate uniforms. Ironically, the only Imperial troops still in their red coats were some "regular" Marines, and that was only because supply hadn't yet filled the need. Shinya was perfectly happy that new uniforms to replace the older but still serviceable ones already in use didn't enjoy the same shipping priority as ammunition and other martial supplies. A young man with sergeant's stripes, noticing their approach, snapped to attention. "Sir," he said, aside to another man who was examining his horse's hoof in the light of an oil lamp. He looked up and saluted as well.

"General Shinya. Lieutenant Freeman, sir, C Troop of the Sixth New London Lancers. Beg to report."

"A moment, Lieutenant, if you please," Shinya replied, returning the salute. He noticed with amusement how the lieutenant's lip curled at the mention of his lettered troop instead of numbered squadron. That change had been made to standardize the regimental organization of all mounted units in the Alliance and was unpopular as well. "My staff is gathering, and I'd like them to hear your news." He nodded at the watching hundreds. "And we might not want the entire army to hear it before they do." The fact that Shinya relied so heavily on a number of relatively junior officers for advice actually endeared him to the enlisted ranks a degree, but was yet another source of discontent among his Imperial brigadiers. Having had it once explained to them by Blair that it was a matter of long use and familiarity to Shinya and no reflection on their capabilities, they'd unhappily acquiesced. Of course, always implied had been the obvious precedent Shinya had set that if they complained too much, they might quickly find themselves *replaced* by relatively junior officers. Ever since the New Ireland Campaign, Shinya had lost all patience with political, egocentric commanders.

"Yes, sir."

Withdrawing to the hardened comm shack/HQ for the lunette, they ran everyone out but a single wireless operator. When Dao Iverson arrived, somewhat breathless, Shinya was satisfied that most of his closest advisors, easily available, were present.

"Very well, Lieutenant Freeman, please make your report."

"Thank you, sir. The Doms are on the move."

Shinya nodded impatiently. That was self-evident. "In what force?"

"All of them, General. It started with some skirmishing in the heights between their native scouts and ours. Not unusual that, but there's weight behind their thrust this time and our scouts were pushed back. Colonel Smith took the Twentieth to stiffen the local lads, and it worked for a while. The firepower of dismounted troopers seemed to come as a nasty surprise for the Doms," he added, a touch grudgingly. "Must've thought we had infantry up there for a while, and they didn't quite know what to do at first. Never occurred to them that mounted troops might actually choose to fight on foot." He shook his head. "Didn't last. There were just too many, and Smith's flanks were unsupported. He had to pull back." He paused, moving to the map on the wall and pointing. "To this descending ridge here, paralleling the road from Chimborazo. He called the Sixth up to support him, but there was little we could add. With a few light guns and some of the new breechloaders, we might've kept them bottled up all day in such a lovely gap, but our smoothbore carbines hadn't the range. In the end, all we could do was watch them watching us while a full division of their lancers—more mounted troops than they even had at Guayak—swept down out of the mountains shortly before dark, screening columns of infantry." He frowned. "We watched them pass, still mindful of our flanks, until the light failed, but they made no further effort to have us off. In the meantime, more local chaps, the 'infiltrators,'" he said, using what many Imperials considered the more polite euphemism for "spy," "joined us with observations of their own. Not sure how reliable they are, sir. . . ."

Shinya made a beckoning gesture.

"Yes, sir. They told us the whole Dom army is coming. Troops, artillery, baggage trains, everything. The environs of Chimborazo are emptying as quickly as a bath with the drain plug pulled, all flooding this direction."

"As High Admiral Jenks and the Governor-Empress predicted," Shinya said. "A coordinated stroke." He glanced around. "Our enemies in this land are evil men, my friends, but not strategic fools. Let us hope their tactical sense has not improved since our last meeting!" He turned to Blair. "Who is deputy COFO at Guayak in Lieutenant Reddy's absence?" He should've known that, but his mind remained muzzy at times.

"Lieutenant Te-Aad, of the Tenth Pursuit Squadron. He has the Tenth Pursuit and Twelfth Bomb Squadrons, both 'heavy,' with a total of nearly forty planes between them, but less than half of what we're accustomed to having at our disposal, of course."

"I want Lieutenant Freeman's gap under continuous aerial assault, beginning immediately," Shinya ordered, knowing full well how dangerous night ops were for his meager air force, Grikbirds or not. He looked at Freeman. "I'm sorry, Lieutenant, but I must ask you to return to your regiment at once. We've lost contact with many of our forward observation posts. Enemy infiltrators have cut our telegraph lines no doubt. But we need timely reports of the enemy advance through the night."

"Of course, General. I'll lead my troop back out at once."

"A question first, Lieutenant," Blair said. "I understand your own perspective has been limited, but you've spoken with our local friends. Have you, through any source, been able to arrive at a better estimate of the enemy force approaching?"

"The numbers vary," Freeman hedged grimly, "and I must dismiss many reports as wild, fearful speculation. But I confess a personal confidence in the figure describing the Dom army at a hundred thousand men."

"Very well, Lieutenant. Thank you for your report. Please express my compliments to your commanding officer. Carry on."

When Freeman was gone, Shinya glanced around at his friends once more, studying their faces in the dim lamplight. "We've prepared for this," he reminded them. "Our own flanks are secure as are the roads to Guayak and Puerto Viejo. The enemy cannot pass this fort in strength. He must reduce it to move beyond."

"Clearly what they mean to do," Blas said, then shrugged. "I don't know why ever'body worries so much how many daamn Doms there are. They all comin' here. We'll get to count 'em ourselves soon enough."

"I worry, my dear Captain Blas," Blair confessed, "because we have half that number, and a large measure of our human troops remains indisposed. What's more alarming, with Second Fleet steaming toward an encounter with the enemy fleet, we'll have no reinforcements."

Shinya smiled mirthlessly, holding up the message form still in his hand. At some time during Freeman's report, he'd unconsciously folded it several times. Now he straightened it out. "Untrue, Colonel Blair. Her Excellency Saan-Kakja and the Governor-Empress themselves have separated from Second Fleet and sail for Puerto Viejo with the forces they brought from the New Britain Isles." He snorted. "Including Sister Audry's . . . interesting regiment of Dom converts. They should arrive at Puerto Viejo in two days, more likely three, and join us here within a week. They've decided, and I agree, that the fever is less of a threat to them than a general fleet action, and without fleet protection, they must come ashore in any event." He shrugged. "And we will need them."

"We're *gonna* need 'em," Finny whispered fervently to Stumpy, but everyone heard. "Doms'll be here tomorrow night. Day after, in force, if they movin' like Free-maan says. A hundred thousands? More, maybe? We daamn sure gonna need a hand—if they's any of us lef' by then."

"Don't sell our defenses here short, Lieutenant Finny," Shinya scolded, but then his tone turned hard. "And don't ever even whisper a sentiment like that where anyone else might hear. I've no concerns about our Lemurian Marines, or even our Imperials." He nodded at Blair who'd been just as frustrated as he in the past. "But we have whole regiments of local, largely untried troops now as well. If they hear you, officers, *respected veterans* talking like that, they'll flee their posts like water at the critical moment, and what I'm morally certain would have been a resounding victory will end in all our deaths. Do I make myself clear?"

Finny and Stumpy both gulped, blinking furiously. "Clear, sur," they chorused.

The morning was late in dawning on Fort Defiance, as usual, in the shadow of the great mountains to the east, and the Chimborazo road that snaked up into the heights remained lost in gloom. Flashes of light and burning trees and clumps of foliage still lit the pass, however, as they had throughout the early-morning hours, as flight after flight of Nancys out of Guayakwil Bay swooped on the advancing columns approaching the crossroads. The pounding had been vicious, if very difficult and hazardous in the dark, and doubtless large numbers of casualties had been inflicted on the serpentine host. But accurate bombing under the conditions was impossible, and Shinya had ordered it more as an assault on the enemy's nerve. Staring through his Imperial telescope, he hoped it had been worth the three planes and crews he'd lost. Two had collided, and one might've fallen prey to Grikbirds, but so far few of the winged devils had made an appearance. He wondered if that meant the Doms were saving them for a bomb attack on the fort, or if the distant fleet action had drawn most away. It was impossible to say since no one had any idea how many Grikbirds the Doms controlled.

Despite last night's losses, Shinya meant to keep bombing the Doms this time, even as they deployed, to give them no respite. He wanted them to rush their attack before they were ready, if only to relieve the torment from the air. With the numbers they were bringing, he hoped not to allow them any more time than possible to coordinate their assaults. His heart sank a bit, however, as he observed the first Dom lancers appear out of the smoky shadows to the east in a long, loose column with a very broad front. They were well-appointed troops, he had to admit, with bright cuirasses, plumed helmets, and flowing banners. Red pennants, like miniature versions of their twisted-cross flags, fluttered at the ends of their lances high above their heads. Looking more carefully, Shinya noted that a number wore bandages, likely earned in the bombing, but they maintained a haughty, professional bearing.

"Don't seem much perturbed by the predawn festivities," Blair observed beside him, also gazing through a glass.

"No. They've experienced our bombs before and expect them now. They stay less bunched up too, as you can see."

"Their infantry as well," Blair grumped, refocusing. Beyond, and somewhat within the advancing lancer formation, was a column of Dom regular infantry, with their white-faced, yellow coats, white knee breeches, and black hats. It was a dense column, perhaps ten files wide and extending beyond view, but still less congested than they'd ever seen before. The better to maintain cohesion while avoiding mass casualties from the air. *They've learned a lot,* Shinya realized. They were still vulnerable, and a stooping Nancy chose that moment to smear fire among their ranks, but the casualties were fewer than they would've been before and there was no panic, no scattering, and the beleaguered force marched relentlessly on.

"I don't like to see that," Blair commented.

"Neither do I. They do learn quickly. More quickly than Grik. I expected their soldiers to learn lessons from the Battle of Guayak, but not their leaders. I'd hoped they'd be less open to change."

"Not many of their 'old' leaders left, if our spies have the right of it. But Don Hernan kept Nerino," Blair added almost wonderingly. "Quite a surprise. But he must be responsible for the changes. Learned *his* lesson, at least."

"Too well."

Blair chuckled. "Do you suppose he'll seek to entertain us before the battle again, as he did last time? I thought that was quite civilized."

"I doubt it," Shinya replied. "He knows us now. And I wouldn't give him the chance if he tried. I've already passed the word to our air to target anything that looks like a command post." He waved. "Nerino commands the army, but Don Hernan commands him, and has their army more afraid of him than us. I'd dearly love to murder that walking pit of wickedness, and maybe we will. Perhaps Nerino might even be reasoned with after that. But Don Hernan's too canny to show himself, and if he even approaches this field, he won't give us an easy target. He knows us too," he finished, remembering how the war had started, and doubting any order he could give would prevent every rifle, musket, and cannon in the entire expeditionary force, human or Lemurian, from opening up on Don Hernan if they caught a glimpse of him.

Far to the east, in a comfortable, shaded overlook, Don Hernan de Devina Dicha and General Ghanan Nerino observed the proceedings as well.

"The Army of God has endured its first cleansing!" Don Hernan hailed sweetly, his arms outstretched. He wore the usual vestments of a Blood Cardinal to His Supreme Holiness—red and gold robes and a bizarre white hat. But there was no great entourage, and only a small concentration of troops around him. Even from the air, he'd be difficult to see, and with the thousands of troops and endless stream of military equipment coursing down the road a short distance away, there were much more tempting targets for the enemy flying machines. "Do not pace, my dear General Nerino!" he scolded lightly. "Rejoice! Your troops have passed their first test! The enemy bombs have flayed them, *burned them*, but they will not break again," he chortled, confident in the power he held over their lives.

Of course not, Nerino thought impiously. *March to battle under threat of an agonizing death at the hands of the enemy, or run away and ensure an even worse end at the whim of Don Hernan. They won't break. Not yet. But this is nothing. Don Hernan cannot know what it will be like when the real battle starts. Then? Who can say.* He silently rubbed the burn scars on his hand. *I cannot honestly answer that for myself anymore,* he realized.

"I am . . . eager to join my army, Your Holiness," he said, and even as the words left his lips, he realized with some surprise that they were true. He'd had enough of battles, and his burns remained painful enough that the last thing he wanted was to risk more injuries, but something had . . . happened to him during his convalescence. He'd suffered terribly, just as so many of his soldiers had, and though he had no new illusions that his troops were his equal in some way, he'd learned much about what was important to them. They didn't want to die or be hurt, but perhaps most important, they wanted to believe there was a reason other than punishment for what they risked. If their leaders were unwilling to risk themselves, how important could the reason be for them? Nerino knew his—Don Hernan's—army would fight. It had no choice. But how much more likely was it to achieve its goal, was it—and he—to avoid punishment, if he was there to lead it himself?

"Your chosen officers know what to do," Don Hernan reminded. "And they know the price of failure. They will perform their duties, and you may join them soon enough. Your experience is of no use to me if you are slain during these opening moves." Don Hernan, a wistful smile on his face, watched another pair of the blue and white flying machines swoop down on the column in the distance, fire bursting within it. "Fire is so beautiful," he murmured, then frowned. "The heretic flying machines are a nuisance. I tried to cause the creation of our own, you know," he added bitterly, "but progress is slow. So many of our first efforts were deliberately flawed." He clenched his teeth in silent rage at Ensign Fred Reynolds. "We do make greater use of the small flying dragons than I ever imagined possible," he suddenly enthused, his whipsaw mood clenching Nerino's gut, as usual.

"But few remain at our disposal," Nerino pointed out delicately. "So many were sent to the fleet for their attack that we can no longer counter the enemy here, as we'd begun to do."

"Concern yourself not, my general. The enemy has only so many machines, and your spies are now certain that few of the ones with markings most associated with the great ship that carries them are present here. That means my broader plan to draw their fleet to its destruction must already be bearing fruit! If all goes well at sea, I assure you that you will see fewer and fewer flying machines above your battlefield." He gestured grandly down at the great, fat serpent of men. "Your officers will absorb the pinpricks from the air and complete your initial investment of the fort throughout the night, and launch the army's first assault with tomorrow's dawn, as planned."

"It seems such a waste to attack with but a tithe of our army," Nerino lamented, again hinting at his disagreement. Despite giving him "command" of the Army of God, Don Hernan had tinkered incessantly with his plans. This aggressive, daylight movement and the first attacks were Don Hernan's additions, designed to test his dream that El Vómito might've left Fort Defiance fatally weakened after all. Nerino was convinced that even if it had, the first hurried assaults could not succeed.

"It will make the heretics focus on a more concentrated defense," Don Hernan argued patiently once more, "and prevent them from more forcefully opposing the advance of the rest of the army, which you may personally join." Nerino bowed, knowing when further resistance was futile. Don Hernan stared hard into the west, the light of day just now falling past the mountains and onto the distant fort. He scowled, gazing at the thing as if it were a dreadful tumor erupting from his own arm. "You will deploy the rest of the army according to your own plans, my general. I will interfere no further. Use the night to good effect and attack with the dawn as I command. The battle will serve its purpose whether the fort falls or not. But I need not remind you that I have great expectations that the day after tomorrow will be decisive."

///// *Fort Defiance*
September 14, 1944

aptain Blas-Ma-Ar sneezed thunderously, earning a bark of laughter from First Sergeant Spon-Ar-Aak, better known as "Spook" from his days as a gunner's mate aboard USS *Walker*. The wind had shifted as the day progressed, and the dust stirred up by the Dom army surging down on their position had aggravated her sinuses. *Just got used to all the smoke,* she inwardly complained. There were always cookfires in the great fort, and the smoke lingered low to the ground all night long. Word was that the smoke might actually be beneficial when it came to controlling the fever that had stricken so many of the humans. *Could be. Not so many skeeters lately, but I do miss the fresh, sea air!*

Nervous chuckles fluttered down the line among her 2nd Battalion of the 2nd Marines. She straightened her tin pot "doughboy" helmet and glared at Spook, but let her eyes stray beyond him to the Marines manning the fortifications just to the right of center in the northwest line. The 2nd Marines had been one of the first military creations of the human destroyermen, raised at Baalkpan soon after their arrival and originally taught to fight with swords, spears, and shields. It had been decimated in fierce fighting time and again, and very few of its first members remained. The tally was even worse for the 1st of the 2nd. It had been with Colonel Flynn at North Hill beyond the Rocky Gap in Indiaa and had, for all intents and purposes, ceased to exist. Most who'd "come up" with the 2nd of the 2nd were senior non-coms and officers now, serving with or commanding other regiments, but all who remained—even the smattering of Guayakans who'd been allowed to join against stiff complaints from Imperial unit commanders who foresaw the eventual integration of their own commands—were seasoned veterans after the Battle of Guayak. She was particularly thankful now for the few salty "originals" who gave comfort to the newer recruits with their stoic silence and confident calm in the face of what was to come. Blas sneezed again, to cover her own laugh at the thought of their Imperial allies—and what they'd say when they learned she'd been lobbying Shinya to let Impie *women*, already serving as Marines on a few American Navy Clan ships, join the 2nd! The notion of women in combat—other than Lemurian females, of course—already gave the Impies fits, and the . . . changed allegiances of people of either sex who joined the, to them, somewhat amorphous "Amer-i-caan Navy Clan," caused simmering resentment as well. They were all fighting on the same side, but some considered it nearly treason that Imperial subjects would swear allegiance to a constitution of a nation from another world—which all "Amer-i-caan" Marines and naval personnel must—and whose supreme representative on this one was Captain Matthew Reddy. They wouldn't complain openly, since even Governor-Empress Rebecca Anne McDonald had specifically protected the practice of allowing her subjects, and particularly women, to join the American Navy Clan as a part of her Declaration of Manumission. How else, at the time, were their allies' ships to replenish crews lost in defense of the Empire? *And more sneakily,* Blas thought, *how would all Imperial women ever get the example they needed to strive for a place in the* Imperial *Navy?*

It was all rather amusing to Blas, if still somewhat confusing. Lemurians from sea-going Homes, at least, were free to move to others, or join with other clans to build and start their own when multiple "parent" Homes had the resources and excess population to help them. That was how it worked, even in the "Amer-i-caan Navy Clan" to an extent, except that people were sent where they were needed. The oath was more restrictive, but still voluntary. She tended to think if the Imperials wanted all their people to stick with Imperial forces, they'd sort out their own lingering institutional issues. She hoped it would get easier for everyone to understand once the new Union, based largely on that otherworldly constitution, was more firmly established. But if there was anything in the world that didn't confuse her at all, it was her duty to her Marines, Captain Reddy, and the cause he supported.

"Dust," she explained conversationally to Spook, who hadn't been sneezing, but was constantly slapping gritty clouds from the white fur on his arms.

"They're doin' it on purpose," Spook griped. "Traampin' up them big ol' clouds an' sendin' 'em down on us. Downright rude. They marched up more polite last time." Blas looked at him, catching his grin and humorous blinking.

"Yes. Well, we ain't greetin' 'em as polite as last time either," she observed. Constant Nancy sorties still hammered the forming army, causing great destruction. But the Doms had learned at least one lesson: they weren't bunching up near as much. They were also deploying considerably farther away to avoid the mortars and exploding shells from the fort. Blas knew they *were* in range, for the bigger guns at least, but with their looser formations, the effect of the artillery would be diminished. *Might as well remind 'em later after they do wad up. They'll have to, eventually, to bring decisive numbers against any part of the line.*

"All the same," Spook said, taking a chew of yellowish tobacco leaves from a pouch. Like many of *Walker*'s alumni, he'd picked up the habit from his human friends, and it seemed to be spreading through the army. "I keep thinkin' I been here before. They call it 'dayjaa-voo,' I think. Here we are, sittin' an' watchin' them daamn Doms come marchin' up ta' hit us." He gestured to the sides. "Even got the same folks around us—though I ain't bitchin'. Finny, with the Second o' the Eighth Maa-ni-laa's on our right again, with the First past him to the middle o' the lu-nette. . . ." He shook his head. "What's 'lu-nette' mean, anyway? Never mind. Then there's the First o' the Fourth Impie Maa-reens on the other side. We got the Fourth Guayak on our left, which is new, but then there's the First o' the Tenth Impies with their squealin' baag-poles just past 'em. Gaah, how can you stand that sound?" He knew Blas rather liked the bagpipes of the 10th. "Just boils down that if all our other people, the hu-maans, wasn't such weenies, we could'a busted the Doms when *we* felt like it." Shinya's explanation had satisfied complaints over why they'd stopped their pursuit of the Doms after the Battle of Guayak, but that didn't mean everyone was happy about it yet.

"Yeah. But unlike in the West, Mi-Anakka make barely a third of *this* army," Blas countered, tiring of Spook's harping on the same old subject. "We'd have felt kinda lonesome chasin' the Doms all by ourselves after most of the rest of the army croaked off. You ain't even a good first sergeant. Quit buckin' for gen-er-aal an' let Gen-er-aal Shinya do the thinkin'."

"Fair enough," Spook agreed and spat. "I'll trust him with his job until he comes around tellin' me mine. Deal?"

Blas shook her head and swished her tail with mock agitation. "They should've left you on *Waa-kur*. At the very least, you'd be on the other side of the world from me right now."

"Hay! I didn't eg-zaactly volunteer! They just took me up, handed me my B-Aay-Aar, an' said 'time to kill Doms, Spook.' I said 'Ay-ay,' like a good destroyer-maan, an' they run off an' left me! Now I'm a Maa-reen!" He looked at her, blinking, suddenly serious. "All of us started different, maybe wanted different, outa' this war an' outa' life too, but here we are. I'd sooner be with *Waa-kur*, fightin' Griks on Mada-gaas-gar. That's *our* real war. But here I am wit' you, fightin' Doms on the bottom o' the world." He hesitated. "It's still kinda' neat, y'know?" Then he blinked and lowered his voice. "An' don't ever think I ain't mighty proud t'be your First Sergeant, Cap'n Blas."

Blas didn't know what to say. Instead of saying anything, she looked to the front. Her ears perked up. "That's weird."

"What?"

"You ain't gonna believe this. I don't. But I think they're gonna come right at us, soon as they finish extendin' their line!"

"What? Why?"

She pointed. "'Cause those on the left are already comin'! Like a etchel-on attack!" She turned. "Runner!"

It became increasingly clear that the Doms had no intention of extending their line after all, but were quickly gathering into a heavy V-shaped phalanx and accelerating directly into an attack. She estimated the force at brigade strength, but it was difficult to tell. The Doms carried so many banners, maybe even down to the company level, that it was nearly impossible to judge their numbers by them, or even identify different units. Blas had always thought they did it to intimidate with *apparent* numbers, but for the first time she saw how they might do it simply to confuse.

"Aye, sir—ah . . ." the runner hesitated. He was one of the colonial frontiersmen from Saint Francis and was clearly unsure how to address a female of any sort on the battlefield. His unit of long-range marksmen with big-bore flintlock rifles built to deal with huge continental monsters had swelled to brigade level but was scattered around the perimeter by companies where they could do the most good since their weapons didn't lend themselves well to hand-to-hand combat. Many, however, like this young man, were too small for the big guns that even Dennis Silva would've admired, and had been assigned to the comm division as runners and messengers.

"Get a message to Col-nol Blair. They're headin' right here, tryin' t' 'catch us with our pants down'!" Yet another expression Blas had picked up from her American destroyermen friends as their two languages merged. No Lemurian ever wore pants. "No," she revised, still watching the enemy mass about seven hundred yards away, "I think they gonna aim for the Guayakans on our left!"

"Their spies have been busy," Lieutenant Finny observed, joining her and breathing hard. "They prob'ly know where all the Guayak-aans are on the line, figure they'll be softer."

Which they might well be, Blas thought. They'd been trained as well as possible, in the short time they'd had, but they were generally very new to this, and just as sick and understrength as any human unit. They were also the least well-armed, having been issued captured Dom muskets at first, then Impie flintlocks (much the same) as Allied cap locks went to the Impies. She glanced at the Maa-ni-laa Arsenal Allin-Silva conversion she carried herself, still new to her. A fine weapon, and shaped just like the muzzle-loading musket she was so accustomed to. The 2nd Marines had been among the first to get them in the West and almost half the army had them now, but the problem of supply on the line kept them from "mixing" the newer weapons with the old, which struck her as a sensible idea. But all they could do was try to support adjacent units with the older weapons. "Yeah," she said, squinting. "That's where they're headed, all right. We'll get some too, but they'll hit the Fourth Guayak hard. Guess we'll see what they're made of." She looked back at the runner. "Ask Col-nol Blair for aar-tillery support, and to have the reserve stand by in case the Guayak-aans break."

"Aye . . . sir," the young man said, and bolted. Blas turned back to the front, trilling at her officers.

"Load!" she commanded, opening the breech of her own weapon and inserting one of the fat, glistening, brass and lead .50-80 cartridges from the box hanging at her side. The Doms *were* coming awfully fast. They'd be exhausted by the time they got here. They might break the Guayak-aans, but what then? Their attack was unsupported. They didn't even have artillery of their own up yet. She shook her head. She looked around to tell Finny to return to his company, but her friend was already gone. "Sights at five hundreds, take aim!" she shouted, watching the Dom ranks near the fluttering range markers. The phalanx was tightening now, bunching up, still tending to her left. Long, bright barrels lowered and wavered slightly over the breastworks, following targets. The Guayak-aans couldn't hope to hit anything much past a hundred tails, so Blas meant to try to slow the charge a little first, as she assumed the Impie Marines beyond the local regiment would do. A pair of lighter field guns, twelve-pounders, snapped out from the line to her left, sending gouts of flame and a cloud of smoke roiling out of their embrasures. There were a *lot* of field guns dug in on the line, by sections of two, every fifty tails or so. Most were twelve-pounders or Imperial eights, but even a few sixes remained with the Eastern AEF. Almost immediately, other guns joined the first, sending case shot, fuses short, arcing into the oncoming mass. They exploded close to the ground, spraying hot fragments of iron, gouging at the Doms. Dozens fell, writhing and screaming, almost silent at this distance, but the rest came on as if they didn't notice. "Fire!" she bellowed at the top of her lungs in that curious tone that carried so far and that only Lemurians were capable of. Her riflemen sprayed a stuttering volley that peeled away an entire layer of the enemy, like the skin of a yellow onion. Banners fell, limbs flailed, and men dropped to the ground. "Adjust your sights on the markers," she trilled. "Commence independent fire!" They thought they'd amassed sufficient ammunition for the new breechloaders for several serious fights, but there was no point wasting rounds with measured volleys when troops **were more** concerned with firing when they were told than with actually **hitting** anything. Her veterans were good enough marksmen to make the most of their exotic ammunition. Very quickly, her Marines resumed their rapid, crackling fire, and the enemy's ranks continued to fall away. She blinked frustration. *What's the point of this?* she demanded silently, at the same time wondering why Colonel Blair hadn't released the heavy guns in the lunettes to open fire. Blair himself, and several members of his staff, suddenly appeared beside her on his horse, gazing at the oncoming rush through his glass.

"They're testing us, it seems," he said mildly, anticipating her questions. "And their own troops as well, I'd wager, to see what we will do—and if they can take it, after our last meeting. Bloody wasteful." He gestured to the north, and for the first time Blas realized that hers wasn't the only fight. The Doms had marched all night, through exhaustion and air attacks, and plunged directly into battle. Counting the five or six thousand men coming at her point of the line, the enemy must've committed nearly twenty thousand to the strike. It made no sense—unless they really thought it would be that easy.

"The fever," she guessed. Blair nodded. "Might as well see how weak it left us. And it's not all madness. They attack with sufficient force at selected points that we can't ignore them. We've been forced to pull many of our Nancys back from harassing their main column, to hold in reserve for us here, and that may be their main goal. Otherwise, they count us, they mean to bleed us—particularly our natives—while testing their own new army. All while they bring the rest of it down relatively unmolested." He looked at her. "We must destroy them, of course, but we mustn't make it look too easy. No heavy artillery, Captain Blas, or mortars just yet either. But if the locals waver, by all means, support them however you must. We can't have those people running loose within the fort no matter how few they may be."

Blas nodded, still confused, but knowing exactly what was expected of her. Blair galloped to the left, disappearing in the smoke behind the Fourth Guayak. At a little over a hundred tails, the Guayakans opened

fire, their volley punctuated by light guns spraying dense swarms of
canister into the surging ranks. The canister performed the greater execution, no doubt, but even as Blas watched, Guayakan infantry me-
chanically tore cartridges, poured powder, drew rammers, and slammed
fresh loads down their muskets. That aspect of their training, at least,
had been well ingrained. Most were firm, determined, Blas saw, but quite
a few were on the verge of panic, staring wide-eyed at the enemy who'd
show them no mercy and had sworn to *impale* their families, drawing
relentlessly closer. The Doms were hitting the entanglements in the killing ground now, slowing at last against the barbed wire and sharpened
stakes. Some, probably veterans of Guayak, had faced similar obstruc-
tions before, but not on as great a scale. For the first time, wails of frustration and panic overrode the screams of agony that permeated the
desperate roar of the Dom brigade, and Blas knew at last what drove
them so maniacally: They *were* more afraid of Don Hernan than they were
of their enemies! They'd storm in against withering torrents of projectiles, against all odds, because there was at least a chance they'd somehow succeed, but the formidable entanglements represented failure—and
failure was certain death. Worse than death. *If they were not yet hu-
maan Grik before, Don Her-naan and his twisted faith has made them
so,* Blas realized. Even faced with the entanglements that stalled them,
helpless in the face of murderous fire, they tore at them, ripping their
uniforms and tearing their flesh, throwing blankets, coats, bodies, anything that came to hand over the wire, so they could continue the
charge, All the while, the Guayakans, now emboldened, stood straighter,
more determined, and poured it in.

"I don't think we'll have to more actively support the Guayak-aans
today, First Sergeant Spook," Blas said, glancing at her rifle again. She
hadn't fired a shot. The fight still raged, all around the northwest perimeter, but she somehow sensed a diminishing . . . urgency, even as the firing grew more intense. She suspected that such an ear, a *feel*, meant
more that she'd been in too many battles than anything else. The Doms
in front of her battalion, and the two to the left, were wavering now,
some finally starting to back away. "Pound them! Kill them!" she roared,
pacing behind her rifle-'Cats now, urging them on. "Let me hear you!"
There'd been remarkably little incoming fire, and the earthen wall had
protected her Marines amazingly well. The usual shouts and curses, and

thankfully few screams, had been the only voices raised among her veterans. That was as much a reflection on their professionalism as it was a throwback to a time when they'd fought behind a shield wall and simply didn't have the reserve air for sustained yells or anything of the sort. Now she wanted a yell that would send the last teetering Doms on their way. Off to her left, the Impies must've had the same idea as the skirling scree of their bagpipes joined the tumult. To her delight, Spook let out a savage, trilling roar, the likes of which she hadn't heard since the Battle of Baalkpan, and it was quickly joined by hundreds more. Now the Guayakans joined in, with a sound all their own, and the Doms still lingering at the wire, trying to fire, trying to do anything, finally broke.

"Keep firing!" Blas roared at the closest section of guns. "More canister!"

"They runnin'!" cried the 'Cat section chief.

"I don't care! You think they won't be back? They got no choice! Kill 'em now while it's easy!"

She steadied her breathing and climbed up past the guns, peering over the parapet that protected them. They'd just broken a brigade of Doms—but what was that? She raised her glass, peering beyond the fleeing force as best she could. She saw Nancys now, finally, swooping low in the middle distance, leaving toadstools of greasy fire in their wakes. Then she saw why. Still forming just as quickly as the first force, was another, maybe bigger, and it was already headed in! No doubt it would sweep up the survivors of the broken brigade and bring them on as well. She took a long gulp from her canteen and sighed. *If Col-nol Blair's right, it makes sense. They can't sneak up on us, so they gotta keep us occupied till they can get their whole army up—and if our spies are right, they got the troops to spare.* "But daamn," she muttered softly. "Gonna be a long goddaamn day."

////// *Fort Defiance*

las tagged along with Colonel Blair to meet with General Shinya after dark. She was exhausted but unhurt and actually somewhat amazed by that. The Doms hit on or near her section of the line five times that day, actually breaking through the entanglements and meeting her Marines' shields and bayonets at the top of the parapet the final time, near dark. (Blas remained a firm believer in the shield wall at close quarters. Shields had been discarded and returned to several times throughout this war, but against spears, swords, and even muskets they'd proved helpful time and again—and particularly in defensive situations. The time for carrying them on the march was probably past, but she was glad they still had them in Fort Defiance.) They'd been forced to practically exterminate the attackers, and the extreme sloping ground before her works, and for half a thousand tails beyond the entanglements, were choked with enemy dead. The last rays of the setting sun had lain on a dreadful sight, bloodred all its own on the red-splattered yellow and white of countless corpses. And beyond it all, in the final glimmer of the day, she could see the even greater mass of the Dominion host assembling in the distance.

The 2nd of the 2nd had been very lucky, its casualties amazingly light, but she knew that would never last. Tomorrow—maybe tonight?—the Doms would finish emplacing their artillery, the chief target for the Nancys that day, she'd learned, and more people inside the fort would start to die. There'd be a response, of course, and no Dom artilleryman's life would be worth much once their positions were revealed, but it would increasingly be a slugging match of guns. They hadn't seen many Grikbirds, comparatively, but they'd been there, employing new ambush tactics that cost them several planes. Unable to replace them or even properly service those seriously damaged with *Maaka-Kakja* away, they'd have to grow more judicious in their use; primarily scouting the enemy and attacking irresistible targets. Blas suspected things would get even bumpier tomorrow.

And, to her surprise, as bloody as the fighting had been in front of her, it had been worse around the northern lunette. The Doms had even briefly managed to occupy the position before the reserves erupted from the inner wall and pushed them out. But they'd spiked a couple of the big guns that *had* been used there, spraying massive loads of canister in a last-ditch effort to keep them out. They hadn't held the position long and their efforts to damage the big naval guns had been rushed and shoddy, but that was what had Blas's attention now, the lamp-lit effort to clear the vents and check for other damage.

"Tough day here," she observed quietly to an exhausted, soot-smudged Impie artillery lieutenant who sat on a crate, staring past the breastworks at the rapidly growing number of enemy campfires in the distance. He just gaped at her in confusion, and she figured her comment had been such a gross understatement, in his mind, that it didn't even register as language. She understood. She'd felt much the same way herself once before, when no words could've adequately described what she'd just been through.

"A tough day," General Shinya agreed, motioning Blas and Blair to join him where he stood before a red-faced Imperial colonel. He turned back to the man. "Despite what you think, your brigade did well, and you should not apologize for their performance here. We regained the position after all. The whole division did extremely well, and we bloodied the Doms very badly. It was my fault that we weren't better prepared for such an impetuous attack. You were at Guayak yourself. You saw how they ordinarily proceed. I expected much the same again and was too comfortable in my assumption that it would take them longer to try something new. I alone bear the blame for that complacency. Clearly, they've radically changed their approach to war with us, and we must be on our guard lest they continue to do so." He paused, blinking apology in the Lemurian way. The apology was probably lost on the Imperial. "I'll make arrangements to stiffen your lines here, and make sure your ready reserve can be deployed more quickly at need. In addition, all heavy artillery and mortars will be better employed against massing formations at whatever distance. They'll probably come at us even more strongly tomorrow, and we'll alter *our* tactics by firing heavily on every massed formation, even at extreme range. Let us show the breadth of the hell they must cross before they come to grips with us again!"

"Thank you, General Shinya," the man said, obviously relieved. "May I express your congratulations to my brigade?"

"Please do."

They exchanged salutes, and the Imperial officer made his way off. Shinya looked at Blas and Blair and nodded stiffly at them. "The same goes for your troops as well, of course," he said, briefly massaging his temples. *He hides very well that he is still quite ill,* Blas realized. *But he'd never use that as an excuse. All the more reason he remains, in spite of any lingering discomfort or confusion, the person to lead us here.*

"It was a mistake," Shinya confessed again. "We should have hammered the Dominion forces from the time we first saw them today, and galled their columns with artillery all the way in. Put the fear of whatever God they worship in their souls, and to hell with Don Hernan."

"We may've begun that anyway," Blair said. "And how long can we sustain operations of the sort you describe? We're fairly well supplied, but such expenditures of ordnance . . ."

"Will kill a great many of the enemy and demoralize the rest. We cannot let them get so close, so easily, again." Shinya let out a breath. "We suffered more than *nine hundred* casualties today," he growled, gesturing around, "most right here. And their advantage was barely three to one. We virtually destroyed those attacking forces," he conceded, "but there will be many more tomorrow."

"True," Blair continued, "but how long can we sustain the ammunition expenditure you envision?" he persisted.

"A few days," Shinya confessed. "Perhaps a week. But High Chief Saan-Kakja and the Governor-Empress will be at Puerto Viejo by then, regardless of how Second Fleet fares at sea, and the relief column will arrive quickly thereafter. We must base our plans on that."

"Our *hopes*, you mean?" Blair asked. From, or in front of other officers, Shinya might have been angered by Blair's question, but now he only grunted. Blas did see a flash of Shinya's frustration, however. It was something he very rarely showed. "Hope, yes, if you insist. I'll plan on what I hope for. For reasons I've already explained, this must be a battle of attrition—the last such battle I ever hope to fight," he added grimly. "Our cavalry slowly improves but is still no match for Dominion lancers in the open field, even given the disparity in numbers. So we can't fight a battle of maneuver as I would prefer. The inferior numbers and . . . relative incapacity of this army at the present time only emphasizes that point. And therefore it comes down to something as straightforward and dreadful as mathematics. We remain shorthanded. It's as simple as that, and we'll lose more troops with each day that passes. But we'll also gain a few as the ill return to their duties. Eventually, we'll have reinforcements as well. The Doms attack with greater vigor than I anticipated, and things got . . . 'frisky,' here today, as I believe the inestimable Dennis Silva might characterize it. We'll use that tomorrow, if we can, to kill a disproportionately higher percentage of their army than they can kill of ours. That's the only plan I can rely on at present. The only 'equation,' I'm sorry to say." He looked intently at them both. "We will savage the enemy at every opportunity, near or far, as aggressively as we possibly can. Hopefully—yes, *hopefully*—we'll grow progressively less 'shorthanded' compared to them, one way or another. If that requires 'profligate' expenditures of ordnance, so be it."

Despite General Ghanan Nerino's best, even somewhat clandestine efforts, he'd accomplished very little in the way of establishing any kind of real, effective, field medicine for the army. There'd been no such thing a century before when the Dominion first clashed with Los Diablos del Norte, and of course, there'd been no other continental battles of note until the current war began. Since then, at the Imperial Dueling Grounds at Scapa Flow, Saint Francis, and then Guayak, few of the wounded had been evacuated, and so there'd still been little need for such a thing. Now, as Nerino had foreseen, there was. Well over two thousand wounded men had been dragged away from the killing ground around the enemy fort, or collected along the line of advance after attacks from above, and gathered here at the foot of the great mountains alongside the Camino Chimborazo. And here they lay. A few of their comrades went among them, bringing water and whatever comfort they could in the darkness, but little actual healing was performed. The Blood Priests examined them, but only to discover which were fit, with a minimum of care, to be returned to the fight. The rest, if already unconscious, were simply allowed to die. Those who suffered noisily enough to distress the others were drugged into insensibility. The result was an amazingly, surrealistically peaceful field of suffering that Ghanan Nerino, having tasted near-mortal agony himself, could hardly bear. Even more difficult for his honor to endure was Don Hernan's strict policy that those too badly injured to contribute to the current fight would be prepared as fodder for the small flying dragons—and the 'gift' from His Supreme Holiness when it arrived.

There'd been a time when he wouldn't have given that a second thought. That was simply the way of things, and even in "peacetime" the dragons had to be fed. Even in garrison, there was always a steady trickle of men either killed or seriously injured by accidents, the depredations of local bandits who styled themselves "rebels," or simply carried away by disease. Dragons couldn't be allowed to run wild and hunt for themselves, or all control over them would be lost, and livestock was expensive. The one thing the Dominion had plenty of was people, and the pagan tribes on the periphery of civilization provided a constant source of conscripts for the army, candidates (mostly female) for sacrifice—and fodder for dragons, of course. But they had to be transported, most often at the expense of local commanders. Dead soldiers were already at hand, and what else was to be done with them? Nerino's honor was disturbed, however, because *these* men had been nobly wounded in actual combat against enemies of God, and many could recover if given the chance. They deserved care and praise, in his view, not what they would get, and he feared Don Hernan's policy would prove corrosive to the valor of others. Don Hernan, on the other hand, seemed convinced that it not only served his stated purpose, but would encourage the troops to avoid serious wounds! As if they *courted* them for their amusement, or to avoid closer combat! Nerino gazed at Don Hernan in the gloom as his retinue drifted among the fitful wounded like the robed deaths they were, and considered. Don Hernan could be serious. In his mind, pain was synonymous with grace, and brought those who suffered it as close to God as they could get in this world. But if Don Hernan truly believed that, why the drugs? Why deaden any pain? One would think, if he was sincere in his own beliefs, he'd gladly wallow in a steady chorus of agonized wails.

A sudden drug-hazed screech of agony, probably elicited by a Blood Priest stepping on a wounded man in the dark, seemed divinely inspired to test Nerino's suspicions.

Don Hernan spread his arms and advanced on the sufferer. "God hears you, my son!" he said, his voice angelically soft. "He is coming! Soon your soul will be cleansed of all corruption and you will be at peace!" The screams continued, incoherent, and Don Hernan crouched over the man, enveloping him in his robes. Something flashed in the starlight, and the screams gurgled to a stop. Grasping the bloody grass in both hands, Don Hernan spoke to the earth beside the corpse. "In the name of His Supreme Holiness, I beseech you to take the soul of this, thy true and faithful warrior, and enroll him in the ranks of your holy army of the dead, there to defend your Heaven from all incursions of this evil world." It was the customary petition for the fallen soldier, normally delivered in a rote monotone by any Blood Priest, but Don Hernan managed to make it sound fresh and sincere, and Nerino was taken aback. *The man is either the greatest pretender alive, and the most dreadful villain, or he truly believes,* he realized. Just then, Nerino didn't know which was worse for his army. He'd watched him during the day, observing the growing, if uncoordinated battle below, and knew that Don Hernan hadn't been prepared for what transpired. By all accounts, the fight at the Imperial Dueling Grounds on New Scotland had been savage, but that had been a mere skirmish compared to this. And Don Hernan hadn't seen much of it in any case. He'd never seen a *real* battle in his life, and Nerino had the impression he'd been a little stunned by the spectacle. Perhaps now was the time to press his case.

"Your Holiness," he said quietly, "have you considered my counsel further?" He gestured at the field of bodies. The moon was finally beginning to rise, more fully revealing its scope.

Don Hernan slowly rose, wiping his hands on his robes. "I have, and do, my general." He sighed. "And must confess, I now have two minds." He waved at the field of men who'd soon be corpses—and worse. "El Vómito did not do our work for us as I'd hoped, and as you warned. God, as ever, stands ready to punish hubris, and those who place too much reliance on Him to accomplish their tasks for them, even when in His name." He pursed his lips. "There is much grace here, much inspiration. So many already stand in the shadow of God." He straightened. "But far too many more lie in His embrace beneath the heretic's position. Too many, too quickly, for our needs, I confess."

Nerino said nothing. He wasn't "inspired" by the waste and suffering he'd seen that day, but he began to hope it had served a purpose after all. "The attack was costly," he ventured. "For the enemy as well, no doubt. But I beg you again to allow me more time to prepare my final assault. Further . . . precipitous . . ." He paused, frantically searching for a better way to phrase it. Failing, he continued. "Attacks such as those we launched today are impossible to coordinate, as you have seen. The enemy's defenses are formidable," he reminded yet again, "and those who serve in his army, both animal and human, are not as weakened by El Vómito as we prayed. I beg you to allow a more thoughtful attack, and fear that more such as we launched today must result in similarly indecisive, and even more costly, um, *delays* to our final triumph." Unconsciously, Ghanan Nerino held his breath.

"It is not that simple," Don Hernan snapped. "I swore an oath to His Supreme Holiness and God Himself that I would not rest once the battle was joined. The battle *is* now joined, yet you counsel a pause!" He released a long-suffering sigh. "You bear no blame, my general," he assured. "Your counsel has been consistent. Yet my oath demands that the attacks *must* continue. . . ."

"The fighting cannot cease, with us now in direct contact with the enemy," Nerino assured, his mind leaping, "and we can proceed with certain attacks while we construct protections, fortifications of our own, for the bulk of God's army. Many will still be rewarded with grace," he added, hiding the bitterness he felt for the euphemism for agony and suffering, "but our army here can continue to grow while Shinya's can only dwindle."

"And the attacks?"

"Still significant," Nerino conceded, "but aimed at their vulnerabilities. We discovered a number of those today. The Imperial Marines were resolute." He hesitated only an instant before adding, "As were the demon animals that style themselves 'Amer-i-caan Marines.'" Don Hernan had seen that for himself now, if only from a distance, but Nerino's reports and warnings had been vindicated. "The regiments of local traitors who joined their ranks remain inexperienced and fragile with fear, however. Without them, the rest would be hard-pressed to man their lengthy walls and cannot be strong at every point. I propose that our frontal attacks be coordinated to commence simultaneously, at unexpected times, and at various places at once, all focusing on those areas defended by Guayakans and Puerto Viejans." He looked down, and then at the carpet of bodies on the ground. "I cannot guarantee any of these attacks will break through. The reserves they hold in the fort move quite rapidly to bolster such threats. But the attacks will continue to weaken the enemy's more unstable elements, which cannot long remain strong of spirit in the face of suffering *they* do not revere." He wondered if he'd gone too far with that, doubting Don Hernan really believed that his definition of supreme grace was quite as devout as his own, but he actually did think that might become a factor to some degree, particularly in conjunction with the rest of his plan. "In the meantime, we should send our lancers beyond the fort, directly against their lines of supply, and perhaps even against the rebellious cities themselves. Unlike a lumbering host, they will be less vulnerable to flying machines and can strike and retire more quickly than the enemy can respond with anything other than its own lancers—which are of little account. Ours are just as useless against fixed defenses and heavy guns. We should use them otherwise."

Don Hernan's brows turned downward. "I see the wisdom of cutting the heretics off from the rebellious cities, though I suspect they have sufficient supplies. They have had long enough to amass them! But I remain less convinced that our noble lancers are of no use in breaking through the defenders in the fort. They move so quickly, with such lethal precision! They are the finest troops in all the Dominion!" The lancers were the elite, and had been for two hundred years. All were from noble families and "Blood Drinkers" in their own right. Nearly all were related to priests in Don Hernan's order. It was only natural for him to expect them to prove the decisive force.

"I cast no aspersions on their quality, Your Holiness, only their utility here. Even without their unholy weapons, the heretics' individual marksmanship is better than ours. Our infantry are peasants, conscripts," he stressed, "and individual marksmanship has never been a priority in their training. Not only was it considered unnecessary, but even a somewhat dangerous skill for them to retain after discharge...."

Don Hernan nodded impatiently.

"My point is, Your Holiness, that whether or not the heretics can consistently hit a mounted man at the gallop, they can most assuredly hit their horses, which has the same effect. That said, I do envision a role for the lancers in our final, coordinated, overwhelming assault against the fort, but I hesitate to commit them unsupported. Let us use them elsewhere for now."

"But the effect? The purpose?" Don Hernan persisted.

"Brings us back to the spirit of the traitors," Nerino said. "Remember, they do not fight for God. Not the One God at any rate. They fight to protect their homes and families from His wrath! If those things are threatened..."

"Ah! I see! A threat beyond the fort where they remain entrapped, against their very homes, would further erode their resolve! They would desire to leave the fort, if only to die defending their squalid kin!"

"Indeed," Nerino confirmed, suddenly feeling vaguely squalid himself. A mental image of a pretty young peasant girl, selflessly nursing him during his convalescence, sprang to mind. He suddenly remembered a fleeting, drug-hazed glimpse of a tiny cross she couldn't have wanted him to see dangling between her breasts. It was the old cross, the unadorned *Christian* cross of the Spaniards, whose followers were considered just as heretical as the Jaguaristas. *How is she any different from those I have just proposed to threaten?* He shook his head. "General Shinya is no fool, and he could never allow that. Both military necessity and his sense of humanity, I think, would prevent it. But if the threat were dire enough, he might have difficulty *preventing* it, and a revolt within the fort could give us just the opportunity we seek, particularly if we are fully prepared."

"By 'fully prepared,' I assume you mean that you desire to continue this strategy until the Blood Drinkers and the 'gift' arrive?" Don Hernan surmised.

"That would be my preference, and what I pray of you." *And that, having given me command, you will finally allow me to do so,* he didn't add aloud.

"Oh, very well. They cannot be many more days away by now, and you are the general here, I suppose," Don Hernan granted a bit grudgingly, though also wistfully, glancing back at the field of wounded. There was a long silence before he continued, and when he did, his tone was steeped in regret. "I confess that I had hoped for a single great battle, not a days-long, lingering, flutter of souls. Just imagine! A single, majestic, *epic* release of divine grace, all compressed into a solitary, glorious day! With such a powerful, focused, effusion of penitent pain, all in one place and at one time, surely God Himself would rise to the surface of the world to stand beside us!" He sighed again, looking back at Ghanan Nerino. "But this will ensure success? That is the most important thing, after all."

Nerino nodded.

"So close to God," Don Hernan whispered sadly, then smiled. "It will be as you say. You will prepare the protections for the army that you desire, while continuing your focused assaults—all while we await the Blood Drinkers and the gift from His Supreme Holiness. I'm sure, in retrospect, that he will be delighted that we made use of it."

Nerino bowed and Don Hernan spun, his robes flaring wide. He then strode away from the field, his priests scurrying to join him. "Just one thing more," he added almost casually over his shoulder. "Do not fail me, General Nerino."

"Never, Your Holiness," Nerino piped, his throat raw with terror at the very definitive position he'd placed himself in. "And I'm sure there will be sufficient 'grace' in the coming days to satisfy both you and God," he added more softly.

*   *   *

"They're digging in," General Tomatsu Shinya said, staring over the breastworks beside Captain Blas in the predawn gloom. It was clear he already knew; had seen it from other vantage points and was repeating his conclusion as he and Colonel Blair made their rounds. Blas looked at him. *He seems better,* she thought, *but that could be an illusion of his personality and the dark.*

"Been at it all night," Spook chimed in. "Gonna be harder to kill 'em now."

"Not when they come at us," Blas said, "but yeah, our long-range aar-tillery won't be as effective. Wonder what they're up to?"

"Another change in strategy, I suspect," Shinya murmured darkly. "Their General Nerino would seem to be a quick study after all, but he jumps to extremes. That can make him predictable as well, over time." He rubbed his forehead, caught himself, and quickly lowered his hand. "Normally, I believe I'd expect a siege from him now. They must know there's a naval battle underway, or at least about to begin, and in their demonstrated arrogance, they'll expect a victory that will leave us dangerously exposed." He shook his head. "But they won't just sit there. Don Hernan's not a patient man. And with such a large army, his supply problems, in the short term at least, will be even more pressing than ours. They *will* do something."

"They're appallingly arrogant," Colonel Blair agreed, "but possibly right about the outcome at sea." He glanced at Blas and lowered his voice. He kept no secrets from Captain Blas, and if she trusted Spook to keep his mouth shut . . . "Yesterday was not a good day for us in that respect. The night before was dreadful enough; Admiral Hibbs being whittled down to a handful of frigates and only six of the line able to keep their distance from the enemy—which we now know boasted more than *thirty* of the line, and at least that many frigates. All steam," he added for emphasis.

"Planes from *Maaka-Kakja* made their attack in the late morning, and did some 'whittling' of their own," Shinya said, "but they were surprised by yet another new tactic employed by the Grikbirds. It seems they've taken to charging straight in, then, instead of attacking with teeth and claws, they pull up and cast bundled *nets* at our aircraft, which foul their propellers! We lost nearly an entire squadron between that tactic and those they've employed before. I've already ordered our aviators to be watchful for such things here," he assured. "In any event, the fleet air attacks were largely distracted from their primary targets and devolved into desperate dogfights for the most part." His tone brightened. "On the other hand, costly as it was to our air, it seems to have been harder on theirs. And the last strike of the day, just before dark, met little air resistance at all and managed to sink several more of their ships of the line."

"Sever-aal," Blas said gloomily. "Out of how many left?"

"Eighteen or twenty," Blair confirmed. "And we didn't do much to weed out their frigates, I'm afraid." He glanced at the distant campfires, listening to the work of tools and men. "The rest of Second Fleet should join what remains of Task Force Eleven sometime today," he said, "in what is shaping into the greatest naval battle ever fought in this hemisphere. Seems a shame to miss it."

"I imagine we'll be sufficiently busy here, Colonel Blair," Shinya reminded.

"Quite."

///// *Battle off Malpelo*
September 14, 1944

"O h no you don't, you furry, flyin' freak!"
Lieutenant (jg) Fred Reynolds shrieked
as he banked hard left in a half roll and
yanked back on the stick, pulling his
now-inverted PB-1B "Nancy" plummeting straight down at the sea.

"Daamn!" squealed Ensign Kari-
Faask through the voice tube near his ear. "You said you don't do that
no more!"

"And I won't!" Fred grated, still pulling on the stick. They weren't
that high, and the sea—and the Dom battle line—was coming up awful
fast. "Not until the next time I have to! Why aren't you shooting at that
damn thing?" Fred had barely missed colliding with a Grikbird arrow-
ing in out of the late-morning sun above his right wing. He'd never even
seen it until it was almost too late, and if it had still been carrying one of

those damn net things, they'd be falling all the way to the water right now no matter what Fred did.

"It ain't chasin' us! It go away!" she shouted in reply from the seat behind the motor. Fred had the nose up now, turning away from the Doms. The Nancy still had two "light" general purpose (GP) bombs slung under each of its wings on this, their second sortie of the day. The "GPs" weighed roughly fifty pounds apiece and were basically the same "common" projectiles fired by *Walker*'s 4"-50 main battery, and all the copies being made that would become the standard light breech-loading naval rifle in the Alliance. The only difference was that GPs had tapered tails and fins attached, which made them respectable little aerial bombs against even lightly armored targets. Dom warships had no armor at all beyond their heavy wooden decks and scantlings, and a single GP was often enough to do them in. But the Grikbird had spoiled Fred's run. Now, close to the deck, he and Kari were the target of a *lot* of Dom guns as two frigates fired entire broadsides at their tiny plane, hoping for a lucky hit. The scary part was, with more than thirty cannon firing grapeshot in their wake, a hit wouldn't be all luck, and Fred and Kari had seen more than one squadron mate swatted from the sky in such a way. *They'd* been knocked down like that before, off Scapa Flow. Fred concentrated on gaining distance and altitude as fast as he could, and tried to ignore the itch between his shoulder blades.

"Aact-ooly," Kari added a moment later when the splashes of small shot no longer rose in their path, "I never seen it, 'cept right when you flopped us over."

"Then keep a sharper eye out! That's your main job right now."

"Wil-co, *Ahd-mi-raal* Fred!" Kari snapped sourly. "Sorry, but I was gettin' ready for my right *then* main job o' droppin' bombs, right after I did my other main job o' answerin' COFO Reddy's order to taagit DDs instead o' waagons. Which came right after my *other* main job o' hosin' them first two Grikbirds that jumped us, and got the 'Two' ship. Oh, an' my shoulder's still sore from my main job o' crankin' up the wing floats after we took off. Still think that's dumb; takin' off from the ship with them floats down."

"That's so we'll float if we lose power and go in the drink. You know that."

"An' get smushed by the whole daamn ship, just bobbin' there in front of her. Seen *that* too."

"Are you finished?" Fred demanded, glancing in the little mirror that let him see behind. Despite her bantering complaints, Kari's head was in constant motion, scanning for threats.

"Nope. I'm back at my main, *main* job, o' watchin' your tail-less aass, so why don't you do your only one main job o' flyin' us back up in the air high enough to take another whaack at our taagit!"

Fred grinned in spite of himself, but it would never do to let her hear it in his voice. "There's that creepy-looking island again," he observed, staring far out to starboard as he guided his plane in a spiraling climb. The island, called Malpelo, or something like that on their charts, had been the waypoint for their first attack that morning, and it had looked to Fred like a freaky huge mountain fish in the gloom. Now the battle below had progressed closer to it and he could see that it was basically a single, giant rock sticking up out of the sea all by itself, maybe a mile long and half a mile wide. *Damn near as tall as it is long too. Weird.* It didn't look like anybody lived there, or even could, but as the only speck for as far as the eye could see, he was willing to bet the whole damn battle would wind up named after it. *Lucky, stupid island hasn't done anything for a million years but sit there, and now it'll be in the history books.* He sobered, his view now on the beleaguered survivors of TF-11. *One way or another.*

Only two battlewagons remained, *Mars* and *Centurion.* Six frigates, or DDs, still paced them, but every other auxiliary, including the transports, thank God, had been sent east, then south, under cover of darkness, escorted by the antiair DEs. The rest had all died, gaining this tattered remnant a final chance to reach the embrace of the rest of the onrushing fleet. Looking south-southwest, Fred knew it would be close. Second Fleet was on the horizon, making full steam and closing as fast as it could. The Dom fleet, still bigger than the whole Allied force combined, had been slowed by the latest sacrificial rear guard, but the fleet was cracking on to catch its prey and finish it before help could arrive. Barring a miracle, they would, and there wasn't much Fred or anyone else could do about it. The Grikbirds were bad news, and had prevented anything like the "turkey shoots" that First Fleet had enjoyed against the Grik in the West. Now, though most of the Grikbirds seemed to be out of it, *Maaka-Kakja*'s 3rd Air Wing had been butchered too. Only the few new P-1 Mosquito Hawks, or "Fleashooters," she'd just received seemed immune to Grikbird attack, being much faster and just as nimble, but they couldn't carry bombs *and* ammunition for their wheelpant mounted SMGs at the same time and still have the speed and agility that kept them alive. Fully loaded, they could barely even fly. They'd been tasked with clearing the sky. Even so, they'd lost several to collisions with Grikbirds or one another. *What a mess.* Nobody out here had any real time in the hot little planes, and that had cost them.

"COFO Reddy's comin' out with the last six o' our Nancys. The other four o' our flight that made it is headed back to the barn to rearm. Reddy wants to know if we still alive an' got our bombs . . . since I didn't report back after we started our last attack. Don't know why he ask that," she added brightly, "since I heard the 'Fifteen' ship tell 'im we're okay!"

Fred groaned. He didn't like formation flying and hadn't done very much. He considered himself a good pilot, but ever since he started, flying *Walker*'s only observation plane, he preferred not having to worry about running into his own people. "He wants to know if we'll join his attack?" he prodded.

"Oh yeah. That. Yes."

"Then send 'yes'!"

Fred kept climbing until he saw the incoming flight. When it passed him, he fastened on to Reddy's plane, easily distinguishable by the bright yellow streamer trailing a few feet behind his wing. Directly alongside, Fred waved at his nominal commander. Orrin pointed at him and then made a spiraling gesture beside his right ear before pointing down at the Dom fleet. Fred looked. The enemy frigates, maybe twenty of them in two lines, were sprinting ahead, trying to stay beyond the reach of TF-11's guns while racing to get between the two Allied forces. The Dom "battlewagons," or ships of the line, were shaking out into a battle line of their own, poising to range up and administer the coup de grace when TF-11 was inevitably slowed by the blocking frigates. Fred craned his neck around. It wouldn't be long after that before the rest of Second Fleet arrived, and he realized that the Doms were trying to bring on a decisive, general fleet action in the shadow of that big stupid rock. They'd *have* to name it *Malpelo*, he thought grimly.

Now on the far right of the formation, Fred would attack the seventh ship back with two bombs on his first run. Reddy would designate the targets for the next—probably the leading ships in the second line.

"Taall-ee ho!" Kari called, receiving the order, and the formation dove, each ship diverging toward its designated prey. Nancys had proven themselves to be pretty good little dive bombers, as long as the angle of attack wasn't too great. And angles always varied somewhat from pilot to pilot based on their skill level and experience. Fred was the first to admit he wasn't much of a dive-bomber yet, and kept his own angle at about forty-five degrees. Not the most accurate, he supposed, but easier to get out of without hitting a tall mast—or the water. And it wasn't like Dom ships could easily evade. . . . He concentrated on the growing form below. *Another side-wheeler, of course, kind of nicely built. Looks more like an Impie DD than the older, galleon-like ships the Doms started the war with. Course now folks figure they already had these for a while. . . .* Men grew more distinct on the bright wooden deck, some scrambling for cover, others still. Some were firing muskets up at him. He bored in.

"Ready!" he shouted.

"Ready!" Kari cried back.

"Drop!" he yelled, and almost instantly, the Nancy bounded upward as a hundred pounds fell clear and he pulled back on the stick. There was a *thwack . . . thwack-thwack* as musket balls hit the plane, more felt than heard, and he shouted back at Kari, always mindful of the time she'd been hit from below.

"I'm fine!" she shouted back, scolding. "Near miss long! Near miss long!" she reported. He frowned, but nodded. Orders were not to automatically retarget a near miss since an explosion close alongside might do as much or more damage than a direct hit, but he still preferred a hit. All seven planes made it through and were climbing now, passing over the second line. More musket fire flared below, but they were out of range. The flight tightened up, still climbing, and Reddy ordered a turn. Finally, Fred could clearly see the effect of their strike. Two Dom ships were dead in the water, burning, and several more were bunched up, black smoke piling high from their stacks. He couldn't tell whether they were damaged or if the shattered line was just the result of the confusion they'd sown. Either way, they'd slowed the advance.

"Near line!" Kari called, relaying the order to attack the second line of ships they'd passed over. Fred's target this time would be the lead enemy vessel and they'd be diving from a lower altitude, but that was fine with Fred. He could still make his forty-five-degree approach. The flight continued its careful, somewhat leisurely turn, and aimed back at the enemy.

"Taall-ee ho!" Kari shouted, her voice high-pitched and tinny.

"Roger that!" Fred replied, waiting a moment longer to get his angle before pushing forward on the stick. "Stand by!"

The ship below looked identical to the first; three tall masts with taut red and gold sails drawing nicely. A tall funnel between the main and foremast belched black smoke. High, thin geysers marched toward the ship just aft of his target, and he remembered that Orrin's plane had a .50-caliber machine gun in its nose, just as a great cloud of splinters exploded from the side of the Dom frigate. *Wish I had one of those! Course, he doesn't have any more bombs. . . .* Refocusing his attention on the top of the mast before him, he mentally adjusted when to call for Kari to drop. They'd be shooting now, he knew, even if he couldn't see them. Most of their shots would go wide, or pass beneath and behind, but he and Kari were doubtless rushing right toward a few that were rising to meet them. "Drop!" he yelled.

"Bombs away!" Kari shouted, and the plane leaped again, just as a sustained *thwack-thwack-thwack* shivered through its frame.

"Near miss short *hit*!" Kari cried, just as Fred began to realize the sound and vibration he heard and felt hadn't gone away. "Big hit!" Kari crowed. "Maybe got the boiler!"

"I think we're hit too!" he shouted through clenched teeth, the stick between his legs starting to rattle violently in his hand.

"Yeah? Oh!"

"What's 'oh'?"

"We fixin' to lose the starboard ale-eron!"

Fred risked a quick glance and saw that it was true. They'd taken a lot of hits, more than he'd have thought possible. *Must've packed the best shots in the whole damn Dominion on that ship,* he realized sickeningly when he saw that several balls had struck amazingly close together and shattered an area around the inboard hinge pin. The aileron, though still attached and still operating, was definitely loose and banging around. Instinctively, he reduced power and pulled the nose up a bit to slow the plane, then applied a little right rudder to throw it into a slip.

The vibration eased slightly, and only then did he notice how fast and hard his heart was pounding. He took a deep breath. "Send that we're all shot up and gonna try to make it back to *Maaka-Kakja*!" he instructed.

"Okay," Kari said. "We gonna make it?"

Fred hesitated only an instant. "Sure, kid. Get the wing floats down, wilya?"

"Sure," came the uncertain reply. "But I'm getting oily. I turn around an' my goggles got all fuzzed. I think they get us in the oil pan."

Fred swore, then looked at the oil pressure gauge. Sure enough, the needle was starting to bounce—and drop.

"Shit!"

"Why shit?"

"Because we've just been shot down. *Again!*" He looked at distant *Maaka-Kakja*, looming large on the horizon and a good five miles beyond the advancing battle line, or about fifteen miles away. Then he looked around at the sea, barely a thousand feet below. They were getting close to TF-11 now, its eight battered ships doggedly churning to meet their friends. "Look, I'm still gonna try to make the *Makky-Kat*," he said. "We could set down forward of TF Eleven and hope they pick us up as they pass—before we sink. But even if they do, we'll be stuck in the same boat as them, with the whole Dom navy roarin' down. I don't know about you, but I'd rather do my fighting in the air from now on."

"Maybe they could pick us up an' patch us up; then we go to *Makky-Kat*," Kari suggested doubtfully.

"No way. They won't stop that long, and I don't blame them. We'd be lucky if they picked *us* up."

"What about the battle line?"

Fred judged the distance, then glanced back at the Dom frigate column. Their last attack had hit it hard, but all the planes were headed back now, to rearm, and the two lines, minus five ships, were already shaking back out and pouring on the coal. They were faster than TF-11 and would likely get ahead of it—which meant *they* might be the first ones close enough to pick up Fred and Kari, if they went down short of the Second Fleet battle line. Fred would rather die than be back in the hands of the Doms, and he knew Kari would too.

Suddenly, all their options evaporated when the starboard aileron tore away. Still attached by the outboard cable, it nearly jerked the stick out of Fred's hand, slamming his knuckles painfully against his thigh. The Nancy rolled hard to the right even as Fred fought against it, the aileron banging and flapping and tearing itself into fluttering streamers of shredded fabric. With a heroic effort, knowing he was probably straining against a damaged cable pulley now as well, Fred managed to right the plane and keep it somewhat level, but he didn't know how long he could. "Send the Mayday! Tell TF Eleven we're gonna set this thing down on their nose after all. They can pick us up or run over us, their choice. But when that cable parts completely, I'm liable to lose horizontal control!"

"I'm already sendin'!" Kari shouted.

USS **Simms**

"We're about to have more guests," Lieutenant Ruik-Sor-Raa told his executive officer, Lieutenant (jg) Gaal-Etkaa, when the latter joined him by the rail. USS *Simms* had already picked up the crews of two planes that day, a total of three battered aviators. One pilot had been lost when her plane sank before she could be hoisted clear, but she might've been dead already. Ruik hoped so. The rest were in the wardroom/sick bay being treated for injuries alongside *Simms*'s other wounded from the last two days. Currently, she was leading a "forlorn hope" squadron of four of the remaining TF-11 DDs, including *Icarus*, *Achilles*, and *Tindal*, in an effort to cut off the Dom frigates before they could squeeze Hibbs's last liners and the two most heavily damaged DDs against the bleak, rocky monolith of Malpelo. The geometry of the chase was such that if Hibbs turned east to round the island, his pursuers would catch him more quickly. If the fifteen or so Dom frigates achieved their goal, the chase would end with the same result. *Simms*, *Achilles*, *Icarus*, and *Tindal* had to keep the choke point clear.

"Yes," Gaal said, "if they make it." The Nancy fluttering down to the sea in *Simms*'s path was clearly in trouble, having difficulty staying level, and gray smoke was beginning to cough from her exhaust. As the plane drew closer, all could hear that its engine was laboring as well.

Gaal gauged the double line of Dom frigates, edging up and closer to starboard, then glanced back at the Nancy. "We can't stop for them," he warned. "Even if they don't wipe out."

"No," Ruik agreed. "But we *will* recover those people. That's Lieutenant Reynolds and Ensign Faask out there."

Gaal didn't reply. He hadn't met the two aviators himself, but they were well-known to all of Second Fleet by reputation, and few 'Cats or men, on land or sea, wouldn't risk everything for them.

"Send for them to try to land ahead of us, then match our speed as we come alongside. We'll do our best to snag them. Signal *Achilles* and the others behind us to try the same if we cannot."

"Ay, ay, sur," Gaal said, pacing to the voice tube cluster by the helm, but Ruik eased farther forward as the battered plane clawed at the sky, trying to stay aloft long enough to meet his request. The smoke was thicker now, and he could hear the engine dying. "Quickly, Bosun!" he called. "Assemble line handlers with grappling hooks along the starboard rail. Stand by to pull that plane alongside, secure, and get its people out!"

"Ay, sur!" *Simms*'s chief bosun turned and blew several blasts on his whistle, followed by bellowed commands.

Close, close, Ruik thought. Even as Fred and Kari's plane struggled to achieve just a few hundred more tails of flight, the battle line of Dom frigates was beginning to close. *Without the waagons to slow us, we will reach position first, so they mean to slow us themselves.* All but *Icarus* had heavier guns than the Doms, and the enemy would soon be in range to receive some serious discouragement—if they could be discouraged. He doubted it. *Simms* had survived heavier immediate odds at the battle off Saint Francis—but she'd been fresh then, and when that engagement ended, the battle had been over. Now she was battered, leaking, and her engine was beginning to wheeze after thirty-odd hard hours of sporadic combat and high-speed steaming. And even if she survived the coming action, she'd quickly face an even larger battle.

Not far ahead, the Nancy dipped abruptly toward the freshening sea; then its nose came up and it stalled, dropping maybe three tails before pancaking down on top of a swell. Ruik held his breath for the instant that it seemed a wing would catch and flip the little plane over, but then it settled, bobbing upright, with gray-white smoke boiling up and away from the still-whirling prop. Even over the machinery sounds of his ship and the crash of the sea against her side, Ruik heard the death rattle of the Nancy's engine.

"Two points to port!" he called to the quartermaster at the wheel. "Steady as she goes!"

"Our bow wave will push it away," Gaal counselled.

"The crew has done this twice already today," Ruik replied. "They will succeed, whether Lieutenant Reynolds can control his plane or not."

Gaal grunted skeptically when they saw the smoldering plane crest the bow wave and quickly dip low, beginning to spin as helplessly as a leaf. With a stunningly loud, clattering roar, the Nancy's prop raced, and the rudder nearly banged against the port elevator. Its spin arrested and the nose pointed at the ship, Reynolds practically aimed to ram— just as his abused engine finally seized and his prop slammed to a jarring stop. Almost instantly, the oil-streaked, superheated engine caught fire with a rush of orange flames.

"Hey!" Fred cried. "Hey! Get us outa here!"

"Heads up!" roared the bosun. "Now!" he added. Half a dozen grapnels arced into the air, trailing lines behind them. Three slammed through the fabric of the port wing, catching in the spars, and one splashed into the water just beyond Fred, narrowly missing him. Flames were licking greedily up around the fuel tank forward of the engine, and if there'd been a leak in that, it would already be too late. Still, they obviously couldn't pull the burning plane toward the ship.

"Cut a rope and grab on!" Ruik yelled. "We'll pull you up!"

"What about the damn flashies?" Fred demanded, his voice high.

"Do it!"

Kari didn't wait. She was covered with oil and coughing uncontrollably, but with a seemingly effortless leap, she hopped up on the wing, cut a line attached to a grapnel with a knife in her hand, and dove into the sea.

"Pull her in!" the bosun roared. "Lively now!" In seconds, Kari torpedoed through the water and came bumping and slapping up the side of the ship like an oily otter. Seeing his friend hadn't been eaten, Fred snatched the rope draped behind his cockpit—but paused. He didn't have a knife. Quickly, he pulled the grapnel up from the depths, snagging it momentarily on the hull of his plane. With a shouted curse, he yanked it clear. Then, with a final glance at the burning engine just behind him, he clutched the grapnel in both hands, closed his eyes, and plunged into the sea.

He was coughing water when *Simms*'s 'Cat destroyermen laid him gently beside Kari, who'd gagged on the smoky, oily phlegm in her throat and vomited on the deck. Fred shook off restraining hands and jumped to his feet. "Gotta sink my plane!" he shouted.

"No need, Lieuten-aant," Ruik told him, gesturing aft. The Nancy was burning fiercely now, sinking already. Fred gulped water from a cup a 'Cat handed him, then nodded aft. "Good riddance. Piece o' crap plane." He appeared to gather himself and looked at Ruik, who seemed to be deciding whether to grab his arm and support him. "I didn't mean that. Got us here, even shot to hell." He looked at Kari. "How'd you know there wasn't any flashies? I thought they're always drawn to ships."

"We didn't, not for sure," Gaal supplied. "But we're going fast, and they're rarely in the bow wave."

Fred turned pale beneath the black smudges on his face, but then shrugged and managed a salute and a sheepish grin. "Oh well. I've been in the water before. Maybe flashies don't like how I taste. And your ship was a fine sight bearing down, even when she almost ran over us! Request permission to come aboard, sir."

Ruik grinned back. "Delighted to have you both. Let's get you down to the wardroom and checked out." He nodded to starboard. "The Dom frigates are closing, and things will shortly get hot, I imagine."

Fred stared out at the double column. Twenty-five heavy frigates, all leaning slightly in the stiffening westerly wind, their bright sails and bronze guns gleaming even at this distance. "COFO Reddy'll be back, whittle 'em down some more. Sorry we couldn't lend a bigger hand earlier, but things are a little different in the air these days."

Ruik waved around, and for the first time Fred realized just how battered *Simms* and her people already were. Some damage had apparently come from Grikbird bombs, but the shot holes in her sails and funnel, spliced cordage, and brightly splintered wood beneath the black-painted rails indicated she'd been in the running surface action as well. Then there was her crew, almost all Lemurians, many lounging tiredly on her dirty fifty-pounders. Most wore peacoats, which surprised Fred. He was used to 'Cats wearing as little as they possibly could, but the wind had a bite to it and the 'Cats, sweat-foamed from battle, had probably been cold. The muzzles of the guns themselves and the normally bright deck and carriage wood were spattered black with fouled water from sponges and buckets, and the area around the vents was a dingy gray. "So we have noted," Ruik agreed.

Fred waved out at the Doms. "So, you trying to get past those guys? Join the rest of the fleet?"

Ruik shook his head. "No, Lieutenant Reynolds. We will soon engage them, as a matter of fact. We must keep them back while *Mars*, *Centurion*, and their remaining escorts 'get past' them. Once they do, we will proceed along behind them, if we can."

Kari had managed to stand, and was looking at Ruik with wide eyes. "But what about this ship, and those other three behind?"

"They are all DDs, and we are destroyermen," Ruik said simply, but the pride in his voice was unmistakable. "We do our job. *Mars* and *Centurion* are sound in their machinery, but both have been the focus of a great deal of fire. In addition to just their two crews being as large as those aboard all my ships combined, they also bear a great many wounded transferred from other ships we were forced to leave behind." He shrugged. "We must clear the way."

Down in the moaning, bloody charnel house of the wardroom, seated on a bench near the hatchway, Fred began to fidget. "Right out of the frying pan," he murmured, staring at Kari to avoid looking at the suffering 'Cats around them. "Maybe we should've run off when we could, looking for Captain Anson."

"No," Kari said firmly. "There's a baattle. Runnin' off then would've really been 'runnin' off.' Can't do that. If we go, we go after the fight."

Fred nodded. "Yeah. If we make it." Still squirming uncomfortably on the bench, he flinched at the muffled sound of shouted orders from above. A sudden, creaking rumble of the guns being shifted made it clear that the action was about to commence. He finally stood up. "And I can't stay down here."

"Cap'n Ruik said to get us looked at," Kari objected without much conviction, glancing guiltily at the harried surgeon, pharmacist's mates, and SBAs going about their grisly work. None had attended them when they arrived. They'd brought themselves down, after all, and obviously weren't emergency cases.

"I'm fine, and I'm not staying down here," Fred stated sharply.

Kari's gaze fell on a 'Cat, seeped to unconsciousness, lying peacefully while his ruined arm was taken off, and she slowly stood beside her

friend. She was no stranger to suffering. She'd endured a great deal herself. And the memories of what she'd been through, now flooding sym-
pathetically back, made her short of breath. "I'm fine too," she gasped.
"Let's get outa here."

Together, they climbed the companionway ladder and peeked up
over the coaming. The gun's crews along the starboard side were poised
by their pieces, waiting for commands, electric igniters ready to be inserted into vents. Shot garlands stood like three-sided pyramids, stacked
with seven-inch solid shot. The exploding case shot was dangerous to
leave lying about and would be brought up by youngling "powder monkeys" when called for. It was lighter and shorter ranged, even atop the
ten-pound charge of powder the big guns gulped, and generally reserved for more confident ranges in any case. Through the closest gunports, they saw that the Doms were a lot closer now, and *Simms* and her
tiny battle line, now steaming almost due west with all square sails
furled, had won the race to cross the Doms' "T." Fred stepped up on the
deck and looked northeast. Admiral Hibbs's two wagons and pair of
DDs hadn't quite made it clear, but they'd formed a battle line of their
own and should be able to keep the Doms at arm's reach with their
heavier guns while Ruik's little squadron punched them in the nose. If
Hibbs's strategy failed, however, his whole force was in danger of being
caught between Malpelo and the whole Dom fleet, still rushing up behind, before the rest of Second Fleet could come to its aid.

"Taagit range, one t'ousand. Speed, ten. Elevation two deg'ees!" cried
the 'Cat in the main top. They didn't have even the rudimentary fire
control system now in use in the West, but they'd come up with a few
expedients of their own out here. Electric igniters had arrived that could
be activated by the gunnery officer who watched a swinging plumb bob
in place of a gyro. This most ancient of instruments would indicate to
him the *approximate* instant when *Simms* found an even keel amid her
constant motion. In this way, *Simms* and her consorts could fire true
salvos, of a sort, and correct their elevation at least. Gunners quickly
proceeded to do just that, turning a heavy screw handle beneath the
breeches of their guns, until an inscribed line corresponded to a numeral "2" engraved on the plate beside it. At a nod from the gunner,
another 'Cat pricked the vent with a long brass rod with a ring on the
end and inserted the priming wire.

"Primed and clear!" cried the first gun captain, stepping back. He was quickly echoed by nine others. "All clear!" trilled the chief gunner's mate.

"Commence firing," Ruik said, his tone amazingly calm as he stared through an Imperial telescope.

"Firing!" shouted the gunnery officer, intently staring at the plumb bob. But for an instant, he didn't fire and the tension grew. Finally catching the exact instant he liked the most, when the plumb tip was pointed directly at a mark on his apparatus, he closed the circuit.

Fire blowtorched skyward from ten vents as the great guns fired, visibly shivering the stout ship as the monstrous weapons trundled inboard amid yellow-orange blooms of flame and a roiling fog bank of white smoke. Fred shook his head and worked his jaw to pop his ears. The first thing he heard was the diminishing, tearing canvas *shoosh* of the outbound shot. "C'mon!" he said to Kari, grabbing her arm and stepping to the rail beside Ruik. The gun smoke was quickly whisked away by the stiff wind and *Simms*'s own speed. He never saw the shot in flight as he might if he'd been able to watch its rise from the muzzles of the guns, but he viewed its fall. The "salvo" raised a curtain of splashes about two hundred yards wide, just short of the closest enemy ship, but the range was amazingly consistent.

"Reload!" the gunnery officer roared, and the gun's crews, already working to clear and service their pieces, now knew to continue their evolution to the end.

"*Achilles* still has her lighter guns. Just as well, because as stout as she is by Imperial standards, I doubt she could hold up to firing sustained salvos, or 'broadsides' like this, with the weight of metal we're throwing," Ruik said conversationally. "But her guns are as big as anything on those Dom DDs, and they'll reach." Fred was surprised Ruik had noticed his and Kari's presence. "*Icarus* will have to wait until they get closer, but *Tindal* is armed the same as us," Ruik continued, taking the glass away from his eye and using it as a pointer toward the top of the main mast. "Signal flags show the range we estimated, and the other ships will adjust." *Achilles* chose that moment to unleash her own broadside, followed almost immediately by Tindal. Splashes rose all around the leading ships in the advancing column, and distant sails shook with impacts. "See?" Ruik said.

"Very impressive," Fred granted, sincerely amazed by how successful such crude expedients could be—but then, the principles were essentially the same as those USS *Walker* had brought to this world. Even
without the sophistication of her gyro and wildly complicated clock-
work gun director, the fundamentals they were based upon had revolu-
tionized naval warfare on this world and given the Allies an enormous
advantage—at least until the Doms figured it out.

"Same range! No change!" yelled the gunnery officer, quickly followed by a chorus of "Primed and clear!"

"All clear!"

"Firing!" Fred barely had time to cover his ears before the ship shook
again, and this time he watched the heavy balls arc up and away. He lost
them as they reached the tops of their trajectories, but the cluster looked
much tighter this time as they disappeared, now falling toward the enemy.

"Why no change?" Kari asked, and Ruik looked at her. "The enemy
is closer this time. The gunnery officer will have calculated how much
closer based on the enemy's apparent speed, and timed his firing accordingly."

He must've timed it very well. Another cluster of splashes rose
around the lead Dom frigate, but at least half the fifty-pound cannonballs staggered the ship. The foremast toppled, dragging the maintop
down with it to lie atop the smoking funnel. Almost immediately,
flames caught the flailing red canvas, sparked by the funnel itself, and
the wind fanned the fire up the mast. A cheer rose even as the gunnery
officer called for the reload.

"Another one down," Ruik said softly. "She was doomed already,
even without the fire." He looked at Fred. "One thing we've learned over
the last few days, and the only reason we're still alive; use our range advantage. Once the Doms close, the only advantage we have left are exploding shells."

"Why? I mean, why was she already done for, so far away?"

"Because of what Mr. Caam-peeti once told me is called 'plunging
fire.' Look, range is key because their shot's not as heavy, at least on their
DDs, and no matter how many more they fire from their 'wagons,' they
can't get near as many on target unless they get close. Then it doesn't
make much difference," he confessed, "because we're both just shooting

through each other." He waved. The burning Dom frigate, wallowing now, erupted in a white cloud of steam and smoke, spraying the sea with a sprawling pattern of falling debris. "Could've been the magazine, but I bet it was the boiler. Water coming in, fast. See, even at just two degrees of elevation, we get 'plunging fire' at this range, when our shot 'runs outa gas' and just drops. Makes it harder to hit a taagit, the old-fashioned way, but as you've just seen, we can do it."

"Great. So?"

"These new Dom ships are stout; the sides, uh, 'scaant-lings,' are really heavy. A fifty-pound shot will still blow through both sides at close range." He managed a predatory grin. "But at long range, they drop on the ship, tear through the decks and right out the bottom!"

"Oh! So then we're okay? We just keep shooting long range and knock 'em off one by one!"

"Normally we could," Ruik agreed, "and we have been. Most of the crippling damage suffered by TF Eleven has occurred in the night when the enemy was able to close the range in spite of our illumination flares and rockets. And, of course, we've been on a necessarily fixed course to keep them from overwhelming us. As you can see, they've had the numbers to absorb great loss while they attempt that."

Hibbs's small battle line had commenced firing now as the range between it and the closing Dom column decreased, with great thunderclap salvos from *Mars* and *Centurion*, which mounted fifty 20- and 30-pounders to a side. Likely glad to have targets of their own, and unable to return Ruik's fire with more than a few bow chasers, the seven frigates in the closest line fired back, the sound reaching them as a sustained, stuttering roar. *Achilles* and *Tindal* punctuated it with salvos of their own.

"Unfortunately, we will soon have to wear our line, coming about across the enemy's path once more to prevent it from closing with Ahd-mi-raal Hibbs."

"I remember the plan," Fred protested. "Then we tack onto the back of his line as he passes that big-assed rock, and we're all in the clear."

"Indeed," Ruik agreed. "But this squadron will first have to sail *very* close to the enemy, perhaps even slowing to prolong the engagement. . . ."

"Oh."

////// *USS Maaka-Kakja (CV-3)*

Admiral Lelaa-Tal-Cleraan paced her bridge and stared out at the developing battle in the distance. *"Degenerating" battle, more correctly,* she thought grimly, since all semblance of order had disintegrated after High Admiral Harvey Jenks, his flag now flying from the Imperial first-rater *Mithra*, slammed his battle line into the bulk of the enemy fleet. What ensued, according to excited wireless reports and the few planes remaining above the action, was a jumbled melee of ships of all sizes, pounding away at one another at point-blank range. That wasn't what they'd planned, but she assumed Jenks had seen some pressing need. *Or had the pressing need to come to close grips with the Doms resided mainly in Harvey Jenks's heart, after all this time?* Lela wondered. She also wondered what had become of *Simms*, her consorts—and Fred and Kari.

She knew *Simms* had picked them up, of course. Orrin Reddy, now teetering slightly with exhaustion and watching her pace, had reported that himself. But wireless contact with all four DDs had been lost when they got tangled in tight with the Dom frigates, and only *Achilles* had managed to join Hibbs's escape. The rest had been engulfed by the chaotic battle that erupted around them. At the very least, all had taken damage to their masts and wireless aerials. They'd done their job, though; flailing at the Doms until Hibbs could squeak past. His battered force had eventually joined *Maaka-Kakja*, where it was currently transferring wounded to the trailing replenishment ships—the only auxiliaries left—and cutting and splicing and making what repairs they could before . . . *Before what?* She paced again, glancing at the bridge watch standing at their posts—and keenly aware of Orrin Reddy's scrutiny. *Can I do it?* she asked herself, remembering what Governor-Empress Rebecca McDonald had decreed, what Saan-Kakja agreed. *Should I?*

"You know, this may well be the last great battle between purely wooden ships on this world. And even now, 'purely' isn't exactly right," she began softly. "All our Amer-i-caan Navy DDs have armor belts amidships to protect their engineering plants. And though both the Doms and Impies still use paddlewheels, the Imperial Navy has applied some armor to its paddle boxes. That's probably the only reason *Mars* and *Centurion* made it back to us, and the beleaguered Task Force Eleven was able to leave so many powerless Dom hulks in its wake. All new Impie ships under construction are being built with screw propellers, just like ours." She paused, sensing Orrin's impatience. He wanted back out there and wasn't in the mood for what he must think were her pointless technical ramblings. But she did have a point. "Also," she continued, "just as in Baalkpan and Maa-ni-la, riveted iron hulls are in the works in the Empire as well, now that sufficient quantities of steel required for the transition are starting to arrive from the West, or the Imperial colonies in North America." She waved at the battle. "And of course, every ship now engaged is a steamer."

"So?" Orrin sighed, aware he was being disrespectful, but too tired to care.

"So, technology marches, for us and the Doms. Even the Grik. Governor-Empress Rebecca's initial strategy may have been . . . flawed, but she's correct that this action must be decisive. I hope—I pray—that our technology may be enough to balance the enemy numbers today, but

even with victory, we will be in poor condition to pursue a beaten enemy to destruction—and every Dom ship we do not destroy we will
likely face again, improved to match our own at the very least."

"What now, then?" Orrin asked, suspecting what was to come. Instead of a direct answer, Lelaa stared ahead. "How many Naancys remain?" she asked.

"Uh, just nine that I'd consider airworthy. We were short to start
with, as you know, even with the ones Saan-Kakja brought. Too many
got spread around," he added, returning to an earlier argument. He let it
drop. He couldn't begrudge the ones sent with the transports to Puerto
Viejo. Shinya would need them. But how long before they could even
arrive, be assembled, and join the fight? It would've been better to put
them together here and fly them ashore—but they'd been too far out.
Particularly for brand-new, untried machines. "The, uh, 'rescue' of TF
Eleven cost the wing more than twenty planes, not counting all the ones
assigned to other ships that've been lost as well—mostly to recovery accidents," he added harshly. The speed of the advance and the choppy sea
had made recovering the little floatplanes extremely difficult. "Fortunately, we haven't lost quite that many aircrews, although it's been bad.
The simple fact is that the guys and gals have flat flown their planes to
death over the last few days, and beyond the nine I reported, any others
will take at least a few days to get back in the air—or even patched well
enough to float." He considered. "We do still have eight of the dozen
Fleashooters they sent us. They've been going out with bombs. The
Doms can't have many Grikbirds left. Haven't seen hardly any today.
Maybe it's just all the smoke over the battle—they don't like it—but
they're all either dead or grounded."

Lelaa turned to him, blinking decisively. "The Fleashooters will
stand down," she said. "They can only recover aboard *Maaka-Kakja*,
and that will soon be impossible. You will lead our last Naancys in a
final bombing sortie. Instruct your aircrews to focus on Dom baattle-
waagons, preferably those engaging any of our ships that seem particularly hard-pressed. I know that may be difficult to discern. . . ."

"Where will *we* recover?" Orrin demanded, "And why will it be
'impossible' here?"

Lelaa blinked at the wild, sprawling battle that seemed to lap against
the high, lonely, rocky island ahead. "Unlike the carriers in the West,

Maaka-Kakja remains heavily armed for surface actions, with fifty of the fifty-pounder smoothbores just like *Simms* and her sisters carry. Even more significantly, she retains four of *Amagi*'s five-point-five-inch secondaries tied into a fully functional gun director also salvaged from the Japanese battle cruiser. We shall use those as we close."

"Close?"

"Indeed, COFO Reddy. I am taking my ship into the fight."

"Lord," Orrin muttered, then shrugged. "Oh well. Why not? I can't fault your strategic logic, regarding Dom survivors, and the *Makky-Kat* might not have armor, but she's hell for stout. She can take a lot." He chuckled. "And just seeing her coming at 'em, like a smaller version of that weird island, ought'a scare the water out of the Doms. She might just turn the tide."

"That is my hope. We will leave our support ships behind, of course. They will recover your aircraft if . . . no one else can."

"Yes, ma'am," Orrin replied, standing as straight as he could. With a lopsided grin, he plopped his battered crush cap on his head and threw her a salute.

Lelaa grinned back. "Really, COFO Reddy. Saluting indoors?"

"Second Lieutenant Orrin Reddy, United States Army Air Corps, ma'am. You keep forgetting I'm not Navy. I just made a report on the state of my air wing." He shrugged again. "And besides, I felt like it. With your permission, I'll go get my planes off this tub before the Doms start shooting holes in her."

"By all means. Bring her into the wind," she ordered the 'Cat at the big wheel. "Make your course three zero zero. As soon as Mr. Reddy's planes are in the air, we will secure from air operations and clear the ship for surfaace action!" She glanced back at Orrin, touching her brow. "May the Heavens protect you, Lieuten-aant Reddy," she said.

"You too, Admiral."

"What a screwed-up mess," Orrin muttered to himself, staring down through his goggles at the vast smoky brawl below. *Looks like somebody set fire to a giant, two- or three-mile-wide amoeba,* he thought with a sick feeling in his gut. There were a number of other ships wallowing helplessly on the periphery, or steaming in impotent circles with one of their paddlewheels shot away, but the bulk of the massive smoking germ was locked up tight. It was impossible to tell who was who, and all he could see was a hopeless scramble of indeterminate ships wreathed in gun smoke, and crisscrossing jumbles of churned-up wakes. The continuous cannonade was audible even over the dutiful drone of the engine above and behind him, and he could feel the stuttering overpressure of hundreds of guns in his chest. It was late afternoon now, the "main" battle nearly four hours old, and the visibility beyond the steaming, flashing, roiling cauldron below was virtually unlimited, with no trace of land besides that big screwy rock.

It was chilly up there, and he was glad for his peacoat, but it really was a beautiful day. Except for the battle, of course. His eight-ship flight—one plane had immediately been forced to turn back with engine problems—was orbiting the battle at two thousand feet, trying to avoid the smoke and figure out who the good guys were. Usually that was easy, with the Doms' red sails, but not now. The chase was over, and every ship had furled her canvas and was fighting under steam alone. That only aggravated the visibility problem, particularly since the Impies and Doms both still used coal. In addition, a lot of ships were burning, and the smoke slanted roughly eastward in multicolored streaks of black, brown, gray, and near white, all obscuring the ships to varying degrees. *Why didn't Jenks stay back?* he wondered. *Hibbs was clear. He could've pasted 'em from a distance, for a while at least. Maybe he, like Lelaa, figured the only way to keep them from running off was to get stuck in. But that doesn't make sense either. Sure, the Doms wanted to pick off TF Eleven after we dropped it in their lap, but they'd obviously come looking for a battle just like this. So why did Jenks turn around and hand it to 'em with a bow wrapped around it?* Realization dawned. *Honor.* Simms, Icarus, and Tindal *are in that mess somewhere; were in it, anyway,* he corrected, *all alone. After all the sacrifices TF Eleven made to get their wounded out, then the final sacrifice of* Simms's *little squadron of DDs, he just couldn't leave them there while it was in his power to provide some relief. His own desire to finally get at the Doms in the same old, instinctive way probably played a part, but when all was said and done, it probably did come down to honor. Kinda stupid,* Orrin grumped, but really, no less than he'd have expected of the man.

He glanced south and sure enough, here came *Maaka-Kakja*, steaming at full speed, with a giant bone in her teeth. Her 5.5s would already be firing if they could pick out targets any better than he could, and they alone would be a big help. But Lelaa wouldn't hang back either. She'd slam her big fat carrier right into the brawl like a pickup truck through a flock of guineas, spitting fire in all directions. She'd been a destroyerman—gal—'Cat—whatever, before she got *Maaka-Kakja*, and it suddenly dawned on him that her first Navy ship had been a razeed Grik Indiaman named . . . *Simms*. That ship was long gone, destroyed by traitorous Imperials working at least indirectly with the Doms. Could her willingness to go for broke be motivated, at least subconsciously, by something as primal as revenge? The hot fury of an old trauma roused by the name of a lost ship, and rising behind her conscious thoughts? Orrin knew in a flash that he was vulnerable to such things. He was still uncomfortable around Shinya after all, just because he was a Jap. He suspected Matt, his cousin, was just as vulnerable in other ways. Jenks as well. He was a man, after all. But Lemurians were different, weren't they? *Might as well've been Quakers before the war, from what I've heard. Practically pacifists.* He knew they weren't *now*, but did that make them more or less likely to act out of hatred? He had to doubt it; *had* to hope what was happening here today was more . . . rational than that. He grimaced, feeling for the first time that he knew how Cousin Matt must've felt at the battle for Grik City when all the 'Cats, people, whoever it was he was always trying to ride herd on, slipped their leash and just . . . stampeded. He took a breath. *Either way, there's a world-class hair-pulling underway down there. Nothing for it now,* he realized. *Question is, what can I do about it?*

He looked in the mirror at the goggled 'Cat in the aft cockpit behind the motor, the brown and gray fur on his face plastered back by the propwash. "Seepy," he said in his voice tube to Sergeant Kuaar-Raan-Taak, who'd been his "backseater" through thick and thin. Even now, Orrin wasn't convinced he and the crusty 'Cat noncom were actually "friends," but theirs was a familiar, bantering relationship that both were comfortable with. More important, they trusted each other. "Send to all other ships in the flight: attack independently, repeat, attack heavy targets of opportunity independently." He was suddenly uncomfortably aware that he didn't even know the tail numbers of all the planes. Everything was so jumbled up, they didn't necessarily correspond to their aircrews anymore. "The two lowest numbered ships'll hunt to the north of the battle, the next lowest, the south. Then east. The highest number . . ." He craned his head around in frustration. His usual plane—with the .50 cal in the nose—was down for a new engine of its own, after the morning sortie. At least that meant he could carry more bombs. "Goddamn it, Seepy, what's our number?"

"Turty-two."

"Okay. The highest number'll join us over by the big rock. Tell them to give 'em hell, but watch out for our guys and make their bombs count. This is our last shot, unless they can find somebody just bobbing around out of the line of fire to refuel and rearm 'em. And for God's sake, tell 'em not to smack into each other!"

"Ay, ay. I send it," Seepy said.

Orrin nodded and banked to the right when he saw the formation begin to scatter. A few moments later he saw a Nancy with a big numeral "20" over the smaller "CV-3" emblazoned on its tail tuck in behind his left wing. "Okay," he said to himself, "let's do some hunting of our own."

Lower down, the battle seemed even more immense, if better defined, with ships flailing at one another with fire that seemed at first to be shockingly indiscriminate. He began to see that such was not necessarily the case, however, and the Allied ships, at least, were making an effort to stick together here and there in twos and threes for mutual support. No doubt that was made easier by their better communications, but that was literally going by the board—with their masts—as the battle persisted. He caught a glimpse of *Mithra*, identified by Jenks's pennant, tailed by another battlewagon. Both were pounding toward a tangled gaggle of fouled Dom heavies that gushed smoke and shot back at them as they approached, even while the two Impies fought both sides against smaller steamers, their masts askew, edging in from port and starboard. He waggled his wings and pointed, the only order his wingman needed to follow him in and attack one of the ships on the left side of the jumbled pack.

"Hang on, Seepy!" he called. "And stand by on the bomb release. I'm going to try to put two on that big mother with its bowsprit hung up in that other one's mizzen rigging. It looks to have the best angle to hit Jenks the hardest.

"Ay, ay. I stand-een by. I hose 'em with my Blitzer too? There ain't no Grikbirds in sight."

"Not this time. Maybe later. Save your ammo in case some of the damn things do jump us. We couldn't have got them all." Orrin pushed the stick forward and bored in. A few musket balls whizzed by, maybe a couple hitting, as he shouted "Drop!" The bombs fell away and he banked right to avoid any jinking his wingman might have to make. Looking down, he saw they'd hit *two* ships—their target, and another just beyond, directly alongside. The "20" plane got a hit and a near miss, and was clawing skyward as well, starting to bank right to join back up. He couldn't tell if they'd done any major damage to their target, although it had stopped firing for the moment, but the accidental hit had blown most of the upper stern and mizzen off the other ship, and flames surged upward amid the cloud of splinters and fragments of men that their bomb had thrown into the sky.

"She'll burn," Seepy declared, also looking back and down. "Prob'ly burn the one beside her too, they don't shove her off. Either way, they be too busy for much shootin' for a while."

Orrin silently agreed, already looking for another target. "What the hell?" he suddenly blurted, his eyes catching sight of a dismasted hulk, close to the great rocky isle. The thing was shot to *pieces*, with only the stump of a toppled funnel gushing gray smoke. It was also visibly low in the water, but still, somehow, underway. What was more, it was towing a smaller, equally battered ship at a meager pace. He blinked disbelief as he realized the thing that really caught his attention was the ragged, practically shredded Stars and Stripes streaming from the stump of its foremast.

"Jeez! That's gotta be *Simms* or *Tindal*, and that can only be *Icarus* she's got in tow!"

"Looks bad," Seepy agreed. "An' there's Doms comin' up to finish 'em off!"

Orrin scanned the battle near the cripples. A few Allied ships were close, but there were more Doms in the way and they'd never get there in time. He banked harder right. "We'll see about that," he ground out grimly.

////// *USS* **Simms**

*T*he gallant DD was a smoldering, shattered wreck. All her masts were shot away, the tangle of rigging still being cleared by the 'Cat sailors who worked the sails, forming roving damage-control parties who chopped at taut cables with axes and cutlasses. Some worked to trim the dangerous, jagged splinters jutting in every direction from the bulwarks, and the blood-soaked deck beneath their feet, the latter making it dangerous to even walk about.

The hull was logy with barely controlled flooding, and only the heroic Lemurian pumps and semiwatertight compartmentalization had kept it afloat this long. The engine and boilers still labored valiantly, with little complaint, preserved for the most part by the armor belt. But the armor was still relatively light, never intended to withstand so much punishment for so long; it was sprung or even shot away in a number of places and its protection had been compromised. Just as bad, after all the high-speed steaming the ship had done, fuel was becoming a problem.

Not only was it depleted, but the bunkers lining the inside of the hull were leaking oil as quickly as they let seawater in to contaminate what remained. Seven guns were operational on the port side, currently unengaged and facing the great stony wall of Malpelo. There were only five guns left in the starboard battery; the rest either dismounted or rendered unloadable by muzzle strikes. It didn't much matter. *Simms* barely had enough gunners and Marines left to serve those few. The wardroom looked more like a slaughterhouse than a sick bay, and the seriously wounded had overflowed it to a degree that there was little point in taking more below. Many just lay on the main deck where they'd been dragged to the illusory safety of the creaking bulwarks, dosed with gulps of seep, and quickly bandaged by well-meaning but harried shipmates.

But the five remaining starboard guns were still in action, firing in "local control" with the new "friction primers," which were little tubes filled with an explosive compound and ignited by briskly yanking a coarse, sealed wire through the mix. Remarkably stable, efficient, and very nearly waterproof, they'd been reinvented by one of *Mizuki Maru's* rescued prisoners of war working in the Maa-ni-laa Naval Arsenal. First manufactured in the Filpin Lands, they were one of the few innovations that might've made it to the "Dom Front" even before they went west. Intended for the field artillery, the Navy had snapped some up to replace the dangerous, smoldering linstocks used to back up the electric igniters, or when guns fired independently. Like now.

Fred Reynolds staggered up the companionway, dragging another pair of powder pass boxes, just as a gunner pulled a lanyard to ignite one of the new primers and sent an exploding shell crashing into an approaching Dom 'wagon about four hundred yards distant. It had just come barreling out of the tighter press beyond and seemed intent on closing. Fred shook his head with a curse. *Simms* had been downwind of the battle all day, and the titanic roar of the entire action had been a continuous, bone-jangling presence. Now, his hearing was so far gone, his head so full of what felt like sloshy wet cotton, he barely heard the shot. The shell detonated amid the enemy's headrails, shivering the foremast with splinters and shards of hot iron, but for all the notice the huge ship took, it might've been her first hit of the day. Fred looked around. Except for them and *Icarus*, under tow behind them and in even worse shape than *Simms*, there was nothing left moving out on this end of the battle.

"Why's that one . . ." He paused, seeing another Dom heavy following in the first one's wake and realized it wasn't alone. "Why're they picking on *us*? There's a whole big-ass battle going on. Don't they have anything better to do? Jeez! We wouldn't be a threat to a rowboat right now, if it left us alone!"

"Gangway!" Kari gasped irritably below him, burdened by pass boxes of her own. He jumped and staggered dumbly toward the gun that just fired, even as the one beside it roared and trundled back. Absently, he tried to pop his ears again, but it was no use. One of the 'Cat gunners—a Marine—grimly took one of his boxes and slung him an empty one. The ship shuddered from a hit forward—the Dom had a pair of big bow chasers—and Fred's knees buckled. Straightening, he staggered to the next gun, aft, even as a powder-stained youngling bolted past him with two pass boxes, each containing a pair of exploding shells.

"Shit! I'm useless!" he railed aloud, realizing the "kid," half his size, was carrying twice the weight.

"Move it!" Kari snapped behind him.

"What's the point?" he demanded miserably, glancing back. Her flight suit was covered in blood from helping move the injured, and it was matted in the fur that showed. He looked much the same, for the same reason. Both had found helmets and still wore their goggles to protect their eyes from splinters and grit. He wasn't hurt, that he knew of, but he was *so* tired. Flying airplanes didn't do much to keep one in shape for this sort of thing. "We're just getting in the way!"

"You gettin' in *my* way!" she snapped, and he glared at her. His only experience aboard a ship in combat had been as *Walker*'s bridge talker. Tabby was technically a communications officer, but she'd never actually done anything but fly with him. With *Simms*'s comm out, there'd seemed nothing else for either of them to do, so he'd volunteered to help the youngling ordnance handlers who'd been decimated along with everyone else.

"That's what I mean," he said with a near hysterical laugh as he waved his empty box at another youngling racing past. "I'm in your way, and you're in their way." Then he pointed at the Dom ships bearing down. "And none of it's going to matter a few minutes from now."

"Lieuten-aant." Fred barely heard, after yet another gut-shaking shot. "Ensign Faask."

They turned and saw Captain Ruik standing between two of the guns, trying to stay out of their crew's way as they feverishly worked. It was the only way he could see anything, but he didn't look good at all. He'd lost his helmet and was having trouble with his telescope since a Dom solid shot had taken his hand off, halfway up his forearm earlier in the fight. He'd had the arm bound and lashed to his body, high across his chest, but that was about it. He'd remained on deck throughout the action. When Fred spoke to him before, he'd merely joked weakly that he'd have to get Prime Factor Bates of the Empire of the New Britain Isles to give him the name of the gunmaker who'd built the long-barreled pistol the one-armed man used for sport shooting.

"Sir!" Fred and Kari choroused.

Ruik managed a pained grin and beckoned them over with his glass. "Please," he said. "With Lieuten-aant Gaal wounded"—(Fred knew Gaal was still alive, but with a big percentage of the top of his head knocked off, he was more than just "wounded")—"and . . . out of the fight," Ruik continued, "and all my other officers either dead or occupied below, I'd raather the only other naval *officers* aboard refrain from tasks such as you are engaged in, laudable though they may be. I've learned that, in the Navy, the example officers set at times like this can be more important than anything they actually *do*," he added wryly.

"How important can doin' nothin' be?" Kari demanded, antsy to deliver her load.

Ruik blinked disappointment. "I assure you, Ensign Faask, standing calmly on the quarterdeck, under the circumstances, is not 'nothing,' and seeing us accomplish it, however challenging, helps others keep their composure."

Fred gestured helplessly around. "Sure, but . . . so? What do you want us to do? Gaal said this would be a help."

"Lieuten-aant Gaal was—is—a very practical person with little concern for appearances. In our current situation, I believe keeping up 'appearances' is the greatest service we can still render to this crew. You may not credit it, but both of you are warmly regarded throughout the Alliance. I'd appreciate it if you'd join me here, and try to affect that things are not nearly as desperate as they seem."

Fred scratched at the grime that had accumulated in his sparse beard. "Oh. Okay."

"Besides," Ruik said, nodding out to the west, where the greater bat-tle raged, "there are sights to see that you will never forget, if you sur-vive this day, and I suspect things may soon take an interesting turn. Look."

Beyond the nearest Dom 'wagon, that looked a little worse for wear now, with dark smoke beginning to billow from beneath her fo'c'sle and behind the gunports along her starboard bow, a new intensity had quickened the fight.

"My God, the *Makky-Kat*'s joined the fight!" Fred exclaimed. Big as she was, he could barely see her through the war-fogged turmoil. She was more than a mile away, churning through the forest of shot, frac-tured masts, flailing canvas in red and white, shell-torn, smoke-streaming funnels, gun flashes, and ragged smoke. Still, from what they could see, the destruction she was wreaking, almost effortlessly it seemed, with her modern guns and many heavy smoothbores, was an awe-inspiring sight. She gave an impression of stubborn indomitability as profound as the great, rocky isle—but an awful lot of Dom ships were starting to turn on her. . . .

"I hope Ahd-mi-raal Lelaa don't beat up our home too much," Kari murmured.

Simms jolted heavily again from a number of hits, and everyone fell to the ruptured deck or clutched the disintegrating rail. Geysers of wa-ter crashed down on top of them. The Dom liner had begun a turn, ex-posing more of the perhaps fifty guns that pierced either side.

"Here it comes," Fred exclaimed, probably louder than he'd in-tended, as he clambered to his feet. He mentally excused his volume with his deafness and the stupendous, continuous roar.

"Look!" someone cried, and they caught a quick glimpse of a pair of swooping Nancys. Bombs detached and plummeted down as the planes climbed and turned. Both weapons from one plane impacted the far-ther ship, and an instant after the initial flash, the whole thing bulged like an over-inflated balloon, popping with a catastrophic ball of orange fire and a towering white mushroom streaked with black. Thousands of unidentifiable fragments slashed the sea for hundreds of yards, and a nearly intact foremast slammed down on the closest 'wagon, toppling masts and spars. That ship had been hit by the closer plane as well, if less destructively, on the port side, throwing a smaller cloud of debris away from the ship. It was still turning, though, and Fred clenched his teeth, waiting for the final, cataclysmic broadside that would surely erase poor *Simms* and *Icarus*.

Well, if appearances are all I've got left, Fred thought, *I'm damned if I'm gonna flinch!* He looked at Kari when his Lemurian friend—the very best friend he ever had—found his hand with hers and blinked an indecipherable measure of fondness at him. He felt lucky that they'd had that long. But the end didn't come, and he haltingly turned to stare back at the Dom amid a tentatively rising flood of cheers.

"They got her port paddle box!" Ruik managed with an understated tone of satisfaction. "And look! She can't control her turn! She's heading straight for that other ship!"

The "other" ship was one they hadn't seen, blocked by the pair of Doms, but coming up fast beyond them.

"She's ours! A *big* one!" came another growing chorus, and Fred suddenly realized that, faced with a possibly equal opponent instead of a pair of virtually helpless ones, the gun's crews preparing to finish *Simms* had stampeded to port, to fight the more pressing threat they couldn't avoid. It wouldn't help them. Already, none of the port guns would bear on the intruder, which unleashed a stunning broadside of its own, directly into the Dom's vulnerable bow. More splinters flew, *huge* splinters, and cables parted and lashed at the sky. A nearly intact longboat cartwheeled away from the waist, ricocheting off the funnel, before flopping, upside down, in the sea.

"She's struck!" came a delirious screech.

Struck? Fred thought. *Surrendered? Naw. Probably just had her flag shot away.* He didn't believe it. But when the now severely damaged enemy ship of the line all of a sudden frantically reversed her engine and still didn't fire at anything, it began to dawn on him. It never before occurred to him that a Dom warship, any more than a Grik, might just . . . quit. But as the moments slipped by and no fire came, he realized it must be true.

"Damage report!" Ruik commanded.

"We're losin' her, Skipper," the blood-soaked quartermaster at the helm stated simply, her ear close to the voice tube from engineering. "Those last shots, they was nothin' left to stop 'em, an' the boiler room's floodin' fast. No boilers, no pumps."

Ruik closed his eyes to hide a pain worse than his arm. When he opened them again, they shone with an inner light. "Right standard rudder. Take us alongside that hulk." He raised his voice. "All hands, draw small arms and prepare to board. No firing unless fired upon, but kill anyone who resists."

"What then?" Fred asked, still a little stunned.

"Then, Lieu-ten-aant Reynolds, we will rejoin the fight from the captured ship!"

Their providential rescuers were none other than HIMS *Mars* and Admiral Hibbs himself, returned to the fight. His own prize crew joined the entire crews of *Simms* and *Icarus* as they gained the deck of the Dom 'wagon without resistance. There *had* been a struggle, however, because there were no officers left aboard. Having just witnessed the traumatic detonation of their consort, and helplessly facing certain destruction themselves, the crew had rioted and thrown their officers over the side. Fred knew that battles drew flashies—and other voracious denizens— into even tighter concentrations that they were usually found in this savage sea, and doubted the Dom officers had lasted long enough to rise to the surface for a final, panicked breath.

By the time the prize was secured and her trailing masts and sails hauled in or cut away, there was no fight for them to rejoin. The battle had moved farther away, largely clustered around *Maaka-Kakja*, and neither *Mars* nor the prize was in any condition to catch up with it. Besides, *Maaka-Kakja* already had help, drawing more and more Allied ships as well as enemies, and though she was clearly taking a beating in return, she'd left an amazing swath of devastation in her wake. Some of that devastation consisted of derelict but still floating ships, and Fred was surprised how many of the Dom variety had hauled down their colors. He had no doubt they'd still try to escape if they could, but for now, on the Allied side of the fight, they had no desire to draw the attention of the few orbiting Nancys that remained above. One of those flew close to the prize, with *Mars* and the two sinking DDs close alongside. Apparently satisfied with the situation, it waggled its wings, signaling its intent to set down alongside the Imperial battlewagon.

"Well done, Captain Ruik! Well done indeed," Admiral Hibbs enthused, his puffy face ruddy with exertion as he came aboard the prize himself, joined by more sailors to augment the Marines he'd sent first.

"I honestly never expected to see you again," he added with a grimacing glance at the shattered *Simms*.

"Ahd-mi-raal Hibbs. Thank you, sir," Ruik replied. "I never expected you to see me again either," he added wryly.

"*Tindal*'s status?"

"Lost, sir," Ruik answered more gravely, "defending *Simms* and *Icarus* while we rigged the tow. *Achilles*?" he asked in return.

"She made it out safe with us, but her Captain Grimsley took her back in behind High Admiral Jenks and *Mithra*." He leaned his head toward the ever-more-distant battle, but had to grab his shako before it fell. "In the middle of that by now, no doubt. If she still swims. Wireless telegraphy is a marvel, to be sure, but like you, we've lost our aerial and have little notion now of what is what." He stopped, his eyes widening. "My God, sir, have you lost that hand?"

Ruik glanced down. "Yes, Ahd-mi-raal. Earlier today."

"You there!" Hibbs barked at a surgeon from his own ship kneeling nearby and inspecting the Dom wounded. "Leave off that and see to this officer at once!"

"I'm quite all right at the moment, Ahd-mi-raal," Ruik protested vaguely, distracted by a low, collective moan along the starboard side where a number of 'Cats from *Simms* and men from *Icarus* were gathered. Without a word, he moved to join them, followed by Fred and Kari. "Cap-i-taan Parr," he said to a young man standing by the rail, head swaddled in bloody bandages above a tear-streaked face.

"Captain Ruik," the Imperial replied. "Glad you made it—and thank you, sir." Ruik waved it away with his good hand. "It was my honor. All of it."

The last of the wounded were being hoisted aboard from the proud DDs, 'Cats and men grabbing lines and scampering up the high wooden sides of the prize—even as *Simms*'s stern dipped beneath the choppy sea. *Icarus* was already deserted and nearly as far gone herself, also low by the stern. Now a lone 'Cat remained on *Simms*, feverishly hauling down the Stars and Stripes, even as the water raced toward him. Wrapping the ragged flag around his torso, he made a knot and lunged for a dangling line. Even as he scrambled up, USS *Simms* disappeared beneath him with a rush and a swirling vortex of floating debris. Gaining the deck, the 'Cat glanced down, then quickly rushed to Ruik.

"Saved this for you, sur," he said.

With tremendous force of will, Ruik managed to tear his eyes from where his ship had just gone down. "Should've left it with her," he scolded huskily.

"But we'll need it, sur, won't we? Aboard here?" the 'Cat insisted. The mainmast still stood, and he gestured with the flag toward its top.

Ruik coughed. "No. If my understanding of the prize conventions is correct, we will all share in some measure of reward, but she is for Ahdmi-raal Hibbs to dispose of."

A sudden crash sounded from alongside, and they looked back to *Icarus*. They'd used her anchor cable for the tow, but the other end was still attached to *Simms* as she plunged to the distant bottom. The cable had torn a jagged gash from *Icarus*'s hawse hole to the waterline and gone impossibly tight—but there was little resistance now. The small Imperial DD's stern was already gone, and now her bow simply vanished with a gush of air, her shot-torn funnel quickly slipping away with the slightest hiss and a wisp of steam.

"My God," Parr gasped. Then he looked at Ruik. "My God," he repeated, but straightened. "Sir," he said. "After all our ships have been through together over the last several days—and before—it seems most fitting that they should remain linked forever when they come to rest at last." He turned to Hibbs. "The same goes for our crews, Admiral. Together, we have sufficient numbers for the prize. Captain Ruik is senior to me—not to mention that I and my crew owe our lives to him and his. I would be honored to second him aboard here."

Hibbs blinked and hesitated. "It won't affect the distribution of the prize money either way," he said speculatively, but Ruik doubted that was his main concern. Finally, he nodded. "By all means." He looked at the 'Cat still holding the flag. "Run it up."

"Thank you, sir," Ruik and Parr both said.

"Yes. Well. We all owe a debt to the American Navy for this day, and others previous." Hibbs nodded at Ruik's arm. "Now please hold still long enough to have that tended."

"Ay, ay, sur."

"Hey!" came the rough call of an overused voice behind them.

Fred and Kari turned. "COFO Reddy!" they said.

"Hi, guys." Orrin grinned at them. "Glad you're okay." He turned to

Hibbs, his expression hardening. "I need gas and bombs," he stated, "and your idiot captain on *Mars* says yours is for your own planes— which you're fresh out of right now." He waved at the distant battle. "Obviously, I can't get any off *Makky-Kat*, and Admiral Lelaa's orders were to replenish from whatever ships we could. You're it." He coughed and cleared his throat. "A drink of water would be nice too, if you can spare it."

Admiral Hibbs was taken aback by Orrin's manner and sarcasm but managed to compose himself. "Water for the Commander of Flight Operations," he called. "And of course you may replenish from *Mars*," he told Orrin, glancing around. "Midshipman Varney, run along there and inform Captain de Spain that he will replenish COFO Reddy's machine at once, or his next command will be of a piece of wreckage alongside. His choice." He turned back to the now slightly mollified aviator. "Will that suffice?"

"Sure. Thanks, sir."

"Here's water, sir," an Imperial Marine said, holding a large dripping ladle.

"*Dom* water? From this ship? No thanks, buster. It's hard enough holding it in a plane when you don't have the squirts."

"Give him your bottle, fool!" Hibbs shouted, and several water bottles were offered. "Our water is properly grogged," he assured, "with good New Britain rum."

"Thanks," Orrin gasped, taking the closest one to hand, pulling the cork, and draining the bottle with several deep gulps. Shoving the cork back in, he handed it back and started to turn.

"A moment, though, if you please," Hibbs said. "Are you in wireless contact with the flagship?"

Orrin shrugged. Seepy could oversee the replenishment. "Not *Mithra*. She's taken a beating, and her wireless is out. I'm still in contact with *Makky-Kat*, some other ships, and what planes I've got left."

"Then tell me, from what you've heard and your . . . elevated vantage, how does the battle progress?"

Orrin rubbed his eyes, red where they'd been protected by his goggles, but sunken into a soot-blackened face. "I'm kind of short on polite ways to describe it, Admiral, but I'd say we're winning—will win—as long as *Makky-Kat* hangs in there." He shook his head. "Lelaa's one crazy 'Cat broad, taking a carrier into a brawl like that, but I guess it worked. The whole damn fight turned into an old-fashioned, hull-to-hull smashup, which I guess you saw here. Not exactly the best way to beat somebody with bigger ships and more guns . . ." He stopped, looking back at Hibbs and realizing he'd let his mouth run away with him. "But yeah, I think we've got this fight in the bag, if you threw half a dozen cats, dogs, and scorpions in it. It'll keep wiggling for a while," he prompted when he saw Hibbs's uncomprehending expression. "Some of the Doms that weren't engaged have already started to peel off, though. Heading northeast, back where they came from. Too many, if you ask me." He sighed. "So I'm not sure exactly what the hell we accomplished here."

"The enemy is fleeing?" Hibbs demanded.

"Some of it."

"Will there be a chase?"

Orrin barked a laugh, but caught himself. It wasn't funny. "Don't ask me. I'm not in charge. But based on what I've seen, I have to ask 'what with'? We've slammed their fleet around but have taken a serious beating ourselves. Worse, even if *Makky-Kat* doesn't take any more damage than she already has, she might be able to operate Nancys over the side, the old-fashioned way, but she won't be flying any Fleashooters for a while—or anything else off her deck. Honestly, it looks like all our fleets did here was pretty much destroy one another. Now, if you'll excuse me, I can still get back in it, so that's what I'm going to do."

"What about us?" Fred demanded.

"What about you?" Orrin asked in return, his voice harsh but his expression slightly amused. "I don't have any spare planes in my pocket. Besides, haven't you already broken enough of 'em for the day? Stay here, rest, relax. I expect what's left of Second Fleet will try to re-form once the shooting stops and you can get back over to *Makky-Kat* somehow. So long, guys."

USS Maaka-Kakja

The sun had finally set on what some were already calling the Battle of Maalpelo, and the fighting was all but done. Furious flashes of gunfire erupted now and then, far to the northeast, when some of the least damaged ships that had sped the Doms on their way happened upon a cripple with some fight left in her, but they'd have to call them all back soon. A pair of fast Filpin-built DDs, undamaged in the fighting, would keep after them through the night, at least, reporting what they saw, but they couldn't let anyone else get too far away or they might run into an undiscovered reserve force and wind up in the same situation that started this mess in the first place—with nothing left to send to their aid. *Maaka-Kakja* had stopped her engines, rolling ever so slightly in a rising sea, sheltering and helping with emergency repairs to several heavily damaged ships in her lee. *Compared to them, we are in fine shape,* Lelaa realized bitterly, *but we're not a carrier anymore. Not right now.* The Grikbirds, apparently expended at the beginning of the fight, had missed their chance at *Maaka-Kakja*, but much of her flight deck had been chewed up by shot from the Doms that had crowded alongside. Firing upward at their maximum elevation, they'd blown through the largely open hangar deck and exited the flight deck in a blizzard of splinters. Unlike the new "fleet" carriers, her flight deck was her weakest feature, and an amazing amount of the planking and structural framing below would have to be replaced. The hull was in pretty good shape; nothing that couldn't be repaired at sea. But they simply didn't have enough timber to repair the flight deck, and the closest place with sufficient stockpiles was the Enchanted Isles.

"What's the plan?" Tex Sheider asked, surprising her in the silence that prevailed on Lelaa's bridge. It was anything but silent throughout the rest of the ship, with noisy repairs underway from the fire-control platform to the engine room, but none of the bridge watch had spoken for some time, recognizing that she was deep in thought. Her executive officer harbored no reluctance to kick-start her mind, however. She almost giggled. *As usual, he actually expects me to answer the question that is foremost in my own mind!* She had to concede that normally, his tactic worked amazingly well, but just then she simply didn't know. She mentally inventoried what she did, beginning with what was most important to her. *My engineering plant is sound, and* Maaka-Kakja's *stout hull turned all but the heaviest shot. Every leak of note is under control and she, at least, can still fight. Otherwise, what little remains of Task Force Eleven is unfit for further combat.* She mentally snorted. *As for the rest of Second Fleet, not a single ship of the line could survive another day of battle similar to what they endured today, and several wouldn't last ten minutes. Some may yet succumb,* she added grimly. *We took a number of prizes,* she consoled herself, *and this Dom fleet was composed of ships roughly equal to anything the Imperials had, but none have been fully surveyed. Whether or not any may yet be used, I must assume they were all gravely damaged before they surrendered.*

"For now, I want one of the fast transports we left with the oilers to collect every aviator in the fleet that we cannot put in the air and stand by to take them to Puerto Viejo. There should shortly be more planes than pilots there, when they get them all put together. That much I can do." *Jenks may not agree,* she realized wryly. *Maaka-Kakja* could still operate Nancys alongside—slowly—but not many more than the half dozen or so that still remained airworthy. Still, as much as she admired Jenks and would—usually—obey him for the good of the Alliance, Captain Matthew Reddy remained *her* High Chief, and she absolutely knew what he would want her to do with her pilots. "High Ahd-mi-raal Jenks will be aboard shortly," she temporized. Thoughts of Jenks reminded her how relieved she was that he was okay. *Mithra* had returned to *Maaka-Kakja*'s side shortly before, confirming by Morse lamp that she was seaworthy—and that Jenks was well. "He will have further orders then."

"He can order away all he wants," came another distinctive, creaky voice that Lelaa enjoyed—and despised at times like this. "I don't give a damn what he says," Chief Gilbert Yeager proclaimed in what amounted to, from him, a petulant whine. "I quit."

As one of *Walker*'s "original" Mice, who'd lurked in her firerooms like an immovable, monosyllabic troll, Gilbert had been introverted to a point of apparent near insanity, but as his responsibilities swelled, so had his personality. Now *Maaka-Kakja*'s chief engineer and de facto engineering officer (whether he liked it or not), and basking in the reflected glow of what his half brother Isak Reuben had accomplished in the West, he'd grown downright insufferable at times. This was despite his having used the precedent Orrin Reddy had set to flatly refuse a promotion to lieutenant.

"You *can't* quit, you weird little creep," Tex snorted.

"Can so," Gilbert sneered at him. "I'm volunteered aboard here as actin' chief o' *Makky-Kat*'s engineerin' division. She's s'posed to be a carrier, which should make that a purty cushy berth. But 'cept for a few o' the new guys you gave me from the other ships, my division's still full o' jugheads an' loafers that don't know live steam from a hot fart. I was wore to a frazzle even before we got shot up. Now, if yer gonna use the ship for a go . . . al danged battleship, I want a transfer back west to my real home on *Walker!*" His lip curled. "If I'm gonna get shot at, an' hafta fix busted crap that's getting' shot at, I'd sooner do it where I nat'rally b'long!"

Tex rolled his eyes. "Of all the . . . Look, genius, since *you're* chief engineer, if your people don't know their jobs, that's at least as much your fault as theirs. You've got to learn to teach people what to do! And even if we could ship you off, which I'd personally *love*, you can't just pick and choose where to fight this war. You go—or stay—where you're needed, and God help us, we need you here!"

Lelaa held up a hand and gave Tex a short, secret blink of assurance, but she spoke in a tone of mock severity. "Enough, Mr. Sheider. No wonder poor Mr. Yeager feels aggrieved!" She looked at Gilbert. "I will forward your transfer request along," she soothed, blinking regretfully now, "as soon as the current situation has resolved itself. Under the circumstances, I cannot promise it will be acted upon as quickly as you might wish, but I will do it. In the meantime, think of the people who appreciate and rely on you; the engines that need you. *Your* engines and boilers, Mr. Yeager," she stressed. "Lieuten-aant Tab-At commands *Walker*'s engineering division now, and Isaak Reuben is her chief. Your expertise would not be wasted there, but your contributions would be infinitely less profound." She paused. "You may certainly go if you wish, when the time is right. But until then, I would consider it a personal favor if you continue the work aboard here that you do so well."

Gilbert opened his mouth, then clacked it shut. "I . . . ," he finally said, but couldn't go on. He just shuffled out of the bridge and down the stairs outside.

"Why do you coddle that nutcase so?" Tex asked incredulously. "He hasn't got the brains of a grawfish."

"Oh, but he does," Lelaa countered. "He is very smart at what he does, and as you said yourself, we need him." She blinked something Tex didn't recognize. "But as you may or may not also have seen, this war has made . . . changes to many of our minds and hearts. It has changed mine in many ways, I know. Most are small, and some have even made me a better officer. But once I would never have dreamed of manipulating the thoughts and feelings of another person for any reason, so I am becoming perhaps a less good person as well." She sighed. "Only time will tell. But Mr. Yeager's mind and heart have changed in big ways, and grown more fragile too, I think. He is *lonely*, Mr. Sheider, and as much as we need him, we need him even more to want to be here, or he will be of no use at all. So, in the future, particularly on days like today when hearts are raw and nerves are frayed and every body and soul is poised on the brink of exhaustion, when you consider calling people like Gilbert Yeager a 'weird little creep,' please do bear that in mind."

A signal-'Cat stepped into the pilothouse from the bridgewing. "High Ahd-mi-raal Jenks is coming aboard," she said.

"Very well," Lelaa said. "Assemble the side party, if you please. Mr. Sheider, do accompany me to welcome him aboard."

////// *Fort Defiance*

t was windy, and even a bit chilly now, and the darkness around Fort Defiance pulsed and flared with fiery lights that left burning, sparkly afterimages in the eyes. The fight had raged all day long, sometimes desperately, and often at widely separated points of the perimeter. Between each assault, a counter battery duel resumed that had been stunning and destructive within the fort, but far harder on the hasty Dom artillery emplacements than those the Allies had erected with thoughtful redundancy. But then the Doms always seemed to have more guns and crews to replace those that were dismounted and annihilated. With yet another dusk attack finally repulsed from Colonel Blair's area of responsibility, the man, red-eyed, almost dead from fatigue, hurried stiffly to Shinya's HQ in response to an urgent summons. He was easy to spot in the gunflashes as he approached because, like other senior Imperial Marine officers, he'd returned to wearing his red uniform coat with yellow facings, insisting it "gave the lads heart."

Shinya was doubtful, particularly since the coat showed dust, grime, powder stains—and blood, of course, on the yellow—much more readily than the green and brown tie-dyed frocks that had become the near-universal battle dress of all Allied armies. Then there was his very real concern that Blair's uniform coat, so distinctive now, made him a more tempting target. Despite all that, there was nothing he could say since no one had ever actually gotten around to making the new battle dress "regulation." Blair would do as he saw fit, and after the long, grueling day, Tomatsu Shinya wouldn't criticize.

Blair managed a sharp salute when he joined his commander, and Shinya returned it with equal formality.

"You've done well," Shinya complimented. "Your troops have done well."

"Thank you, General," Blair said, his voice raspy. "A hot day."

"Indeed," Shinya agreed with a frown. "For everyone. Here and at sea." He proceeded to describe what they'd heard of the naval battle that raged that day, complete with the initial assessment by some that it had ended less conclusively than anyone would've preferred.

"So," Blair said, the exhaustion seeping into his hard-used voice, "what does that mean to us? I mean, here, of course."

"Second Fleet must disperse. For a time, at least. Some of the least—and most—damaged ships will come to Puerto Viejo and Guayakwil Bay to help protect the approaches. Others will have to retire to places where better repair facilities exist." He looked squarely at Blair. "That means the Enchanted Isles, or even as far away as Saint Francis. The new American harbor at San Diego is not yet complete."

"Are there any ships there that can augment Second Fleet?"

"Only support vessels. No warships beyond a couple of DDs necessary for their protection."

Blair removed his helmet and ran his fingers through sweat-plastered hair. "Some of the worst damaged are coming here, you say?"

"Under tow if they can't move themselves, or are in particular distress," Shinya confirmed.

"Why?"

Shinya sighed. "Because, if early reports are correct, Second Fleet has virtually ceased to exist as an effective fighting force. We can only hope the Doms suffered equally or worse, but we cannot know that for certain. Jenks claims a victory, if a pyrrhic one, but the Doms may have yet another fleet they did not send. So at present, whatever survivors of the engagement that retain significant combat power but may founder on a longer voyage will come to Puerto Viejo or Guayak—and be beached in the harbors as static batteries, if necessary." He watched Blair's reaction, guessing his thoughts. "There are no dry docks, permanent or floating, any closer than the New Britain Isles. Those that need a dry dock to stay afloat . . . won't. If they make it here, whether we need them or not, perhaps they can be refloated at a later date." He clasped his hands behind his back. "In the meantime, just as our surgeons must quickly decide whom they are most likely to save in the heat of battle, repair work must focus on ships that can be most quickly returned to action, since even the facilities at the Enchanted Isles are limited."

Blair seemed to absorb that. "What of *Maaka-Kakja* and our air support?"

"Our air here will improve for a time as planes the Governor-Empress brings are assembled, and we will soon have more pilots as well. But *Maaka-Kakja*'s ability to launch and recover aircraft was seriously damaged. She will retire to the Enchanted Isles with the highest priority for repair—but that could take weeks."

"So, one way or another, whether the Doms can strike Puerto Viejo and Guayak by sea or not, supplies will soon grow tight—and the only reserve we can count on for the foreseeable future is only just arriving at Puerto Viejo with the Governor-Empress."

"Essentially, yes."

Blair grimaced, the news and exhaustion visibly deflating him further. Shinya grimaced as well, with a new determination. "We shall *still* win here, Colonel Blair," he promised.

Blair sighed. "What makes you so sure, sir? Because frankly, it seemed to me that we very nearly lost today—and beyond that, I can't help but feel that the enemy is somehow . . . holding back."

Shinya nodded. "Good. I'm glad you saw that. From the thick of the battle, I wasn't sure you would notice the . . . pattern that has emerged."

"I noticed that the Doms didn't support their near success at certain points as vigorously as I'd have expected," Blair said, "but my attention was somewhat focused," he added dryly, "and I'm not sure I saw a pattern to it."

"There was. Please, come inside my headquarters. Sit, have refreshment, and I will show you on the map what I saw."

Blair was nodding. "Thank you, General. I could use a drink and a chair. I must admit I feel quite stupid right now."

Shortly after, with a glass of watered rum on the table that jostled with the concussion of guns outside, Blair leaned over a map and followed Shinya's tracing finger with bleary eyes. "It took a while for me to realize it myself, Colonel," Shinya explained, shaking his head. "I have . . . recovered significantly, I believe, but the aftereffects of the fever have left me feeling quite foolish as well. In any event, it's become clear to me that the Doms are deliberately focusing on what they must consider 'weak' points along our perimeter, defended by local troops from the liberated cities. Those troops have done remarkably well," he stressed, "and remain highly motivated, in spite of the enemy's obvious efforts to exhaust and dispirit them." It was unnecessary to repeat that the locals knew they'd get no more mercy from the Doms than their new allies. Less, most likely. "But the enemy's ostentatious redeployment of their lancers today, in clear view of the fort, in an attempt to edge past around us to threaten the cities beyond, caused great distress."

"Yes, sir." Blair nodded. "Until we reminded their officers that there were probably more than enough militia and support troops remaining in Guayak to see the lancers off. And your orders to our own lance—our own *horse soldiers*, to intercept them in any case, reassured them amazingly."

Shinya shifted uncomfortably. "Yes. Well. As you know, I consider the mounted troops our weakest branch at present, but practice may improve them. I do think Guayak is secure, and believe the move was designed more as a psychological assault on our already hard-pressed allies."

"The Puerto Viejans were less reassured," Blair warned.

"Their city can fend for itself, and the Governor-Empress, Saan-Kakja—and Sister Audry"—he raised his eyebrows—"are landing nearly five thousand fresh troops of their own." *Troops that we need here,* Shinya thought but didn't say aloud. "In any event, the locals should no longer fear for their homes and families. That's the main thing. But the problem they face most keenly now, besides the disproportionate attention of the enemy, is arms." All the Lemurian Marines had recently received the new Baalkpan and Maa-ni-la Arsenal Allin-Silva breechloaders. There'd been yet more resentment from the Imperials over that, but even they had to admit it was only natural that the Lemurians should get the first shipments sent by their own people. As some consolation, the 'Cats had turned their old weapons over to the Imperial Marines. Those were still smoothbore muskets, but they were better made and used the more reliable percussion ignition system. With at least slightly superior weapons in hand, the Imperials then turned their flintlock smoothbores over to the local regiments. These were essentially identical in function to the captured Dom muskets they'd used at the Battle of Guayak, but their offset socket bayonets allowed them to keep firing even with bayonets fixed, whereas Dominion troops used plug bayonets that, once installed in the muzzles, had to be driven out, turning their weapons into little more than short spears. Still, the Doms had discovered these "soft points" where the rate of defensive fire was least, and their spies had confirmed who was standing there.

"I agree," Blair said. "But what can we do about it? Pull the locals off the line? God knows they deserve a rest, particularly the Fourth Guayak. But Blas's Second of the Second has suffered nearly as badly supporting them, as has the First of the Tenth Imperial. We *can* put them all in reserve for a day, but then I'd think we should replace them with other tested battalions from elsewhere on the line." He exhaled and closed his eyes briefly. "I do fear tomorrow will be even worse than today."

"I'm not sure it won't get worse *tonight*," Shinya said broodingly. "Doms do fight at night, you know, so there can be no question of a major shift of forces." He tapped his nose, staring at the map. "What we can do, is pull the Fourth back, as you suggest. They are down nearly thirty percent, even beyond the fever depletion they had before the assaults began. Pull them back and reinforce them from the general local reserve. They *are* good troops, and that way we can plug them back into the line if we must." He paused, a slight smile forming on his face in the lamplight. "But they will leave their flag," he said, "and beneath that flag we will shift the Second of the Second. The two battalions to their right will shift left as well, and we'll put a fresh Imperial battalion in the northeast lunette. The Doms have begun to avoid those."

"I see your plan. The Doms will likely keep at the locals, but will instead be met by troops with the highest rate of fire instead of the lowest." He frowned. "But those battalions, and particularly that of Captain Blas, have been sorely tested as well."

"And passed the test, as always. Exactly why we need her—our best," he stressed, eyebrows rising again, "there. But they'll have help. Captain Blas and . . . Let's give Lieutenant Finny a brevet to captain, at last, shall we? Both have fought alongside your colonial frontier troops before. We will directly reinforce them and the First of the Tenth with the Third Saint Francis Regiment."

Blair considered, then nodded. "If anyone can get the most out of those undisciplined ruffians, Blas and Finny will."

"Excellent. That's settled." He smiled, but shifted uneasily, staring at the map. "We *will* win," he stressed again, "but it will be costly in many ways." His smile faded. "We built this fort for a larger force than we currently have. It's as simple as that, and the outer wall is just too long to sufficiently defend. In strictest confidence I must tell you that I consider it inevitable that the Doms will breach it at some point, probably in yours—and Captain Blas's—sector. We must bleed them white before they do, and that's why your men and Lemurians, our very best," he stipulated again, "must remain in place: to kill as many of the enemy as they possibly can before they're pushed back. I'm making other preparations based on that assumption, pulling men and guns from the southwest ramparts. Those have thus far only been lightly engaged and are likely to remain so. No large force can march entirely around the fort to exploit a breakthrough there in any case, so I'll use those men and guns to bolster our inner defenses." He looked hard at Blair, who'd grown suddenly more alert. "The enemy will get in," he predicted darkly, "but I truly believe that the deadly space *between* the walls is where we'll finally break them." He paused, before continuing in a quiet tone. "Even if it breaks our hearts to do it."

He took a long breath, gauging Blair's reaction.

"Strictest confidence," Blair repeated slowly. "Surely that does not exclude Captain Blas?"

"I'm afraid it must," Shinya said, his eyes narrowing. "By that I mean that you are to tell no one at all. Spies concern me."

"But spies are a constant concern. I'm sure our local ranks are thick with them. And they'll see the redeployments anyway, and report them if they have the means."

"That's why we do it now, at the last moment, so to speak. But I think the enemy will now do what they mean to do regardless. We can respond to changing dispositions more quickly than he. What I fear more than his knowledge of our redeployments is his understanding of what they mean—and what our underlying expectations might be. That's why you must tell no one"—he looked away—"and because even Captain Blas must not suspect that we expect her to lose the wall. She loves her Marines and might pull them back sooner if she knew." He shrugged. "I would. But we need her to stand as long as she can not only to kill more Doms, but to make them absolutely sure that when she does pull back it was because she *had* to—and so they'll send everything they have left in after her. In *between* the walls," he added grimly. "Now," he said, suddenly brisk, "having expressed my concern for a night attack, I find myself somewhat anxious. I don't know how far back it goes, so you may not know it, but our American friends have a saying: 'Speak of the devil and he will appear at your door,' or something like that. Orderly!" he cried, to be heard over the cannonade outside.

"Sur?" replied a Lemurian corporal, bursting through the entrance.

"Paper and pen, if you please, then have runners stand by to take orders. He glanced apologetically at Blair. "You'll see that the redeployment in your sector is complete before you sleep?"

"Of course, General Shinya," Blair said, his tone still tired, but now sounding sick at heart as well.

"Thank you. I'll send the instructions we've already discussed immediately, so hopefully there won't be much left for you to do when you get there. While we wait, however, let's see what we can come up with for these other 'weak' points I've identified."

CHAPTER 28

////// *Puerto Viejo*

*T*rying to stand out of the way on the hastily built docks in the torch-lit darkness, Governor-Empress Rebecca Anne McDonald, High Chief Saan-Kakja, and Surgeon Commander Selass-Fris-Ar, who'd accompanied them to help with (and protect the two leaders from) the fever—and the battle casualties to come—watched with mounting frustration as their reinforcements tried to disembark at Puerto Viejo. All had seen confusion before, in similar circumstances. They'd even seen what they might've defined as chaos. But in her anxiety to move immediately to General Shinya's relief, Rebecca was convinced that what she now beheld was something even worse, though she had no name for it. All three wore what had become regulation female naval officers' uniforms for their respective powers. Saan-Kakja and Selass were in white tunics and kilts, and Rebecca wore a dark blue tunic with white knee breeches and black boots. Sergeant "Lord" Koratin stood silently nearby, conspicuous as usual in what had become the Lemurian-Amer-i-caan Marine "dress" uniform of a blue smock and kilt and white rhino pig armor. Their dress was the only thing in view that seemed remotely ordered. Koratin remained Sister Audry's primary military advisor, but also directly commanded the detail of men and 'Cats protecting the two leaders. Despite his well-cultivated outward calm, his own exasperation was clear in the guttering orange light by the way his tail whipped back and forth.

Smaller than Guayak, Puerto Viejo was otherwise similar in architecture and culture, with its mixture of stone and brick public buildings surrounded by adobe huts and ultimately, wood and thatch shacks. Unfortunately, directly on the coast, its harbor wasn't nearly as well protected or really even suitable for large ships. Somehow, the Imperial surveyors hadn't sufficiently stressed this to any of the planners involved when it was decided that Puerto Viejo should become the primary forward supply port for General Shinya's forces at Fort Defiance. Only now, when supply was critical and a major effort was underway, did the inadequacies of the early studies fully reveal themselves. For example, there'd apparently never been any kind of real docks at the small coastal city before; the local fishermen and traders had merely pulled their bright-painted boats straight up on the dun-colored sand. And the new docks, still under construction by Imperial engineers and local labor, were hasty, ramshackle affairs, not nearly up to the task of dealing with the sudden, frantic influx of ships, troops, and material.

It hadn't begun so frantically, when the first ships began dribbling in several days before Rebecca and Saan-Kakja's greater force appeared, but instead of clearing the way for them and making it easier to land the reinforcements they brought, the early arrivals only fed the stirring bedlam to come. To be fair, they'd been former "company" ships for the most part, merchantmen still manned by old crews with new commissions. They'd been dispatched with cargoes from the fleet or the Enchanted Isles weeks before, and without wireless, had no notion of the logjam they were creating when they leisurely choked the ridiculously insufficient docks with their cargoes. Some of those cargoes had been crated Nancys and their support—but no one had reported that there were no facilities whatsoever to receive them either, and the energetic surf made it impossible to operate the planes directly from shore. It was discovered that Imperial engineers had been preparing ramps and docks at a small lake northeast of town for their use, where a small squadron of overworked Nancys already made its base, but that information and the necessary coordination had been neglected as well. Now the crates languished, in the way and dangerously exposed to damage while their irate ground crews tried to arrange their transport.

And as bedlam has a tendency to do, it only got worse from there. The Puerto Viejans themselves were a mixed blessing. Just as isolated from and persecuted by the Church and Blood Priests of His Supreme Holiness, they'd learned of Guayak's resistance, with the help of the strangers from the West, and joined the rebellion against the hated Dominion. Now, as news reached them of the terrible battle raging beyond the rising foothills to the east, and word inexplicably but inevitably spread of the great battle at sea, they were fearful of the Dominion's wrath. They remained helpful, even hopeful. What choice did they have? It was much too late to turn back now. But in their fear-stoked zeal to help the Allies help them, they'd wildly compounded the prevailing confusion when nearly the entire population of the city; men, women, even children, almost spontaneously took it upon themselves to swarm aboard ships crammed haphazardly against the freshly planted piers—and now one another—to "help" unload them. Ships waiting farther out were dragged ashore, leaning in the surf, and hundreds of small boats mobbed them as well. Faced with letting them "help" or killing them, Rebecca had finally ordered everyone to join the locals in unloading everything and getting it ashore as quickly as they could, however they could.

The 1st Maa-ni-laa, Saan-Kakja's personal guard and the only Lemurian regiment she'd brought, and Sister Audry's Regimento de Redentores, her former Dom prisoners of war, had been the only reinforcements to get ashore in reasonably good order before the chaos struck. They'd landed slightly down the coast as if assaulting an unfriendly shore before marching into the city where, after unsuccessfully trying to regain order, they simply guarded and tried to sort the growing, jumbled mountains of supplies, guns, horses and paalkas, more crated aircraft—everything they'd brought to this place—as it piled up on the beach. But the other troopships with the majority of the Imperial Marines hadn't been equipped for a combat landing, having been meant to off-load at Guayak where the already-better docks had been further improved. They remained anchored offshore like outcast geese, still thick with troops for the most part, as boats of every description belatedly scurried to carry their human cargoes to the same beach the 1st Maa-ni-laa and the Redentores had used.

"May the Heavens preserve us—and General Shinya—from such good intentions in the future," Saan-Kakja murmured dryly.

"I agree with your sentiment," Selass said, "but it is pleasant to be appreciated."

"They appreciate us because they're terrified," Rebecca said more harshly, the tone seeming unnatural from her elfin face. It was a tone she'd used almost exclusively over the last few days; a tone directed more at herself than anyone else. She remained sure that her own meddling had caused what she considered the near disaster at sea and blamed herself for all the damage, deaths, and looming impotence of the fleet. Now, as an extension of that, she was just as sure the turmoil here was her fault as well. "And they have reason to be terrified," she added amid the uncomfortable blinking of her friends, "because if we can't bring some order to the calamity I've set in motion, the entire war in the East may well be lost."

"Skuggik shit," Koratin pronounced in his once-soft voice turned gruff, then blinked at Rebecca as innocently as his rough countenance would allow. "'Shit' is right? Sometimes the proper words still hide from me." He shook his head at her. "Perhaps your orders to High Ahd-mi-raal Jenks *were* ill-advised. Only time will tell, and to dwell on such things now can only do harm. But have you considered that, without Taask Force Eleven as bait, the Doms might have *refused* battle against the whole of Second Fleet, and drawn it back in pursuit to a place of their choosing, where many great guns on shore could add to their advantage? Or how would the whole fleet together have fared had the Grikbirds not largely spent themselves on the smaller force? Discovering the truth of that is a task for the tellers of tales—the, ah, 'histori-aans'—when the war is done. What we do know is that the Dom fleet Ahd-mi-raal Jenks met will not threaten us here." He gave a very human shrug. "Perhaps another will, but I do not think so." He nodded toward where Sister Audry's regiment was deployed around the growing mounds of supplies. "I am no sailor, any more than our interesting Col-nol Araano Gar-ciaa, but I have learned much from him about the enemy. Possibly as much as he has learned about himself," he added with a blink of irony. "As a junior officer, he knew nothing of the eastern reaches of the Dominion, the 'Pass of Fire,' or any more fleets they may have had beyond it. But he confirmed what I have long suspected. The Doms do not hold back, straa-teegic-ally, any more than the Grik once did. They use what they have, all they have, to achieve their purpose. They may 'hold back' on the battlefield for an advantage there, in much the same way we always try to keep a reserve, but I believe, and Col-nol Gar-ciaa agrees, that if the Doms *have* yet another fleet, they would have sent it too—unless they need it elsewhere."

That left them to ponder that, as well as the implication that Fred and Kari's mysterious "other Americans" were already being of help, somehow, somewhere. But Koratin's statement reinforced Rebecca's primary worry over Shinya's somewhat cryptically reported sense that the Doms *were* "holding back." Aerial observers updated the disposition of the enemy forces around Fort Defiance as often as they could, but the picture was far from complete. There weren't as many dragons as they'd been facing in the past, and it was assumed many had gone north to the Pass of Fire, if not to the Dom fleet, but there were enough to make things difficult for the few planes still in action. The only thing that seemed certain was that Don Hernan's army still numbered upward of a hundred thousand men. No reinforcements could reach him unobserved down the military road from the north, but what might be moving to join him from beyond the mountains to the east? Was he waiting for something else? Was that why he was "holding back"? She feared that must be the case, and that made the situation here even more agonizing for her.

Koratin waved again at the surging, shouting mob. Crates of weapons, bundled tents, casks of food, ammunition, and barrels of everything from gunpowder to rum and musket flints were flowing ashore, the civilian bearers being guided, funneled, and sometimes physically shoved in the general direction that roaring sailors thought they should take their burdens. Sometimes they got the gist of the foreign commands, but more often they just deposited their loads on the closest pile and went back for more. Horses shrieked and whinnied in alarm or annoyance as they thundered down the gangways, and paalkas mooed resignedly as they dragged guns, limbers, caissons, forges, wireless carts. . . .

It was chaos, surely, but every imaginable thing an army needed in the field *was* very quickly going ashore.

"This is not so bad, after all," Koratin continued. "I have seen worse—far worse when Aryaal fell, if you recall. But worse also when our armies have landed on other shores, even unopposed." He snorted. "It is confusing. War always is. You forget that my people, Aryaalans like General Protector Lord Muln Rolak"—he showed sharp, yellow teeth at some secret amusement—"were among the very few Mi-Anakka who always fought wars. We boasted so among ourselves of what ambitious, important things they were, and bragged of our courageous deeds," he said as if reminiscing, but his eyes blinked self-mockery. "And yet even the insignificant *arguments* those wars were compared to this were just as disorderly when viewed from within at the time."

"If that is true, Lord Koratin," Selass said, nodding at his swishing tail and addressing him with the old title he'd worn when they met but no longer liked or claimed, "why are you so anxious?"

"Is it not obvious?" Saan-Kakja said. "He is little concerned for us at present, but believes Don Hernaan has brought 'all he has' to destroy Gener-aal Shinyaa."

She feels it too, Rebecca realized. "And worries what he 'holds back,' as General Shinya suspects, and when it will be felt," she reaffirmed, looking at Koratin with her large eyes reflecting the torchlight.

Sergeant Lord Koratin bowed to her.

"General Shinya has not begged that we come at once," Selass speculated, "but then, he would never 'beg,' would he?"

"No," Saan-Kakja said with certainty. "But he has described his situation and concerns—and will expect us to act accordingly."

"We must go to him at once," Rebecca stated firmly, "but it will be *days* before our entire force can move to his relief!" she added, almost snarling.

"Then we take what we can," Saan-Kakja said mildly, soothingly, patting her "sister's" arm.

Rebecca glared at the rough, uneven planks of the dock for a moment, then looked at Koratin just as intently. "It comes down to it at last, then, I suppose. Do you truly trust Colonel Garcia?"

"I do, Your Majesty," he said. "But what is more important, Sister Audry does—and the entire Regimento de Redentores would throw themselves in the terrible sea if she demanded it." He blinked irony. "Having saved them from their evil faith, they believe perhaps more strongly than you recognize that they owe her their very souls." He paused and gazed casually down beyond the waterfront where a company of Redentores was trying to form itself in the crush. "As do I," he added softly.

Koratin had probably been Sister Audry's very first Lemurian convert to Christianity, if not true Catholicism. He openly admitted that before he'd experienced a very personal tragedy and met the Dutch nun, he'd been as vain and corrupt as any lord of Aryaal, and more infamously conniving than most. But even then he'd had his principles—and an adoration of younglings. Having lost his own, he found that Sister Audry's teachings had helped direct his quest for a meaningful life—beyond the personal vengeance he'd sought—and he'd devoted his soul to protecting younglings. His cause then naturally became the war against the Grik, and then the Dominion, because both enemies represented the most direct, existential threats to younglings everywhere, human and Lemurian. Despite his past, he could've risen to a position of leadership in the Alliance, as a representative from Aryaal, at least. Instead, he'd defended Baalkpan along with all the other huddled refugees from other lands and Homes when the Grik came there at last. Distinguishing himself in battle, he'd become a Marine, and earned the rank of sergeant. That title meant far more to him than "lord" ever had, and he'd declared he'd stay a sergeant forever. He knew the power of higher rank would only corrupt him again, and as a sergeant he could protect and serve the "youngling" leaders of Maa-ni-la and the Empire of the New Britain Isles, while continuing to protect and advise Sister Audry—who cared nothing for rank in any case.

Rebecca nodded, recognizing one of Koratin's introspective moods and respecting it, as well as the wise counsel they often inspired. Thinking of wisdom and guidance, she caught herself desperately missing her one-armed Prime Factor, Sean Bates, who'd very reluctantly stayed behind to preside over her government in her absence. Bates *was* wise, but she also knew he couldn't trust Garcia as much as Sister Audry and Koratin did—as much as she suddenly realized *she* did, based on Koratin's assessment. Much as she missed him, Bates's absence most likely prevented a momentous argument over the decision that was forming in her mind. She couldn't help but fear she was making yet another terrible mistake, but she no longer doubted Garcia. Only herself.

"Then send for Sister Audry and Colonel Garcia at once, if you please," she said at last. Then turning, she bowed to Saan-Kakja. "You directly command the First Maa-ni-la, of course, but would you care to send for other of your officers?"

A short while later, with the shoreside tumult undiminished, all those summoned had gathered far enough away that they could speak in near normal tones. Sister Audry had dispensed with her habit at Rebecca's insistence, but there was a simple white cross painted on her helmet—just like all her troops—and her small golden cross hung as always between her breasts upon the tie-dyed fabric of her frock. Knowing the woman well, Rebecca found it amusing that Audry was also armed. Around her waist was belted a Maa-ni-la Arsenal copy of a 1911 Colt .45, and a pattern of 1917 cutlass. Rebecca couldn't imagine the young, straw-haired woman ever drawing either weapon, but understood her own troops had insisted she have them. The rest of her regiment, nearly eight hundred strong, carried Imperial flintlock muskets, just like those given to the locals, but the nearly one thousand Lemurians in Saan-Kakja's 1st Maa-ni-laa had Allin-Silva breechloaders, and every platoon had at least a pair of Blitzerbug SMGs.

Rebecca looked searchingly at Sister Audry who stood stiffly, as close to the position of attention as she'd ever attempted. Sister Audry had been in charge of gathering local maps and intelligence since being flown ashore with Colonel Garcia two days before. The plane had gone to the lake.

"I fear that General Shinya is in distress," Rebecca declared abruptly, "and as you can see, this force as a whole is in no condition to assist him. The First Ma-ni-laa and the Redentores can, however, and I must know how quickly they can march to the relief of Fort Defiance, and how long the march will take." She already knew what Saan-Kakja thought. Without hesitation, Audry turned to Colonel Garcia.

"Arano?" she asked, using his first name as always, which clearly made him uncomfortable.

Garcia wore an anxious expression on his dark, handsome face, little different from the one he'd worn every time Rebecca saw him. His face itself had changed, however, as had most of his men's. Nearly all now wore impressive "Imperial" mustaches, and Garcia's was long enough that he'd started modestly braiding the ends, like Admiral Jenks. "As did the First Maa-ni-la, the Redentores landed with rations for three days and a combat load of eighty rounds per man," he said. "We're somewhat scattered at the moment, as you can see, but I can assemble my regiment and be ready to march in one hour." Rebecca thought he was boasting, but when he bowed to Saan-Kakja, his expression grew more confident. "I am sure the First Maa-ni-laa can do likewise," he said, then looked back at Rebecca. "Fort Defiance is nearly fifteen leguas—" He paused, mentally calculating. Distances were reckoned by the *"legua de por grado"* in the Dominion, which equated to roughly four sea miles by Imperial measurement. The sea mile equated well enough to the nautical mile the Americans had brought to the Lemurians, who measured everything in "tails," close enough to a yard. Therefore, a thousand tails was half an Imperial sea mile of a thousand fathoms, and Fort Defiance was sixty miles away, as Garcia translated in a way all the others would understand. "The road rises, but is good enough that a man may easily walk, ah, four miles in an hour. Mathematically, that means we could reach Fort Defiance by noon tomorrow."

"With half our troops dead from exhaustion, and the rest unfit to fight," Sister Audry scolded him. "You have nothing to prove, Arano!"

"With my dearest respect, we do," Garcia objected.

"I must agree with Sister Audry," Selass said. "The march alone would destroy all eighteen hundred troops before they ever met the enemy."

"Sergeant Koratin?" Rebecca asked.

Koratin blinked speculation. "The Redentores could have done it during their training on New Ireland. Their instructors were Maa-reens, after all," he added without modesty. "But they have been at sea for months." He looked at Saan-Kakja. "And the First Maa-ni-la, good as they are, could never have done it." Strong as they were, Lemurians generally had less endurance than humans and shorter strides. And, of course, the First Maa-ni-la wasn't a Marine regiment, with the more intensive training they received. Koratin was simply stating what he considered a fact.

"With rest stops, then," Rebecca demanded of Koratin, expecting him to give the most realistic assessment. "How long?"

"Not before tomorrow evening, and even then they will be of no use—and helpless if we must fight our way through the enemy to enter the fort. I recommend a pace that would bring us there in the night, and rested enough to join Gener-aal Shin-yaa the following dawn."

"That may be too late," Rebecca murmured, biting her lip.

"We can do it!" Colonel Garcia insisted, but Audry fluttered her hand at him. "Do shush, Arano," her gentle tone softening her impatient gesture. "God knows your men serve Him now, as do we all. Let them do so to a purpose."

There was near silence for a moment within their midst as they all considered the problem and tried to find an answer. Another paalka lumbered down the gangway, pulling a limbered battery forge. A group of wide-eyed Puerto Viejans, who'd never seen a paalka before, tried to lead the oversize, vaguely moose-shaped beast in contradictory directions as soon as it reached the pier. Losing patience, it jerked a man who refused to release his line through the air, and then slammed him into a native-born horse that was waiting to haul a cartload of barrels away from a jumbled stack. The paalka, like the rest of its kind Rebecca and Saan-Kakja had brought with them, was among the first to ever set foot in the Americas. *It* had met horses before, and probably wouldn't have cared if it hadn't, but the horse had certainly never met a paalka—or been struck by a flying man. Already nervous in the excitement and press of people, the horse reared and squealed, then bolted down the waterfront, scattering people as it went and tipping over other carts that spewed their contents on the sand. The paalka, possibly even a veteran of combat, saw no reason for all the excitement and simply plodded on, now dragging the rest of its squawking handlers.

Sergeant Koratin hacked a Lemurian chuckle while doubtless those around him were even more appalled by the expanding chaos in the city. He cleared his throat and scratched the graying mane around his face. "Actually, Col-nol Gar-ciaa may be right," he said, grabbing everyone's attention once more. "I doubt there is any way to reach Fort Defiance before tomorrow evening, but we may still be fit to fight when we get there." The others leaned forward, eager to hear his idea, and he gestured around. "This is a lost cause. The rest of our force will not be ready to move in 'days.' It may not be ready for a week."

Saan-Kakja reluctantly nodded, joined by the others. "What do you suggest?"

"The animals here, the horses and paalkas, only add to the problem right now. Let us solve that one as well as our own. We start right now, gathering every animal and every cart in the city, marshaling them on the road east of town. We can't use the First Maa-ni-la or Redentores for that; they would get swallowed in that madness. They march around the city as soon as they are assembled and wait for the animals and carts to arrive. We use the locals and whatever Imperial troops have already landed to get them there."

"Then?" Rebecca asked, already knowing.

"We pack our troops on the animals and in the carts, and *ride* to Fort Defiance, as fast as the animals can go!"

"Are there enough horses here, with those we brought?" Rebecca asked Garcia.

"It would take them all, perhaps three or four hundred, but . . . *sí* . . . yes, Your Majesty, I think there are. But it will take more time before we can leave."

"Then we make them go *faster* than they can," Koratin said.

"Many will die, so heavily loaded and pushed at such a pace," Selass stated simply. It was a warning, not an argument.

"Then we leave them and load the troops on the live ones until they *all* die, if it comes to that, and march on from there. But I see no other way."

Sister Audry looked unhappy, but she spoke. "You are so certain that the moment of decision draws near for General Shinya, Your Majesty?" she asked.

Rebecca looked at Koratin, his argument about reserves still fresh in her mind. "I am."

Audry looked at Garcia. "Then we must go at once, and perhaps with the beasts gone from the city, the rest of our army can march more quickly as well."

I doubt it, Rebecca thought, *but it's possible*. She mentally pulled her hair. *Too much is possible, good and bad, and I've already made one terrible mistake. How can I be so sure this is not another? I split my force again? How can that be good? But Shinya is already "split" from us, like Task Force Eleven was, and none of its ships would've survived at all if we had not acted.* She closed her eyes. *I am not a general. I am a child playing at war, playing at ruling a nation. A child who has made dreadful mistakes that have cost lives—and now I endanger the lives of those few left who remain most dear!* She shook her head. *High Admiral Jenks remains CINCEAST in name, but child or not, this is "my" theater, "my" war, and I must lead—just as Captain Reddy must lead in the West just now. Oh, how I wish he were here, and Dennis Silva, and Chack . . . and Abel Cook. Do they ever feel as I do? How could they, and accomplish what they have so often? Perhaps it grows easier with use, but I so wish they were here! I know I could lead better with any of them at my side.* She finally took a deep breath and sighed. *I doubt the rest of my troops will march much sooner, but the unloading probably will grow easier with less congestion at the waterfront. Enough that the planes might then be assembled and ready when the pilots from Maaka-Kakja arrive. That will be a help. But either way, I'm as certain as I've ever been that the time to move is now, and if we move, we must do so decisively.*

She looked at Saan-Kakja and took her friend's hand. "Let us pass the word, Sister, without further delay."

Camino Chimborazo

The Blood Drinkers had come, more than seven thousand of them, which was more than even Don Hernan had hoped for. They were still streaming in, down the mountain pass, but the vanguard was already deploying inside the edge of the forest, taking positions laid out behind the forward works. Don Hernan, General Nerino, and about a hundred of Don Hernan's priests had found a rocky promontory overlooking a ragged clearing the host must cross, to observe as best they could. There could be no lights and visibility was poor, but they saw the dark columns marching past under the hazy glimmer of a shrouded quarter moon.

"I am so pleased! Now you can make your night assault with the decisive weight of the cream of the Holy Dominion, General Nerino!" Don Hernan practically bubbled. He'd grown increasingly impatient with Nerino's probing attacks, and sensed that had they been more focused, one or more might've broken through on its own.

"I am pleased—and relieved—myself, Your Holiness," Nerino temporized. He still—gently—insisted that, with their internal lines, the heretics could quickly reinforce any point so threatened, but realized during the previous long, bitter day of indecisive fighting that he was no longer really sure about anything anymore. He'd been a soldier all his life and had considered himself a professional. He was regarded as a master of the board game *ajedrez*, brought to this world by the Spanish, and played it with anyone he met who could learn the rules. When no one was available, he played against himself. He'd drilled his old Army of the South to perfection and orchestrated mock battles for the amusement of priests and visiting nobles. He'd engaged in games of strategy with his senior officers or colleagues in other provinces when he traveled and thought he was quite good. Based on this, he'd been so sure he already knew what a battle would be like if he was ever privileged enough to fight one that his greater interest, his hobby, became the forms and ceremonies that surrounded them. That had been his focus at Guayak; to enjoy the pageantry of it all, because he'd considered the outcome preordained. The irony of that still stung. But with his defeat, he'd learned the greatest lesson of all: war was not a game with fixed rules for moves and countermoves that resulted in utterly predictable outcomes to the master. And it was most certainly nothing like *ajedrez*.

What that meant then was that even as he tried to project continued confidence to Don Hernan, the only thing he was really certain of was that he was the farthest thing from a "master" of battles, and he doubted such a general could exist. A *better* general might have been more confident with what he had, but Nerino knew his limitations now and believed the only thing that would absolutely ensure success was the utterly overwhelming power the Blood Drinkers and the gift had brought him. Now, of course, he had to make sure even that power was not frittered away by Don Hernan's impatience.

"Perhaps we should . . . delay the attack a short while longer, until just before dawn," he said tentatively. "Heroic as they are, the Blood Drinkers have marched all day and must still get into position. They are tired, Your Holiness, as will be the gift, no doubt. Let them rest awhile; refresh themselves." He paused, waiting for Don Hernan's displeasure, but the Blood Cardinal was silent and Nerino couldn't judge his expression in the darkness. "And honestly," he continued, "I fear the difficulty of coordinating so many men in the darkness, not to mention managing the gift. I've never even seen that done. But given the greater part of the night, I'm confident we can have all in readiness for the final great assault before the morning comes."

"Yet another delay," Don Hernan said broodingly, but he seemed to see the sense.

"A *final* delay, Your Holiness," Nerino stressed, "just one more, before the great . . . cleansing battle you have dreamed of, and after tomorrow the heretic's fort will be yours—as will all that lies beyond."

Don Hernan sighed. "Very well. A *final* delay." His voice turned wistful. "I had so looked forward to the night attack. The fire of the great guns is beautiful in the night, is it not? A night battle on the scale we will launch would rival the fires of El Paso del Fuego. Surely that would draw the attention of God Himself!"

"We should begin the battle before dawn," Nerino consoled, "and I suspect it will be sufficient to draw His notice in the night or day."

A low-frequency gurgling moan rumbled in the darkness, echoed by others, and Nerino peered eastward. Massive shapes were moving down the Camino Chimborazo, emerging from the gloom. Some seemed as tall as the mighty trees flanking the road, while others, smaller, moved on either side.

"The gift!" Don Hernan crooned, spreading his arms as if to embrace the monstrous shapes. "The gift is here! Oh, look at them, General Nerino! Are they not magnificent?"

Nerino gulped. He was terrified. In the dark, he couldn't see what controlled the things, though he suspected it had something to do with the smaller shapes on either side. Those he recognized as armabueyes; giant armadillo-like beasts with long, spiked tails just like the army used to draw its heaviest guns. There were hundreds of the things, pacing the dozen or so larger monsters that had resolved themselves on the road, and despite his growing awe, he felt an instant of resentment considering how many great guns could've been brought to the battle if so many armabueyes had been made available earlier. He shook his head. The gift should certainly offset that. Surrounding the lumbering draft animals were as many as a thousand much smaller shapes, he realized. Men.

"Dragon monks," Don Hernan proclaimed grandly, guessing the object of his attention. "A very exclusive order, as you might imagine." He chuckled. "Did you know they will not speak a human tongue?

Though it is said they speak directly to the armabueyes." He actually snorted. "I do not believe it. Speaking to animals is impossible, of course. But they do control them." Ghanan Nerino frowned, troubled. He'd spoken to an "animal" himself, one named Captain Blas. So either that was not true, or she was not an animal. But he was not about to make that observation aloud to Don Hernan. "And the armabueyes control the gift by keeping tension on the chains you will soon see," Don Hernan continued. "All you must do is tell the dragon monks where to go. Ah! The escort commander!"

Several Blood Drinkers scrambled up the rocks and went to their knees before Don Hernan, kissing his hand as he passed it before them. Now closer, Nerino could see the dark red facings on their yellow coats, where ordinary uniforms were faced in white. "My sons," Don Hernan greeted them, as he did all the soldiers of his order, "stand and salute your general, His Excellency Ghanan Nerino!"

"General!" they chorused, covering their hearts with their right hands. "Your orders?" the one with a captain's braid asked harshly. Nerino tried to look stern. Though undeniably the most elite troops in the Holy Dominion, Blood Drinkers were also the most privileged and arrogant, and somewhat notorious for ignoring commands from regular officers outside their order whom they didn't respect. That shouldn't be a problem with Don Hernan present, but they knew Nerino had lost a battle to animals and heretics, after all.

"Captain, you will lead your charges down the road a quarter *legua* farther, where my officers will direct you to the staging area we have set aside. There you will find provisions for your men." He paused, then added, "And the gift you bring from His Supreme Holiness. Rest yourselves, but the entire Army of God shall begin its general assault in the hour before dawn. The gift will follow, aiming at specific points at which you will be directed. The rest of the Blood Drinkers will exploit the breakthrough I expect of you. Is that understood?"

Don Hernan de Devina Dicha beamed, his happiness seeming to cast more light than the frail moon above.

///// *The Battle of the Crossroads*
Fort Defiance
September 15, 1944

Captain Blas-Ma-Ar had fallen asleep, scrunched down on her haunches against the wall at the top of the earthwork. She'd been exhausted by the previous day and then the confused, nighttime redeployment that followed. Most of her 2nd Battalion, 2nd Marines had found some rest, but she'd felt compelled to help her friends, the newly brevetted Captain "Finny" Staas-Fin and Lieutenant "Stumpy" Faal-Pel, shift their 8th Maa-ni-la as well. Then there'd been the even more confusing job getting the 3rd Saint Francis "Frontier" troops plugged into the line. They hadn't liked being split up and she didn't blame them. However, their long rifles wouldn't accommodate bayonets, and she didn't dare allow them to man even a company-size section of the wall, so she stuck them in by squads so they could at least "fight alongside their mates." The 4th

Guayak was gone now, reassembling behind the high inner wall behind her position that protected the compound beyond. Much of this had been done under a galling bombardment that, while largely ineffective, had been a nerve-racking distraction. But the guns on both sides fell silent sometime after 0100, and without even realizing it, she'd slumped down and slept.

"Cap'n Blas," came a soft voice, and a hand gently squeezed her shoulder.

"Yes, First Sergeant," she said, her voice amazingly clear, though her mind was still fuzzy. Her eyes opened, but it made little difference. The overcast was heavier now and the moon had set, leaving the world beyond the works in utter darkness. She could see around her to a degree because the fires in the fort reflected light against the smoke and haze above.

"Sump'ins goin' on," First Sergeant Spon-Ar-Aak "Spook" told her quietly. He nodded over the dirt wall. "Doms've put out all their fires an' our observation posts say they's a lotta noise out there, some pretty screwy noises too. But they figger the Doms is on the move."

Blas rubbed her eyes and stared hard, then shook her head. "I'm sure they're right. First smart thing they've done too. Try to move closer to us in the dark. How long until daylight?"

"About a hour."

"No order to stand to?"

"Just verbal. Word's passin' along to be ready for . . . loom-inaton."

Blas realized then that all the Marines and colonial men around her were beginning to stir as sergeants moved down the line, waking them and telling them to be ready.

"Stinks here," she observed absently. "I didn't notice before."

"Them Guayakans," Spook snorted. "Filthy buggers. Couldn't be bothered to run fifty tails to the latrine, an' crapped right here." He shrugged philosophically. "Course, they been a little pressed these last few days, an' at least they buried their turds. Mostly."

"How's ever'body holding up?"

"Swell," Spook said, but his tone was less sure. "To say honest, a buncha' the fellas ain't happy about leavin' our flag over the Eighth, an' us fightin' under that Guayaak raag. What is it, anyway? Looks like one o' them flyin' squid critters First Fleet seen, standin' on the moon."

Blas shrugged. "I don't know. Haven't even looked at it before. But orders are orders, and they kinda make sense."

Blas grabbed the water bottle hanging from a strap over Spook's shoulder and took a long gulp before returning it. All the water bottles of the wounded and dead had been filled and spaced along the defensive line, but she couldn't see one right then, or even where she'd dropped her own when she fell asleep. "Got anything to eat?"

"Just crackers. Hot chow's on the way—if we get time," he added ominously.

Blas thought about it. "Hand me a cracker, wilya?"

She heard a dull shriek, then another, as rockets soared into the sky trailing tails of sparks. A dozen more quickly followed, all popping high in the air and making bright orange glares that were usually hard to look at as they drifted downward. The clouds were quite low, she realized, and there was fog as well that dulled the eye-searing lights, but they cast sufficient illumination to reveal long, thick ranks of massed Dom infantry, less than five hundred tails out, rolling toward them as relentlessly as the surf.

"Shit!" Spook growled.

"Yeah," Blas agreed.

Muskets popped and flashed out across the killing ground as the men and 'Cats in the forward OPs opened up, then scrambled back toward the fort.

Drums thundered and Imperial horns sounded their calls to "stand to," but there was little point by then. Those not already alerted had seen the rockets or heard the mounting shouts of alarm.

"There's a lot of 'em this time," Spook said without inflection.

"I think it's *all* of 'em this time," Blas said, gazing as far to the left and right as she could see under the guttering flares—and then the Dom artillery opened fire. Either they hadn't been using all their guns before, or they'd brought up more, because it seemed like the entire distant tree line erupted in flaring strobes of yellow-red light. Cascades of sparks arced out, quickly followed by the choking smoke, and roundshot began impacting the earthworks, causing the very earth to shake. The Dom artillery still couldn't do much damage or inflict many casualties, but the clouds of earth and shattered wood from the entanglements were making things very hot.

More rockets *whooshed* into the sky, and there was Colonel Blair, trotting his horse along behind the line, yelling for the protected guns to commence firing at the advancing infantry. "Ignore their damn guns. They can't hurt us!" he cried. "Captain Blas!" he said, seeing her there. "Have your riflemen hold fire until the enemy is in musket range! They think you're Guayakans, remember. Mustn't frighten them away!"

Blas looked at the advancing Doms, then back at Blair. "I don't think that much matters now, sur, an' they were close to musket range when we saw 'em!"

"Nevertheless. At least keep your rate of fire down a bit until they're committed. Don't want them to veer off, into the First of the Tenth for example. When they're in musket range, you may go to rapid fire."

Blas felt her ears lie flat. "I'm tellin' you, Col-nol, they're daamn near in musket range *now*, so why don't you come up here and see for yourself if they're 'committed'! Have you even looked? It's a gener-aal advance! Their ranks look deeper in front of us, sure, but there's nowhere for 'em to bloody veer *to*! And if we don't start killin' 'em right daamn now, as fast as we can, they gonna 'veer' the hell all over us!"

To her surprise, Blair actually urged his horse to claw its way up the embankment onto the fighting step behind her. More flares popped just as he arrived at the top, lighting the grim expression on his face. "General Shinya was right," he murmured. "Quite right, Captain," he said louder. "My apologies. You may certainly commence firing at once."

Blas nodded. "Battaalion!" she roared. "Load!"

The roughly four hundred 'Cat Marines under her command raised their weapons, pulled their hammers to half cock, flipped the hinged breech blocks up, and inserted fat cartridges into the chambers. The failing flares glinted dully on the brass. Spook stood beside Blas with his cherished BAR and handed her an Allin-Silva rifle and cartridge box. She already had a cutlass and pistol on her belt. She slung the box, taking one of the new cartridges—new to the Allied troops in the West at least—and looked at it. *Quite ingenious,* she thought. *That monstrous Dennis Silva has never been as silly as he pretends, and this conversion was his idea. The weapon is identical in appearance and function to those we've used so long, but now they can be loaded from behind and, being rifled, are much more accurate.* The only thing people had to get used to was how easy they were to load. She inserted the cartridge, latching the breechblock closed behind it.

The colonial "frontier" troops checked the priming on their massive flintlock rifles, already loaded, and leveled them. "Runner," she called aside, with a quick glance at Blair. "Hurry over to the right and get our own flag back from the Eighth Maa-ni-laa, if you please." A satisfied cheer followed that, and Blair didn't object. She turned back to the front. "Take aim!" Four hundred rifles went to shoulders and pointed toward the enemy. The Imperial Battalion to her left with their smoothbores would have to wait a little longer, but they were ready. On her right, the 8th Maa-ni-la might as well have been following her commands, so quickly did Captain Finny repeat them. Cannon started firing, their sputtering shells arcing out to explode among the enemy ranks, now little more than three hundred yards away, and mortars emplaced on the ramparts of the inner wall started thumping, sending bombs rising over their heads. She waited an instant longer for the smoke from the guns around her to clear, but it just hung there in the still, humid air. It didn't matter. The Doms were visible even through the smoke, and she opened her mouth. "Fire!"

It wasn't a perfect volley, but considering it was still dark and most who fired it had been asleep shortly before, she thought it was fine—particularly considering the effect. The front rank in front of hers and Finny's battalions staggered amid the delayed, resounding, stuttering *blop!* of heavy lead bullets slamming into men. Blas figured that maybe a quarter of the volley hit somebody, but, as usual, more were struck by slugs passing through men in front of them, or pieces of things the bullets shattered such as equipment or even bone. A roundshot hit nearby, throwing up a geyser of dirt and broken rocks. "Carry on, Captain Blas," Blair said, coaxing his frightened horse back down the slope.

"You heard the col-nol, First Sergeant," Blas said. "Pass the word to all company commanders: commence independent fire."

"Ay, ay."

Blas was a big believer in volleys, under certain circumstances, but except for the initial impact they produced, she preferred to let her Marines pick their targets and fire when they were ready instead of when someone else told them to. They got a lot more hits that way. And her Marines were good, certainly among the best marksmen in the Alliance even before they got the newer weapons. Almost immediately, the clatter of fire resumed from her position and became a continuous roar.

More rockets burst in the sky, illuminating the enemy, and the battle became a slaughter—but the Doms kept coming, and it grew increasingly clear that she'd been right: They *were* bringing everything they had this time, and they wouldn't stop. No matter how many men her people killed, heaping the ground behind the advancing ranks with bodies, the Doms would hit her line—probably the entire sector at once, she thought—with a remorseless, senseless abandon reminiscent of the Grik. Her Marines *were* slaughtering them, but she began to grow concerned. There were just so many! And the Dom guns didn't stop even when their shot started falling among their own men. It was madness—but it might just work. She began calculating how many Doms they could kill before they reached the top of the wall.

When an approximate answer formed in her mind, she grimly joined the firing line and began the mechanical process of firing, loading, and firing again as quickly as she could, the rifle slamming her shoulder and her bullets trailing vapor in the humid air before knocking another Dom to his knees or to the ground.

"Fix bayonets," she called. "Don't stop firing all at once, but fix bayonets! They'll charge us soon, and you won't have a chance." At one hundred tails, about where the thickest entanglements began, the Doms stopped to dress their lines even as men tumbled to the ground, dropped their weapons, and fell in grotesque heaps, screaming and clutching themselves.

"Here it comes!" someone shouted. The commands they heard were clear.

"Apunten! Fuego!"

Several thousand musket balls struck near the crest of the berm, sending dozens of 'Cats who hadn't ducked in time flailing backward down the slope. A pair of guns near Blas sprayed the massed enemy with canister and whole companies went down, but those in the second rank leveled their muskets and fired again, hitting more of her Marines. "Keep your stupid heads down, for the sake of the Heavens!" she roared. More canister whirred through the air, but so did the balls of the third Dom rank. That volley didn't catch as many of her people, but when she glanced over the crest, she saw two things. First, a gray-yellow light was staining the sky, silhouetting the great mountains to the east. Second, the enemy was now *advancing* between volleys, getting closer! *They're learning,* she thought grimly. Before, they would've just stood and exchanged the unequal fire until they couldn't take it anymore, then fixed their bayonets and charged from where they were. For an instant, she contemplated the inevitable casualties to come but realized there'd be far more if the Doms reached the top of the wall. Nothing for it.

"Let 'em have it!" she roared. The staccato crackle immediately resumed, and continued even when the whirlwind of the fourth volley engulfed them. More of her Marines fell back, most struck in the head, and loose helmets rolled and clattered down the slope. The big rifles of the colonials, meant for giant game on the northern continent, boomed intermittently. Cannon, mostly six- and twelve-pounders, but mixed with a few Imperial eights and who-knew-what-size Dom guns captured at Guayak, fired all along the line. Blas suddenly realized the scope of this fight was beyond anything she'd ever seen, in firepower if not numbers. The noise was tremendous, and the thick smoke made her body try to reject the short, rapid breaths she took. Coughing, she pushed another shell in her rifle and cocked the hammer. She couldn't see! The sun was still far from cresting the mountains to the east, but the brightening day on the smoke and fog actually made visibility worse. She searched the smoke, found a yellow-coated shape, and squeezed the trigger. Even more white smoke jetted from her rifle, and she had no idea whether she hit her target or not. She didn't know how long she fought like that, loading and shooting at blurry shapes, but it felt like moments and hours at the same time. It couldn't have been the latter even though it was somewhat brighter when, through the maelstrom of roaring fire, drifting dust, grit, and flying lead, she heard a muffled command. The shout was picked up by other throats, indistinguishable in the streaming, dirty white haze.

"*Armen la bayoneta!*"

"Keep firing!" she screamed, her voice now rough.

"*Calen bayoneta!*"

A high-pitched, desperate roar followed that command, and the massed, fuzzy ranks surged forward.

"Keep it up! Keep firing! *Wait* for it. . . ."

The firing around her intensified, the big colonial rifles still booming, but soon those men would draw pistols for the up-close work to come, then eventually the long, two-handed "hunting swords" they car-

ried. The first Dom troops to squirm through the entanglements appeared at the bottom of the works about thirty feet below. They died in
a hail of bullets, but more quickly replaced them. The barbed wire
stretched between the planted stakes had grown choked with dead over
the last few days and lost much of its effectiveness despite attempts to
clear it. A bigger mass of Doms lapped below, clawing at the slope, pushing men ahead of them. Blas could see their faces now and though the
meaning of human face moving was still somewhat mysterious to her,
she clearly recognized the desperate terror she saw, but there was also a
kind of frenzied determination as well.

The yelling had all but stopped on both sides. Her Marines were too
busy loading and shooting, and the Doms' cries had been replaced by
gasping, grunting, and short, sharp calls she didn't understand. She saw
they were getting closer, though, heaving one another up the berm,
climbing bodies, a wall of glistening plug bayonets bristling slowly but
remorselessly nearer. Dozens of times, she'd trotted up and down that
very slope herself, taking only seconds to do it. But only now did she
realize what a dreadful, unattainable height it must seem to those men
now scrabbling upward under such a murderous fire.

Blas's Marines weren't the only ones doing murder, though. More
enemy ranks had moved up to replace those that charged, and were still
firing, killing Blas's Marines as they were forced to expose themselves to
shoot downward. Cannon still sprayed them with clouds of canister, but
there were just so many! The flag ruse was unnecessary now, but the
Doms had clearly assembled a heavier force to assail the Guayakans.
Maybe too heavy even for her. She considered sending to Blair for reserves; the Doms climbing the berm would reach its top in moments.
But she decided Blair had to know what was going on and doubtless saw
the same thing all along his line. He'd trust her to stem the tide with
what she had, and she would try.

"Now! Gree-nades!" she roared, taking one of the lumpy hand
bombs from her cartridge box strap. They didn't have many grenades in
the East yet, but the few crates they'd received had been distributed
along the line. Now her Marines pulled pins and tossed or rolled the
things down the slope as fast as they could. She threw hers a little farther, hoping to catch an officer she'd glimpsed waving his sword in the
press. With a stuttering *whump*, the grenades went off, showering them

with more dust, rocks, and a fine red mist. Momentarily, there was a kind of stunned silence below her position, then a mounting, horrifying roar that seemed to combine fury, anguish and terror in equal parts. That was when she knew she couldn't break this attack with bombs and firepower alone. The men coming for her were already dead. They'd die attacking her, or die much more horribly later if they failed. Victory was their only hope. More grenades rolled down among them, throwing bodies and clouds of dirt in the air, but the greater mass of Doms still surged upward. The first to reach the top were met with a withering fire; they tumbled back, screaming, but their bodies only widened the shifting, rolling platform for others. Their footing was unsure, but they had the numbers, and more and more reached the crest.

"Shields!" she coughed, hoping she was heard, but other voices carried the command.

"Up an' at 'em!" sergeants bellowed. "In their faces! Meet 'em at the top!"

Shields, fearful weapons themselves, slammed against the unsteady men, throwing them back. Those that stood were shot or bayonetted by 'Cats behind those banging their shields forward. The distant ranks of Doms stopped firing, already hitting too many of their own with their inaccurate weapons, so most of what little shooting remained came from Blas's Marines—and the cannon in their protected embrasures.

Blas fired past a shield, its holder crouching low behind it, grunting with the effort to stem the tide of men. Muskets pounded or slammed down on it, trying to knock it away, and Blas caught glimpses of desperate faces, mouths open in silent or unheard roars. Some sprayed spittle as they gasped; others managed short, defiant cries she couldn't understand. She shot as many of those faces as she could, and her ammunition was dwindling fast, but most of her attention was devoted to stabbing with the long, triangular bayonet on the end of her rifle. She stabbed at eyes, throats, arms, anything that appeared before her. She didn't always connect, but when she did, she drove in hard and twisted savagely before pulling her weapon back.

A huge man, swinging a pair of muskets by their barrels, flailed at the tiring 'Cat in front of her. He absorbed the blows on his shield with loud grunts of pain as the muskets shattered, but a Marine beside Blas drove his bayonet into the man's upraised armpit. He shrieked and tried to knock the shield 'Cat over with his dying bulk, but already sliding backward, he merely grabbed the shield and took it with him. For an instant, the brave 'Cat had no defense, and a pair of the wicked, sword-like Dom bayonets found him before he could scrabble back. Blas stabbed at his killers, and the shields closed up over his corpse. A pair of colonials flanked her now, laying into the Doms with their long swords, like axes, and slinging blood in all directions. They didn't have the reach of bayonets, but at such close quarters, they could hack the enemy with flesh-cleaving, bone-smashing strokes. She wondered briefly why they'd chosen to fight at her side; colonials could be cliquish. But ever since Saint Francis, they'd shown a fondness for Lemurians in general, calling them "kitties," to mixed annoyance and amusement, and she was grateful for them.

The fighting raged like that for at least an hour, maybe more. It was impossible to tell. And the bayonet work was the most prolonged and grueling Blas had ever endured. The new rifles made a huge difference since they could be loaded much more quickly and she doubted she'd have held if not for them, but her Marines were exhausted, the grenades were gone, and their ammunition was spent when the pressure on the faltering shield wall suddenly just . . . ended. Her hearing was destroyed, but she did perceive the sound of trumpets braying beyond the second massed ranks of Doms that had never advanced. Those opened fire again as their comrades melted back, scurrying over the heaped bodies and through the corpse-choked entanglements.

"Back!" Blas shouted, not recognizing her own voice. "Get down, back behind the wall!" She needn't have exerted her voice. Her Marines were already dropping down to the firing steps.

"Thanks, guys," she managed to the two blood-smeared colonials.

"Our pleasure!" One of them grinned. "An' a rare fightin' kitty, ye are!"

She contemplated a retort, but then just grinned back. The small cats that had spread across the Empire of the New Britain Isles, arrivals with the same ancient "passage" that brought its people to this world, did look a little like Mi-Anakka, and she wasn't offended by the diminutive, considering the present source.

"It was the shields," First Sergeant Spook declared as he joined her, handing her his water bottle again. She drank greedily. He was just as bloody as the two men, and his beloved BAR hung from his shoulder with an empty magazine well. She suddenly realized she'd never even heard him fire, but apparently he'd shot everything he had. He tugged on his sling, noticing her gaze. "I'm not completely dry," he said, blinking irony. "Savin' a couple maag-a-zeens back for if it gets *really* bad."

Blas barked a laugh, and Spook peered carefully over the wall, watching the retreating Doms near the next ranks, still firing over their heads. It was scant protection. Mortar bombs and canister still clawed at the enemy, and Blas didn't know how they could just stand there and take it. The smoke and lingering fog beyond made the world invisible past the ongoing slaughter.

Spook's tail flicked annoyance. "I was hopin' those others'd kill the ones that ran, but I guess the Doms ain't Griks after all."

"No," Blas managed, handing the bottle back. Her throat was better, and she also felt a growing sense of triumph. Not that they'd won; she didn't really believe that, and suspected the fight was far from over. Just that she was still alive. "And they didn't just quit. They were *called* back. But why?"

"They were gettin' wasted." Spook shrugged. "We'd have killed ever' daamn one." Blas wasn't so sure, but she said nothing. The sun had risen above the distant mountains, and she could see it up there, amid bright blue gaps in the streaming white haze. It would be a clear day once the last of the fog burned away. But the smoke remained dense down low, still being generated as fighting raged on at other points along the wall. She expected the Doms to come back, but she'd enjoy the respite no matter how brief.

"The shields did it. Again," Spook declared. "So maybe the guys an' gals'll quit bellyachin' about waggin' the heavy daamn thing around."

Blas nodded. Decisive or not, the shields had been a help. Undeterred by cannon, accurate rifle fire, and even grenades, the Doms had finally driven through every obstacle to reach the shields at the top of the parapet. But difficult as all those other obstacles had been, the final one couldn't be avoided or climbed, and it battered at them mercilessly even as the bayonets and bullets still slew them from behind it.

"Yeah," Blas agreed at last. "But just like the war in the West, one of these days this war'll move too fast for shields, and we'll have to quit 'em. I hope that's soon," she added bitterly.

"Well, maybe," Spook allowed, but paused. There was a growing commotion among the Marines around them, and together, he and Blas peeked up over the earthen wall.

"What the hell's that?" Spook muttered.

Beyond the Dom ranks, straight out of the ground haze and the overhead glare of the sun, something was moving toward them. Something huge, and more than one.

"I don't know . . . ," Blas murmured, but then she thought she did. Everyone had heard the tales Fred Reynolds brought back of the momentous beasts to the north, and Suares, the "vice alcalde" of Guayak, had confirmed there were many horrible monsters, "great dragons," on the other side of the mountains where the land was wild and choked with impenetrable jungles. Some of the monsters were mythical things, Blas was sure, but she was equally convinced not all of them were. Certainly not the ones Fred and Kari described. And as these things drew closer, she knew they must be similar creatures. Spook apparently thought the same.

"How'd they *train* them?" he suddenly muttered in awe.

The Dom ranks were peeling back, doubling at a trot and leaving a large gap for the monsters to pass through as they approached. Blas could see them fairly clearly now; enormous cousins to the aal-o-saur-like creatures Dennis Silva had dubbed "super lizards" that haunted the interior of Borno. Super lizards were bad, measuring up to twenty tails in length and able to reach as high as the main yard on a ship, but these, with the same terrible jaws, were possibly twice as big. They seemed to be all head and tail, perched atop long, powerfully made legs. It struck her as odd that they didn't have any forelegs at all that she could see, like humongous skuggiks, which were common carrion eaters in the West. She shook her head, and for an instant she railed to herself that the air corps should've warned them. But there weren't many planes left, and she hadn't heard any over the battle today. And even if they'd been present, they might not have seen them. Colored like dark tree bark, the monsters might've approached invisibly in the dark, then the shadow of the mountains, finally to come closer under cover of the smoke and fog.

Blas suddenly realized the method the Doms used to control them was almost as amazing as the creatures themselves. Their jaws were chained shut at present, and more chains spiderwebbed away from great iron collars fastened around their necks. The chains were secured to a dozen of the big, fat, armored creatures the Doms used to move their heavy artillery, that strained against the chains at the urging of hundreds of men in bright red and black hooded robes. The Dom infantry, still under fire, shuffled more tightly together to make the gap wider as the "super-duper lizards" (Fred's name for the things reemerged in her mind) were led nearer by their bizarre handlers. As the first monster passed them, the Dom infantry advanced. Near panic had erupted, even among Blas's Marines, because it was obvious what the Doms meant to do with the things.

"Stand fast!" she bellowed with all she had left, her shout carrying in that peculiar way only Lemurians' voices could, as far away as the two lunettes on either side of her Marines and the Maa-ni-la 'Cats to her right. "Runners! Take to all stations, and personally ensure that Col-nol Blair and Gener-aal Shinyaa are aware that the Doms've led Fred and Kari's monsters against us! Tell 'em we need ammo *now*, and probably the reserve! Go! Aar-tillery, commence firing!" She paced a few steps, heart pounding, even as the first load of canister sprayed the closest beast. Hooded figures went down all around it, but it shook itself and trudged on, apparently unconcerned. "Solid shot!" she screamed. "Solid shot only at the monsters! Save your canister for the Doms!" They'd need every bit, she realized, because *all* the Doms were coming now, including those that had retreated. And in the distance, beyond the monsters, she could just make out more infantry with red-faced uniforms. . . .

Hooded figures pulled cables leading to the terrible jaws, and the confining chains slackened and fell away. Awarded partial freedom, the first great beast opened its mouth and roared its triumph, a sort of thunderous gobbling sound, before stooping to snatch one of its handlers. At the same time, the other chains attached to the iron collar dropped to the ground. The big armored creatures that kept it confined rolled in the dust when the tension left, but quickly rose and lumbered to the side, dragging their chains and flailing their tails to discourage pursuit. The giant lizard took a couple experimental steps, seeming tempted to chase them, but rifle fire was peppering it now and it didn't like that a bit. *Has to sting*, Blas snorted to herself, but the sarcastic thought was edged with a creeping terror. Even the big guns of the colonials were apparently not penetrating sufficiently to do serious harm. But they did make it mad—and Blas suddenly realized that was what the Doms had counted on. It lunged forward, past its scattering handlers, toward the source of its torment. Several guns fired at once but missed. The thing was amazingly fast for its size, moving like a two-legged serpent, its head and tail swaying from side to side as it quickly negotiated the entanglements, tearing barbed wire as if it were rotten vines and scattering stakes like twigs. In just a few more steps, it started up the slope, meeting a hail of bullets, and churned directly at Blas.

In that moment, as had happened long before, and for the first time since that dreadful night in *Mahan*'s steering engine room, Blas was silenced and immobilized by panic. She'd been a youngling then, in every sense of the word, and there'd been nothing she could do. But her powerlessness in the face of such an unimaginable violation still haunted her, as did an obsessive determination never to experience such a feeling again. That's why she became a Marine, even reveling in the risks that entailed, because she could confront them with friends at her side and a weapon in her hands, and each time she did so, the memory of that terrible night faded a bit more from her mind. But in the face of the monstrous juggernaut of flesh stalking toward her, she felt like a helpless youngling again. She didn't run, as all her senses demanded, but she didn't do anything else. She just stood there, stunned, as the great jaws opened toward her.

A twelve-pounder in a covered embrasure just below her feet fired directly into the monster, and it staggered back. The concussion of the report struck her like a slap and she shook her head, clearing the unnerving trance that had engulfed her. A great bloody hole had bloomed on the monster's belly, smoke and black blood coursing out, but Blas gathered with amazement that the shot didn't exit! Comparably speaking, shooting the thing with a twelve-pounder was probably like shooting a rhino pig with a .45. Chances were it would die—eventually—but the wound only enraged it further. Like a striking snake, it chomped down on the protruding muzzle of the gun and dragged the whole two-ton weapon through its embrasure, shattering its wheels and casting it away like a toy. Another gun, atop the parapet, hit it in its narrow chest from the side, and that shot *did* exit, blowing a gaping, jagged-ribbed hole, and warbling off into the distance. The beast fell then. Perhaps its spine was broken? Its body slid down and lay still over the embrasure it had opened. Blas, still recovering from the shame and terror of what she considered a flare of cowardice, had no time to appreciate that small favor because there were more monsters coming. Just as bad, the Doms were sweeping forward in their deep ranks, followed by hordes of Blood Drinkers.

"Quit shootin' at the daamn lizards! We just pissin' 'em off! Fire at the Doms!" she screamed at her Marines. "All aar-tillery between the lunettes will target the big lizards!" She coughed. "Runner!" she managed.

"Col-nol Blair is here!" First Sergeant Spook declared, pointing and breathing hard. He'd been shooting at the monster too and now returned to her side. Blair and a small staff were still mounted, just below her, amid men carrying crates of ammunition up the slope to the 'Cats above. She shouted down at him, "It's here! All is coming *here*! We must have our reserves!" She could see nothing of the battle elsewhere around the fort, but couldn't imagine the Doms had the resources to make such an effort in more than one, maybe two places at once.

"Are you sure of that?" Blair demanded.

"*Sure* I'm sure. The monsters and Blood Drinkers had to have come last night!" she explained desperately. "They would've been seen from the air or by the spies still reportin' if they'd been assemblin' long enough to build a bigger force than that!" She waved at the monsters and men coming for her. "An' this is the closest point of contact! They came in last night, and Nerino's thrown 'em straight at the closest 'weak' point we showed him! It's here!"

Blair finally nodded, seeing the sense of that and trusting her instincts. But then, to her surprise, he hesitated. "I'm sorry, Captain Blas, but my new orders from General Shinya are that no reserves be committed to the outer wall for any reason." He waved helplessly up at one of the observation towers behind the inner wall. "I suppose he has his reasons, or sees—and hears by wireless—what we do not." He looked at her earnestly. "That said, I will find *some* reinforcement for you, from an unengaged portion of the outer wall if I must. Can you hold long enough for troops to come from the west side of the fort?"

Blas turned, feeling violated again in a different way. She'd been promised the Guayakans as a reserve, and they were ready and waiting less than a hundred yards away, atop the wall behind her. *They* could get here in time, but could anyone else? A furious fire was stripping men from the advancing Dom ranks, and a cheer announced that another of the monsters had been struck by a gun, its head becoming a ragged, bloody mass of shattered bone and teeth, and it fell in the path of another huge beast. But she reckoned it had taken ten or twenty shots to hit it, and those behind—she counted ten more at a glance—had all been released and were charging forward as if confident that a huge feast lay beyond her wall. She suspected they'd been conditioned to that belief somehow; to race toward shooting, expecting to feed. Cannon were very difficult to aim at moving targets. Even with the instantaneous ignition of the new friction primers, one had to point the gun where one hoped the target would be when it was fired—after its crew had a moment to get out of the way. The monster behind the dead one simply leaped the corpse and hurried on, its long strides devouring ground.

"No," she answered bitterly. "We can't hold 'em that long, and any disorganized reserves dribblin' in will only block our path of retreat."

Blair nodded again, as if that was what he'd expected her to say. "Then hold as long as you can. Fall back to the second wall when you must. The Guayakans will provide covering fire. I'll join you there after I spread the word—and see the situation elsewhere for myself." With that, he spurred his horse southward, followed by his staff.

And just like that, In Blas's mind, and entirely without warning, General Tomatsu Shinya had sacrificed the 2nd of the 2nd Marines, the 3rd Saint Francis, and the entire 8th Maa-ni-la. Three more monsters quickly died in a barrage of cannon fire, crushing dozens of screaming men when they fell. And not all the monsters were content to delay their feast until they breached the fort. A couple, at least, strolled through the enemy ranks, leisurely eating men packed too closely to flee. The screams that rose above the roar of battle were terrible to hear. But when the first wave of Dom regulars, many returning for a second time, slammed into her Marines' battered shields, Blas finally realized that trying to fall back now would likely prove just as difficult as holding her position. With the artillery largely devoted to firing at the monsters, only the Imperial guns in the lunettes could sweep the Doms. Those were *big* guns, but even more impossible to aim at moving monsters.

They laid a terribly destructive, enfilading fire into the enemy's flanks, but it simply wasn't enough given the weakness on the ramparts and the greater weight of the new attack. Granted, most of the Dom infantry was just as exhausted and terrified as the defenders, but they had the Blood Drinkers pushing them on. There'd be no lull, no momentary respite she could use to disengage and pull back to the inner wall. Maybe her Marines and the Maa-ni-los to her right were making time for some other plan to unfold, but that went increasingly beyond their concern. They fought for their lives, and when any hope for survival faded, they fought to take another breath. Everyone knew that as soon as the first Doms broke through, they'd be overwhelmed.

Blas found herself closer to the Maa-ni-los, where their left had become mixed with her right. She stabbed past the shields with her bayonet as her self-appointed colonial guards stayed close by her side. She still didn't know why they stuck so close, but they were good fighters and she certainly didn't mind. Spook stayed near as well, occasionally stepping into a gap and hosing the enemy with his BAR, but his "couple more" magazines had to be nearly exhausted by now. The slope below was choked with corpses and the footing was terrible for the attackers, but still they surged and roared, banging on shields and stabbing past them with their plug bayonets. A monster lizard had paused, just beyond the raging fight, to snack on the unprecedented buffet, when a cannonball slammed into the meaty part of its tail, just behind its mighty haunches. It roared indignantly, spewing gobbets of men from its mouth, and lunged at the wall. Doms screamed and tried to make way, but the crush was just too tight. Many were pulped beneath its feet as the ranting beast stepped almost effortlessly to the top of the rampart and paused to gaze around.

It was too much. The 'Cats nearest its feet fled first, tumbling back, and then ran to the rear. The Doms didn't take advantage at first—they couldn't—but after a long moment, apparently surveying the delicacies to be had within the fort, the great lizard marched down the slope and the northeast wall of Fort Defiance was broken.

Everywhere else, all along the northeast line between the lunettes, a great shout arose, and the Doms streamed through the gap or over the crumbling shield wall.

"Fall back!" Blas croaked. "Fall back to the second wall! Captain

Finny!" she said, seeing her friend's blood-matted face fur. "Spread the word! Fall back!" Something grabbed her arm, and she lashed out, hitting Spook in the chest.

"That means you too!" he yelled, pulling her along. "You," he shouted at the colonials. "Help me get her out of here."

They dashed down the slope, at first pulling, then following Blas as she sprinted back to gain enough distance to see. The wall was going fast, eroded under a yellow tide that crested over it—and her Marines—before streaming down toward her. There was still desperate fighting, but 'Cats fought and died alone now, or in pathetic little clumps. It helped some that the Doms were so terrified of their beast because they avoided it, even while Lemurians fled past it, not realizing it was so close. Vicious struggles erupted around gun embrasures where, with some protection, larger clots of Marines made their stand. Added to that, the Guayakans directly behind them on the second wall opened up, their muskets flailing at the swarming Doms. That threw them into further confusion and bought time for a couple hundred more Marines and Maa-ni-los to escape.

"Lieu-ten-aant Stumpy!" Blas called, seeing her other old shipmate limping away from the fight. "Where's your cap-i-taan?"

Blinking misery, Stumpy waved back at the firing step above and Blas gulped back a sob. She'd just seen Finny—and now he was dead. She shook it off. No time now.

A lone cannon barked at the monster, striding away toward the northeast lunette. The gun was incredibly loud down between the walls, even though Blas saw that it was just a six-pounder. That meant that the three 'Cats working it, the last bloody, limping remnant of its crew, must've dragged it all the way down from the top of the rampart where the lighter guns had been. The shot grazed the monster deeply along its side, and it spun to face them. "Leave it!" Blas shouted. "Come on!"

"You go!" cried the 'Cat gunner, his crew already reloading the weapon from satchels they carried. "We gonna kill dat teeng an' save our gun! We had dis gun sinst Aryaal!"

Blas blinked, then turned to Stumpy. "Get our people to safety. Then cover us! I want ten volunteers!"

"But!"

"Go!"

Blas wasn't sure why it suddenly became so important to her to save that one little gun when they'd just lost twenty. And six-pounders, considered obsolete by many, were the lightest, least powerful they had anymore. That struck her strangely, considering there'd been *no* artillery just a few years before. But she was determined to make up for what she considered her cowardice in the face of the first monster, and now the loss of her position—not to mention her fury at the enemy—and General Shinya. All those things drove her now. And it might've also been because that gun had suffered at Aryaal too. . . .

The Doms held back, afraid of the charging monster and the fusillade of fire from the second wall. The gunner centered his sight on the middle of his target with a glance, pierced the charge through the vent, and stepped away. Another 'Cat inserted the primer with a lanyard attached, stretched it taut, and nodded at his gunner.

"Fire!"

The gun roared and jumped back, the wheels grumbling and the trail skating across the gravelly earth. The shot was well placed, striking the monster high in the belly, but if a twelve-pounder couldn't exit there, a six-pounder certainly couldn't. The monster staggered, but shrieked and advanced.

"To the rear!" yelled the gunner. "To the gate!" There were two small gates in the inner wall, heavily reinforced, and they were closer to the more southerly one—but so was the monster. They had to go back. More than ten willing pairs of hands grabbed the gun's trail handles, wheels, anything they could grasp, and accelerated to a clumsy trot. "Load!" the gunner cried.

"I only had the one!"

"Me too!" cried the other cannoneer breathlessly as they ran. The satchels were used only to bring a single fixed charge to the gun at a time, and there wouldn't have been any in them at all if they hadn't been firing so fast. The gunner reached into his own satchel that he'd hastily grabbed and pulled out a shot strapped to a wooden sabot atop a wool-like powder bag.

"Case shot," he gasped, disappointed. Then he grinned, pierced the paper fuse at the one-second mark, and trotted over to shove the whole thing in the muzzle. "Raam it!" he ordered.

The female 'Cat with the rammer staff was limping badly, having trouble keeping up. She glanced over her shoulder at the monster, closing. "What good dat do? Is too light! It not even go as deep as solid shot!" she trilled.

"Raam it!" the gunner roared. She did—and then spun to the ground as musket balls began striking around them. The Doms may not have wanted to get in the way of the charging monster, but they were still in the fight.

"Drop it! Drop it now! Staan clear!" the gunner cried, and Blas and the others let the trail slam down. The gunner only glanced at the lay of the gun; there wasn't time to aim, and it looked close enough. Instead, he pierced the charge, stuffed a primer in the vent himself, and, hopping away, pulled the lanyard.

The gun bellowed almost in the monster's face, sending smoke gushing up around it. The shot struck close to where the second one had, with no more apparent effect—until it detonated inside the beast. A cascade of dark flesh, bone fragments, loops of entrails, and a few hissing shards of iron joined the smoky fountain of blood that sprayed across Blas and her impromptu artillerists. The monster had been blown over onto its back, and its feet flailed at the sky.

"Let's go!" Blas shouted, reaching for the trail handle again. A great cheer erupted from the Guayakans, and strangely, few Doms fired at them before they finally reached the gate and dashed inside. By then the enemy had swarmed down into the lane between the walls and filled it with their thousands. For the moment, they had nowhere to go. The inner wall was sheer and couldn't be scaled without ladders—which the Doms hadn't expected to need. It wasn't until after the gate closed behind her and she was half-carried up to the top of the inner rampart to view the battle from above that Blas finally understood the genius—and cold-blooded ruthlessness—of General Shinya's battle plan. She glanced at her wall and saw the Blood Drinkers cresting it now, swarming down to join their comrades. She knew that if any of her people had survived to that point, in the gun embrasures, for example, the remorseless Blood Drinkers would quickly wipe them out. The fur on her face was thick and crackly with drying blood, but tears filled her eyes and she looked up at the sky. She was amazed to see that the sun stood nearly overhead. This time it felt like she'd been fighting for hours, but she couldn't account for them. She looked down and caught sight of Colonel Blair, bailing off his horse and rushing up the ladder to one of the observation towers.

That's where Gener-aal Shinya must be, she thought bitterly. *Baastard.*

With the lane between the walls now clear of all of Blair's retreating defenders, and the space quickly filling with more thousands of roaring, triumphant men in yellow uniforms, new embrasures opened halfway up the high palisade and vomited fire into the milling enemy from perhaps forty guns.

Sister Audry's horse stumbled, nearly pitching her over its head. It was one of those lightly wounded earlier that day, and even under her minimal weight, the killing pace they'd set had finally worn it down. Colonel Garcia caught her and quickly, effortlessly, plucked her from the animal and placed her behind him on his own.

"Colonel!" she protested, but said nothing more.

"Your animal is finished, Santa Madre," he said gently. "Mine also," he admitted. He'd been pushing his harder than most, occasionally scouting ahead. "But we are near," he added grimly. "Teniente Pacal!" he shouted. "A horse for the Santa Madre!"

"Stop calling me that!" Audry demanded fiercely. "I'm a simple servant of the Lord Jesus Christ, who does her best not to stretch too many of the blessed Saint Benedict's rules, nothing more. And you promised!"

"You are far more than that to your men," Garcia corrected, then smiled. "And I only promised not to call you that in front of people."

"You just did!"

"Teniente Pacal is one of *your* people."

"That doesn't matter! And there are others here as well," she sniffed, nodding farther back where Rebecca and Saan-Kakja shared a horse surrounded by Koratin and their remaining escort. Koratin was riding double with Selass. "And I do not need a horse to myself. Few enough remain to go around." There was no doubt of that. They had a total of six "spares" left, and the animals had begun failing them at an ever-increasing rate, utterly spent.

Sister Audry rolled her eyes impatiently, but allowed herself to be placed on one of the captured Dom horses that one of Pacal's men brought. She watched with remorse as her previous mount stopped trotting and sagged with exhaustion. She hoped it would recover. They'd destroyed so many of the precious beasts, still not terribly numerous on this world, during the arduous trek. She glanced forward, toward the roiling cloud of gun smoke rising above the distant, still-hidden fort. The smoke glowed orange brown under the lowering sun. *But Colonel Garcia is right*, she realized. *We are almost there at last.*

The sixty-mile march from Puerto Viejo to Fort Defiance had turned into a grueling, bloody torture test. It started well enough, with the Redentores and 1st Maa-ni-la riding atop or behind every animal they could find, and they made good time in the misty dark. Dawn found their strung out, ragged column more than a third of the way to their destination, despite the delays, but suddenly faced by two thousand Dom lancers, apparently headed for the city they'd left behind. The Doms quickly and professionally deployed from column into line, lowered their terrifying lances, and charged.

Probably only the Maa-ni-los' breechloaders saved them from being slaughtered. The breechloaders—and Sergeant Koratin. Without even thinking about it, he essentially took command, roaring for the carts and animals in the lead to curl back down the road to the rear, while the back of the column raced ahead. He'd hoped to form an impromptu square. What resulted was more of a blob—but a *compact* blob that assembled just in time to receive the lancer's charge from behind the protection of its carts and animals. So what should've been a massacre of the relief force in the open, rolling hills, became a slaughter of the cream of the Holy Dominion as a thousand breech-loading rifles and eight hundred muskets loaded with buck and ball stalled the charge at the last frantic instant with a stunning volley. The lancers were disciplined, hardened veterans of frontier clashes with bandits, rebels, and even monsters, and they fought hard; wheeling and stabbing at horses with their lances, or firing back with their carbines. They reaped a terrible toll among the animals and unprotected defenders, but while they did, they were swept from their saddles by a volume of fire they'd never endured before.

Time may occasionally be needed to shift mental gears, when one confidently expects a certain outcome, only to be confronted by something utterly unexpected, and that brief, precious moment was all it took in this situation to empty a great many Dom saddles. More were killed as they tried to regroup, still stunned by their first encounter with breechloaders and the impossible rate of fire they maintained, but then they shattered and fled, galloping off to the north, their glistening, well-ordered squadrons reduced to a chastened mob half its original size. But that left the aftermath.

Hundreds of Doms lay dead or wounded, and nearly a hundred Allied men and 'Cats had been killed or seriously hurt in the sharp, close fight. Too many animals had been killed or wounded as well. Quite a few riderless Dom horses were quickly rounded up, but many of those were injured. Then there was very nearly a fight between the 1st Maa-ni-la and the Redentores when Lemurians began killing Dom survivors. The 1st was an elite regiment despite its lack of combat experience, and it had been formed with the expectation that it would fight the Grik. The Grik gave no quarter, and the notion of mercy to the enemy had never been explored by Lemurians before, so they only did what came naturally. Doms didn't take prisoners either, except as slaves or to feed their dragons, and they rarely surrendered—but the Imperials did take prisoners, and the Redentores were the beneficiaries of that. A tense moment flared when these two conflicting philosophies clashed. Ultimately, Rebecca and Sister Audry prevailed on a confused Saan-Kakja to help them break up the confrontation, and the shouting, escalating altercation between furious men and baffled, angry 'Cats subsided without bloodshed. But the original plan was done.

"How many troops can we mount double on the horses that remain, including the ones we captured?" Rebecca had demanded, thinking fast. It was quickly discovered that they had about four hundred uninjured animals, and another hundred with light wounds. Three Lemurians could ride an animal that could carry two humans, so it was decided to push on with roughly half of each regiment, entirely mounted, while the rest stayed to guard the wounded and the carts with enough of the lightly hurt horses to either continue the march or return to the city as ordered. In the meantime, they'd stay where they were and the corps-'Cats would set up a field hospital.

So the relief force was cut in half, but it could move much faster. It would have to, to reach Fort Defiance before dark. The little battle and its aftermath had cost them two hours.

Now they were close. Their animals were finished, but the combined regiment, though tired, could still fight. The question was, where and how? Shinya knew they were coming. That had been sent before they left. And a couple of Nancys had seen them approaching as the day wore on, one dropping a message trailing a streamer that described the battle at Fort Defiance. The news was grim. The northeast wall had fallen, but untold thousands of Doms had been slaughtered between the walls before the Blood Drinkers turned guns that hadn't been spiked or brought up their own, using the captured wall as their own fortification. For most of the day, the battle had degenerated into a close-range slugging match between the two walls, like immobile, unsinkable ships, just blasting away at each other. Shinya still had one advantage; his north lunette, with the 1st of the 10th Imperial, still held, firing down the flank of the Doms. The east lunette had been taken with the help of one of the monstrous lizards the message described, but it was believed that all of those terrible beasts were now dead, or had simply gone away. There'd been no word after that.

"Colonel," a scout cried from a distance, his lathered horse's tongue lolling, incapable of more than a brisk walk. "Santa Madre!" Audry took a sharp breath and glared at Colonel Garcia as the man drew closer. Rebecca, Saan-Kakja, Koratin, and Selass managed to coax their horses forward to hear the expected report.

"What did you see?" Garcia demanded.

"The battle looks much as described before," the swarthy man replied in Spanish, thickly accented with something else, and Garcia quickly interpreted. "It is difficult to see through the smoke," he confessed. "The enemy attacks from everywhere now, but only in sufficient strength, I think, to prevent General Shinya from further weakening those points to thicken his defense on the eastern side. There is one exception. The enemy now makes a strong assault on the northern-gate bastion."

"That is where we must strike," Garcia said to the others.

Koratin was nodding. "If we can hit them from behind or on the flank, we might break that attack, and so enter the fort at least."

Garcia nodded back. "At least," he agreed. "Can we approach unseen?" he demanded of the scout.

"Perhaps. The terrain is still somewhat rolling, and there is a depression we might use, along the bed of the stream that passes through the fort."

"There will be scouts," Koratin warned.

"I expect their attention to be largely inward, toward the fight," Garcia agreed, "but we will send skirmishers ahead." He looked at the two leaders. "With your permission, I propose this as our strategy: The horses are useless to us now, so we should dismount and quick-march the rest of the way, using cover to get as close to the enemy as we can. Then we attack." He spread his hands apologetically. "It is risky, and surprise is our only hope. If we are caught short, with fewer than a thousand troops, we may not be able to break through to the fort, so I must insist that you all"—his gaze swept across Audry, Rebecca, and Saan-Kakja—"remain safely back."

Saan-Kakja barked a laugh. "Safely? We could not escape on these weary beasts if we wanted to, and we would no doubt be safer among our troops, even fighting." Her tone turned to iron. "And speaking for myself and my sister, I can tell you that we did not come here to run away!"

"Indeed. Don't be ridiculous, Arano," Sister Audry said. "As you say, the Redentores are *my* troops. My warriors of God. I know I am not fit to lead them properly, but I will certainly accompany them into battle!"

"It is decided, then," Rebecca said firmly. "Sergeant Koratin, please pretend you have been the colonel in command of this combined force, if only for this day."

Koratin blinked resentfully at her, but nodded. "Very well. For this day. Dismount and form the troops, Col-nol Gar-ciaa," he said.

Garcia gave the order, then turned to Sister Audry. "Before we make our attack, might I beg a prayer from you? For all of us?"

Sister Audry's face grew soft. "Of course, Arano. Of course."

Fort Defiance

Captain Blas-Ma-Ar and Colonel Blair had rounded up what remained of the 2nd of the 2nd Marines, the 8th Aryaal, and the 3rd Saint Francis into what amounted to a single understrength regiment. Most were bandaged and all were exhausted, but they'd assembled in the vicinity of the inner-wall gate to the north lunette, resting, tending wounds, and trying to push the morning's trauma to the back of their minds for a time. They also waited for the inevitable command to plug back in the line, somewhere, as the thunder of battle roared beyond the palisade. The Doms still held Blas's wall, and they were still pouring into the gap between it and the palisade, so it might've looked to General Nerino that they were making headway. But those who actually entered the fort were being torn apart by the guns in the palisade and the rifles and muskets on top. It was the only breakthrough the Doms had managed, and Nerino was obligingly dropping chunk after chunk of his army into the meat grinder that Fort Defiance had become, and that General Shinya had, apparently, envisioned it would be.

"You knew," Blas said to Blair as they sat together on the rocky ground.

"Yes," he confessed.

"Why didn't you tell me?"

Blair sighed. "I don't know. I should have, I suppose. General Shinya told me not to, but I should have."

"Did he think I wouldn't have fought as hard?"

"I doubt it," Blair replied, considering. "But he probably thought, rightly, that you would've prepared a more orderly withdrawal, more conscious of saving as many as you could."

"So, in other words, he needed it to look like the disaster it was, to convince the Doms to pour everything they had in after us," she suggested bitterly.

"I expect so," Blair agreed softly.

"With help, we could've held them," Blas insisted.

"Against the monsters?" Blair asked. He shook his head. "No one expected *them*, and I think they would've broken through *somewhere*, no matter what we did. Better that they did so where we were best prepared, and that they spent themselves in the effort." He looked at her sternly. "And what if you had held? Good for you, but not perhaps for the battle. The biggest problem with any defense of the sort we've mounted here is getting the enemy to commit the bulk of his force exactly where we want him, where we could mass sufficient numbers to destroy him! Hate General Shinya if you like, but as your focus has been the well-being of your battalion"—he paused—"and my first concern has been my division while I have been his second in command, he seeks to win a war. He must bear the guilt for what he did to you—to me—today, and all the fine troops we lost. But his strategy seems to have worked, after all, and thank God he was willing to shoulder that burden for us, Captain Blas!" he ended firmly.

A new commotion was rising beyond the gate to the north lunette, and the big guns there, silent for some time, were roaring again.

"It seems not *all* the Doms are content to be funneled meekly to Shinya's slaughter," Blas observed coldly.

A mounted 'Cat courier galloped up in a cloud of dust, saluting Colonel Blair as he stood. "Report!" Blair demanded.

"Gen'raal Shin-yaa's compliments, sur, but the Doms is hittin' the north lunette, tryin' to widen the gap. He figgers it's their last chance to break in here, an' they gotta know it too. Thowin' all they got lef' at it. He asks can you lead your division thoo the gate an' reinforce the lunette? You about all the reserve we got lef, not engaged."

Blair helped Blas to her feet, then dusted off his uniform coat and straightened it. "Inform General Shinya that Captain Blas and I will lead what's left of my division not still in action—please stress those combined regiments number only about eight hundred effectives—to the relief of my last *intact* regiment in the north lunette. Please also tell him that if we ask for further help, it is because we need it rather badly and he'd better find it somewhere if he truly wishes us to hold the position. The absence of necessary reserves in this case will indicate to me that he *wants* the north lunette to fall, and I will attempt to abandon it in as noisy and apparently disorganized fashion as I can manage with the least loss of life."

Blas snorted beside him and he glanced at her. "Let that suffice," he told her. "I do thank God for General Shinya, but am somewhat unhappy with him myself. He should know who he can trust by now, in any situation." He looked at the wide-eyed messenger. "Go," he ordered, then turned to the heavy gate leading to the north lunette. It wasn't barred, since corps-'Cats were still carrying wounded out, and Blair had visited the regiment there himself. "Open it," he shouted to the guards on the rampart to either side, manning stout levers that could also be latched in place. As the gate swung wide, the roar of battle intensified and the battered remnant of Blair's division wearily, painfully, filed into the crucible once more.

"Charge them! Charge them now!" Governor-Empress Rebecca Anne McDonald urged Sergeant Koratin. Assisted by the failing light, they'd crept within two hundred yards of the north gate of the fort before the gully abandoned them and left a closer undetected approach impossible.

Koratin glanced at the setting sun, then looked back at the Doms now swarming around the lunette. The firing was intense and the great guns churned bloody gaps in the Dom horde surging against the earthen wall, but the Doms weren't breaking. It was if they sensed that here, at last, they'd found the weak point that would take them past the inner wall. They might be right, since there weren't nearly as many guns backing the lunette, nor could as many troops fire down on them from above once they broke through. Koratin considered. The attack also had the feel of desperation to him. He didn't know what was happening on the other side of the fort, but the volume of fire was amazing. The main attack must still be there. But this one was pressing as hard as it could, five or six thousand strong, and heavy as it was, there appeared to be no reserve. "We can't just charge them, Your Majesty!" he objected with an amused blink. "We owe it to our audience to perform for maximum effect!" Rebecca hesitated, then smiled while Saan-Kakja blinked uncomprehendingly.

One of Koratin's greatest joys in his former life was helping to organize little dramas; plays, performed by younglings in the forums of Aryaal. At the time, his life had been focused on drama and intrigue of a far more serious nature, but the innocent little plays he arranged had been his sweetest pleasure. All that was gone and dead, as was the person he'd been, he hoped, but he'd learned a little about creating a vivid impression. "With your permission, Your Majesty?"

Rebecca nodded. "Of course. I told you that you command here today."

"Col-nol Garciaa, Your Excellency Saan-Kakja, and . . ." He grinned. "Col-nol Santa Madre," he said to Sister Audry, "when I give the word, I want the entire force to rush forward one hundred tails and form into line, facing the enemy, with our backs to the setting sun. The line will be long and with the glare, the Doms cannot know it consists of but a single rank. At my command, the Redentores will fire a volley. That should get the attention of the enemy and our friends—we don't want to be shot down by our own people! The Redentores will reload as quickly as they can, and the entire command will fire a volley together. More will be looking then, and it will appear most impressive!" He looked at Rebecca. "*Then* we charge, with the first Maa-ni-la firing their breechloaders as we go! They will think a third rank charges with us that had not yet fired, and our nine hundred troops will seem two or three thousands at least!"

Rebecca grinned back at him. "Very well. But if we are to perform a drama, let us make the most of it!"

Horns and whistles trilled and blared, and the Redentores and 1st Maa-ni-la erupted out of the draw and ran forward, their polished weapons glaring red beneath the setting sun. At one hundred yards, the horns blew again and the entire force slammed to a stop, quickly dressing their line, and poising their weapons high in the prescribed manner of Imperial troops. Behind them, exhausted horses, tied together, were led forward as well; not that they'd be of any use in the attack, but to create an impression of additional mass and movement. Flags were uncased at intervals to stream in the freshening afternoon breeze. There was no "Union" flag as yet, but the Stainless Banner of the Trees unfurled, as did the striped flag of the Empire of the New Britain Isles. The regimental flag of the 1st Maa-ni-la, a golden sunburst in a black field, was joined by the flag of the Redentores, which represented Sister Audry's chief contribution to the formation of "her" regiment. Painted on another stainless field was the image of Saint Benedict holding a cross and his book of rules, surrounded by several prayers and phrases, roughly translated into English, which the Imperial troops who fought alongside them could easily understand and embrace. All seemed particularly appropriate to the soldiers fighting under it: "May He protect us in the hour of death," "May the Holy Cross light my way," and "Begone Satan!" Perhaps most fitting on that day were the phrases "Let not the Dragon be my guide" and "The drink you offer is Evil. Drink it yourself!" Above all was the simple word "Pax" that Sister Audry had insisted on.

The Doms saw none of this. The flags were only dark silhouettes against the sunset. But they'd also learned their enemies didn't fight beneath nearly as many flags as they did, so four of them added to the impression of numbers. "Volley fire, present!" Sergeant Koratin roared, his voice carrying all the way to the enemy. "Fire!" The volley roared, amazingly tight, and slashed the Doms' right flank with "buck and ball"—four hundred musket balls and twelve hundred pieces of buckshot. Koratin allowed a pause while the Redentores reloaded their muskets, ramrods flashing above their heads and drums thundering behind the lines, ratcheting up the tension. A few shots came at them, but the Doms were likely mostly empty, shooting at the Lunette, or, having fixed their plug bayonets, were unable to fire anymore. A moan swept through them, punctuated by the shrieks of the wounded.

"Present!" Koratin yelled again, and every rifle and musket was leveled this time. "Fire!"

The second volley was devastating, collapsing the whole right flank of the Dom attack like hundreds of human dominoes. The defenders in the lunette, taking quick advantage, furiously poured a renewed fire into the enemy as well.

"Fix bayonets!" Koratin bellowed, repeated by Garcia, Rebecca, Saan-Kakja, dozens of noncoms, and even Sister Audry. With feral shouts, the Redentores and 1st Maa-ni-la drew their long, wicked blades, and flourished them at the enemy as if to show them what was coming before fastening them onto their barrels. Then, with the drums still thundering and the panic in the Dom ranks reaching a fever pitch, Sergeant Koratin gave a final command as loud as he could:

"Charge bayonets!"

In the lunette, Blas saw it all. She'd miraculously avoided any real wounds throughout the long, bitter day, but had just about decided she'd die of exhaustion anyway. The fighting was brutal, and had quickly gone to the bayonet in spite of the big naval guns emplaced there that fired torrent after torrent of canister. The noise was stupendous in the confined space, and through that and all the firing, she never heard the first horns and drums blaring from the relief force to her left. All she could do was concentrate on the fight right in front of her. Her arms ached so badly that she could barely heft her rifle anymore, much less parry and thrust with her blood-blackened bayonet. Her breath came in ragged heaves, and the smoke remained so thick that no breath seemed very useful. One of her two "bodyguards" had been killed, but the other stuck with her—as did Spook, though he'd replaced his beloved BAR with an Allin-Silva at some point. There was no more ammunition for the automatic rifle. Stumpy was still alive, the last she saw him, and Colonel Blair still survived, though the yellow facings on his uniform had turned just as red as the rest of his coat. He appeared occasionally, helping out at critical points with a mobile reserve he'd formed.

It had grown increasingly clear that with the bloody stalemate in the gap between her old position and the inner wall, this was where Nerino hoped to end it and had sent everything he had left. A few Nancys bombed the advance and their dwindling mortars clawed at it, but they quickly exhausted their mortars and just as had been the case all day, there wasn't enough air to make a serious difference. The planes *had* confirmed that no other significant enemy force remained in close reserve, however, and Shinya had reinforced the lunette from the south wall before he was even asked. Nonetheless, the planes had evidently reported something else, because General Shinya himself suddenly appeared at Blas's side.

"Check fire on the left!" he shouted. "Check fire on the left! We have friendlies approaching out of the sun!" It was then that Blas saw the ranks deploying across the field, their flags unfurling to stand out from their staffs, the muskets poised high and coming down. . . .

"Duck!" she croaked, dragging Spook to cover. Only a few balls *verped* by over her head, most striking the enemy—that was completely stunned by the unexpected fusillade. Even over all the noise and the deafness it had caused, she thought she heard a familiar voice call for a second volley. This had an even more devastating effect than the first, and the Doms right in front of her fell squalling and writhing in the dirt. The "Charge bayonets!" command was clear in the near silence that followed, and she stood to join Shinya, who'd never even crouched down.

With a mighty roar, the new formation, utterly unexpected by her, surged forward at a sprint—and the Doms that had pressed her so closely, in the face of such terrible slaughter, just gushed away. There was no other way to describe it. One moment they'd been standing, fighting for all they were worth, and the next they simply turned and fled, flowing past her like she'd heard the Grik once had between Fort Atkinson and Baalkpan at the great battle there. She lowered her rifle, her fingers numb around it, until the butt-plate rested on the ground, and watched the spreading rout.

"Friends! Friends! We're friends!" came a growing shout in front of the lunette as fleeing Doms were replaced by another force and the firing gradually tapered off. "Gener-aal Shinya!" shouted Sergeant "Lord" Koratin, a Lemurian Blas knew well, as he trotted breathlessly up the berm, between stunned troops and gory bayonets. He seemed not to notice them, but Blas knew everybody there recognized *him*.

"Sergeant Koratin," Shinya replied, getting the old 'Cat's attention, and Koratin saluted. Shinya returned it. "The Governor-Empress and their excellencies Saan-Kakja and Sister Audry are with me," Koratin said loudly, for the benefit of Shinya and everyone else.

"Cease firing!" Shinya ordered, though only a few were still shooting at the fleeing Doms. "Cease firing at once!" The three female leaders puffed up the rampart, avoiding the carpet of bodies, to a great, rising shout.

"General Shinya," Rebecca managed between deep breaths, "the First Maa-ni-la and the Redentores, around half of each at any rate, are at your service." She smiled. "Considering the day we had and the march we made, they are remarkably fresh, if you consider it appropriate that they should continue the pursuit."

"Indeed?" Shinya asked, looking at Garcia, just now cresting the wall. Saan-Kakja, not as reserved as her "sister," immediately embraced the Japanese officer she considered a dear friend. Shinya felt the same about her, but stiffened in her arms—as she'd expected he would. Sister Audry was also breathing hard, and beaming with pride.

"Indeed," Garcia confirmed. "The Redentores came to fight, as did the First Maa-ni-la. Let us pursue them!" he almost pleaded.

"I've heard a great deal about you, Colonel," Shinya said, "and I am glad you have justified our trust. By all means you may continue your pursuit—but wait a moment first. Open the gate!" he bellowed behind him, and as the gate swung open, all could see gathered there a large force, which immediately began filing into the lunette. It was led by Major Dao Iverson's 2nd Battalion of the 6th (Imperial) Marines, but many more waited to follow. Blas felt a surge of resentment. None of the troops she saw looked like they'd been closely engaged that day. "As soon as I heard of your approach," Shinya continued. "I hoped you would arrive in time to create the opportunity I have sought, an opportunity just like this. I've been preparing to break out here on my own, but you've provided a greater, less costly enemy reverse than I could've managed and I mean to make the most of it. Let the Doms, the 'Blood Drinkers' still on our northeast wall, see the enemy run from here a moment longer. Let the panic you caused infect them as well. *Then* we will all pursue them, those that can," he added, glancing at Blas and blinking his version of something like regret.

"What if the Blood Drinkers don't run?" Blair demanded sharply, hobbling up to join them. "They usually don't, you know." Blas hoped he was just exhausted and not wounded, but she couldn't tell in the deepening gloom.

"Then we'll surround them, take them between fires from inside and out, and exterminate them to the last man if we must," Shinya said mildly. He sighed. "I told you before. We *will* win a great victory today, and many have contributed to it far beyond my expectations. You, for one, Colonel Blair." He nodded at Sister Audry, Koratin, Garcia, Rebecca, and Saan-Kakja. "You as well." His eyes found Blas, leaning now on her rifle. "And you perhaps most of all. I won't forget."

"Neither will I," Blas promised, her tone tired and dark.

Shinya nodded understanding. "You will rest," he told her, "as will all who fought on the outer wall. But our larger force that your valor allowed me to keep within the inner wall has exercised only their rifles and guns today and remains ready to join the chase. *You* bought me that luxury, Captain Blas, and now we'll begin what you've so long desired." His voice rose so all could hear. "We will *chase* the Doms at last! We will chase them without pause or mercy!"

"How?" Sister Audry asked. "Our supply lines will be tenuous at best, we are still outnumbered, and we have no air support."

"Our supplies are tenuous—for now," he agreed. "And we're outnumbered, though I expect that to change with your help. Do you think Guayak and Puerto Viejo are unique? This entire continent chafes beneath the heel of the Dominion. I have no doubt our ranks will swell as we advance. And as for air cover, I know you brought more planes to Puerto Viejo—and we are perhaps not as short of them as I have been leading the enemy to believe, in any case," he added cryptically, then shook his head. "We can discuss all that later, but I believe you will appreciate my plan. For now, you, Saan-Kakja, and the Governor-Empress must retire inside the fort while we complete today's victory. None of you can be spared, nor should you ever have personally come here," he lightly scolded. "But now that you are here, please believe that this army, *your* army"—he smiled—"this 'Army of the Sisters,' I believe we shall call it, will soon have the initiative. And Don Hernan and the wicked empire he serves shall not draw a tranquil breath for the rest of the short time either one survives."

Gales in the West

Battle of the "Go Away Strait"
"2nd Grik City"
USS Tassat
September 17, 1944

I t was dawn over the Comoros Islands, and the southeast-ernmost one, the one infested by the largest number of Grik, was just a couple of miles to the southwest of Task Force Jarrik. The sky was like dull, weathered lead, and the sea was a similar, wetter, darker color, topped with slashes of near white. A stiff, northerly breeze stirred the sea and made it warm and humid—for now, but it was clear to all that a storm was brewing. USS *Tassat*, under Keje's cousin, Captain Jarrik-Fas, and her consort, USS *Haakar-Faask*, under Lieutenant Commander Niaal-Ras-Kavaat, constituted TF-Jarrik, and had been cruising south of the islands under topsails alone, keeping the watchful station they'd been assigned when the rest of First Fleet South steamed northeast to deal with the gathering Grik menace at the Seychelles.

Both DDs were *Haakar-Faask* Class square rig sailing steamers. Measuring two hundred feet in length with a beam thirty-six feet wide and displacing around sixteen hundred tons, they were not the newest wooden DDs in the Allied fleet, nor the oldest, and were two-thirds as long as *Walker* and actually heavier. Both were capable of making fifteen knots even with the new armor applied to protect their engineering spaces, and they were well armed with twenty 32-pounder smoothbores, Y guns, and depth charges.

Haakar-Faask carried 224 officers and enlisted, while *Tassat* had 230, about a quarter of whom were "exchange Impies." These were Imperial sailors and Marines assigned to "Lemurian-American" Navy ships to put more Imperials in the war in the West, while all Imperial ships remained in the fight against the Doms. It was a satisfactory arrangement for all concerned. The influx of volunteers from the Great South Isle would help the war effort amazingly—eventually. But those volunteers still had to be trained, and "Aus-traal-ans" didn't depend nearly as much on the sea as their cousins from the great seagoing Homes, or even those in Borno or the Filpin Lands. Most didn't even have the basic knack for seamanship that had made other Lemurians such quick learners. Factoring in the dreadful losses sustained by those more experienced 'Cats and the pace of operations that kept the rest so long deployed instead of rotating home to teach their skills, the shipyards at Baalkpan and Maa-ni-laa had outstripped the Allied ability to provide trained crews for even newer, more complicated designs. A simple lack of trained crews had created the greatest bottleneck to the deployment of ships that, had they been available, might already have turned the tide in the war.

Conversely, the Empire of the New Britain Isles was a seafaring nation. Its sailors were already well acquainted with steam power and relatively sophisticated ship designs, and Imperial vessels now under construction should have been able to cope with armored Grik warships. But those they had in service, with their exposed paddlewheels, were as hopelessly outclassed in "western" battle lines as dedicated sailors like *Donaghey* had become. Therefore, a growing number of "Impie" officers, particularly from nearer possessions such as Respite Island, were coming west to learn their trade while ships were made for them back home.

One such officer was Lieutenant Stanly Raj, who was acting as Jarrik-Fas's executive officer on *Tassat*. He now stood beside his shorter, bear-shaped Lemurian captain on the DD's quarterdeck near the exposed helm. The ship was currently hove to and still at morning GQ, her Nancy scout plane being prepared for launch. *Tassat* had no catapult and had to set the plane in the water where it would take off on its own.

"A little rough for this, don't you think?" Raj asked, gauging the wind and sea.

"Almost," Jarrik confirmed, "but my pilots are good. They've lifted from seas like this many times." He blinked. "Any worse and I wouldn't let them, though, and I might still have them divert to Grik City instead of trying to recover aboard here later, if the sea gets any friskier." He scratched the reddish brown fur above his eyes. "Especially since *Haa-kar-Faask* lost her plane, an' we couldn't get it replaced. Ours is the only one left out here. But it's also the only eyes we'll get in the sky today, and we gotta stay on guard."

"It does feel a bit . . . lonely out here at times," Raj observed wryly. "I concur that the Grik on the islands are no real threat, but with only our two ships standing between Grik City and the continent to the west— where all the Grik in the world reside . . . I certainly hope Captain Reddy is right about the Seychelles."

Jarrik grunted. "Me too. And he probably is. Reports have a *lot* of Grik ships gathered there." He blinked. "But I known Cap-i-taan Reddy a long time, an' sure as he might be, he's gonna want to watch for sneakin'." He grinned. "That's why we're here!"

The Nancy slapped the water and tried to surge against the side of the ship, but the boom held it away. Moments later, its observer propped the engine and when it was running smooth, the pilot pointed it away and the shackle attaching it to the boom was released. Immediately, the plane wallowed away from the ship.

"Secure from special air detail!" Raj called. "Resume course!" Piercing whistles shrieked, and men and 'Cats heaved on lines, bringing the yards back around where the sails could bite. Almost immediately, they felt the ship surge ahead.

"By the way," Jarrik said to Raj, "congratulations! It seems the victory at the Battle of Malpelo was more complete than first suspected. A large number of Dom ships that were thought to have escaped were later captured, severely damaged, and unable to keep up with their friends. Combined with reports from Fort Defiance, it seems things may be looking up in the East at last."

"Indeed, and thank you. The aftermath of battles on land and sea is often quite confused, it appears," Raj observed. "What seems like a defeat, or perhaps a draw in this case, may turn out to be a great victory, under further scrutiny."

"It is natural," Jarrik said. "I've been in enough battles to understand that one rarely knows what's happening beyond one's own view, much less how an entire, sprawling battle proceeds. And it's equally natural to concentrate on one's own wounds before devoting much interest to how badly one's opponent is hurt." He snorted a Lemurian chuckle. "And in this case it seems High Ahd-mi-raal Jenks was quite busy gently probing his broken nose while what remained of the Dom fleet dragged itself away, trailing its entrails!"

"An appropriate, if somewhat disrespectful metaphor," Raj conceded a little stiffly.

Jarrik blinked amusement. "No disrespect. He won a great victory, as did Gener-aal Shinya. And like all victories, it remains to be seen how complete they were. But certainly the war in the East can now proceed more briskly?"

"Let us hope so, and hope also that Captain Reddy can achieve a similar victory north of here."

"As you say, 'indeed.'" Jarrik swished his tail, watching the Nancy disappear in the sky to the south. "Malpelo was a helluva fight, and there will be another one today. Just two days ago," he said, his tone turning somber, "*Santy Cat* and *Arracca*'s battle group finally joined *Walker* east of the Seychelles after a hard voyage. They immediately proceeded to a point fifty miles south of the islands, and already—right now, most likely—the first planes from *Salissa* and *Arracca* are closing on the enemy anchorage. Soon the bombs will fall, the new Grik rockets will rise, and destruction will reign. People will die. Let us hope that surprise has been achieved and the cost will be light. But there will be a cost."

For the next half hour, *Tassat* and *Haakar-Faask* cruised on companionably, alone in the "Go Away Strait," with nothing but the Co-moros Islands to share the sea as far as the horizon in all directions but to the east, where Madagascar's low, dark form could be seen. And there was near silence aboard *Tassat* except for the pounding rush of the sea and the wind in her rigging. Everyone knew a great battle was shaping up to the north and time must pass before any reports were made. It remained unknown whether the enemy had the ability to monitor their wireless transmissions, but they proceeded under the assumption that it did. The codes had been changed, after cryptic orders to do so were received, and traffic was being kept to a normal minimum to prevent *any* listening enemy from suspecting anything was up, just in case.

Tassat's Lemurian signal officer scampered up the companionway from below and stood before Jarrik and Raj, eyes wide and blinking distress.

"Well? What is it?" Jarrik demanded. "Has the attack begun?"

"I, aah, not have news of the Saay-shells attaack yet, Cap-i-taan, but our scout makes a report!"

"Then spill it!" Jarrik demanded. "What have they seen?"

The 'Cat gulped and swished her tail in agitation. "Grik ships! Hundreds of 'em! All old Indiaa-maans like they use to carry warriors only, is thirty miles sou-sout'west o' here an' comin' this way!"

"How many 'hundreds'?" Jarrik snapped.

"I—I don't know."

"Then find out—and send to all stations: whatever the Grik are doing in the Seychelles, they're also hitting us here, *now*. Ask Gener-aal Safir Maraan to release all armed auxiliaries to join us near our current position. With this wind, they might just make it in time. Tell her also that we'll direct her aircraft as best we can, once we get a better fix on the enemy position." He paused. "And tell her that if the Grik are indeed in their 'hundreds,' we can't stop them alone and she must be prepared for a ground assault upon the city." He continued grimly. "Even if no surface elements survive, she should be able to predict where the enemy will strike by air observations, and deploy accordingly." Blinking irony, he looked at Lieutenant Raj. "It seems there'll be a 'helluva fight' here today as well."

Over the Seychelles

Captain Jis-Tikkar, COFO of Salissa's 1st Air Wing, and back with his Home where he belonged, led *Salissa's* and *Arracca's* combined air wings against the Grik anchorage in the Seychelles from the single seat of "his" P-1 Mosquito Hawk, or "Fleashooter." Much as he'd have preferred to fly "his" strange P-40E configured as a floatplane, that aircraft, draggy as it was with the big Japanese pontoons bolted on, was still too fast to keep formation with his other planes. Besides, as strapped as they were, he considered the P-40 too valuable to risk in this role—whether he survived to fly it again or not. *Big Sal* had only two short squadrons left, just under twenty Nancys, but *Arracca* had sent forty, plus a dozen "Fleashooters" configured for antiship attack, with no guns and a pair of fifty-pound bombs. Not since the air attacks preceding the First Battle of Madras had he had so many planes under his command—and now he had far better bombs, and voice communications via the miniaturized TBS sets now installed in all planes in the West! As his planes approached the anchorage, it looked like they'd achieved complete surprise. The ironclad Grik battleships, or "waagons," just lay there, moored nose to tail, and there was no smoke rising from their funnels. They didn't even have steam up! None of the cruisers was in view, so perhaps they were clustered around one of the other islands? But there were plenty of the ubiquitous Grik Indiamen that the enemy used to transport troops and supplies.

"Taally ho!" he cried into the clumsy microphone mounted on a boom in front of his face. "Odd-numbered flights target the waagons. The rest of you, burn down those transports!" Replies came fast and his planes bored in. It was then that he realized that not all the Grik were asleep. He'd examined the new antiair rockets they'd captured at Grik City. They were about two tails long and very narrow, with a nose shaped like a bullet and topped with a rather delicate-looking contact fuse like a big musket cap glued to a piece of tubing. Three fins were positioned toward the rear. In most respects, they looked just like oversize signal rockets to him, and if they hadn't already lost some planes to the things, he might've discounted them, imagining how hard it would be to hit a plane with a signal rocket. But he'd never seen them in action before and when clustered *shocks* of the things jetted into the sky in initially dense, but diverging patterns, he was surprised both by their speed and their sheer numbers. *Just like everything the Grik do, numbers are what make them dangerous,* he realized. A lot of the rockets went wild, cartwheeling in the sky, disrupting the flight of others, or just flipping manically along the ground until they went off with small explosions. But a truly stunning number rose to meet his planes. His first "vee" was already past; they'd fired late, but when he looked back, he saw smoky tendrils intersect the next formations, followed by several flashes of light. At least four planes fell out of formation, one completely out of control with its wing peeling away. Another drifted down almost lazily, in scattered, smoldering pieces.

Grimly touching the polished 7.7-mm cartridge case piercing his left ear for luck, he bored in on the ships below. Closer he got, closer, his left hand fingering the bomb release lever, caressing it gently, waiting for the exact instant he'd practiced so often. The first great ironclad loomed large below him—and he suddenly began noticing things.

"Abort! Abort the run! All planes abort!" he cried into his mic as he pulled back on the stick, still not sure if he'd really seen what he thought. Banking right, he looked down and saw that several planes had already released, and bombs exploded on or near two of the huge ships below. Great wooden splinters blasted away from one ship, leaving a gaping wound in the sloping casemate, but there was no secondary explosion. Most telling of all, the damage seemed too extensive to have been caused without setting something off inside.

"Abort your runs, daammit!" he shouted.

"What's the dope, sur?" "Why? What?" "Did I hear 'abort'?" "What's goin' on?" came a flurry of queries.

"Those waagons have no guns! *No armor!* Their boilers are cold, an' there's nobody home!"

"You mean they're not *real*?"

Tikker continued his orbit, still looking down. "They're real enough, just not finished, I bet. No armor bolted on, an' no iron shutters over empty gunports. They're just wood, painted black. No iron but the funnels—an' I bet the funnels're dummies!" He saw more explosions, crackling among the anchored Indiamen and the flies where they'd assumed the enemy encampments were. "Even-numbered flights, abort!" he shouted. "*Everybody* abort, I said!"

"We do!" came an immediate response. "Rockets is fallin' on our taa-gits!" Tikker stared a moment, then barked a laugh. That was something even he hadn't thought of. With their contact fuses, of *course* any Grik rockets that didn't smack a plane would go off when they hit the ground—wherever that might be. Just further proof they didn't much care what happened to the ships and equipment they'd gathered here.

"Skipper," came another tinny voice. "The Indiaa-mans—they's *wrecks*! Old, they look like, an' no way fit for sea. Half are beached or sunk in shallow water!"

"But why?" came a confused shout.

"The rockets are real! Griks is still shootin' at us!" someone else warned.

Tikker took a deep breath. "All pilots, listen up," he shouted, and the chatter died away. "There're Grik down there, all right, but I bet just enough to shoot the rockets. We'll take a closer look, but I think there's only one thing that can possibly be goin' on here."

USS **Walker**

"They suckered us," Matt said grimly, handing the message form to Spanky, who passed it to Herring.

"I think it's obvious why the cruisers are absent," Herring said. "They towed the decoy fleet here and then pulled out."

"Obviously," Matt agreed. "But why decoys—and expensive decoys at that, even if they're just empty hulks—and why here?"

Herring pursed his lips. "The Grik are not stupid. Not any longer. They've seen that their large battleships, at least as currently designed, are expensive in time and materials to produce, and not particularly effective. They're extremely vulnerable to our torpedoes as well. My guess is that they expended these incomplete hulks, minus the iron they mean to use on other projects, expressly because they knew how tempting they would be to us."

"To sucker us," Spanky repeated sourly.

"Indeed. The cruisers were complete, just as capable in a surface action, and far less costly to produce and crew. They have saved them for later."

"Probably be better protected from the air when we see them again too," Bernie Sandison supplied.

Matt nodded. "But they drew us here for a reason," he said, staring out at the gray day. Ed Palmer raced onto the bridge with another message form and breathlessly handed it over. Matt scanned it quickly, then slapped it against his leg. "Here's why," he snarled. "Jarrik-Fas on *Tassat* reports a big Grik fleet of transports approaching the Comoros Islands from the south, and all he's got to stand in its way are *Tassat, Haakar-Faask*, and whatever Safir Maraan can scrape up to send him, which isn't much. A few lightly armed DEs and fast transports! *Boy*, did we get suckered!" He took a deep breath and gazed around the bridge before his eyes settled back on Ed. "Message to all ships," he said. "Recover aircraft as quickly as you can, and turn 'em around for an immediate flight to support Jarrik. They'll have to rearm and refuel at Grik City."

Herring stepped to the chart table and put his finger on the cracked, filmy Plexiglas protecting the chart above their position. "It's about two hundred and fifty miles, Captain, and the weather is deteriorating," Herring warned.

"I know. But they can get there in about four hours, counting turnaround. It'll take us eight to ten hours at flank speed in this sea."

Spanky whistled. "Hard on the boilers, and we'll be sucking fumes by the time we get there," he pointed out.

"I know, but maybe we'll be close enough to pick up any aircrews that can't make it."

Herring cleared his throat. "Do I understand that you mean to steam *Walker* to aid Jarrik-Fas all alone? What difference can this one ship hope to make?"

"No choice," Matt said. "And we're not going to be much help to Jarrik. Whatever he's gotten into—what *I've* gotten him into," he added bitterly, "will probably be over by the time we get there. Let's just hope he can hold them long enough for us to get between what's left of the invasion fleet and Grik City. *Santy Cat, Salissa, Arracca*, and the rest of the escorts will proceed at their best possible speed, but we're looking at sixteen, eighteen hours before they can get there. That's too long." He turned in his chair to face Herring full on. "And as for the other, I'd have thought by now that you'd have a far better appreciation of what 'this one ship' and her crew can accomplish!" He turned back to Ed. "Send it! Helm, make your course one eight zero. All ahead flank!"

///// *Grik City*
September 17, 1944

"I ser' you, Lord!" Hij Geerki exclaimed, throwing himself on the swept stone floor of General Queen Safir Maraan's HQ in the former "Celestial Palace." All conversation halted for a moment, in surprise at the strange creature's behavior. Lieutenant Colonel Saachic had been suggesting using his me-naak mounted cavalry—essentially dragoons now—as a rapid mobile reserve, while General Grisa, commanding 6th Division, and General Mersaak of the 3rd were arguing over where Major Risa-Sab-At's 1st Raider (Chack's) Brigade should be placed. Risa had ideas of her own and remained adamant that the regiment of "Maroons" her raiders had been training must stay close to her brigade. The Maroons, still represented, if not commanded by the man named "Will," was equally insistent on that. General Safir Maraan, dressed as always in black cape and silver-washed armor had listened just about long enough, and Geerki's intrusion gave her the break she'd been about to create.

Competing with the moaning wind of the building storm, rushing explosions throbbed outside the thick stone walls as formation after formation of Grik zeppelins pasted the city—in daylight, for the first time—and there was nothing she could do about it. All her remaining air reserves had gone to attack the fleet of Grik transports Jarrik had sighted and she'd ordered them to ignore the zeps they saw approaching. As usual with the near nightly raids, this new, bolder bombing remained largely ineffective and still focused on the waterfront. At least that was the supposition. The wind was shoving the zeppelins around so badly that it was hard to tell what they were aiming at, and their bombs fell largely at random. Even so, it galled her mightily to just sit there and take it. It galled her even more to "hide" in the Celestial Palace, and she hated the dreary place. But it was centrally located to her various defensive positions and provided her headquarters section good protection from the occasional bomb (the Grik clearly didn't want to damage their holiest temple) that hit the place no matter how careful the Grik tried to be. *Stupid,* she thought. They couldn't hurt the structure with their puny firebombs, but they might burn everybody out if they concentrated on it.

Safir looked at Geerki, still groveling on the stones. "Does he still do this all the time?" she asked one of the Aryaalan guards who'd accompanied the creature from General Rolak. They weren't there to prevent his escape, not anymore. They'd been sent to protect the ancient Grik "prisoner" that Rolak now trusted implicitly.

"Almost always, my queen."

"Stop that, Hij Geerki!" Safir commanded. "And stand. I will speak to you in a moment."

"O' course, Lord . . . Qyeen!"

"The rest of you . . . silence. You've all told me what you think. Now prepare to hear my orders. What are you hearing from Cap-i-taan Jarrik?" she demanded of the comm-'Cat seated at the bank of wireless equipment. She'd learned Morse herself, just as voraciously as she learned any new language, and had identified *Tassat*'s current code prefix amid the clatter of the keys.

"*Tassat* and *Haakar-Faask* smite the enemy, my queen. They rake its vanguard and keep their distance. The lead enemy ships are all the older style, but mount guns in their sides. Staying ahead of them allows Cap-i-taan Jarrik to take a heavy toll while receiving little return fire."

"Does he slow the enemy advance?" Safir demanded.

"Some," the comm-'Cat hedged. "*Tassat* and *Haakar-Faask* have destroyed or disabled seventeen ships, by Jarrik's best count. Our nine planes certainly destroyed five—before they were forced to return to rearm and refuel. . . ."

"But the airfield and seaplane docks are under constant threat from the air," Safir added.

"Yes, my queen. And the sea is worsening. Even the bay is perhaps too rough to continue operating Nancys."

"All planes will continue operations at any cost," Safir Maraan said, her voice cold but her eyes closing briefly in prayer. "In a few hours, we will have all of *Salissa*'s and *Arracca*'s planes. They will attack the Grik swarm and rearm and refuel here as well."

"Further taxing our damaged facilities," Mersaak murmured.

"Yes!" Safir snapped. "And they'll continue operations regardless of that as well, even should the weather turn to the fiercest strakka ever known!" She moved to the map on the great table fashioned of timbers from one of the sunken Grik dreadnaughts in the bay. "We have our warning—now," she said flatly, "and should be able to place troops in response to the enemy landing. But I do not want to *respond*! I want the Grik to land where they will be most concentrated and we can best concentrate against them—to most easily slaughter them. That means, one way or another, we must drive them ashore as quickly as we can." She pointed to the northwest side of the island beyond the "Wall of Trees" that encircled the city. "I want them to land along *this* coast, between the abandoned city to the south and the enclave of starving Grik."

"I thought you did not want to fight them there, from behind the Wall of Trees?" Risa speculated. She was wet and muddy and had been working hard to improve the defenses along the point Safir now indicated.

"I did not *expect* to, but would if we can manage it." Safir grinned at her. "If they round the northern point, they can land anywhere, or several places at once. Force them to come ashore directly to the west of us and they must attack through the jungle before they even reach the Wall of Trees." She looked around. "If we can make them land there, all of them, then we can concentrate all our forces against them at that one place. The jungle is not hospitable, as you know, and not only will it slow them, but their leaders will also have great difficulty maintaining cohesion and control."

"But how do we 'make' them?" Saachic asked. "*Waa-kur* will not arrive until late this afternoon or evening, and the rest of the fleet cannot be here before tonight at the earliest."

"The weather will help us, to some degree, even as it makes things more difficult. I suspect some Grik ships, damaged in action, have already been driven ashore." She took a long breath. "As for the others, I've dispatched every vessel but our oilers from this harbor that can carry cannon, except the 'Pee-Tees,' which do not and must guard the narrow port channel with their torpedoes in any case. The others will join *Tassat* and *Haakar-Faask*. Their mission, and that of our air-craaft, will be to 'herd' the Grik fleet toward shore, damaging as many ships as they can. My hope is that as more and more Grik seek the supposed safety of land—and many are wrecked in the attempt!—the rest, their leaders, will realize they must also land if they mean to preserve a large-enough concentrated force to menace the city."

Risa stared at her, wide-eyed. "To inflict such damage before the enemy rounds the northern point, *Tassat*, *Haakar-Faask*, and the others must *press* their attacks! Two DDs and what, six or seven DEs? Perhaps a dozen auxiliaries? Against *hundreds*? They cannot survive!"

Safir said nothing.

"And what if the Grik do not oblige us in this plan? What if, after such sacrifice, the greater part of the Grik fleet still survives to land elsewhere?"

"Then a smaller force will be needed to defend the Wall of Trees. Yours and the Maroons alone, in that case. And the rest will face fewer Grik elsewhere." She blinked a sudden flash of helplessness that belied her ruthless tone. "As Cap-i-taan Reddy sent to me; 'we have been suckered.' My understanding of the term is imperfect, but I think sufficient for me to agree it is appropriate. We have managed the feat often enough ourselves, but now we must cope with an imaginative Grik besides Gener-aal Halik. I pray they don't have many more." Finally, she turned to Hij Geerki. "Your report?"

"I ser' you, Lord Qyeen!"

"Yes, thank you. What have you learned?"

"I talk to the . . . encircled Griks, like you say. They is not all hungry. They let Geerki eat!" Safir's lip curled in disgust, imagining what they'd fed him. "They is gettin' less an' less o' them, though," Geerki continued. "Less than, ah, sixteen thousands o' they still there. The rest get eat. They said the soldier Griks all killed one another and get eat right at start. Just regular Griks, like Geerki, is all that's there," he added a little skeptically.

"Did you tell them what I offered?" "Offers" of various sorts were things that Grik warriors understood, when "offering" to let others join their eternal hunt. Presumably, they "joined" other Grik hunters, from other regencies, for joint operations. That was probably how they amassed their "swarms." But no one they'd considered "prey" had ever asked a group of Grik to join *them*. Obviously, there was no question of anyone actually allowing these Grik to join the *Alliance*, but Safir had promised they'd be fed, in return for labor . . . and they'd live.

"I did, Lord," Geerki replied. "An' I told they to look at Geerki! I a *great* critcher now, nearly a . . . ph-erson! They is a'nazed," he added modestly.

"What did they say?"

"They say they see. They is not soldier Griks," he stressed, "and they know you kill they all easy." He hesitated. "They also know General Es-shk is returning, though, too. Think he kill you." He shrugged strangely. "He *not* kill you, they surrender," he ended simply.

"But they won't fight to aid him if he comes?"

Geerki made a fluppering sound with his tongue behind dull yellow teeth. "They can't! They not soldier Griks any 'ore than Geerki!"

"But you *have* fought," Safir pointed out. "Alongside Lord Muln Rolak."

The old Grik looked to the side, then stared down for a moment before he spoke.

"Geerki still not a soldier Grik," he finally said quietly. "'Ut Lord Rolak turn Geerki into a . . . else thing. Not just Grik. I nearly a ph-erson! A ph-erson do soldier things, he has to, e'en he not a soldier."

*　　*　　*

The action that would come to be known as the Battle of the Go Away Strait grew much more furious with the arrival of the six DEs and ten "fast transports" from Grik City to join the already weary DDs under Jarrik-Fas's command. All the new arrivals had once been Grik "Indiamen" themselves, identical to those they came to fight, before being captured, cut down to lighter, sleeker lines, armed and provided with steam engines. Unlike the DDs, they had no applied armor to protect their engineering spaces, and if their guns were better than those on the Grik warships, they didn't have as many. Even so, Jarrik was sure his meager force could've savaged the old-style invasion fleet the Grik had sent—given time, replenishment, and most of all, sea room. The problem was, he had none of those things. Safir Maraan had told him where she needed him to force the enemy to land his troops, and that meant he had to get "stuck in."

The sea was getting rougher, the sky darker, and the normally tight Grik formation, which had always spoken well of their seamanship if nothing else, was spreading out. But to keep from being hopelessly scattered, Jarrik figured the whole force would have to shoot the gap between the easternmost island he'd been cruising near that morning, and the coast of Madagascar. That was where he chose to face them with his combined "fleet," and that was where he wanted all the Allied planes to focus their attention as well, concentrating on the ships farther back in the formation for two reasons. First, that was where the highest concentration of dedicated transports was likely to be, and second, he didn't want the planes hitting any of his own ships when things got tangled up.

He looked aft, northeast, across the rising swells. *Tassat* led the puny battle line he'd formed, and seventeen ships, bare-poled, steamed dutifully behind her. *Haakar-Faask* was near the center of the line.

"It certainly *looks* impressive," Lieutenant Stanly Raj observed.

"It does," Jarrik agreed. "And they're all of similar size and rig to us, who have already bloodied the Grik's ugly snouts. They can't know how weak most really are. Maybe the prospect of a lot more of what we've already given them will make 'em think twice."

"Do you really think that?"

Jarrik blinked thoughtfully. "No," he confessed. "But not because the Grik we fight today are particularly formidable, except in numbers." He saw Raj's confusion and explained. "These come on like the 'old'

Grik we fought early in the war. To you, Grik are Grik, but there's a difference. The old Grik fought ferociously but with little thought. They
came in swarms, like those ships: bunched up in a great, lethal mob that
couldn't be stopped without practically killing them all. Sometimes, if
they got suddenly surprised or somehow scared enough, they might
rout"—he grinned toothily—"caat-a-strophically. And we got good at
making interesting setups to bring that about. But the Grik learned and
became much more . . . difficult." He paused, gauging the distance to
the enemy across the heaving sea. Less than a mile now. Soon, the battle
would begin in earnest. "The thing is, the plan, the . . . straa-ti-gee that
brought this all about was very good. *Too* good. And now we're in a
jaam. This 'Gener-aal Esshk,' or whoever we face, is like that daamn
Halik. He has a noodle," he said, tapping his head. "But right now, I
think, he's usin' old tools to shape a new, good plan. Does that mean
that's all he has left?" He shook his head. "I don't think so. Tikker seen
organized army camps when he first started scoutin' Aaf-ri-caa in his
Pee-Forty. I think, like them old ships that was at the Seychelles, and
those comin' at us"—he pointed—"Gener-aal Grik—whoever he is—is
tryin' to hurt us as baad as he can, throwin' all his old tools at us, hand
over fist, before he sends his new stuff." He blinked irony and waved at
the following battle line. "The funny part is, if this is all we can scrape
up, he might not even *need* his new stuff!"

He considered awhile, and Raj was quiet as *Tassat* pitched into the
foaming sea, her engine and shaft rumbling beneath their feet. The Grik
ships were close enough now that they could've commenced firing to
some effect even in such a boisterous sea, but *Tassat*'s earlier long-range
nibbles had depleted her shot locker more than Jarrik liked, and he
wanted to get closer before the rest of his ships revealed how lightly
armed they were. "Just for hoots," he suddenly said, "I'd better send my
notions off in case nobody else has thought them up—and just in case
they're right. I kind of doubt I'll get a chance later." He quickly summoned a young Imperial midshipman and dictated a note to be taken
below to the comm shack. Then he turned to Raj. "We'll cross their
bows at least twice, firing as we go," he said, just above the noise of the
sea, wind, and engine. "That should jumble them up. Slow them down.
Hopefully, by then, our air-craaft will arrive."

"Then?"

"Then we'll try to do the same on the western flank of their 'formation,' causing as much mischief as we can. Maybe 'herd' them east, as Safir Maraan desires. At some point, though, I expect our battle line to fall apart. It's inevitable in this sea. I've already passed orders that if any ship finds herself separated or surrounded, she must engage the thickest concentration of Grik she can reach."

Raj blinked surprise in the Lemurian way. "That is suicide! And they would invite capture!"

Jarrik shook his head. "No Lemurian, and no Amer-i-caan Navy ship will be captured by the Grik. The, ah, 'proto-col' for that was established long ago by the first USS *Revenge*, and there are fuses of several types in the maag-a-zines of all our ships." He grinned at Raj's horrified expression. "Believe me, you don't want to be captured by the Grik!" He turned to face the growing enemy fleet, its red hulls and dingy sails darkening the heavy sea, even as the sky above continued to darken into a malignant black swirl. "I believe we may be building to a true strakka!" he said gleefully, and spread his arms. "I, for one, embrace it! A strakka of wind and fire! Starboard baattery!" he roared. "Run out your guns and stand by to commence firin' in local control! Pass the word to all ships," he cried to the talker standing by the cluster of voice tubes beside the helm. "Local control" merely meant that the guns would be individually aimed instead of controlled by *Tassat*'s crude but effective gun director in her main top. Since the aim was not necessarily to sink a few ships but to damage as many as possible, salvos would not be used.

Raj managed to compose himself—what else could he do?—and watched the gunports open and the great guns roll to their stops. He'd heard how ferociously his Governor-Empress's furry allies fought the Grik, but he'd never imagined himself in his current situation. He was here to *learn*, not die. But it looked like he was about to die regardless. His subconscious railed against that, but his conscious mind, the part ruled by honor, supposed that to die in such company would be a privilege, after all.

"Are strakkas more intense than the great cyclones, the 'typhons' in the East?" he asked conversationally, trying to sound steady and unconcerned.

Jarrik blinked at him with respect. "I do not know," he answered. "I've never been east of Maa-ni-la. But they're brisk enough to suit anyone in a ship as small as this, and if we're lucky and the Heavens smile upon us, it might do much of our work for us." He grinned. "And who knows? We may even ride it out ourselves!"

Jarrik-Fas turned to gauge the distance once more. "Fire as you bear!" he commanded. One by one, or occasionally in pairs, ten great guns roared and rumbled back, spitting their heavy shot screeching at the enemy. The smoke was quickly swept away, and glancing back, Jarrik saw white puffs and yellow flames jet away from the ships astern. Looking back at the Grik, he saw tumbling splinters and toppling masts torn aside by the freshening wind, and the closest ships twisted and collided, dragged around by trailing wreckage—but exposing their own batteries as well. One ship fired a heavy broadside, just a couple of hundred tails away. Most of her shot went wild, but a few ripped the air above *Tassat*'s deck or slammed into her hull. One caromed off her tall funnel, leaving a tremendous dent, and whined away to splash into the sea. Jarrik grinned at Raj. "Isn't it wondrous how when the shooting starts, all concern immediately fades?"

Raj nodded dutifully, but he didn't necessarily agree. He was still afraid.

Captain Jis-Tikkar had been in the air all day, first for the aborted raid on the Seychelles, and now on this long-range raid on the Grik fleet that Jarrik was jamming up east of the Comoros Islands. There'd been a longer-than-expected delay, rearming and refueling all the planes. None could land on water or decks with bombs still slung, so they'd quickly dropped their ordnance on the Grik ghost fleet after all, before returning to their ships. No sense in leaving anything for the enemy to make use of. But the weather was worsening even then, and what should've been accomplished in half that time wound up taking more than two hours. Now midday, the two Naval Air Wings were finally closing on Jarrik's reported position after flying through the worst weather Tikker had ever experienced in any plane, much less anything as tiny as a P-1 "Fleashooter."

The little windscreen and the propwash of the five-cylinder radial kept most of the rain off him, but he couldn't see through it. Every time he peeked over the top, his goggles quickly went opaque, and he spent the next few minutes drying them on his damp flight suit—smearing them, mostly—before taking another peek and doing it again. He'd been forced to fly into the darkening sky and increasing wind almost entirely by compass, and his little plane bounced and swooped as erratically as a leaf. Often glancing from side to side and behind, he was gratefully amazed to see that most of *Salissa*'s and *Arracca*'s planes were still with him. All "his" pilots were experienced veterans now. Still, he knew he'd lost a few. Most of those had simply become lost or separated from his straggling formation, and he'd ordered them to make for Grik City. Some had gone down, though, and even if *Walker* had been close enough to pick the pilots up, he doubted she'd ever see them in the heaving sea below. "What a mess," he mumbled to himself for perhaps the hundredth time.

They were close now, though; close enough to hear garbled TBS traffic between Jarrik's scratch task force, which meant at least a few of his ships remained in action. He told them repeatedly that they were coming and had the *Arracca* Nancy flying on his wing send the same by wireless, but nothing coherent came back from the ships. He did get Safir Maraan's latest assessments from the Cowflop, however, based on earlier wireless reports she'd received from TF-Jarrik and the last planes she'd had over the action. None of what he heard was very useful. Flying conditions had deteriorated so badly that Safir had finally relented and suspended further sorties from Grik City. She couldn't justify the sacrifice anymore. In addition to combat accidents—the Grik weren't even shooting at her planes—she was losing planes and pilots every time they tried to land on water or the airstrip. The water was too rough, and the strip had turned to mud.

"The Gen-raal say to land," came the crackly voice through Tikker's left-ear speaker. "She say you lose too many ships when you attack in dis wedder, an' maybe not hit nuttin' anyway. The Griks *is* gonna get past Task Force Jarrik, an' Lib'ty City's defenses is bein' shifted to center where dey can deploy to face any Grik land-een."

"No!" Tikker snapped back. "We didn't fly all this way just to dump our bombs on nothing—and crack up landing at Grik City. If we're gonna lose ships anyway, we're gonna bomb the Grik first!"

"Okay," said the comm-'Cat, as if he'd been expecting that response. "But be aad-vised; we lost wireless contact wit Task Force Jarrik an' hadn't had eyes on the strait for over a hour, so we don't know what's goin' on there."

"I'm getting some TBS, but I can't make much out."

There was a moment's hesitation before General Queen Safir

Maraan's own distinctive voice replied. "Then you must be extra care-ful, Cap-i-taan Tikker," she said. "Jarrik's remaining ships must have taken damage to their masts—and aerials. They are also probably quite mixed with the enemy by now. Try not to harm any of them. They will have likely suffered enough."

"Ay, ay, Gener-aal. We'll try," he said, knowing all his planes would've heard. He risked another peek over his windscreen, and in the moment that he had, he saw bright gun flashes against the dark sea to the south. "We got 'em in sight!" he cried. "And somebody's still fighting." He squinted, frustrated. "You're right about one thing, though. A lot of Grik ships are past the fighting, making for the northwest headland that opens on Grik City Bay! They're all scattered out, but there's a bunch of 'em!"

"Can you see if any, what, uh, fraaction of the enemy fleet may have been driven ashore?"

"No, not yet."

There was another long pause. "Then we must continue to assume the greater fraaction has bypassed Task Force Jarrik and will land along the northern shore. It will be the most protected from the weather in any case, and they will know that." The wind had turned around out of the south, turning colder and starting the rain. "If you must make the attempt, your orders are to attack *those* ships, Cap-i-taan Tikker, and destroy as many as you can."

"Ay, ay, Gener-aal," Tikker replied, wiping his goggles again while fighting to keep his plane under control. It was *so* hard to see, and the dingy white enemy sails were difficult to differentiate from the heaving, white-capped sea, but he thought there must be at least two hundred still coming relentlessly on. A fist clenched his heart. With three to four hundred warriors on each ship, that could mean as many as *eighty thou-sand* Grik were still poised to strike at Grik City's defenses. He and his planes *had* to thin them out because if even half that many made it ashore, they'd outnumber Safir Maraan's entire force.

"You heard the gener-aal," he said grimly into his mic. "Pair up and hit 'em, north to south, then west to east. *Try* not to run into each other!"

"What about Task Force Jarrik?" asked one of his flight leaders.

"Whatever's left of it must still be fightin' to the south. Try not to hit anything flying the Staars an' Stripes . . . but I don't think you gotta worry about it much. All planes! Taallyho! And good huntin'!"

////// *USS* **Walker**

hief Isak Reuben amazed himself and everyone around him by suddenly puking on the rattling deckplates of the forward fireroom. He'd been gleefully and loudly recounting a particularly vomity episode he and Gilbert once endured in the Philippine Sea in the old destroyer tender *Blackhawk*'s fireroom—their first Asiatic Fleet assignment back in 'thirty-nine—when he just suddenly . . . spewed. It was damn rough in the fireroom, and everybody was holding on to something as the ship wallowed and pitched. The roar of the blower and the boiler was almost insurmountable by his reedy voice. Everyone not already puking—the ex-pat Impie gals had it *bad*—was leaning forward, trying to hear, when what must've been half a gallon of the subversive coffee they brewed in the fireroom so they didn't have to drink Earl Lanier's swill just hosed right out of his mouth. Some got on a shedding 'Cat leaning close, and she turned and spewed as well—on the only Impie gal not already afflicted. Isak kind of hated that. He supposed he was sort of sweet on her. She immediately doubled over and added her stomach contents to the disgusting mix of sweat, condensation, oil, soot, rancid bilgewater sloshing up past the plates—and now vomit—that had combined with the fur 'Cats always shed in the hellish firerooms to create a kind of dark, creeping ooze.

In mere seconds, everybody was puking and retching—and Isak grinned. That had been the point, after all, to test the power of his developing social skills. He didn't know what made *him* puke; he felt fine. Maybe it was being ashore so long? Or maybe just going on about puking long enough would do the trick on anybody? Didn't matter. If he'd known he could start the ball rolling so easily, he'd have just conjured up some retching noises and saved his coffee. Amid the continuing sounds of gastric misery, he wiped his mouth on his skinny arm. "Well, *anyway* . . . ," he began again.

The airlock hatch to the aft fireroom banged open, accelerated by the motion of the ship, and Tabby glared at him. As usual, and like everybody—even human females—in the ferociously hot firerooms where temperatures often hovered around 130 degrees, she wore no shirt. That had driven Spanky nuts for a long time, and she'd finally had her department keep T-shirts handy in case Spanky came down, or for whenever they went topside. But with the storm and Spanky's gimpy leg making it unlikely he'd visit, and the extra heat of the high-speed run, she hadn't given a damn about T-shirts that day. "What the hell?" she demanded when she saw—and smelled—what had happened. She shook her head. "Never mind. C'mon, Isaak! We got problems!"

"Tabby says we've got a bad condenser leak, salting the feedwater," Spanky quickly reported when Matt trotted up the stairs aft, into the dank, dark pilothouse. Rain had lashed him during his brief exposure, and he wiped it out of his eyes. "Cap'n on the bridge!" Minnie shouted belatedly, but Matt merely waved his hand, saying, "As you were," as usual. He'd been in the comm shack with Ed Palmer listening to developments at Grik City when Spanky called him. Stepping toward his chair where Spanky sat, he nearly slammed into his friend when the ship's bow buried in a heavy swell and the sea pounded the pilothouse.

They would've already lost their new glass windows if the battle shutters hadn't protected them. Of course, that left nothing but small slits to see through. It didn't matter. Right then there was nothing to see but the dark, malevolent, rain-swept waves. "And the firebrick in the number three boiler is starting to crumble. Isak thinks it may collapse completely. All this banging around," Spanky apologized. "I told Tabby to split the plant so only one boiler gets the contaminated feed—but that means running one engine off one boiler and the other off two—"

"And different RPMs on the shafts if we maintain speed," Matt agreed grimly, noting that Paddy Rosen was already straining harder at the wheel than he'd already been. It would soon get much worse.

"I've called a relief to double up with Rosen at the helm," Spanky said, reading his mind. He hesitated. "Skipper?" he began.

"We're not slowing down," Matt said firmly.

Spanky nodded resignedly. He didn't need to tell Matt that the salted feedwater would eventually ruin the boiler tubes. If just one let go, the feedwater would flash, snuff the fires, and turn all the other tubes into busted guts. The whole boiler could be finished, maybe for good. Spanky contemplated pressing his point. They had spare tubes to fix the condenser, or they could just plug the leaky tubes. But they had to take the boiler off-line to make the repair. What he choked back was that they couldn't *rebuild* a wrecked boiler. Not out here.

"The condensers always leak," Matt pressed.

"Not like this."

"The tubes'll hold until we finish the job," Matt stated stubbornly. "Tabby and Isak will fix them when this is over."

"But what about the firebricks?" Spanky asked.

Matt braced for another big wave and then sighed. "The firebricks will hold up too. They have before; they will again. Then we'll rebrick the boiler like always. Spanky." He paused and rubbed the grit in his eyes. "You're not the engineering officer anymore. You're my exec."

"I know."

"Then you also know, as much as we love her and as careful as we try to treat her, when this ship has an important job to do, the job becomes more important than the ship, see? Sometimes, the way this war, this *world* has turned, it's hard to keep that straight, but it's still the truth." Matt went on to describe what he'd heard in the radio room; that two hundred plus Grik ships had made it past Jarrik and were heading straight for Grik City. Tikker's two wings had accounted for maybe fifteen or twenty of those, losing half a dozen planes in the effort, and then cracking up twice that many trying to land. Tikker himself would try to fly again, but he wouldn't risk any more pilots unless the weather improved. "So we're *it*," he said at last. "This old, worn-out, leaky ship is it. Again. Now, we don't have much farther to go, and if we can keep this speed, we might get there before the enemy. Even if we do, we'll be running and gunning like never before, and Tabby *has* to keep our feet under us that long." He waved his hand. "We don't have to sink 'em all, at least. Just whittle 'em down to a bite-size chunk for Safir Maraan. But we've got to do that, and it'll be tough. Afterward?" He nodded at Spanky's crutch, "You can spend your deferred 'convalescent leave' helping Tabby patch things up."

"In case you haven't noticed, I'm not arguing with you this time," Spanky said. "So who are you trying to convince? Me or you?"

Another wave pounded the ship and she shook beneath their feet, but then surged ahead to meet the next one as if emphasizing that she was game. Matt smiled but looked away. "Habit, I guess," he said, then shook his head. "I don't know," he finally added, barely loud enough for Spanky to hear, "but I just have this *feeling* that we're right on the edge, at last. We smash this Grik fleet and they'll probably send another. Maybe bigger and even better. One of Jarrik-Fas's last transmissions included a theory about that, and I think he's right. But we'll have all of First Fleet then, and two more corps as well. Not to mention another *front* to get the Griks' attention when the Republic attacks. It may not seem like it now, but I think the Grik are close to breaking, right down to the core."

"So are we," Spanky pointed out.

"Yeah, I've thought about that too," Matt confirmed. "So are we."

They passed another hour like that, slashing through the heavy seas, the old ship rising and plunging and fighting her way back up. Making the ride even worse than usual, she was getting low on the fuel that not only fed her boilers but also provided much-needed ballast. Combined with all her extra topside weight, she'd invented a new, intermittent, corkscrewing roll in the rough, disorganized sea that had even the saltiest hands feeling a little green. It did begin to moderate ever so slightly as they neared the northernmost point of Madagascar, however, long in view from the crow's nest above, and even visible from the bridge when the ship heaved herself up to the crest of a wave. The wind wasn't as fierce, with a shorter run off the big island, and the swells weren't as high with the seafloor coming up. It was still raining, but not with the same storm-lashed intensity as when it began.

"Crow's nest report Griks! *Many* Griks, bear-een two two seero!" Minnie cried. "They hard to see through the rain, but the closest is about fifteen thousand yaards!"

"Very well," Matt said, glancing at Spanky. "I guess we made it, barely. Reduce speed to two-thirds. That'll take some of the strain off the boilers—and the rest of the ship." He shrugged. "We'll have to slow down to hit anything in this sea anyway." He raised his voice. "Sound general quarters—wait!" He caught himself and grinned. "Belay that. Pass the word for the bugler instead. I believe we have time, and I'd like to do this right."

Other than their Hij leaders, Grik were not generally social creatures. They worked and fought together under close supervision and direction, but the average Uul warrior possessed barely enough language to follow the most basic commands. Predatory, pack-attack instinct took over after that. It was already clear to the Allies that this wasn't because they didn't have the *capacity* for more, but because they were so rarely allowed to live long enough for their mental maturity to match the physical maturity and lethality they achieved so quickly. The current war had begun to change that to various degrees, and there'd always been exceptions. Particularly bright Grik, if recognized, were allowed to mature, to be "elevated," to the status of Hij, though the privilege had rarely been extended beyond the offspring of already long-established Hij with the influence to persuade a regency's choosers to "recognize" and elevate their own young. Hij shipmasters were particularly adept at this, and the growing need for experienced Grik sailors was long established. Further exceptions had been made during the current crisis, creating leaders for vastly expanded armies and changing the very nature of the armies themselves. General Halik was a prime example, having been elevated from a successful sport fighter to commander of all Grik forces in India. He'd lost most of his battles there, but he'd learned. And though his peers couldn't know it, he'd taken things a long step farther. At first of necessity and then by design, he'd preserved as much of his army as he could for long enough that a fair percentage had begun to "elevate" itself. Having influenced the program that elevated Halik and others like him, "General of the Sea" Hisashi Kurokawa was doing much the same independently, and also by design, as was General Esshk to a more limited degree. Such had never been done before, in the long history of the Grik, and it remained to be seen what the result would be.

But on that wild, stormy day when the "traditional" forces commanded by Regent Consort Ragak of Sofesshk made their great attack to recover the Celestial City from the grasp of the prey, the only Hij to attend Ragak were the usual generals and shipmasters. The generals were of the "traditional" sort as well, whose only role was to design battles and then set their Uul warriors loose. Due to the limited nature of those designs, they had little to do until they reached the shore and generally stayed out of the way. But the shipmasters and Regent Consort Ragak, who'd taken the role of "General of the Sea" for himself, had been quite busy indeed. Ragak's plan to quickly shift his horde across the Go Away Strait to the southwest coast of Madagascar itself before the prey organized its meager patrols far enough south to discover its passage had worked perfectly. There his swarm had waited until the bait was laid in the Seychelles to draw off the more powerful elements of the prey's fleet. That had worked even better than Ragak hoped, and spies that remained among the trapped survivors near the Celestial City had signaled watchers beyond the Wall of Trees with colored cook-smokes that the prey had taken the bait. They, in turn, raced south in relays along the coast. Many were slain by the various preys inhabiting the island, but enough survived to bring Ragak word that the time to strike was at hand.

Ragak was already imagining himself as Regent Champion of all the Grik, and contemplating how General Esshk should be destroyed when things suddenly became . . . tedious. First, after several days at sea without the least sign of the prey's flying machines—Esshk's air raids had drawn them back to the city, no doubt, he grudged—his great fleet encountered troublesome weather that roughened and slowed its voyage. Then, that morning near the Comoros, they'd run into a *most* troublesome handful of ships that, combined with the worsening weather, had thrown his entire swarm into disarray. More than half his ships had been swept or diverted to the west coast of the island, and their warriors would have to make their attack there. The remaining swarm struggled on, sped by a turn of the wind, and was now rounding the northeast point of land, its objective in sight at last. He was content. The flying machines had been grounded by the storm, with one lone exception that had suddenly reappeared but merely watched from above. The rest of his fleet was turning into a quartering wind that would send the ships racing across a milder sea beyond the harbor mouth and the great guns he knew awaited him there, to the broad, flat beach he'd chosen to slam his ships ashore. After that, his warriors would leap into the surf. Some would be eaten by the ravening fish, of course, but the storm would keep most of those from the shallows. Few enough would die. Then it would merely be a matter of loosing his proud, *pure*, Uul, untainted by General Esshk's revolting experiments, to quickly scour the Celestial City of the feral vermin prey infesting it. He fully expected to be feasting on the defenders in the Celestial Palace by nightfall.

"My Lord Regent Consort!" The shipmaster hurled himself at Ragak's feet on the sodden deck of his flagship, the *Giorsh*. Ragak stared suspiciously at the creature. *Giorsh*, with her white-painted hull and lavish appointments reminiscent of another time, had been the flagship of all the Grik for a hundred years. Ragak had been astonished when Esshk gave her, and the prestige that went with her, to him. But he was suspicious of her master's constant caution.

"What is it, Shipmaster?" he growled.

"The lookout describes a ship, Lord, a ship of *steam* with *four smoke pipes*, approaching from the north-northeast!" the shipmaster wailed at the deck.

Ragak was taken aback. He remembered Esshk had described such a ship as having something to do with their misfortunes in the past, but by all accounts it wasn't very big. He was sure Esshk had blown the little steamer's contributions far out of proportion to further excuse his failings. But why should this pathetic creature seem so terrified, so close to turning prey himself? He hadn't even commanded *Giorsh* during the earlier . . . setbacks the Grik suffered at Baalkpan, for example. That one had gone on to command one of Esshk's new iron steamers. Seeing the nervous slouching of the other Hij officers nearby, Ragak slashed at the shipmaster with the talons on his feet. "Get hold of yourself—or destroy yourself at once!" he snarled.

"Of course, Lord Regent Consort, at once!" the shipmaster agreed fervently, and dragged himself away, blood seeping from his back to drip and spread on the wet deck. Rising, he trotted aft, down a companionway by the wheel, leaving Ragak with no idea which he meant to do.

What Ragak didn't realize was that shipmasters and their officers, as a separate class of Hij and as required by their trade, were particularly social creatures. Other Hij—generals, engineers, artisans of every sort, even choosers—jealously guarded their methods and thoughts to promote their own value, but shipmasters had to share their knowledge of the sea, the weather, and the meticulously crafted charts they were taught to make. They also shared tales of places they'd been, shores they'd seen—and enemies they'd fought. That information spread much more widely than any passed by comparatively insular regency generals, and the one ship that had entered the collective nightmares of Grik shipmasters everywhere, particularly those still commanding the hopelessly outdated "Indiamen," was USS *Walker*.

"*Waa-kur, Waa-kur,* come in *Waa-kur*! This is Cap-i-taan Jis-Tikkar, COFO of *Salissa's* First Air Wing! Do you read me, over?" Tikker was orbiting a thousand feet above a loose concentration of Grik ships and what he saw below might have been the most stirring sight he'd ever witnessed. All alone on the wind-tossed sea, USS *Walker* lanced through creamy waves, shearing foam and spray from her knife-edge bow, wisps of smoke peeling away from three funnels behind the big battle flag that streamed taut behind her foremast. Before her, the range shrinking fast, was a vast armada; still somewhat scattered, but numbering more than any single ship should ever have to face. Bright jets of flame flashed from three of *Walker's* four 4"-50s. A moment later, two water columns rose beside a Grik Indiaman about six hundred yards away. At the same time, a mighty blast shook the ship and debris flew in all directions. A few Grik were already firing back, peppering the water around the old destroyer with roundshot splashes. *Not many of the enemy here is armed,* Tikker thought. Most of those had stayed to tangle with TF-Jarrik, but there were enough to be a threat.

"Hi, Tikker!" came Lieutenant Ed Palmer's voice, scratchy in Tikker's ear. He and Ed had been friends since they flew together with (now Colonel) Ben Mallory in an old, battered PBY Catalina they'd almost literally worked to death, and finally lost at the Battle of Baalkpan. They'd all been lucky to survive, and though Ed never flew again, all three shared a special bond.

"Ed! I'm up here, ah, your eleven o'clock, about two miles an' a thousand feet. Is *daamn* windy up here!"

"We got you, Tikker! What do you see?" Ed's voice on the TBS was punctuated by the crash of guns that Tikker saw lash another Grik ship, though he'd have never heard it otherwise.

"The Griks are spread out, straggling bad, but starting to concentrate as they round the point. Some rounded it too quick," he added with satisfaction, "an' hit the rocks off the harbor mouth. Guns there are firing on those an' others that get too close. The rest . . . The rest *look* like they're makin' for pretty much the same beach Safir Maraan hit with Second Corps."

"It's the best, for the way Grik land; just running their ships up on the beach. All sandy," Ed agreed. "Anything landing northwest of the harbor, where the Grik civvies are?"

"Not on purpose. Geerki must be right. Griks have to know they're there, but them not bein' warriors, they probably think they'll just get in the way, slow their rush toward the Cowflop."

"General Safir will *stomp* their rush!" Ed replied.

"*We* know that," Tikker agreed.

Walker was charging into a bigger cluster of Grik ships now, her guns flashing in all directions, smoky tracers arcing from the 25-mm gun tubs in her waist and the red tracers from "old world" ammunition brought by *Santa Catalina* seared bright across the dark water from the two .50-caliber machine guns mounted on each side. The smaller rounds probed wildly for Grik ships from their leaping platform, but mauled them when they touched. They'd finally solved the brass problems with the 25s and .50s. The ammunition for them wasn't as rare and precious as it had been for so long, but *Walker* had apparently picked up some more of the "good stuff" when she rendezvoused with *Santy Cat* off the Seychelles. *At least something good came from that,* Tikker thought grimly. Two more Grik ships were hit and one erupted in

flames, its magazine of "Grik fire" igniting. The other spun beam on to
the sea, pulled around by a toppled mast, and simply rolled on its side.
There was no perceptible pause before *Walker*'s guns sought new targets.

"Say, Ed. You're a helluva sight down there," Tikker managed.

"I bet. Can't see anything from the radio room. *Nobody* can see
much from down here. Skipper wants to know if anybody's heard from
Jarrik, and whether any large force landed on the west coast?"

"I don't know," Tikker confessed. "General Maraan's deploying to
face this bunch and wants me to spot for her—and you."

"Well, tell us what you see here and then hightail it southwest and
have a look!"

Tikker hesitated just an instant. He knew Safir's comm section was
monitoring them and she'd hear of the exchange. And Captain Reddy
was Supreme Commander . . . but his plane was using a lot of fuel. The
weather *seemed* better here, on the surface, but not up high, and he'd be
pounding right into the wind to check to the south. He'd have to refuel
before he went, or on his way back here if he wanted to stay in the air
long enough to do any good—which meant he'd have to land. *Great.
Another chance to break my neck!*

"Wilco," he said, "there's a *lot* of daamn Griks down there. Most are
gonna get past you, and Gener-aal Maraan will have to stop 'em on the
beach. But near the center of the concentration you attack is one of
those big white-hulled jobs." They'd seen those before and knew they
were the Grik equivalent of flagships. Take their leaders out and the
Grik would still attack; that was what they did. But they'd lose whatever
ability remained to them in this mess to coordinate anything at all, or
react to the resistance Safir Maraan was preparing.

"Thanks, Tikker. I'll tell the Skipper."

Feeling conflicted since he didn't want to leave his friends below,
Tikker made his own report to Safir Maraan and turned his Fleashooter
into the wind, southwest, and started to climb. He figured it would take
an hour, bucking the storm, to reach the coast opposite the Comoros
Islands.

He didn't have that long. He hadn't quite reached the harbor mouth
when his engine coughed and the spinning prop in front of him skipped
a beat.

"Oh, you better *not!*" he warned. The Alliance had been very lucky with its aircraft engines from the start. Granted, they'd had a functioning prototype to study and keep going—for a while—and then they'd been gifted with the still-underused (in Ben Mallory's opinion) P-40Es. They'd also had fine manuals that covered the basics very well, not to mention all the original destroyermen with their wide and varied technical expertise—and then actual airmen who'd had to learn the very basics covered in the manuals, and had practical experience applying them. The four-cylinder Wright-Gypsy–type engine in the Nancys had been a great success and was used in a wide variety of applications now. The five-cylinder radial powering the newer P-1 Mosquito Hawks had been fairly successful as well, but failures were more common. And the engine on Tikker's plane had already been through a lot. Add the adverse conditions, the moisture it was sucking, and the wild ride that had to be annoying the carburetor, and there was no real telling why the engine suddenly quit.

"Shit!" Tikker shouted when the prop wound down and the plane almost immediately tried to stall. He pushed the stick forward to get the nose down and looked frantically around below, since he'd only about doubled his altitude before losing power and didn't have time for much of anything but to try to figure out where—and if—he could set the plane down. He couldn't bail out. He had the altitude, barely, but the wind would carry him over the bay and drop him in the water. Nope. He couldn't even report his situation: his high-frequency transmitter was powered by the engine. And one thing was sure; he'd never glide all the way back to the airstrip. The harbor sprawled before him, and even if he made it across, only the jagged ruins of Grik City lay beyond. The fort guarding the eastern mouth of the harbor was just below, and the ground past that was laced with trenches and other defensive positions facing the beach. The beach. That was his only option, the only flat stretch he could possibly reach. The wetter sand would be the firmest, probably better than the mud at the airstrip—but the surf was breaking hard and washing far up the beach. Grik ships that had evaded *Walker* were coming in and the defenses manned by Safir Maraan's 3rd and 6th Divisions were preparing to give them a hot welcome, but the beach between them was his only hope. He considered jumping out there, but he'd be too low by then. Besides, even if the wind brought him down among his friends, his plane might crash among them too. He was just going to have to ride it down.

Turning, he lined up on the beach, trying to hold his northwest to southeast glide path and struggling against the crosswind that threatened to flip him. He eased the stick a little farther forward to gain a bit more speed, remembering the last "dead stick" landing he'd been a part of, when he and Ben tested the very first Nancy over Baalkpan Bay. This was worse. The world was coming up awful fast, and the P-1 kept drifting toward Safir's first trenchline. He tried to compensate and wound up over the water. That wouldn't do at all, even if he'd been in a Nancy. He adjusted again, aiming for that imaginary line on the beach that the sea only occasionally reached, but the line was capricious and he could only control his touchdown to within a few instants, either way. He expected Safir was watching now, along with thousands of her troops, and figured she was praying for him—and cursing him—with every breath. The time for thinking was over, and only his sense of the wind and his aircraft could save him now. He'd *feel* his way through this or die. He thought he caught a glimpse of the sea fading just as he pulled back on the stick, flaring out, trusting the mushy Indiaa rubber "balloon" tires not to sink and stick in the sand—and they didn't! The plane bounced, but it continued forward, smacking the wet sand again, again, slowing each time. Then he saw white foam surging forward across his path, and a geyser of spray erupted around him. The plane tipped up, slamming hard on its nose. His forehead smacked against the crude tube gunsight piercing the windscreen, and he saw bright purple sparks.

For a moment, his eyes didn't work, and he heard and felt a big wave rush around the plane. He figured it would topple it over on its back and drown him, but instead the tail slammed down again with a splash. He felt dizzy, twisting this way and that; then another wave pushed the tail hard to the right, and for an instant he caught a hazy glimpse out to sea. There were still gunflashes far out over the water, and bright flares danced in the dim-lit day where Grik ships burned on the heaving sea. *Walker* was invisible beyond other dark shapes of distant ships, but she was still fighting; that was sure. Despite that, other Grik were coming in, lots of them, and one ship seemed aimed right at him, all sails hastily set to drive it as far up on the beach as possible. Its bow shouldered the sea aside as it drew closer, bigger, until it looked like it would crush him.

He felt all alone, just waiting for the Grik to smash him in the plane, tear him apart. Eat him. Then, just fifty or sixty yards away, the ship surged to a stop, sending the foremast toppling into the surf trailing a long red pennant. Instantly, Grik poured over the side, splashing into the sea. Most disappeared entirely and he thought they were drowning themselves, but then he saw them as they thrashed through the marching swells or somehow rode them in, their heads and weapons held high.

"Get him out! Hurry!" a 'Cat cried, tugging at the harness holding him fast to the wicker seat. "Cut it!" someone else shouted urgently. He drifted away. A short time later—he didn't know how long—he coughed water and sputtered as he was dragged up on the beach and across the sand by panting forms that clutched him tightly under his arms.

"Hey, fellas!" he managed. "Let go! I can do it!"

"Just a moment, Cap-i-taan! We almost there!" one gasped. Tikker didn't argue. He didn't feel like it.

"What about my plane?" he asked instead. "The motor craaped out, but it's a good plane."

"You get another plane!" came an insistent voice. "The waves get that one, flop it over. An' when the Griks gather 'round it, an' they will, *blooie!*"

"Shut up! Is gonna be 'blooie' for *us* right quick, we don't get him in the trench! This whole beach gonna be 'blooie'!"

Tikker felt himself dropped, and then dragged up over a wood and earthen ramp of some sort before he fell down into a muddy pit. "Hey, daamnit!" he cursed, spitting sand—just as the second 'Cat was proved correct and the world around him erupted in thunder.

 *The Wall of Trees*

ajor Risa-Sab-At could barely see USS *Walker*'s battle at sea; she could just make out sharp, distant gunflashes through the rain that was falling on her position west of the Cowflop atop the Wall of Trees. The growing fight northeast of where Safir Maraan had landed to help take Grik City in the first place, a stretch called "Lizard Beach One," was partially obscured by the bulk of the ugly Grik palace, but she could see it better—and it was a "doozy." More and more Grik ships were crowding in, piling up in the surf, spilling warriors. Cannon and mortar fire met them as they swarmed against the primary defensive line, and she imagined that the surf was quickly turning red. She snorted. The Grik were so wasteful! They built decent ships, good enough that the Allies were glad to make use of them, and the older "Indiamen" were particularly well made. She knew their wrights had Hij supervisors, and she sup-

posed the rest worked like insects constructing intricate hives, time after time, but to her, a Lemurian who'd always considered *Salissa* her
Home, it remained difficult to comprehend the abandon with which the
Grik destroyed their ships. They were wasteful of themselves as well,
just as wasteful and careless as insects at war with others. At least *these*
Grik remained so, she amended. Not all were like that anymore, and it
had been a long time since they fought Grik that attacked with so little
concern for loss. But did that mean the war had drained them of the
"new" Grik such as Halik led, or that they were ridding themselves of
the "old" Grik—the old ways of thinking—here, at last? The battle on
the beach would be fearsome, she knew, and Safir Maraan's divisions
would be hard-pressed before it was done, but Risa was confident, particularly with *Walker*'s help, that they'd ultimately slaughter the invaders. Her greatest frustration just then was that the 1st Allied Raider
Brigade, the 1st Maroon Regiment, and part of Lieutenant Colonel
Saachic's 5th Division Cavalry—numbering a little more than five thousand troops—under her command, wouldn't be in on the kill.

Turning back to the west, she peered at the jungle across the killing
ground through the driving rain and saw absolutely nothing. She
growled exasperation deep in her throat.

"Our position is a strong one," Major Alistair Jindal observed, twisting his long, dark mustaches with a wet grin and nodding at her 7th
(Combined) Regiment standing on the newly built platform behind the
towering, rotting, mountain-range-like pinnacle of the Wall of Trees. The
platform was a firing step made from the remains of Grik City, or hacked
directly from the mighty decaying trunks of the ancient Galla trees that
the Grik had used to build the astonishing wall. They'd even cleared embrasures and built platforms for a number of light guns. She looked at her
troops, both Lemurian and human. The 7th was composed of the 2nd
and 3rd battalions of the 19th Baalkpan, and the 1st of the 11th Imperial
Marines. Then she glanced back at Jindal, blinking, because his voice
held a trace of irony that mocked her mood. Jindal was a good man and
commanded the 21st (Combined) Regiment composed of the 1st and 2nd
battalions of the 9th Maa-ni-la and the 1st Battalion of the 1st Respite.
Ordinarily, he was Chack's executive officer, but Chack had left his sister
in charge. If Jindal resented that, he made no sign. Risa was more experienced. But he'd clearly guessed the source of her frustration.

"But a useless position," she replied. "They might need us at the shore."

"They might need us here," he countered philosophically. "We *know* a lot of Grik landed on the western coast this morning. That was what Captain Jarrik was trying to force them to do."

Risa didn't reply, but she secretly doubted Jarrik and his tiny, weak squadron had been very successful. Still, without aerial observations or communications, it was impossible to know, so there her brigade had to stay. She had scouts out; me-naak mounted cavalry accompanied by Maroons who knew the jungle, but there'd been no reports. She glanced resentfully at the roughly three thousand troops detached from 6th Division that were dug in to the brigade's far right, guarding the starving Grik "civvies" bottled up between the harbor and the northwestern-most section of the Wall of Trees. *Should've wiped them all out,* she thought, vaguely surprised by her bloody-mindedness. She'd understood and supported why they hadn't at the time. But now, if they had, *that* force could've taken this useless post and hers would've been free to fight.

"I doubt Colonel Yaar-Aaan is happier than you with his assignment," Jindal said, noting the direction of her gaze. She huffed. Brevet Captain Enrico Galay, a former corporal in the Philippine Scouts who'd survived *Mizuki Maru* and who now commanded the 1st of the 1st Maroon, joined them with another man. Despite his dress that was just like everyone else's, this other man was obviously a Maroon because he wore a long black beard, and the hair gushing from beneath his helmet reached past his shoulders. "Maroons are getting edgy," Galay reported.

"Why? What do they say?"

"Christ," Galay snorted. "How should I know? I can barely understand 'em." He nodded at the man beside him who was supposed to be his exec, and Risa wondered how that worked if they couldn't communicate. The "English" the Maroons spoke was very heavily—and oddly—accented, but Jindal and his Imperials seemed best able to decipher it. All their NCOs were Impies, but the Maroons were very strict about chain of command. This man had insisted they report to him, and he to Galay. . . . Risa shook her head. "You need to get that sorted out," she warned Galay. "Learn to understand them, teach them to understand you, or get an interpreter! If you can't do one of those things, I'm sure Major Jindal can find someone who can."

"Yes, Major," Galay agreed.

"Ay unnerstan', Cap'n Galay," the man insisted.

"Very well," Jindal said, "Then please repeat your report to us."

"Aye." He hesitated. "Ay fare tha Garieks is camin'!"

"What makes you think that?"

"'Tis tha baesties! Tha baesties in yan jangle!"

Risa peered over the peak of the wall. The rain was slacking, but she saw nothing alive below. "How can you tell? What're they doing?"

"Thay's camin. Lak!" he said, pointing. "Look!" he repeated carefully. Risa still saw nothing—at first.

"The lizardbirds?" she asked. Colorful flocks of the things were swirling through the trees as far as she could see in any direction like thick wisps of smoke, surging back and forth and exploding into the sky with muted, raucous cries. She supposed she'd noticed them, but there were always lizardbirds—or were there? "It's raining," she stated.

"Aye. Bards danna fly mach an tha rain, less samthin' scares am ap—an' nathin' scares sae many!"

Far below, a me-naak burst from the jungle, bearing two riders, followed by several more, equally burdened. The long-legged crocodilians bounded directly toward the wall and scampered straight up amid the clatter and jangle of their riders' dangling carbines and cutlasses like no horse ever could. Their claws made them far better at scaling steep slopes, particularly when they were made of spongy, eon-old tree trunks. The cav-'Cat on the leading me-naak urged his mount toward the 1st Raider Brigade flag, rain pasted tight to its staff, and Risa and her companions trotted to meet him.

"Griks!" he shouted, saluting. The Maroon riding behind him made a parody of the salute and cried out, "Garieks!" as well.

"How many? How far?" Galay demanded.

The cav-'Cat blinked at him, then looked back at Risa and Jindal. "Thousands of 'em," he stated simply. "An' they is spreadin' out in the jungle right behind us. Fixin' to attack, I bet."

"What took you so long to report?" Jindal asked.

"Garieks ain' tha anly nasty baggers in tham jangle!" growled the Maroon.

"We lost some troopers tryin' to break back through," the cav-'Cat confirmed. "The Griks is pushin' all the bad boogers ahead of 'em, but then they break to the side, like, before they reach the clearing. We had to bust through. Some guys're still out there"—he waved—"tryin' to find the flanks. Maybe they get stuck behind 'em?"

"They're not all breaking to the side," Galay said, pointing down at the killing ground between the wall and the woods. A pack of something like oversize Grik, but with spikes down their backs, bolted from the trees and raced to the south. Other, smaller creatures—just as bizarre—were doing the same, and what began as a trickle quickly became a flood. The 1st Raider Brigade—and the Maroons, of course—had encountered many of the island's predators before. The Raiders couldn't have told how many creatures fled their advance through the jungle when they marched across the island to attack Grik City, but an awful lot *hadn't* fled. So, to see so many running now implied that a lot of weight was pushing them. And all the while, lizardbirds screeched and flocked overhead, nearing the edge of the jungle.

"Thank you, Corp'raal," Risa said, and nodded to all the riders. "Go join your companies. Messenger!" she called. "Get on the horn to Gener-aal Safir Maraan and tell her that an apparently sizable force of Grik is preparing to attack us here." The Raiders had no wireless set, or even field telegraphs, but they did have the new field telephones that connected them to Safir's HQ by the same wires used elsewhere. They also had other "new" technology of a more lethal nature that had proven itself in attack. Now they'd see how their still somewhat experimental equipment would fare at defense, it seemed. "I'll report further when I know more!" she added, turning to the drummers standing beside the brigade standard, their instruments covered against the wet. "Beat 'stand to,'" she ordered, then glanced at Jindal with a swish of her tail.

"They might need us here after all," he said, blinking irony.

The drums thundered dully and whistles blew, not that they'd needed them to assemble their troops. Everyone was already in place, watching and waiting. The exodus of jungle predators finally thinned, and a pregnant near stillness ensued. Suddenly, here and there, Grik warriors crept out of the jungle, glancing around. None carried the now-ubiquitous Grik matchlock muskets—as if those would've been of any use on such a wet day—but were instead armed with the traditional spears, crossbows, and sickle-shaped swords that had equipped Grik armies since the beginning of time. Their crude leather armor and round leather shields strapped to their backs drew the thoughts of all the veterans who saw them back to earlier times, earlier battles, and most were surprised. The Grik scouts seemed surprised as well to find themselves in the open at last, but the high, massive Wall of Trees that loomed before them quickly caught their attention and they yipped back behind them at the jungle. Bellows-driven horns *blapped* in the trees, robbed of their impressive, menacing volume by the damp, but then the "thousands" of Grik they'd been warned about began to gush from the dark woods.

Risa was stunned by the numbers that just kept coming, beginning to snarl and yip and bang their shields with weapons as they emerged— and they didn't even pause or wait for their lines to firm up before they advanced. They just surged forward across the killing ground while more and more poured out of the jungle. Risa suspected there were already more Grik in view, appearing in a matter of moments, than she had defenders to stop, and knew that however many ships got past him to assail Safir Maraan, Captain Jarrik-Fas had been far more successful in his mission than anyone had imagined.

"Tell Gener-aal Safir Maraan that we have many thousands of Grik attacking here, and that they come in the 'same old way.'" She paused. The "same old way" hadn't been much used for some time, but everyone still knew what it meant. More, from what she could see of the battle beyond the Cowflop, the seaborne Grik were doing the same. She couldn't make sense of it, but despite their growing numbers, she much preferred that they approach like this than the ways they'd begun to use elsewhere. She turned to the Maroon standing beside Galay, suddenly transfixed by horror. "Get back to your battalion at once," she ordered, "and remember one thing. Your people asked for this, and we've trained them as best we could in the time we had. But spread the word: if they break, all is lost and we'll kill them ourselves. Is that perfectly clear?"

The bearded man turned to her and a deadly resolve replaced the terror in his eyes. Apparently, he could understand her just fine.

"We willna ran," he said. "The Gareiks've kapt us as thar spart, thar playthans sance befare are paple can remamber. We willna ran," he repeated simply, firmly.

"Good," Risa said, suddenly wishing Chack and Dennis Silva were there. Her brother had once been a pacifist, unable to fight, but had become one of the greatest leaders in the Alliance. She supposed she could lead here, for this, just as ably as he. But he'd also developed a talent she thought she lacked for inspiring troops under his command. Of course, the sight of thousands of Grik swarming to slaughter you would inspire just about anyone, she supposed. Anyone who knew the Grik—and the Maroons certainly did—fully understood that the Grik gave no quarter and their only hope lay in cooperative defense. Running only ensured defeat and death for everyone. Why did she wish Silva were there? She wasn't sure. He was no leader, beyond the small-unit level, but he could inspire others in a singular way—if he was in the mood. And they were still great friends even now that their—mostly—pretend affair had run its course. Mainly she just yearned for his uncomplicated enthusiasm for a fight, his irrepressible humor—and his lethal competence, of course. She wished he were there to talk to just then, to lend her his peculiar confidence. And to fight beside.

"Good," she repeated. "Return to your posts—and good luck." She raised her voice to that carrying tone unique to her species. "Blitzerbugs and flame weapons will hold until I give the command. All other guns, mortars, and riflemen—commence firing!" A sheet of fire, lead, and iron rolled down the extreme slope toward the enemy, shrouded in a dense white-yellow cloud of smoke, tearing at the leading edge of the mass of Grik already nearing the base of the wall. The Second Battle of Grik City had become a general engagement at last.

///// *USS* **Walker**

*T*he staccato hammering of *Walker*'s 4"-50s, firing in local control, was almost constant now, as were her 25s and .50s. Even the six scattered .30 cals, up on the fire-control platform, the amidships gun platform over the galley, and the aft deckhouse, opened up now and then when they got close enough to spray Grik crammed aboard the enemy ships. The old destroyer had moved into the tightest concentration of Grik Indiamen she'd tried to squirm through since Aryaal, and she was doing a terrible slaughter—but the Grik were fighting back, and even their wallowing wrecks were a menace. Light roundshot slammed her hull from a Grik warship far enough away that they didn't penetrate, but they opened seams and more reports of flooding reached the bridge. Her funnels leaked smoke, and her searchlight on the tower aft had been shattered. The auxiliary conning station on the aft deckhouse had been damaged as well, with several casualties, and Matt felt a selfish sense of relief that Spanky's bad leg had kept him from his usual battle station there. Its launch in the heavy seas unsuccessful, yet another Nancy had been turned to wood and fabric wreckage on its catapult. *We've lost an awful lot of them that way*, Matt thought glumly, but he'd always hated throwing perfectly good planes over the side. At least it hadn't caught fire—and he'd given Bernie Sandison permission to use his torpedoes to get them off the ship before she closed with the enemy—all but the "spare" stuck in the inoperative number two tube. Torpedoes and their heavy, sensitive warheads were much too dangerous to have aboard in this kind of fight, and the five fish Bernie hurriedly fired at high speed in the chaotic sea had still managed to spectacularly account for two enemy ships. Granted, the range was ridiculously short, but after all the trouble they'd had with torpedoes—on this world and the last—it was nice to have weapons they could trust.

"Caam-peeti says we gettin' low on common shells in the for'ard maag-a-zeen!" Minnie reported. "An' it's not much better aft. We got less than tree hundreds left, total!" Matt considered. They'd begun the action with two hundred "common," or contact fuse exploding shells for each of *Walker*'s four main guns. They had some of the new "Armor Piercing" (AP) shells as well, but they were less effective against wooden ships.

"We've fired more than five hundred rounds," Herring stated, impressed, "and accounted for what? Sixty enemy ships?"

"The sea makes it tough," Bernie defended.

"No!" Herring objected. "I'm amazed how *well* we've done!"

"Not well enough," Spanky growled. "They just keep comin'! And too many are getting past us and piling up on the beach in front of Safir Maraan!"

"And they keep throwing themselves between us and that white ship," Matt added, stepping close to the battle shutters and peering through the slit. He couldn't see anything.

"Caam-peeti says she's right ahead," Minnie encouraged. "But . . . more ships is get in the way!"

"We've done good work," Herring began tactfully.

"But we need to get that white ship—and whoever's on it. We've been fighting the Grik awhile now, Mr. Herring, and you don't need to be a snoop to know where their honchos are. Taking them out might not make any difference in the short run, but it could damn sure kick in later!" He paused. "Have all guns that will bear forward concentrate on the ships between us and the white one. Have them take potshots at it too, if they get a target." He looked around the pilothouse. "We're going after that ship."

"We'll take a beating from those we pass," Spanky warned.

"We already are. But not many of those left out here have cannon, and the secondaries will have to take care of them."

"Aye, aye, Skipper."

"Does that mean I can lift the shutters?" Paddy Rosen begged. He was clearly frustrated—and exhausted, after fighting the uneven thrust of the screws so long. It was better now, at their reduced speed, but the long sprint had taken its toll. "At least the one in front of the wheel?" he pleaded. "I can't *see* anything, Captain."

"Very well, but only if you take a break." He started to direct one of the 'Cats that had been standing, waiting to relieve Rosen, to take the wheel. "*Now*, Skipper?" Rosen demanded incredulously. In the ship- and wreckage-tangled sea, Rosen was still the best choice at the helm.

"Not just yet, I guess," Matt relented. "But soon. Raise the battle shutters in front of the wheel," he ordered, and 'Cats sprang to comply. It was immediately lighter in the pilothouse, and they could all better see the confusion of fire- and storm-lashed destruction ahead. The salvo bell no longer rang, and the bright flame and overpressure of the number one gun on the fo'c'sle gave them a slight start, rattling the now-exposed window panes. A Grik ship, its red hull dark and marred with streaks of black, reared into view directly in their path. The number one gun fired again, joined by the number three, and the muzzle blast of that gun, so close behind the bridge, was stunning. More stunning to the Grik. Both shells struck near the waterline, amidships, and exploded in a welter of spinning timbers. The masts didn't fall, but the hull buckled when the sea lurched up fore and aft. Its longitudinal integrity lost, the ship jackknifed, its back splintering, and quickly began sliding under, spilling hundreds of struggling Grik into the frothing waves.

"Left standard rudder!" Matt ordered, and Rosen heaved at the wheel.

"Left standard rudder, aye!" he gasped. Lancing through the debris-choked sea, *Walker* had to avoid the sinking ship that, perversely shifted by the waves, seemed to chase them even as it disappeared. Heavy pieces of wood banged against the hull, and the pitching bow came down on something that rattled down the ship's length before they felt it no more. Matt had been gritting his teeth, half expecting whatever it was to foul the screws. "Rudder amidships!"

"Rudder amidships, aye, Skipper!" Rosen cried just as Campeti reported from above.

"There she is!" One or two of the ships still screening the white one had at least temporarily been displaced by the sea, leaving their target exposed less than four hundred yards away. But *Walker* was now aimed directly at one of the others. It had no guns, but its tossing deck teemed with Grik.

"Right standard rudder! All guns fire on the white ship!" Matt commanded.

"Right standard rudder aye!" Rosen replied, straining once more. "Here! Gimme a hand!" he shouted at one of the 'Cats. The Lemurian obeyed and grasped the big wheel with him, heaving it to the right— until it suddenly spun wildly and sent them both crashing to the deck strakes.

"All astern, emergency!" Matt roared, realizing they'd had some kind of steering casualty. The 'Cat clutching the lee helm immediately shifted the levers, and the answering bells responded with a speed that made Matt proud—but they were still aimed right at the side of the Grik ship! The guns tried to fire at their target, but it was quickly concealed by the closer vessel and they fired at it instead, blasting great chunks out of its bulwarks and shredding bodies huddled behind them. The ship itself, however, seemed to remain relatively motionless as *Walker* bore down, and there seemed nothing they could do to avoid a collision. The screws wound down with a juddering vibration that shook the deck, but before they could bite again, Matt took a desperate chance. "Port engine, full ahead! Starboard engine will remain at full astern. Let's see if we can twist her tail!"

The 'Cat at the lee helm didn't hesitate, but slammed the left lever forward. The starboard screw was turning now, throwing sheets of seawater all the way up to the top of the aft deckhouse. *Walker* slowed just a bit, but the sea was relentless, and waves kept trying to heave the ships closer together. Matt grabbed the back of his chair that Spanky still occupied, bracing for the impact that seemed sure to come. He was about to order Minnie to sound the collision alarm, when the port screw wound up.

"C'mon, baby!" Bernie Sandison crooned nervously. "C'mon!"

Only a combination of the engine orders and the capricious sea saved them. Ever so slightly, the waves pitched the Grik forward and *Walker's* stern began shifting to the left. Even so, a collision seemed inevitable, side to side now instead of head-on, but that could be just as bad—or worse. "Port engine, full astern! Starboard engine, ahead full! Now we'll try to twist around it!" he explained to the men and 'Cats around him who all seemed to be holding their breath. Slowly, the old ship responded, her momentum carrying her bow past the Grik's stern galleries while the stern twisted slightly right. A sudden hail of crossbow bolts sheeted in at the 'Cats crewing the number one gun, and they tried to hide behind it or the splinter shield. One was struck in the back and fell, but another dragged him to safety. Machine guns raked the Grik, blasting bright splinters among its thick horde of warriors, mowing them down, toppling them into the churning water. None of the big guns fired, all their crews were taking cover, but only because Campeti, who knew they didn't want to do *anything* to slow the enemy's forward progress, told them to. Now, as the range gradually increased and fewer crossbow bolts touched the ship, Campeti ordered the number two gun in the port side of the amidships gun platform to "blow that damn thing all over the water."

"That was . . . a close one," Commander Herring said, his shaky tone belying his calm words. "I . . ." He was interrupted by a roiling explosion to port as the number two gun found the Grik Fire magazine aboard the ship they almost hit. Matt didn't speak at all for a moment as he paced quickly out on the wet starboard bridgewing. "All ahead one-third," he called over his shoulder. "We'll steer with the engines. Damage report!"

"Steer-een casul-tee!" Minnie answered.

"No shit," Spanky seethed. "Beggin' your pardon, Skipper."

"No need," he said, staring out to starboard at the white-hulled ship, now at their mercy. It had tried to turn directly away, an act of sheer panic, but the wind was still blasting out of the south and it simply stalled there, tossing drunkenly, as its bow came back around. "How bad is it?" he asked.

"Tabby says we fight uneven thrust so long, the steer-een engine work too hard, blow a steam line. Space all fulla' steam, but they bypassed fast and is ventin' it. The chains from the helm just broke. Too old, too rusty, an' too much stress from uneven thrust again, to turn the rudder without the steer-een engine . . . Tabby says we can splice the chain, but wi'out the engine, it'll prob'ly just break again, someplace else."

"I get the picture," Matt said. Of all the things they'd replaced on his old ship, they'd left the steering chains alone because they were, well, chains, and not only difficult to make, but hungry for iron. They could've used rope or cable, and probably should have, but the chain seemed better—at the time. He was tempted to view the failure as another example of how his ship was getting too old and beat-up to keep fighting her like they did, but she *wasn't*, he insisted to himself. She'd been rebuilt and maintained on this world better than she ever had been at home. Just a stupid chain. "With the auxiliary conn damaged, Tabby'll have to rig the tiller on the rudder post between the depth charge racks," he said, knowing the wet, dangerous duty he was ordering; to manually steer the ship from the confined space, entirely exposed to the elements. "We'll steer with the engines in the meantime," he repeated, but pointed out at the white Grik ship. "But let's kill that damn thing first, if you please."

Having broken through the thickest mass of Grik still offshore, Matt was surprised to see so few left at sea after they left the burning white hulk in their wake. A lot of Grik were still afloat, waiting to join the attack on Safir Maraan, but they were stacked up, grinding together in the shallows, beginning to break on one another in the churning surf as their warriors crossed from ship to ship to gain the shore. He was about to order a turn to the southeast, taking them to point-blank range to fire on those ships from seaward. It would be a largely ineffectual gesture at this point, but it was something his battered, balky ship could still do. Then, one of Ed's signal strikers brought a hastily scribbled message form. Matt read it and scowled. *Ed Palmer's always been good about that,* he reflected, *delivering news like this by message form instead of just calling it up. Lets me think about what to do before everybody knows the situation—and he obviously thinks I'll want to do something about it.*

The Wall of Trees

Despite all her "modern" weapons, Major Risa-Sab-At wished the 1st Raider Brigade still had shields. Shields had been taken up, discarded, and then taken up again numerous times by various outfits as their tactics changed. They might've saved Flynn's Rangers on North Hill in Indiaa if they'd had them. They *had* saved *Walker* when her Marines defended her decks, and the Marines in the East, fighting the Doms, still used them to good effect. But the whole purpose of the 1st Raider Brigade was to move swiftly with its lethal weapons mix and plenty of ammunition. It wasn't an outfit intended for defense, and shields were heavy.

It was a passing thought she had no time for now. She'd seen—participated in—numerous epic slaughters of Grik before, but had to think that nothing she'd experienced could possibly compare with this. For one thing, she had more Grik coming at her than she'd ever seen so concentrated in one place, and for another, she had more terrible weapons than ever before to slay them with. *But shields would be nice, when they reach the top of the wall,* she added wistfully, and it looked like, in spite of her cannon, mortars, Blitzerbugs, grenades, rifles, and even flamethrowers, the Grik *would* reach the top.

Cannon, light six-pounders mostly, that had been easier to build platform embrasures for and haul close to the summit, spat double loads of canister into the howling horde, mulching great swaths of Grik into mewling heaps, but the mob closed over the bloody mounds and pressed on. Mortar bombs exploded near the tree line, making chaos in the mass still rushing into the open ground; but all was already chaos and the Grik knew the direction of their prey. Allin-Silva rifles crackled uninterrupted as human and Lemurian troopers fed their hungry breeches and Maroon muskets on the right made duller, slower, popping sounds, but not terribly slower after all. They were holding firm so far. Grenades thumped as they were rolled down the slope to geyser earth and rotten wood, mixed with downy fur, into the sodden sky.

"Blitzers!" Risa cried, hearing the command passed along. Almost immediately, the distinctive clacking stutter of the little submachine guns added to the noise, spitting their .45-caliber bullets into Grik, now almost crawling to the summit. Scores screeched and rolled away, but more surged past them. Risa now wished she'd been given some of the new .30-cal "Brownings," copies of the M1917 "light" machine guns that *Walker* brought to this world that were just now making their appearance. Though they might be considered "light" compared to a .50, it still took four men or 'Cats to lug the weapon, tripod, and enough ammunition to make it worthwhile, so none had yet found its way to the Raiders.

One "heavy" weapon the Raiders had was a number of "flamethrowers," essentially just wands with an igniter attached by a hose to a fuel tank that was pressurized by a pair of 'Cats on a hand pump. Originally enclosed in a small, wheeled cart that could be drawn by a pair of men or 'Cats, the wheels had made the things impossible to transport through the jungle. The wheels were done away with, but then the same two troopers had to carry the cart/crate around. Everyone hated that duty, and most were terrified of the things—but so were the Grik, they'd learned.

"Flamethrowers!" Risa roared, judging that the climbing Grik were getting close enough for the short-range weapons. Pairs of Raiders went to work on the pumps while "fire-'Cats" edged their wands over the summit and pointed them down. Crossbow bolts sleeted over their heads or skated off their helmets, and they hunkered as low as they could before turning their valves and depressing their ignition triggers. A dozen gouts of orange flame roared down the slope in a rush of roiling black smoke, scorching the wet, rotting wood of the giant palisade and searing Grik. An unearthly keening wail accompanied the stench of burning flesh and fur that joined the fuel smoke, and the Grik beyond the reach of the flames recoiled as those in front writhed in agony or rolled and flopped amid horrible squealing screams like young rhino pigs being eaten alive.

"Cease fire, flamethrowers!" Risa called. There was little fuel in the weapons, and she had to reserve it. "Riflemen, pour it in!"

The torrent of flame receded, and the rifles and Blitzerbugs resumed their fire. The Maroons didn't have flamethrowers and had never stopped shooting. Far to the right, she could see the familiar wave of their bayonet-tipped muskets rising to be loaded, gray steel ramrods pushing charges of buck and ball down smoothbores, or heavy slugs down rifled barrels, and then lowering to fire. It hadn't been that long ago that all Allied troops had carried muskets like those, but then it hadn't been long since they'd used longbows and spears either. Yet those few short years felt like an eternity.

A crossbow bolt glanced off Risa's helmet, knocking it askew. Sheets of bolts came now, from below and afar, but those from a distance were slow, wobbly things, falling from high trajectories. The Grik bowstrings were damp and that affected their power, but they were still lethal and there were so many! 'Cats and men around her screamed or roared in pain and anger. Others simply slumped down, silent, as the wickedly sharp bolt points plunging from the sky nailed their helmets to their heads or struck gullets and spines. A man from the 7th Regiment to her left where Jindal had gone ran to her on the firing step, crouching low. "Major Jindal's compliments," he yelled over the fire, wind, and rain, "an' he begs ta' report he's runnin' low on ammunition for his rifles an' Blitzers! Voracious buggers they are!"

Risa gestured behind and below. "More is coming." One of their magazines, the closest behind the 7th, had been hit by errant bombs dropped by a wind-tossed zep formation that morning, but they had several more. She wasn't much afraid they'd run out of ammunition, for the rifles and cannon at least. The mortars and Blitzers were another matter. But right now it was taking time to bring it forward, up the rain-slippery reverse slope of their position. "Tell him to send more bearers. Take all you need from the other bunkers."

"Can't spare too many from the wall," the man said, peeking over it. Ever more Grik surged from the jungle, even as the mortars kept slaughtering them, and they were building for another push.

"Tell him to do it now," she began, but a bolt slammed down past the man's collarbone to bury itself deep in his chest. With a blood-hacking moan, he clutched the dark feathers at the end of the shaft and sank to his knees. "Corps-'Cats! On the double!" she shouted, then snatched a 'Cat out of the firing line. "Did you hear what I told that maan?"

"Ay, Major."

"Then take the message to Major Jindal, and hurry back as quick as you can!"

"Ay, ay!"

She glanced back over the wall at the seething mass of Grik, still climbing relentlessly against the merciless fire from above. "Flamethrowers, stand by!" she cried, making her way to the comm-'Cat crouched over his field telephone, protecting it from the rain with his body.

"You still connected?" she demanded. The delicate wires they strung behind the "Double E-ates" somebody had dubbed the things for no reason she could imagine, were always breaking. They needed braided wire for strength, and that she understood. "Get Second Corps HQ on the horn. Gener-aal Maraan if possible, but don't let 'em give you the runaround! I know they're busy too, but the Gener-aal has to know that we're in a jaam here, with probably just as many Grik as she has. Sure, our position's better, but we got just a brigade, the Maroons, an' a few of Col-nol Saachic's cav to stop 'em. An' if we *don't* stop 'em, it won't matter what she does, 'cause they'll be climbin' up her aass! You got that?"

"Yes, Major!"

"Then wind it up!" She turned and looked down, from the relative peace and security that momentarily surrounded her to the surf of yipping, roaring Grik clawing close once more. "Flamethrowers! Fire!" she yelled again, and once more the leading edge of the Grik horde withered under the hellish flames, shrieking, squealing, leaping in the air, trying to jump over those pressing from behind. Those were immediately slain in the "same old way" the Grik had always killed those that tried to flee, that "turned prey," she noticed with interest, but the rest kept coming this time. One reason she saw to her dismay was that the flamethrowers didn't reach as far or as vigorously, and she knew they must already be running out of fuel. Not quite, unfortunately, she saw to her horror, because amid startled cries to her right that rose to shrieks of terror, a fire-'Cat stumbled back, a crossbow bolt jutting from his eye, and he went down—his wand spraying his last flaming fuel on his comrades nearby. Most recoiled away in time, but more than a dozen Impie Marines of the 1st of the 11th got a murderous dose, and the screams tore her soul. She shook it off; she had no choice. These Grik might be the same mindless monsters they'd faced early in the war, but they'd definitely see and exploit an opportunity like the smoldering gap that had just opened before them.

"Fill that hole!" she roared, racing forward, stepping over burning, bawling men, and unslinging her own Blitzerbug. Others hurried to join her, but it might have already been too late. "Meet 'em with your bayonets!" she cried, racking her bolt back and firing quick bursts into slathering, toothy faces that appeared in front of her. Bayonets stabbed into the mass, thrusting, twisting, and rifles fired the big .50-80s to tear through two or three Grik at a time. Even the comm-'Cat she'd just spoken to was beside her now, hacking with his cutlass at a leather shield. Risa fired through it and the Grik fell away with a squawk, but another barged up, trying to skewer her with a spear. An Impie Marine drove his bayonet into the monster's neck, and she shot a Grik trying to hack him with its sword.

"I got through!" the comm-'Cat gasped beside her.

"What did they say?" she demanded, slamming another magazine in her Blitzer.

"Dat dey got a wider front, an' the Griks is maybe get past aroun' dem. Dey can't spare nobody right now. But dey say you right!" he added with a quick, angry blink. "We got de 'better position,' an' we got to hold it!"

Risa fired a long, frustrated burst that toppled several Grik. The gap was closing, finally, but more Grik were reaching the top of the Wall of Trees at last, all along the line.

"Right," Risa said grimly.

USS Walker

"Risa and Chack's Brigade, and all our new 'Maroon' friends under her command are catching hell on the Wall of Trees west of the harbor," Matt told the others in the pilothouse. Spanky rubbed his chin, and Bernie looked alarmed. Herring just stared, his expression unreadable. Doocy Meek had rejoined them on the bridge. Though he didn't know Risa well, he knew she was important to these people. "And Safir says she doesn't have anything she can send to help," Matt added.

"That's tough," Spanky growled. "Wish *we* could help." He gestured at the mass of Grik ships ahead. "But we got a target here that needs attention," he reminded. "Can't be two places at once. And even if we steamed into the harbor, we couldn't give Risa any supporting fire with the Griks so close under the wall. Shooting high enough to clear it, all our fire would fall way past, back in the jungle."

"That's better than nothing," Bernie insisted. "The Grik hitting her are coming from the jungle."

Matt shook his head. "Too dangerous. Even the water in the bay is too rough to risk shooting right over our friends' heads. One short round and we're Grik heroes. But Spanky's wrong. We *can* be in two places at once." Spanky looked at him, brows arching, and Matt turned to the signal striker. "Have Mr. Palmer instruct the PTs to meet us in the lee of those big rocks off the harbor mouth. We'll hook on and transfer as heavy a landing party as we can, with all the thirty cals and modern small arms on the ship. They'll take us ashore and join us with their new thirties too. The PTs can't do much else today," he added, looking at the surprised expressions.

"We?" Spanky growled.

"Well, not you, of course," Matt answered.

"That's not what I meant!"

"I know, but *you* can't go. Starboard engine back one-third. Port ahead two-thirds," he called to the 'Cat at the engine order telegraph. "That area just off the harbor mouth is liable to be the calmest place we can find. We'll hold the ship so the PTs can approach under our lee as well." He looked back at Spanky. "You'll stay with the ship. They should be finished rigging the tiller soon enough, and I want *Walker* back off the beach as soon as you can get her there, to keep blasting the Grik in front of Safir Maraan. You'll still have the twenty-fives and fifties, but I'd rather you didn't get any closer than they will reach."

Spanky grimaced, glancing at his crutch wedged between the chair and the forward bulkhead, then finally nodded. "When I said I figured you might have to whip things in shape ashore for a while, this isn't what I had in mind."

"Me either, but we do what we can. And this is what we can do." Matt looked at Minnie. "Pass the word to issue small arms and dismount the thirties from the rails. We'll take everybody not shooting, passing ammunition, keeping the screws turning, or fixing leaks." He considered. "That'll give us maybe fifty, counting the Marines. I'll take one of the gun crews off the amidships platform and one of the twenty-five-millimeter crews too. That's a dozen more. You'll *stand off*," he stressed to Spanky, "so you won't need to fight both sides at once." He looked at the others. "The rest of us are going to help Risa."

Transferring sixty-five men and 'Cats from the wallowing destroyer to the three bouncing, capering MTBs was a harrowing experience, but with a spiderweb of lines and cargo nets prerigged for safety as soon as the word was passed, and a long fender supported by the lifting boom on the mainmast aft, it all went fairly quickly. Everybody had friends with the Raiders. Matt turned Pam Cross away, even though his ship had suffered few casualties in the fighting so far. Those on the aft deckhouse had been either lightly wounded or killed outright. She might still be needed aboard, and there were plenty of corps-'Cats where they were going. He was still amused when she tried to swing down to one of the pitching boats anyway, just like she'd done to go with Silva's party to assault the Cowflop, but where Silva couldn't really give her orders, he could, and he harshly commanded her to remain with *Walker*. He also had to order Juan Marcos to stay behind, but the short, one-legged Filipino took it more gracefully until the bloated cook, Earl Lanier, whom Matt had somehow missed sliding down the line—and what a spectacle that must've been—waved jauntily at his little nemesis. Juan became exercised then, shouting unheard epithets, complete with imaginative gestures. Earl just grinned. Matt didn't know what use Lanier would be until he saw that the fat cook was possessively supporting the muzzle of one of the .30s, its grip end lightly gouging the PT's deck. Earl was a blob, but he was strong. Commander Herring had volunteered, somewhat to Matt's surprise, with a vague mention of something important he had to tell him when they had the chance. Commander Bernard Sandison came against his wishes, though he hadn't ordered the young man to stay. Of all *Walker*'s remaining human officers still with the ship, Matt probably felt most protective of the young torpedoman. Others could carry on his torpedo work by now, but Bernie was just . . . a really good kid. And he'd been grievously wounded before.

Most of *Walker*'s landing party carried Springfields, pistols, and cutlasses, but they also had four Thompsons, a BAR, and a dozen Blitzerbugs. Still, it was the .30-caliber machine guns, nine of them counting those they'd take from the PTs, that Matt hoped would turn the tide atop the Wall of Trees—if they could get there in time.

"All set?" he demanded of Chief Jeek, who was directing Gunner's Mate Pak-Ras-Ar's (Pack Rat's) number three gun crew in getting the weapons and ammunition secured.

"Ay, Skipper!"

"Then unhook from the fender and take in the lines!" He gestured for those still on *Walker* to pull up the cargo nets. "Let's go!" he shouted at the Lemurian ensign commanding the MTB. Nodding, the ensign spun his wheel and advanced the throttle. The two other boats quickly followed, roaring out of *Walker*'s lee and back into the heavier seas. From there they steered almost due south, trying to keep to the channel through the harbor mouth. It wasn't raining just then, though the heavy spray made that irrelevant, and the battle on the beach was only evident by the darker smoke smudging the gray day above it. The sound of the sea and the roaring engines drowned any battle noise they might've heard. They could barely even see the peak of the Wall of Trees where the Raiders fought; the haze was too thick and there was more rain between them. Matt turned, and for a moment he watched *Walker* toss and roll in the swells as she gathered way, throwing streamers of spray aside as she churned east-northeast. Her sides were streaked with rust again, except for the bright dents where Grik shot had knocked away both rust and paint. Her number two and four stacks bled wisps of smoke from new punctures, and the shattered aft searchlight gaped at him like an empty eye socket. But she'd performed heroically that day, as she always did, and the big battle flag streaming from her foremast left a proud, wistful lump in his throat. He was glad Sandra was away from here, she and the child she carried, but he was almost as glad that whatever happened to him that day, his ship and all she represented *should* live to fight on and remain the inspiration she'd been for so long, for so many. But he couldn't help but wonder if he'd ever set foot on her again. He shook his head.

The three PTs thundered through the channel, past the point where *Walker* had been stranded during the fight to take the city, the place where "Super Bosun" Fitzhugh Gray had died along with so many others. The only visible monument was the charred skeleton of a Grik cruiser that had grounded and burned beside Matt's ship, but Gray's real monument still lived in the hearts of all who'd known him.

"So much sacrifice for such a crummy place," Bernie Sandison shouted beside him, gazing at the same spot, full of the same thoughts.

"Yeah, but like I told Spanky, we do what we can. And after the Battle of Baalkpan, our priority has always been to take the fight to the

Grik's front porch instead of our own." He waved around. "And here we are, past the porch and right in the middle of their home. It's a crappy 'home,'" he conceded again, "and I wouldn't give two bits for it if they gave me a choice. Christ, the city's a dump, and even the rest of the island is a wild, monster-infested nightmare now. Nothing like the 'sacred homeland' Adar and all our Lemurian friends dreamed of and hoped it would be. I doubt even they still hold much regard for the place as anything *but* a place to fight the Grik."

"I hope you're right, Skipper," Bernie said, almost too quietly to hear. "But our problem—yours, mine, and all the gals and fellas on *Walker*— is that we always bring *our* home *to* the fight, wherever it is. And it always takes a beating," he added bitterly. "We fight here to keep the Grik out of Aryaal and B'mbaado, Baalkpan, and Maa-ni-la, and the rest of the world eventually. But no matter what this new nation, this 'Union' Mr. Letts is cooking up, winds up looking like, *Walker* is still the only 'home,' the only 'nation' Chief Gray was fighting for at the end, and her people, human and Lemurian, you, me—his *shipmates*—were the only 'countrymen' he was defending."

Matt nodded. He'd been thinking much the same ever since that fight—but he'd been wrong, and so was Bernie. "But that's the way it always is," he insisted. "In the heat of action, you fight for yourself, your buddies, your ship"—he waved at the crest of the Wall of Trees ahead— "and your position. That's what keeps you going. Sometimes it's the only thing. But that doesn't mean you're not fighting for something bigger too." He smiled. "My wife once told me, a long time ago it seems now, to 'decide what was right and then fight my ship.' Well, that's what I've tried to do. Not always well," he admitted, "but I try. And by doing so, I, *we*, also fight for the bigger 'right thing' of defeating the Grik so our people, old and new, will be safe. Period. *Our people*, Bernie: human and Lemurian, my wife and child, our friends back home or on other ships, other battlefields—even that pretty Impie gal you're sweet on back in Baalkpan!" he added, and saw Bernie blush. "I don't know as much about this 'Union' Alan Letts is cooking up as I'd like, but I know he hates fascism and communism—and do you think any 'Cats would join a system that stank of totalitarianism? So I think he'll get it right, and I bet he's doing his best to make sure its first goal is to keep the people we care about safe. And if that's the case, I'm fighting for it too, and no 'Home,' not Aryaal, Baalkpan, even *Walker*, is more important than the people that make them one—and make that 'Union.'" He shrugged. "You're right about Chief Gray, though. And at the very end, his focus narrowed even further; from defending his 'home' ship, to saving my life. And insignificant as that may seem in the grand scheme of things, that doesn't mean he ever stopped fighting for his ship, the Alliance, or even the 'Union' he didn't know any more about than I did. Does that make sense?"

"I guess so," Bernie grudged. "It's just hard to keep things in perspective sometimes."

"You're telling me!" Matt agreed. "I always preferred to keep things black-and-white, good and bad, but it's just not always that simple. Sometimes I envy that idiot Silva. Even he's run into a gray area from time to time, I understand, and he sure thrives on stirring them up! But generally he's still a light switch. Switch on; let 'em live. Switch off; kill everything you're pointed at. And he sleeps like a rock," he added wistfully.

"I wish he were here. And Chack too," Bernie said.

"Yeah. Look, time to get ready. We're getting close to the wrecked Grik BBs, and as soon as we squirm through them, we'll go ashore at the dock. When we do, make sure all the heavy weapons are organized. You're in charge of them."

"Aye, aye, sir."

When Bernie moved aft, against the pitching motion of the boat, Matt realized Commander Simon Herring had replaced him. "Did you mean what you said, about nothing mattering but the people we defend?" Herring asked.

"Of course."

"No land, no 'Home,' not even your ship, in the end?"

"That's what I told Bernie," Matt stated, implying that Herring was intruding to listen. Herring caught the reprimand and spread his hands. "I'm a snoop, remember? And your position is somewhat . . . modified from others you've taken in the past."

"I don't know what you mean."

"Perhaps not. The subtle progression of attitudes from one to another, often quite diverse, is rarely noted by those who experience them."

"You've been using shrinkery on me!" Matt suddenly realized.

"Shrinkery! Ha! Excellent. I'll have to remember that." He looked at Matt. "Of course I have. That's part of my job; a large part, if I ever return to Baalkpan and the specific duties I was assigned. As you should certainly know, my initial evaluation of, and esteem for you, have both undergone a significant 'progression' as well, but I've remained . . . concerned about certain aspects of your overall strategy." He nodded at Bernie. "Now I wonder if I've clung to that concern too long."

"What are you getting at, Commander?"

"Only that, as I hinted earlier, I'd like to request a private, perhaps even lengthy discussion of an idea I have."

"If you've got an idea that might help out now, you'd better spill it," Matt warned. Herring waved it away. "It can have no bearing on today's events, I assure you. It's . . . much too late for that. But it could well have a decisive effect at a later date."

"If we survive today," Matt interjected, and Herring blinked.

"If, indeed."

Matt looked forward as the boat bounced close to a bomb-ravaged dock. 'Cats were waiting there, backed by others mounted on vicious-looking me-naaks, or "meanies." There were more than a hundred, and all were dirty, powder smudged, even blood streaked, and he wondered where they came from. "We'll have our talk, Mr. Herring, as soon as we finish up here," he said, hopping across to the dock and returning the salute of a Maa-ni-lo cav-'Cat, standing by a meanie with its jaws lashed shut. "Corporal," Matt said, "what are you doing here?"

"Col-nol Saachic sent us, to fetch you an' your destroyermen—an' your weapons—to Major Risa-Sab-At an' Major Jin-daal. Tings is tight, an' there's not a moment to spare. He figgered you wouldn't want to run all the way."

Matt stared at the me-naak. He'd never ridden one of the terrifying creatures and didn't want to, but like the corporal said, it beat running. "Commander Sandison, Chief Jeek, get our people paired off and mounted up." He stared dubiously at Earl Lanier, stepping across the gap between the boat and the dock, "his" Browning machine gun, one of *Walker*'s originals with its battered water jacket resting heavily on his shoulder. Earl stopped and took a wide-eyed step back when it became clear he'd have to ride a meanie.

"He ain't too heavy. Barely," the 'Cat assured. "You hafta ride him single, less you strap that gun on another," he called.

Earl set his jaw and stepped forward again. "I'll keep my gun," he snarled. "And I've rode a horse before. How different can it be? He'll just follow along, right?"

Another 'Cat snorted a laugh. "Sure—if you can hold on. You fall off, bust open, he gonna eat you! Them straps won't hold his mouth shut long, he gets tempted by too sweet a snack!"

"Shut up, you fish-faced little monkey!" Earl roared. "I'll stay on! I can ride anything with feet. Gimme a hand with this gun!"

Matt rode behind the corporal, his Springfield slung across his back. He was a little unsteady and wasn't sure what to do with his hands until the 'Cat told him to "grab on me"! After that, it was easy. The me-naak had a smooth, sure-footed gait even through the muddy debris, and its back was steady as a rock. Matt knew the creatures grew tolerant, even apparently fond of longtime riders, and the cav-'Cats often became very attached to them as well. Their thick thoracic case and rough hide made them nearly bullet- and arrow-proof, and they were more terrifying that any medieval warhorse when their muzzles were removed in close combat. If it weren't for their occasional tendency to try to eat their riders in a fit of pique, they'd be better than horses. *Of course, horses bite, stomp on your feet, and sometimes try to throw you,* Matt reflected. He looked around.

The column that left the docks was making good time, and there was a minimum of straggling. He knew his destroyermen and 'Cats had been just as hesitant to ride as he, but riding double, there seemed to be few problems. One beast was far behind, acting up, but it was starting to rain again and he couldn't see who rode it. *Probably Lanier,* he supposed, *with one of the guns. Never should've let him keep the thing, but there's nothing for it now.* Passing the rearward trenches of the troops guarding the Grik civvies, he saw another cluster of riders trotting toward the charred hovels those creatures dwelt in, and wondered what that was about. He looked forward. Suddenly, they were at the base of the Wall of Trees. Looking high above, he saw the flash of rifles and the cloud of gun smoke swirling at its peak for a good distance to the left and right.

"Hold on!" the cav-'Cat warned. "We goin' straight up, an' it's kinda steep!"

"Straight to the center?" Matt asked as the meanie made its first lunge upward.

"Ay. The Maroons is holdin' well enough on the right," the 'Cat admitted grudgingly, "but these Griks is hittin' the center hardest. Major Risa don't know if they doin' it on purpose, to break through an' roll up either side, or they doin' it by accident, just chargin' at the middle like they always used to do. Don't matter. It'll work just the same if the Raiders break." Matt could see that was close to happening. The firing was intense, and crossbow bolts fluttered by them even here, but now bayonets flashed and the defenders were edging back as more and more Grik gained the crest.

"Bring us up behind the Raiders, parallel to their position!" Matt ordered.

"That's what I's gonna do!" the 'Cat shouted back to be heard over the fighting. Curving to the left on the high angle, reverse side of the wall, the ride was much more frightening—but it didn't last long. "Off here!" the 'Cat cried. "Holders!" he shouted. Even as Matt's landing party dropped from the animals, one 'Cat in four gathered the reins to hold the me-naaks as their riders raced up the slope with their carbines.

"Riflemen! With me!" Matt shouted, taking the Springfield off his back and affixing the bayonet. Others were doing the same.

"What about the machine guns?" Bernie shouted back.

"We can't just shoot up there from here!" Matt answered. "Put 'em together and bring 'em up ready to fire." He looked at the others. "We have to push the Grik back over the edge first, see? Follow me!" With that, he staggered up the wet, mushy slope toward the sagging line, followed by forty-odd 'Cats and a ragged cheer. Their puny numbers and gasping cheer had no effect on the Grik. They couldn't see it or hear it, most likely. But the exhausted 'Cats and men of the 1st Raider Brigade knew what it meant, and with cav-'Cats and their carbines first, then Matt's destroyermen joining them, they fought back with renewed vigor.

Springfields boomed, not as loud as the Allin-Silvas up close, but with greater pressure that pounded eardrums in the press. They fired faster too, bolts working feverishly and stripper clips reloading five rounds in the time Allin-Silvas took to load one. Blitzers stuttered, and the distinctive *Ta-ta-tat! Ta-ta-tat!* of Thompsons joined in, accompanied by the *Wham-wham-wham!* of Packrat's BAR. Matt shot a Grik in the face, right in its open mouth, and it fell away, but another was there before he even worked his bolt, swinging its curved sword in a wide arc aimed at his head. Simon Herring shot it, then gave a high-pitched yell and lunged forward with his bayonet, toppling it backward. Matt nodded at the wide-eyed man, who was wiping spattered blood off his face with his hand, and finished chambering another round. He fired. Chief Jeek was suddenly there beside him, firing a Thompson. Rain sizzled on the hot barrel, and smoky brass spewed in the air. Matt realized the battered weapon was the same one Gray was using when he died, and Jeek was doing the same thing with it—protecting *him*.

"Thank God you're here!" Major Jindal yelled in his ear, jabbing past him with a bayonet at a Grik trying to slink in low. The creature squealed and another tripped over it, taking three rounds from Jeek's tommy gun that spewed steaming gobbets back at them.

"Where's Risa?" Matt demanded, fending off a spear aimed at his face and slamming the rifle barrel down hard on a Grik head. Herring shot it.

"God knows! To the right, I think! The Maroons are fighting well, like devils in fact, but they were having a hard time of it where their lines touch ours. She took a squad with Blitzers to bolster them!"

"When?"

Jindal gestured helplessly.

"Doesn't matter," Matt said. "We have to push them over the crest to use our machine guns, and this looked like the toughest spot from behind. Kill them!" he roared, his voice cracking in the dense smoke flowing back over the peak, but he doubted his words went far in the more violent wind and heavier rain that assailed him now. *The wind's come around more out of the west,* his subconscious sailor's mind told him without asking. Herring screamed, dropping his rifle in the rotten wood, mud, and churned-up vegetation that grew from it. He went to his knees, clutching his abdomen, and a Grik clamped jaws on his shoulder and tried to pull him away. He screamed again and fell forward, flailing his hands and feet for purchase to resist. Matt shot the Grik in the head and its jaws slacked, allowing Jeek and another 'Cat to drag Herring back. "Corps-'Cat!" Jeek shouted.

"Keep pushing!" Matt yelled, stuffing rounds in his rifle and throwing the stripper clip away. He'd reached the peak at last, but the fight was desperately close and he *had* to clear a spot for the .30s! Something wet and slimy was underfoot, and he slipped and fell. Jeek and Jindal crowded around him, firing and stabbing, as he tried to climb his rifle, but something grabbed his leg and claws pierced his calf. He looked and saw the Grik whose guts he'd stepped in trying to drag him to its teeth. Flipping open the flap on his holster, he drew his 1911 Colt, thumbed the safety down, and blew the thing's eye out. Its claws spasmed and he yelled, but then the claws relaxed.

"Gangway, you buncha fuzzy monkeys!" Earl Lanier bellowed, waddling up behind, the heavy machine gun cradled in his arms. "Here! Next to the Skipper!" he ranted, and a 'Cat dropped a tripod that spattered Matt with bloody mud. Lanier splashed to a knee and dropped the pintle in the hole. "Feed me!" he roared, and Matt couldn't help barking a laugh, considering the source, and Lanier glared at him while the 'Cat quickly positioned a long ribbon of shiny brass shells.

"Get the Skipper back, Jeek," Earl shouted over the wind and rain and battle. "He's in the way!" Jeek seemed to notice Earl for the first time, as well as the fact that Matt was down, and he and Jindal dragged Matt behind the gun. "Get a load o' this!" Earl growled, racking the bolt and pointing the weapon at a new surge of Grik, but instead of the expected chattering spray of copper-jacketed lead, there was only a muffled *clack*, barely heard. Earl's face lost all expression. "Now, ain't that the god-awfulest sound you ever heard?" he murmured, and frantically racked the bolt again. Jindal had helped Matt to his feet, and for the first time he finally looked down on the swarm of Grik below, choking the area between him and the jungle. At a glance, they seemed numberless, but Jindal pointed at the trees, indistinct in the storm-lashed rain. "No more coming!" he gasped. "No more coming out of the jungle! This must be all of them, at last!" He seemed . . . relieved, and Matt took his word, but looking down, he still saw a hell of a lot of Grik climbing toward them. What, "only" twenty or twenty-five thousand more?

"Get that thing shooting or get it the hell out of the way and let somebody else in!" he ordered Earl. "Bernie!" he yelled back down the slope. "Get them in! Anywhere you can!" He couldn't see more than a few paces to either side, but it looked like this was the only position so far. Or maybe not, he reevaluated, hearing rapid fire from one of the gun embrasures he'd seen coming up. Most were still spitting canister, but maybe that gun was damaged or out of ammunition. Bernie might find other places. He looked at the swarm and again at Earl, who was slapping and cursing his weapon. No time. Earl would get his gun going or he wouldn't. The others would find their own positions or not—there was nothing left to do but fight. His leg ached where the Grik had clawed him, and his eyes were blurred by rain and blood, with a near wall of water pouring off his helmet rim when he looked down. Crossbow bolts still fluttered thickly, but their strings were wet and they were much less powerful. Blitzers and rifles still chattered and cracked in response, but there were so many Grik—and they just kept coming. The ones they'd pushed back were having a tough time regaining their ground, scrabbling up the slippery slope on all fours, the rain directly in their upturned faces. Many had even discarded their weapons, coming on with just their teeth and claws. *Nothing left to do but fight*, Matt told himself again, and thrusting his pistol in his belt, he raised his Springfield once more. "Let 'em have it!" he shouted at those around him.

Hij Geerki slid down from the me-naak he'd ridden to this ravaged area between the "civilian" Grik and the frustrated troops guarding them. Not far away, to his left, the battle raged at the top of the Wall of Trees, and he yearned to be there, fighting as he'd done in Indiaa. *What a strange craving that is*, he reflected. *I am no warrior, and I am old and nearly useless. Yet, I feel . . . compelled somehow, to help these friends of my master, General Lord Muln Rolak. Very strange indeed.* The same apparent "First Hij" of these resident Grik that he'd spoken to before was waiting for him in the rain, as Geerki had requested. That had been simple enough to arrange. English was considered the "scientific" tongue, and enough upper-class Hij could read it, at least. A message had been sent to the commander of the entrenched brigade to write out the request, put it in a water bottle, and then just throw it toward the surviving Grik huddled under whatever shelter they could find. That was how he'd first made contact. That had been a much different situation, however, and he wasn't sure they'd meet him this time, but this one did. Geerki peered at the First Hij standing before him, warm rain soaking his thick, finely woven, hooded cape, and wondered how best to proceed. Summoning himself to behave as he'd seen his master do in similar situations, he did his best to project an air of confidence.

"You have had ample time to consider 'The Offer,'" he said. "I must hear your reply."

"A strangely generous 'offer,' made by hunters to those who do not hunt," the creature observed. "And not an offer to *join* the hunt. You ask me to consider a proposal so distressingly unprecedented that I may as well contemplate walking across the sea—or flying, like a winged beast! It seems impossible that anyone could even imagine such a thing."

"We fly," Geerki pointed out dryly, "as do Ghaarrichk'k now. Nothing is impossible. Even offers such as the one I brought you, to those such as us, from *warriors*. My masters make 'offers,' alliances, accommodations, of all sorts among themselves—and to other folk like us that I have seen." He clasped his breast. "I serve them myself, and I thrive."

"So you say," the First Hij replied skeptically.

"You can doubt me? Here I am before you!"

The First Hij sighed. "It is so difficult to know what to do in these strange times. Prey has come to the Celestial City, slain our Giver of Life, and now 'offers' to give us life in her stead. I am not able to believe such things even as I see them." He jerked his snout toward the battle. "And perhaps I should not. Warriors *have* come. If they destroy your masters, all will return to as it was before, for us. It is so much simpler to wait for that than to contemplate the unsettling thoughts you bring. I believe we should wait."

"If you wait for all to be as it was, then you wait in vain. The Ghaarrichk'k will not win this fight. And even if they do, they will slaughter you for what you have seen. They have done it everywhere else." He cocked his head. "But I come to tell you that you *may* wait," Geerki said to the other's surprise, "as long as 'wait' is all you do." He stared up at the dark, heavy clouds and let the rain wash his face. "I was once as you, so I understand your hesitation. But having seen and done the things I have, *lived* as I have, since accepting my own 'offer' from my master, I am no longer Ghaarrichk'k, and I despise the miserable existence you would again embrace. Even so, I will force you to make no choice *except* to do absolutely nothing until you do decide."

"What could we do? We are not warriors."

"You might cause a distraction, as I suspect you've been urged to do by the warriors who remain among you." He held up a hand. "Do not protest! Do not lie. I know it is so. Coordination was required for this attack, and it could have had no other source." He made a very human shrug like he'd seen General Pete Alden make so often. "Still, the offer remains. You may contemplate further, as I have said, whether you wish to truly live for the first time in your life, and you may do that for as long as you like. But you must decide this instant whether you will do absolutely nothing while the battle proceeds—or die."

"How can you know which I choose, in truth?"

"Choose to live by destroying the warriors among you and casting them here upon this muddy ground. They will not die easily and there will be fighting. They are warriors, after all, and your only weapons are those you were born with. The brigade behind me will see the fighting and will leave you to join the greater battle. If they do not see you do what I say, they will destroy each and every one of you—and *then* leave to join the battle. It's actually quite simple."

"What you propose is not 'doing nothing,'" the First Hij grated uneasily, glancing behind him.

"From my perspective it is," Geerki suddenly snarled, "as it relates to the outcome of the battle here today." He sneered. "Even this, my masters here would have done for you, had you made the greater choice sooner. Consider it the price of indecision." Geerki turned to stalk away, but the First Hij called to him. "How soon must you see us . . ." He paused, probably glancing behind him again, toward where warrior Hij doubtless watched. "How soon must you see us 'doing nothing'?" he pleaded.

"Now," Geerki replied. "I go to stir the troops that guard you to march to battle—or destroy you all. You have until I reach them to begin . . . doing nothing," he almost spat, amazed that he sprang from the same species as that loathsome creature. He knew many of his master's friends remained skeptical that he truly was as devoted to them as he tried to prove each day, but he forgave them. What else were they to think, given the evidence of the Grik at large? But he knew the difference between what he was and what he'd been, and thanked the Lemurian's Maker of All Things that he'd been captured that day in Raan-goon. He did spit then, hacking a gobbet of phlegm from deep in his throat, and quickened his pace. Long before he reached the trenchline, he heard the growing tumult of fighting behind him.

"Now you can go," he told the Lemurian officer waiting expectantly below. He looked northeast to where the "main" battle led by General Queen Safir Maraan raged on the beach across the storm-ripped harbor. "I ser' you, Lord!" he said aloud, fervently.

The Wall of Trees

Five machine guns were up and running now, steaming, hissing, crackling, spitting fire, and scything Grik away like twigs from a broom. They tumbled back, falling on others, tripping them, sliding or rolling down the slope. More crawled over them, clawing at mud and bodies, roaring defiance and rage. Canister gusted from embrasures, sweeping dozens down, right in front of their muzzles, and .50-80 Allin-Silvas, .30-06 Springfields, and .45 ACP from Blitzers, Thompsons, and 1911s continued to slay and maim. Bayonets did their grisly work as the Grik lapped at the summit, tearing bowels, gouging eyes, ripping throats—but the Grik were killing too, with their wicked spears, swords, claws, and teeth, and the Raiders' line was thinning. The slope ran with blood and gore mixed with feces, and the wind slammed the stench in the defenders' faces, causing many to retch even as they fought. Nothing Matt had seen in this war, except maybe the fight for *Walker*, compared to the concentrated killing he and his friends were doing. But still the Grik came on. Worse, since they hadn't been able to use the machine guns all at once and mass their fire, they hadn't been able to create the sudden, decisive edge Matt wanted—and they hadn't been able to bring enough ammunition to keep them going long. So now they were feeding five guns with the ammo they brought for nine, and they were already running low.

Matt emptied his Springfield again and drew his pistol, firing quickly into faces and bodies that writhed in front of him. The loud popping of the pistol was muted now, barely heard by his tortured ears over the thunderous roar of battle.

"Gen'raal Maraan can send nothing!" came the cry of the comm-'Cat behind him. "She holds, even wins, she thinks—but the last Grik landed farther down the coast, and she must shift forces there to stop them!"

"Well, we ain't gonna win here, if we don't get some goddamn *help*!"

Earl Lanier shouted excitedly to the right of Matt's leg. He'd fixed his gun, but he was helping a 'Cat insert another belt. He had only a couple more. Packrat was firing another Browning to Matt's left, chewing Grik with short, clattering bursts. Matt looked farther to the left, but the rain was worsening as the storm built strength and he couldn't see far. For all he knew, the Grik might've hit the Wall of Trees in other, more feebly defended places as well, but he didn't think so. These were "old-style" Grik—there could be no doubt of that now—and having found their enemy, they'd attack it with a single-minded ferocity that still amazed him. Whether those that faced Safir Maraan were any different he couldn't know, but he doubted they were, and only the accident of the weather had driven their ships ashore where they might force her to extend her lines. "She says she already sent all she can!" the comm-'Cat yelled, and Matt blinked bitter amusement at that. He and his destroyermen were the only reinforcements that had reached the Raiders.

"Goddamn it!" Earl shrieked when his gun quit again. "An' this ain't even one o' those new pieces o' shit! It's a *Colt* for God's sake!"

"It's a hard-used Colt," Bernie shouted, carrying a pair of ammo cans and tossing them down in the mud. "Pitch it. Here's another one!" A 'Cat behind him was carrying one of the newly made weapons, the rain beading on the oil that covered it. "I doubt this one's even been fired. You take Packrat's gun. Packrat! Over here!"

"What the hell?" Earl bawled. "No damn 'Cat . . ."

"Can cook like you," Bernie finished, letting others decide what he meant. "Packrat knows guns better." He joined Matt, his pistol in his hand. "That's the very last ammo," he shouted in his ear. "When it's gone . . ."

"We keep fighting," Matt said simply, holstering his own pistol. His Springfield was stabbed in the mud by its bayonet beside him. "I'm already empty." Reluctantly, he drew his battered Academy sword and ran his hand down the notched blade. Bernie looked at him, rain-thinned blood spatter running down his boyish face. He paused, then nodded grimly.

"We keep fighting," he agreed. The semicircle of Grik in front of them that had been kept open by the pair of machine guns began to close. Earl *splapped* down behind Packrat's gun, cursing at the Grik guts he'd landed in, and Packrat and his assistant were jamming a belt into the new one. The fighting remained close everywhere else, but they'd have one more brief respite before the Grik closed over them here and Matt would have to use his sword yet again—one more time.

It was hard to hear, but it suddenly seemed like a new kind of yell was building on the right. At first, Matt thought it was the roar of the mounting wind. But shouts raced toward them down the line, excited, exhausted shouts of hope—then glee, which turned to screams of triumph and encouragement.

"What the hell?" Matt murmured, straining to see. The Grik were too close, too thick to see beyond them, and they were still pushing forward, snarling, yipping in anticipation, but he sensed that something was happening. Something the Grik wouldn't like. "Get those guns firing!" he shouted. "Everyone! Let 'em have it with everything you've got!" The firing had diminished as those who still had ammunition tried to conserve it, but now they let loose with a last, stunning flurry that mowed the closest Grik down. Packrat's new Browning opened up, chopping across the faltering Grik behind, side to side, and then Earl's finally joined in, doubling the slaughter. The roar on the right continued to mount, and Grik started looking that way, pausing, staring, mouths gaping wide in sudden confusion. They were winning, grinding down their prey—but the sounds of triumph were not Grik and even if they couldn't see what was happening either, they instinctively knew it wasn't right. Major Jindal practically crashed into Matt, gasping, and Matt held him up before he could fall, avoiding the bloody bayonet on the rifle the man still clutched.

"Risa!" Jindal grated, and cleared his throat. "God, how can I be so thirsty on such a day!" He looked at Matt, at Bernie. "Risa is charging the Grik flank with the Maroons!" he finally managed.

"They'll be torn apart!" Bernie objected.

"No! The brigade guarding the Grik below has joined her! Nearly the entire brigade! That creature, Geerki, I believe, says even if the 'civilian' Grik wanted to cause any mischief, they are somewhat too occupied at present to achieve it!" Matt tried to see again, and suddenly he could. A sudden easing of the torrential rain revealed a roaring tide of tie-dyed, helmeted troops and gray steel bayonet-bristling muskets surging down the slope from the right, backed by far greater numbers than they'd had before. And the Grik were responding, recoiling, being driven under, and starting to flee. Even as they did, others behind them, as yet unaffected or unaware, slew the ones that turned on them, fighting to get away, or were killed themselves in the growing panic.

"Grik rout," Matt said, amazed.

"What's that?" Jindal asked.

"Grik rout," Matt explained. "Courtney Bradford's term. Something you've never had the pleasure of seeing before, and I never thought I would again. Don't you get it? These are 'old' Grik, probably 'pure' Grik. They only know attack, and if they're not attacking, they're losing." He smiled grimly. "And if they're losing, they run away, useless to continue the fight!"

"What can we do?"

Matt stared to the right, watching the entire line at the summit begin to follow Risa's charge, peeling down to join it as the companies to their right, one by one, did the same.

"Charge them!" Matt replied, grinning now. "Pass the word! Charge bayonets, by companies, from the right! Probably not a proper command, but I'm a destroyerman, not a Marine. Cease firing as soon as the guys around us go!" he shouted at Earl and Packrat.

"What?" Earl yelled back. With a feral yell that seemed to release all the tension and terror of that long, vicious fight, the men and 'Cats who moments before had been preparing to make their final, bitter stand, leveled their bayonets and raced down the slope at the Grik who'd already started to turn away.

"Cease firing!" Matt repeated.

"Which I already did, didn't I?" Earl snapped back, his tone surly. Matt just stared at him and then started to laugh.

"I ser' you, Lord!" Matt heard a breathless, rasping call, and saw Hij Geerki—protectively surrounded by six Lemurian Marines to keep him from being murdered, no doubt—being ushered into his presence.

"You certainly do, Hij Geerki. You certainly do," Matt said seriously. Geerki looked down, almost modestly, Matt thought.

"I too old to . . . join that killing," Geerki said. "'Ut I do all I can," he added piously.

Matt was struck by how similar Geerki's intent had been to his own not long ago. "You did swell. Escort this . . . person to General Maraan's main HQ in the Cowflop. Make sure he's comfortable and well fed," he told the Marines. "He's going to be busy, and he'll need some rest."

"Ay, ay, Cap-i-taan Reddy!"

"Skipper," Bernie said, touching Matt's sleeve. Matt looked at him and saw him nod down the slope behind where corps-'Cats feverishly tended the many wounded that had been dragged away from the fight. A pair was kneeling over a man in mud and blood-spattered Navy whites. Matt didn't even look behind him. The battle here was over as soon as the Grik turned away. Many more would die, chasing them down, and he'd tried to tell Jindal to stop the pursuit at the jungle, but he'd bolted to join the charge before he could. *Risa will stop them,* he thought. *She knows. Any Grik that escape us today will belong to the jungle,* he added grimly to himself. A few might make it to one of the abandoned Grik cities down the west coast, but they'd be no threat. Unlike the "civvies," they probably would murder one another to the last. "Round up *Walker*'s people," he told Bernie. "Make a count, and find some cav-'Cats and meanies. I want to get down to Safir as quick as we can if she needs us there. There's got to be more ammo someplace. Hopefully, not too many of our people joined the charge," he added, then stepped down the slope.

Simon Herring was looking up at him as he approached, his eyes wide and surprisingly clear, considering how much seep the corps-'Cats had probably given him for the pain. But his face was terribly pale, and there was far too much blood soaking the bandages on his torso past his unbuttoned tunic.

"It was a spear," Herring explained almost apologetically. "Would you believe it? A spear. How could I let myself be killed by a spear in 1944!" He snorted and tried to sit up, but the corps-'Cats held him down. He relaxed but looked back at Matt. "Another famous victory, Captain Reddy. I salute you." Matt was surprised that there was no sarcasm in his tone, and he sat in the mud beside the man, grunting a little from his wounded leg and aching joints and muscles. He stabbed his sword into the ground and just stared past the Cowflop and the jumbled battle beyond, out to sea. The wind was milder in the lee of the great wall and though the visibility was better now, the storm on the water seemed even stronger. That was when he knew he wouldn't be riding to save Safir Maraan next; she wouldn't need him.

Past the pounding, surf-racked wreckage of the mighty Grik fleet, there were now *two* shadowy gray shapes in the distance. One was his beloved *Walker*, of course, and he saw occasional deliberate, unheard flashes from her guns. Steaming ahead of her, however, the odd "dazzle" paint job further obscuring the lines of her much larger form, was the converted freighter turned armored cruiser, USS *Santa Catalina* (CAP-1). She'd clearly outpaced her consorts to arrive so soon. And unlike *Walker*, she had plenty of ammunition and was pounding the Grik to smithereens with her more numerous, more powerful weapons. *No*, Matt thought tiredly. *I won't be going anywhere.* He looked forward to seeing Russ Chappelle, Mikey Monk, Cathy McCoy, and all his other friends on the doughty old ship, but right then he belonged where he was, with the people who'd held the back door to this crappy place—and the strange, dying man beside him.

"*Santy Cat*'s here," he told Herring.

"Leave us!" Herring ordered the corps-'Cats, who looked at Matt. He nodded, and they moved to another patient. "I've been watching her," Herring told Matt. "I saw her arrive some time ago." He closed his eyes and took several careful breaths. "A famous victory," he finally repeated, "and I don't know why I'm surprised anymore. You do seem to have a curious aptitude for creating them, regardless."

"I didn't create anything but a mess," Matt said.

"Untrue. We were all 'suckered,' but as usual, you ensured that the enemy did not benefit. That is perhaps your greatest talent. You are always making bricks without straw, and yet they somehow endure." He coughed, and a blob of mucous and blood came to his lips and slid down his cheek. "So much for that 'long talk' I requested," he murmured, "so I will just tell you what I have to say and let you decide what to do with the information. I'd hoped to counsel you, but there won't be time for that." He blinked. "Remember the organic weapon that Adar authorized and Mr. Sandison helped create?" Matt looked at Bernie, still standing beside them, and saw his confusion.

Bernie had indeed helped make a weapon that Courtney Bradford considered worse, and far more insidious than gas. It was made from the collected seed-thorns of a kudzu-like plant they'd discovered on Yap Island. The terrible thing about this plant was that it grew in the living tissue of whatever creature was pierced by the thorn, very quickly consuming it and sprouting from the body to produce more thorns. In addition to the dreadful nature of the plant as a weapon—spreading or dropping the tiny seed-thorns where they might fall on enemies, or be stepped on or ingested, could kill uncountable numbers of them in the most horrendous way—Bradford feared such a deployment would spread the plant uncontrollably, and might ultimately render entire continents uninhabitable.

"Mr. Sandison didn't know," Herring assured him, "but the weapon, the 'kudzu bomb,' as I believe he referred to it, is here."

"What?" Bernie gasped. "How?"

"I brought it," Herring simply said. "And it's perhaps not precisely *here*—I don't really know anymore. But it was aboard *Salissa*, packed in several barrels labeled as a dietary supplement for captured Grik. A kind of fish hash, I believe." He chuckled and more blood came up. "Grik food," he managed. "An amusing irony I indulged in." He looked at Matt, seeming to have trouble focusing now. "It may have been moved. In fact, I suspect it has."

"If Bernie didn't know, who else does? Keje? Adar?"

"Neither, at first, though I told Adar after the battle to take this place. He said he'd move it to the Celestial Palace, the uh, 'Cowflop,' but I don't know if he ever did. He may have told Keje himself, and left it aboard *Salissa*. Other than Adar, I told only two others. One is Corporal Ian Miles, who accompanied Mr. Bradford, Chack, and that interesting Mr. Silva on their expedition south." He looked troubled. "I no longer trust Corporal Miles for various reasons; nor should you. He is a capable Marine and should pose no threat to his companions on their mission, but his only real loyalty is to himself."

"Who else, Herring?" Matt demanded.

Herring's eyes flickered. "I didn't use it," he defended. "I only brought it because I didn't think you could win, and saving our people here has become as much my cause as yours. But you amaze me again, and along with my most sincere esteem, I shall leave you with this final gift, this weapon, to use or not as you see fit." Herring closed his eyes.

"Who else!" Matt insisted.

"The perfect person, really," Herring mumbled, then smiled vaguely. "I had a desk in the War Department, you know. It was a small, ugly, metal thing with a green linoleum top. The Navy dearly loves green linoleum! I actually *begged* to be sent to China before the war, just in time to flee to the Philippines and be captured by the Japanese. Imagine that!

Oh, how I missed that horrid little desk." He opened his eyes and grasped Matt's arm. "And then, in spite of everything, you turned me into a destroyerman. I thank you, Captain Reddy." His last words came as a whisper, and Matt gently shook him.

"You've become a *good* destroyerman, Simon, but tell me the name!" he whispered back, expecting nothing and not surprised when Herring's head rolled to the side and he could say no more.

"Damn," Matt murmured.

"Yes, sir," Bernie said, then looked at him. "I'm sorry, Skipper, for the kudzu stuff."

"Not your fault. I said so then. You were just doing what you were told."

"What if it's not on *Big Sal* anymore?"

"Then we find it."

"How? It's not like we can whistle up Adar or Miles and ask them. Mr. Garrett and that Choon guy are sure the League is reading our mail, and our codes may not matter. I don't think we should be sending any messages asking where our ultimate weapon might be."

Matt smiled in spite of himself. "No."

"So what do we do?"

Matt waved around. "After all this is sorted out, we'll look for Herring's 'fish mash,' in *Big Sal* and the Cowflop. Chances are, we'll find it without the other name."

"What then?"

Matt sighed. "I honestly don't know, Bernie. I used to think I did, but after today, after everything, I can't tell you right now whether I'll burn it—or use it. Either way, this is between you and me, clear?"

"Of course, Skipper." Bernie frowned. "You and me—and whoever else already knows."

"Yeah."

Bernie finally grunted and sat beside him, and Matt stared back at the sea, another round of driving rain from the mounting storm soaking him to the bone. Together they waited with Simon Herring's corpse while that terrible day, and the Second Battle of Grik City, slowly came to an end. *Liberty City was a fine name, and an even better idea,* he thought, *but the old name is too set in the minds of those who fought here, and on the graves of those who'll never leave. Probably just as well.*

Change the name of the place, and eventually the names of the battles will change as well—and that'd change the whole meaning of what we fought for here . . . or would it? He was suddenly unsure of that after all, but "Grik City" would stick, regardless.

"At least *Amerika* and . . . well, everybody on her, was out of here before the fight," Bernie said at last, mirroring Matt's own, earlier thoughts, thoughts he now returned to.

"You can say that again," he agreed, "but I won't be happy until I hear she's dropped anchor in Baalkpan Bay."

////// *PT-7*
Mangoro River

nything for *us* yet?" Dennis Silva grumped at the comm-'Cat in the Seven boat's cramped wireless office. He completely filled the small hatchway and unconsciously shifted his weight to compensate for the boat's still somewhat energetic bucking. PT-7 had crept as far as it could up the sluggish, narrow red waters of what Bradford called the "Mangoro" River about six hundred miles south of Grik City a couple of days before. There it moored offshore, using the mighty carcass of a fallen Galla tree as a dock of sorts to ride out what threatened to become a full-blown strakka. It hadn't turned as bad as that, as far as Silva could tell, at least not here. But it sounded like Grik City had been harder hit, on top of the Grik attack. It had been a "bit brisk," however, and the torpid river had become a boisterous torrent. Silva had wanted to go ashore, of course, even during the worst of it, but Courtney and Chack vetoed the scheme. They'd seen firsthand how dangerous the Mada-gaas-gar interior could be and didn't want anyone, even Silva, tromping about in a storm ashore. That left them largely battened down together in the small MTB, riding it out like sardines in a can. The group comprised Chack, Bradford, Lawrence, Corporal Ian Miles, an Imperial Marine sergeant named McGinnis, Ensign Nathaniel Hardee, his Seven boat's six-'Cat crew—and Dennis Silva. Silva had been excruciatingly bored and had begun contemplating numerous antics to relieve the tedium by the time the blow finally eased, and Bradford assured him they'd all soon be on the loose. But in the meantime, Silva pestered the comm-'Cat almost hourly for news from the north.

"*Still* nuttin' for us, spaacsiffically," the 'Cat groaned. "I send, but I guess we ain't gettin' through. Them mountains Mr. Braadf-furd says is between us, I bet, gets in the way. I still pickin' up stuff, now an' then. Some clear, some not." He paused. "*Amer-i-kaa* get to Diego okay. That come through good early this mornin'. Still dark, here. Better, ah, 'aat-mos-pherics,' I guess. She gonna lay over for some few repairs before steamin' on to Baalkpan. Mr. Braad-furd got some traffic from *A-mer-i-kaa* then too, but run me out to take it, an' I don't know what it was about," the 'Cat said, then added thoughtfully, "Chairmaan Adar prob'ly askin' him what bugs an' such we seen so far, I bet."

"Swell," Silva snapped, thumping Petey on the head. The little tree-glider was perched on his shoulder, a small, clawed finger picking in his ear while Petey stared inside in apparent amazement. Petey blinked. "Goddamn!" he shrieked, shaking his head.

"'Goddamn' is right, you little shit. Did you hear that? You'd be ca-vortin' on shore with plenty to eat, an' all them Diego 'Cats—them 'Lalaantis'—fawnin' over you an' stuffin' fish down your miserable gullet if you'd'a just gone back to Miss Sandra like you should'a." Silva still wasn't sure why the Skipper's dame hadn't just taken the little creep back. She'd seen him often enough.

"Eat?"

"No, damn you, an' keep your fingers outa my ear!" He looked back at the 'Cat. "How 'bout *Walker*? She get in okay?" The last they'd heard, *Walker* had gone to search the strait for survivors of Jarrik's task force. She found two ships. One was Jarrik's own *Tassat*, dismasted, her boilers wrecked, and wallowing dangerously close to one of the Comoros Islands. The other was one of the fast transports in similar shape a little farther north. No other member of the gallant little task force had been seen or heard from. *Walker*, still using a hand tiller while her steering gear was repaired, and then *Santa Catalina*, had been attempting to tow both ships back to Grik City.

"They musta made it okay," the 'Cat said. "I get reported that the tows got in, when they send the caas-ulty lists."

"Hmm. Damn it, we should'a *been* there. Feel like we was playin' hooky from the fight, on this here pleasure cruise." He held up a hand. "Not that I'm against playin' hooky in general, but I surely hate to miss a fight."

Despite his first irritated inclination, the 'Cat wisely didn't comment on how little difference Silva's presence would've made to the outcome of the battle. Besides, even still slightly weakened by his wounds, Silva had proven many times just how much difference he was capable of making.

"We'll return soon enough, Mr. Silva," Courtney Bradford consoled absently. The balding Australian had crowded in behind him in the cramped passageway between the berthing space forward and the engine room aft. He looked tired, disappointed, and . . . frightened? That wasn't like him. "But we're here, after all, and must at least have a look about while we are." Even stranger, he sounded like he was trying to convince himself of that. "By the way," he asked too casually, "have you seen Sergeant McGinnis? Or Corporal Miles? I need to have a word."

"A word with both, or just Miles? Silva asked, then shrugged. "I dunno, but they ain't pals. I doubt they're together. Miles is prob'ly hidin' from the water. Look someplace dry. Shouldn't take long. Ain't many places to hide in this little teacup." He squinted. "Last I seen Miles was just before dawn, I guess, pukin' over the fantail, right out in the rain. Worst case o' Marine Pukery I ever saw; worse than Gunny Horn. What is it with those guys?" He frowned. "But Horn's a right guy. Miles is a sneaky, squeaky, chickenshit little possum turd. Don't know why he came. Prob'y playin' hooky for real. What do you want with him?"

"It's none of your concern, Mr. Silva," Bradford assured somewhat forcefully, and that, of course, was the absolute worst thing he could've said if he wanted Silva to leave it alone. Without another word, Bradford squeezed past and worked his way forward.

"Silva!" came Lawrence's voice down the companionway. "Chack and Ensign Hardee are calling you on deck! You take a look at so'thing."

"Oh, all right, you goofy little skink." He turned to the comm-'Cat. "Sing out, you hear anything new."

The 'Cat sighed. "Sure."

Silva crouched and took a couple steps aft, careful not to conk his head on the low deck beams, then poked it up through the companionway. The rain had finally stopped and a small gap had opened in the clouds, letting a stream of morning sunlight touch the misty jungle to starboard. Far beyond, to the west-northwest, high, hazy mountains reared to the sky. He grunted and climbed the steps to stand on deck behind the conning station beside Chack, Lawrence, Nat Hardee, and Nat's Lemurian XO. Two others were hurriedly rigging the .30-caliber machine gun on the hard point newly attached to the starboard splash-guard bulwark. Nat was clearly upset and trying hard not to show it. "Yep," Silva said seriously, "it's a jungle."

"Look closer," Chack said grimly, blinking furiously and pointing at the nearby shore. They'd all seen the jungle for the last couple of days, of course, but that was all they *could* see through the rain.

Silva squinted his good eye, then widened it. "I'll swan," was all he said. Erected at the shoreline near the massive, rotted, tangled roots of the great Galla tree they were moored to was a lattice of bright green bamboo-like stalks, lashed together and obviously positioned so they'd easily see it. Spread-eagled and tied to the lattice was a naked man. At least it *looked* like a man. The corpse was horribly mutilated, with the flesh flayed from the bones of the arms and legs. The torso, though roughly intact, had been split from pelvis to sternum, and glistening loops of entrails dangled down past the hide-lashed feet. Empty eye sockets gaped upward, and the lower jaw and tongue had been hacked away.

"Miles and McGinnis both have black hair," Nat said simply. A bloody black mop of hair was the corpse's only distinguishing feature. Courtney climbed from below, shaking his head, followed by a pale Ian Miles. "Sergeant McGinnis is not aboard," he said. Miles quickly saw what they were all staring at and took a step back toward the companionway, his mouth working.

"Poor bastard," Silva said. "I kinda . . . didn't hate McGinnis." His tone and convoluted statement made it clear he'd have preferred it if Courtney found the sergeant alive instead of Miles.

"But who gitteem?" cried Nat's XO. "They had'ta come aboard! Along the Galla tree!"

"And they could've gotten us all," Chack agreed. "Why not?"

"'Cause whoever it is either figgered they couldn't take us all—or mainly wanted to scare us off," Silva said, looking at the deck. "Too bad I can't see no tracks. No way to tell *what* they are."

"What," Chack said. "You mean 'what kind of people.'" It wasn't a question.

"No 'people' did that, but yeah. Whether it was humans like the Maroons—or the 'Cats we came lookin' for."

"Scaring us off worked on me," Nat said abruptly. "We're getting out of here."

"Damn right!" Miles agreed.

"No, we're not!" Courtney said harshly. "Not yet!"

"But, Mr. Bradford!" Nat objected.

"I'm in charge here!"

"No," Chack said softly. "I am. You're in charge of any negotiations our presence may bring about, but I'm in charge of the mission." He took a long breath. "That said, we came here for a reason, and we *must* go ashore and discover exactly who is responsible for this."

"What *you* mean is, to find out whether it was 'Cats or not," Silva said. "The very folks we came to meet!" Chack jerked a nod. "Well, I'm game, Chackie, you know that," he said, louder now, but still looking at his friend. They all knew the Grik were capable of terrible things. So were the human Doms. But they'd never encountered any Lemurians in all their travels even remotely capable of what they now beheld. They were always the 'good guys,' generally peace loving, friendly, even possibly *better* in their own minds, in some indefinable moral way. And if it had been a tribe of Lemurians who did this thing, it could surely shake things up. Silva loved to shake things up, but even he wasn't sure this was the best time for a racial, psychic shock like this. "If it was 'Cats, it was probably just one crummy little tribe that tries to scare folks instead of fightin'," he consoled, "but my money's on none of 'em bein' quite as shy an' peaceable as them Maroon fellas made out. And if I'm right, I wonder why they went on like they were?"

"Because this may not have been done by Lemurians at all," Courtney stated, still more harshly than his custom, "or as you say, it could've been the work of a single, isolated tribe."

"Or they told you that 'cause you ex'ect to hear it," Lawrence speculated, "and didn't tell the truth 'cause they ha' just joined our struggle against the Grik, a struggle o' 'Cats. They not anger us."

Silva appraised his Grik-like friend with rising brows. "Makes sense, an' that's what I woulda' done," he agreed. "Never piss off the guys with guns, fightin' on your side." He looked at Chack. "So we're stayin'?"

"For a while."

Silva nodded and opened a locker on the bulwark, retrieving his "personal" Thompson. He removed the magazine, checked it, then reinserted it and pulled the bolt back.

"What are you going to do?" Courtney asked, suddenly alarmed. "We will stay, but in light of this new . . . development, we must carefully plan any explorations!"

Silva looked at the gruesome display ashore and then touched the guard on the cutlass hanging at his side. "Whoever done that—a nutty human offshoot o' the Maroons, wild, cannibal 'Cats, or the goddamn tooth fairy— they sneaked up on us to do it, and I doubt they gave McGinnis any kinda chance. Buncha *cowards!*" he suddenly bellowed, and Petey jerked on his perch around the back of Silva's neck. The shout echoed dully off the surrounding jungle, and small flying creatures leaped into the air with raucous cries. He stepped around the bulwark and headed for the bow and the fallen tree beyond. "Somebody's gotta go cut him down," he growled.

Chack hopped over the bulwark and pulled his own cutlass. "I will go with you, my friend," he called, then looked back. "No one ever goes anywhere, or even stands on the deck of the Seven boat in this terrible place alone!" he said.

"I think we need to get the hell out of here," Miles insisted quietly.

Palace of Vanished Gods
Sofesshk

First General Esshk, now wearing a long red robe instead of the shorter, customary cape over his armor, paced within the vast sunlit chamber of the Palace of Vanished Gods that he'd made his own. The new robe proclaimed his elevated status of Regent Champion of all the Ghaarrichk'k, and it swayed and dusted the tightly fitted stone floor as he strode back and forth, hands clasped before him in contemplation. The walls of the chamber were covered by dense, climbing ivies reminiscent of Tsalka's lost palace on Ceylon. Together with the sunlight that bathed him by ingenious reflections through various openings, it was a far more inviting abode than the similarly arranged, but dank and dreary halls within the Celestial Palace on Madagascar.

He wondered again how the slain Celestial Mother and her ancestors could've chosen to dwell in such a place when this one still existed. Perhaps her removal had been originally inspired by a desire to keep her remote from her subjects? A distant, unseen, idealized god was always easier to worship than one visible to all, he supposed. And though the previous Celestial Mother had been cunning in her way, and wore her authority with a sublime assurance, she'd been naive and suffused with too *much* assurance, perhaps, that her divinity should be universally accepted. Even by their foes. Better that she'd been so far away, Esshk decided. Her appearance had certainly been impressive and intimidating, even beautiful in his eyes, but liable only to inspire a fanatical, emulative gluttony in the elite Hij that might have had contact with her here. And her death, such as it was; revealed so publicly, so traumatically . . . He didn't know how that would've affected the continental population. All knew she was dead and remained in a vengeful mood, but only he and the Chooser, through spies the Chooser had left behind—and no longer had access to, he fumed—knew how the Celestial Mother's very pathetically dead head had been displayed on the palace steps. . . . He pushed that thought aside.

"Lord Regent Champion!" came a satisfied voice from the single arched opening in the chamber, and the Chooser himself swept past the silent guards stationed there. He alone was allowed into Esshk's presence without permission or announcement.

"Not 'First General'?" Esshk inquired. The Chooser made a throwing-away gesture.

"That too, of course, but today you are Regent Champion first and foremost, with no remaining opposition!"

They knew Ragak's Swarm had been destroyed, by accounts from the few shipmasters who'd returned. The scope of his defeat was revealed only by observations made by the first zeppelin raid they'd been able to make since the terrible storm abated. They'd lost many more airships than on previous raids as well, which meant the enemy—Captain Reddy—Esshk was sure, now had more flying machines of his own with which to destroy them. Still, Ragak's destruction had left Esshk—and the Chooser—secure in their positions, and the enemy more tenuous in theirs. It had not been a waste.

"By all accounts, Ragak very nearly succeeded despite his handicap," Esshk gurgled. "His was a rather brilliant plan, after all. A similar plan, better supported, would have succeeded, I believe. It is unfortunate he did not survive. I would have honored my pledge to make him a general. Perhaps even First General, in my place." He hissed a sigh.

"Truly?" the Chooser inquired. "Despite his ambitions?"

"Truly. He may not have been as skilled at designing traditional battles as I, but we do not have those anymore. And he was imaginative. Cunning. Without General Halik, or any knowledge of whether he remains loyal—Kurokawa's bizarre scenario aside—or whether Halik even still lives, Ragak showed the most promise. In the absence of others and in spite of his intrigues, I would have let him lead our armies." He sighed again. "You forget, Lord Chooser, that I early recognized the threat our enemy poses to the very survival of our race, and that survival will always be more important to me than my own. I am the tool of our race—and of our new Celestial Mother when she gains the wisdom to lead."

"How fortunate then that you shall remain her sword as well until that happy day—and beyond," the Chooser said, carefully picking his words. He lowered his voice. "She *cannot* rule effectively for some time yet, and I think, of necessity, the position of Regent Champion, supreme above all other regents, must maintain significantly greater influence than in the past. Even after the new Celestial Mother comes into her own."

"You are not wrong," Esshk conceded. "The world has changed too much to return completely to what we had before. As has our race," he added thoughtfully.

"As must the status of First Chooser to the Regent Champion," the Chooser lamented convincingly.

Esshk regarded the creature for a moment, then made a diagonal nod. "Indeed. But in the meantime, I must continue to carry the sword as First General as well," he said almost wistfully.

"So, as First General now, what next?" the Chooser asked.

Esshk paced again. "With Kurokawa returned to the hunt, our fortunes should improve at sea if half of what he claims about the forces he has assembled are to be believed."

"Do you trust him? And these 'new hunters,' this 'League of Tripoli' that has sworn him their allegiance. What of them?"

"Of course I do not trust Kurokawa, or any creatures that associate with him. Not anymore. But I do trust that his ambition, his most base desires, can be made useful to us—as Ragak's were. Nothing motivates Kurokawa more than his lust for power and his desire to avenge himself on our enemy—and 'Captain Reddy' in particular." Esshk grimaced the equivalent of a toothy grin. "We shall give him the illusion of the first while affording him the opportunity for the second. Our air raids on the Celestial City will continue regardless of losses. We can make them good for a while longer yet. Our new army, raised, trained, and equipped under the New Principles of war, is ready. And with Ragak and his army of merest Uul no longer consuming supplies, we can gather it at last. All that remains are the final improvements to the battle fleet and the resurrection of the Ancient Fleet with which we will strike. When all is done, and Kurokawa comes down, we will make our *own* thoughtful attack that will drive the enemy from the Celestial City and all the world, and turn them back to prey once more!"

Chimborazo

eneral Tomatsu Shinya slid down from his horse and stood on the rocky ground, staring up. Impaled high on a modest, narrow tree trunk, which had clearly been stripped and sharpened for the purpose, was a corpse. The barkless trunk, covered with blood all the way to the ground, had entered the corpse between its legs, forced its way upward through the vital organs, and then exited through the ribs just in front of the collarbone. The head hung back and to the side, and the face was unmarked except for the blood that had spewed from the mouth—and the pinkish burn scars on stubbly cheeks.

Major Blas-Mar-Ar dismounted to join him, as did Colonel Blair and several others. Blas remained tense and resentful around Shinya, but she stood close. Around them in the cold, high air, the Allied Expeditionary Force (East), or the "Army of the Sisters" as it had been quickly reorganized after the Battle of Fort Defiance, marched past under the bright, cloudless sky the great mountains pierced. Before the army lay the charred remains of what must once have been a rather large and picturesque village nestled in a shallow, timber-bordered vale. Wisps of smoke still rose above it and nothing moved that they could see, even livestock. A great many other trees had been festooned with ghastly ornaments similar to this first one they encountered.

"Is that . . . ?" Blair began, and Shinya nodded.

"Yes. General Ghanan Nerino."

Blas tilted her head. She was one of the few Allies who'd seen the man before, but it was hard to tell. Sometimes, if she didn't know them well, she found it difficult to tell humans apart. And if this was Nerino, he looked a lot different from the last time she'd seen him. She shook her head. Shinya sounded sure.

"Coldhearted, evil, bloody-minded bastards," Blair said, gazing now at the other impaled corpses.

"All it takes is one truly evil man to lead others to do such things," Shinya said.

"Don Hernan," Blair spat.

"He didn't stick him up there by himself," Blas pointed out.

"Is it 'evil' to do that to a man, knowing if you don't, it will happen to you?" Shinya asked her.

"Yes!"

"Many foul fruits grow from a single vile seed," Blair said, as if quoting a passage, and Shinya looked at him. Finally, he nodded. Colonel Garcia joined them then, staring up in horror.

"Go back," Shinya told him. "Keep the Governor-Empress, Saan-Kakja, and Sister Audry away until we can deal with this," he said, waving at Nerino and the many others.

"Why?" Blas demanded. "I think they oughta see it. The whole daamn army oughta see the . . . sickness we fight!"

"She has a point," Blair admitted—and then cringed at his accidental pun. He was glad that not many caught it.

"This is no surprise to anyone here," Shinya objected, "but that doesn't mean I'm comfortable letting young ladies view it if they don't have to." He paused, slightly disconcerted by Blas's incredulous blinking. "The only 'surprise' is that they were all allowed to die so quickly," he added. "Vice Alcalde" Suares had described the "usual" way Doms impaled their victims, and it could take them days to die. The way this had been done, death was no doubt agonizing, but also fairly quick. "Go, Colonel Garcia," he ordered. The former Dom nodded quick agreement and galloped back down the column. He, at least, agreed with Shinya.

"Those 'ladies' are our leaders—and just viewed a *battle* and its aftermath!" Blas snapped hotly, but managed to calm herself; she couldn't let her anger at Shinya affect her professionalism. She finally gestured around. "These men who so obviously disappointed Don Hernaan died quickly only because he was in a hurry to light out of here," she stated.

"Precisely," Shinya agreed, relieved that the confrontation with Blas had ebbed. "Which tells us a great deal."

"More than that they were soundly beaten?" Blair asked.

"Much more. Look at the terrain. They could've contested the approaches to this place and delayed us, at least, for a considerable time. They didn't. We slew a large percentage of the Dom army, but didn't destroy it. A force even larger than ours has run away. What does that tell you?"

Blair considered. "That though they had the numbers and ability to fight, and certainly the ground, they lacked the will?"

"That's my hope, confirmed by the atrocity here." Shinya nodded. "Don Hernan has made his 'example' to his army, and fled to put as much distance between it and us as he can while he uses that—and surely others—to rebuild his army's will to fight. We can't let him, of course."

"How will we stop him?"

"We continue the chase."

"And our supplies? Second Fleet's victory was greater than we first imagined, but it remains in disarray. How will it support us?"

"Well enough," Shinya said, climbing back on his horse. He managed a smile. "Captain Reddy earned a degree, but I was also a student of history. No doubt you know Alexander?" he asked Blair, and the Imperial nodded. Blas only blinked confusion. "There were others, just as great if not so famous. Captain Reddy might be surprised to learn that I hold his country's Winfield Scott in equal esteem and believe he had the ability to surpass Alexander had he lived in a different time and desired conquest for its own sake." He shook his head and took up his reins.

"The one thing all the leaders now springing to my mind shared in common was a tenuous, if not abandoned line of supply. And yet they prevailed—through boldness and maneuver, and by gaining the good-will of the populace in the lands they invaded to varying degrees. They employed ruthlessness at times, but it had *rules*. It was not the sort of twisted, capricious ruthlessness that Don Hernan uses to terrify." He looked down at his officers. "We will prevail in the very same way. We will chase Don Hernan, liberating the oppressed, terrified people of this land as we go, using his own weapons and supplies against him if we must." He looked right at Blas. "We will chase that evil, murdering madman to the very gates of their capital city itself, where I intend to destroy him once and for all—and the greater evil, the 'seed' he sprang from!"

Northeast of Puerto Viejo

Orrin Reddy walked briskly, following his "backseater" Seepy, as the 'Cat led him through the cool, damp, predawn dark toward the still building docks, ramps, and canvas-covered hangars at the south end of the small narrow lake northeast of Puerto Viejo. Almost all of Second Fleet's airworthy Nancys had come here, crowding the nascent, insufficient facilities, when battered *Maaka-Kakja* steamed by offshore on her way to the Enchanted Isles for repairs. High Admiral Jenks had left a light picket of DDs in the vicinity of Malpelo to give warning if any elements of the Dom fleet came nosing around, and a few of Second Fleet's more lightly damaged warships would remain in the vicinity of Puerto Viejo or Guayak, to join the "gun hulks" already beached or moored there. The rest would accompany *Maaka-Kakja* for repairs of their own, or to help untangle and rebuild General Shinya's supply line.

Orrin had remained with his homeless air wing for the time, to oversee the completion of proper support facilities and create some form of organization, much like Mark Leedom had done in the West until Ben Mallory arrived; combining all the scattered air assets under a single command. He'd stay to coordinate air support for Shinya's advancing column and supervise the construction and supply of forward-operating bases as suitable places were discovered, at least until

Maaka-Kakja's repairs were completed and her own wing reconstituted. It was a dreary, miserable, thankless job for a man who only really wanted to fly—and kill the enemy who'd cost him so many of the fliers he'd grown so protective of. But he was it. Increasingly, he understood the frustrations and concerns his cousin Matt had to endure—had been enduring—since long before he came to this world aboard *Mizuki Maru*.

At least El Vómito Rojo had passed. Some new cases were still being reported, but they had treatments now. And the greatest defense they had, besides the fact that most of Orrin's pilots were 'Cats, was the growing throng of seasonally migratory lizardbirds that blackened the air over the lake at dawn and dusk, gorging themselves on the guilty mosquitoes. Weird, but evidently benign bugs—also clearly seasonal—joined them in their feast, but different kinds often came and went on an almost daily basis. Together, the profusion of airborne life made flying extremely hazardous while they were active. That was why Orrin and Seepy hurried now. They'd discovered that someone intended to fly, regardless of the risk.

"Is up here, the second hangar," Seepy hissed. Orrin nodded in the dark, and they proceeded to the next large structure bordering the lake. Pausing to listen, they carefully eased the canvas entry flap aside. Inside, in the muted light of a single lantern, two indistinct figures were heaving gas cans aboard one of four Nancys that shared the space, their urgent whispers indecipherable. Orrin sighed, and, stepping fully into the hangar, he loudly cleared his throat.

"Oh crap!" came Fred Reynolds's distinctive, boyish voice.

"See?" accused Kari-Faask in a louder voice, equally recognizable. "I *tole* you somebody would blow! We should'a took longer to gather supplies!"

"Why are you doing this?" Orrin demanded, his tone harsh. "I know you think you're everybody's fair-haired brats, but disobeying a direct order is still a serious offense. I ought to send you both back west to *Walker* and Captain Reddy! You could spend the months it takes to get there, missing all the action, wondering how much mercy *he'll* give you!"

"I'd love to go back to *Walker*," Fred said miserably. "But we're here, and this is something we need to do."

"Flying off God knows where—do you even have any idea?—to find a man, a *spy*, who could've just been blowing smoke up your ass. That's nuts."

"We've got captured Dom maps that show most of the route," Fred defended. The region around the capital city of New Granada where the Dom Pope dwelt was always strangely blank—but Fred and Kari had been there and had filled in some of the gaps. "And somebody has to make contact with Captain Anson—or his people!" Fred insisted. "They hate the Doms as much as us. If we could just coordinate with them . . ."

"Seems to me their 'don't call us, we'll call you—*after* you whip the Doms at the Pass of Fire for us' was pretty damn definitive. Well, we did that—kind of—and not a peep."

"Yeah, but maybe we took 'em by surprise and they aren't ready. Or maybe they don't even know. Stuff like that, communications, takes more time for them than us, and if we're going to do anything together, now's the time. While the Doms are on the ropes!"

Orrin considered. "Okay. Maybe you're right. But I repeat: how do you aim to find that Anson guy, and why does it have to be you?"

"We don't have to find *him*!" Kari said. "Just find *any* of 'em—an' tell 'em what we know of him and them, and what we been up to. Look, the Dom fleet we fought came from the east, right? From the . . . Caari-beaan. The 'other Amer-i-caans' had to notice the withdrawaal of such a large force an' come lookin'." She looked at Fred. "We figger we get past the pass, flyin' low to the south, avoidin' the Grikbirds gathered there, an' head out to sea east o' there. We almost *gotta* run into some o' Aan-son's people."

"No, you don't. It's a damn big sea," Orrin pointed out.

"A sea that *Donaghey* is sailing into," Fred countered. "I left a note, but I'll just tell you. Pass the word west for Commander Garrett to be on the lookout for us. If we run into trouble or run out of gas before we find who we're looking for, we'll find an island. There's *lots* of islands. Even the Dom charts show that. We've got a hand-crank generator for the wireless, and we'll . . . make do until *Donaghey* gets close enough to hear us and pick us up!" Fred knew it was thin, and so did Orrin; he could tell. Still, it was better than nothing.

Orrin frowned. "What if *Donaghey* never makes it?"

"Then we'd have the same chance we were willing to take before we even knew she was headed that way. Not much of one," Fred admitted, "but either way, somebody's got to *try* before the Doms get their 'shit back in the sock' as Pete Alden always says."

"Okay," Orrin agreed. "I already granted that point. And maybe you make better sense than I gave you credit for. But again, why you?"

"Because we found 'em and we deserve the chance," Fred said stubbornly. "And besides, at least one of whoever goes needs to be an American too." He smiled impishly. "Somebody who can amaze whoever we find into listening to us *especially* if we don't find Captain Anson. Who else is there out here? You? You've got a whole wing to command. Gilbert Jaeger? You want *him* talking for us? Even if *Maaka-Kakja* didn't need him so bad, you might as well send a talking mole." He shrugged. "I'm just a pilot. You've got more of us than you have planes right now. And I have met one of them," he repeated. "Even if we never find Anson, we can throw his name around. Somebody's bound to have heard of him."

"But why Kari, after all she went through?"

Fred looked at his friend, suddenly realizing that *she* didn't really have to go, and as much as he wanted her with him, he didn't want her hurt.

"I go for the same reason," she stated firmly. "What other 'Cat has ever met one o' them before—an' speaks as good Amer-i-caan?"

Orrin stifled a sad chuckle and sighed. "Okay. I guess I knew this was coming sooner or later, and at least you seem better prepared than I expected you'd be. I just wanted to make sure you really had a plan other than just flying off." He gestured vaguely. "It's still not much of a plan," he added sternly, "but the *Donaghey* angle, slim as it is, makes a difference." He glanced at Seepy, then back at Fred and Kari. "I'll take the heat, try to lay it out better than you did. I'd just as soon they replace me anyway." He shrugged. "Just a few things: First, don't be afraid to use your wireless. Tell us what you see as long as you can. Things may be different in the West, but there's absolutely no reason to think the Doms can pick you up. If you're determined to go on this suicide mission, might as well make the most of it and at least make it the deepest scout we've had. Second, you'll have an escort part of the way. Two planes that can carry enough fuel to replace the extra gas you're taking. There'll be two because I don't want anybody flying all alone over country you might've stirred up. And be extra careful wherever you set down, because the area around any lake big enough to land a Nancy is liable to be crawling with Doms. Third, and most important, don't get caught. Period. And by that I mean don't let the Doms get their hands on your plane in one piece, whatever you do, and you can't let them take you for questioning. You know way too much."

"Don't worry, Mr. Reddy," Fred said softly. "After last time, we won't let them catch us. One way or another."

Orrin nodded. "Okay. Then I've got just one more thing." He waved at the lake beyond the hangar. The lake was just beginning to brighten, and the air above the water was becoming thick with flitting shapes. "Wait until after breakfast, then Godspeed."

SPECIFICATIONS

American-Lemurian Ships and Equipment

USS *Walker* (DD-163)—Wickes (Little) Class four-stack, or flush-deck, destroyer. Twin screw, steam turbines, 1,200 tons, 314' x 30'. Top speed (as designed): 35 knots. 112 officers and enlisted (current) including Lemurians (L) Armament: (Main)—3 x 4"-50 + 1 x 4"-50 dual purpose. Secondary—4 x 25 mm Type-96 AA, 4 x.50 cal MG, 2 x.30 cal MG. 40-60 Mk-6 (or "equivalent") depth charges for 2 stern racks and 2 Y guns (with adapters). 2 x 21" triple-tube torpedo mounts. Impulse-activated catapult for PB-1B scout seaplane.

USS *Mahan* (DD-102)—(Repair suspended at Madras). Wickes Class four-stack, or flush-deck, destroyer. Twin screw, steam turbines, 960 tons, 264' x 30' (as rebuilt). Top speed estimated at 25 knots. Rebuild has resulted in shortening, and removal of 2 funnels and 2 boilers. Otherwise, her armament and upgrades are the same as those of USS *Walker*.

USS *Santa Catalina* (CA-P-1)—(Protected cruiser). (Initially under repair at Madras). Formerly general cargo. 8,000 tons, 420' x 53', triple-expansion steam, oil fired, 10 knots (as reconstructed). Retains significant cargo/troop capacity, and has a seaplane catapult with recovery booms aft. 240 officers and enlisted. Armament: 4 x 5.5" mounted in armored casemate. 2 x 4.7" DP in armored tubs. 1 x 10" breech-loading rifle (20' length) mounted on spring-assisted pneumatic recoil pivot.

Carriers

USNRS (US Navy Reserve Ship) *Salissa*, *"Big Sal"* (CV-1)—Aircraft carrier/tender, converted from seagoing Lemurian Home. Single screw, triple-expansion steam, 13,000 tons, 1,009' x 200'. Armament: 2 x 5.5", 2 x 4.7" DP, 4 x twin mount 25 mm AA, 20 x 50 pdrs (as reduced). 50 aircraft.

USNRS *Arracca* (CV-3)—Aircraft carrier/tender converted from seagoing Lemurian Home. Single screw, triple-expansion steam, 14,670 tons, 1009' x 210'. Armament: 2 x 4.7" DP, 50 x 50 pdrs. 50 aircraft.

USS *Maaka-Kakja* (CV-4)—(Purpose-built aircraft carrier/tender). Specifications are similar to *Arracca*, but is capable of carrying upward of 80 aircraft—with some stowed in crates.

USS *Baalkpan Bay* (CV-5)—(Purpose-built aircraft carrier/tender). First of a new class of smaller (850' x 150', 9,000 tons), faster (up to 15 knots), lightly armed (4 x Baalkpan Arsenal 4"-50 DP guns—2 amidships, 1 each forward and aft)—fleet carriers that can carry as many aircraft as *Maaka-Kakja*.

"Small Boys"

Frigates (DDs)

USS *Donaghey* (DD-2)—Square rig sail only, 1200 tons, 168' x 33', 200 officers and enlisted. Sole survivor of first new construction. Armament: 24 x 18 pdrs, Y gun and depth charges.

***Dowden* Class**—Square rig steamer, 1,500 tons, 12–15 knots, 185' x 34', 20 x 32 pdrs, Y gun and depth charges, 218 officers and enlisted.

****Haakar-Faask* Class**—Square rig steamer, 15 knots, 1,600 tons, 200' x 36', 20 x 32 pdrs, Y gun and depth charges, 226 officers and enlisted.

*****Scott* Class**—Square rig steamer, 17 knots, 1,800 tons, 210' x 40', 20 x 50 pdrs, Y gun and depth charges, 260 officers and enlisted.

Corvettes (DEs)—Captured Grik "Indiamen," primarily of the earlier (lighter) design. Razeed to the gun deck, these are swift, agile, dedicated sailors with three masts and a square rig. 120-160' x 30-36', about 900 tons (tonnage varies depending largely on armament, which also varies from 10 to 24 guns that range in weight and bore diameter from 12–18 pdrs). Y gun and depth charges.

Auxiliaries—Still largely composed of purpose-altered Grik "Indiamen," small and large, and used as transports, oilers, tenders, and general cargo. A growing number of steam auxiliaries have joined the fleet, with dimensions and appearance similar to *Dowden* and *Haakar-Faask* Class DDs, but with lighter armament. Some fast clipper-shaped vessels are employed as long-range oilers. Fore and aft rigged feluccas remain in service as fast transports and scouts. *Respite Island* Class SPDs (self-propelled dry dock) are designed along similar lines to the new pur-pose-built carriers—inspired by the massive seagoing Lemurian Homes. They are intended as rapid deployment, heavy-lift dry docks, and for bulky transport.

USNRS—*Salaama-Na* **Home**—(Unaltered—other than by emplace-ment of 50 x 50 pdrs). 1014' x 150', 8,600 tons. 3 tripod masts support semirigid "junklike" sails or "wings." Top speed about 6 knots, but ca-pable of short sprints up to 10 knots using 100 long sweeps. In addition to living space in the hull, there are three tall pagoda-like structures within the tripods that cumulatively accommodate up to 6,000 people.

Commodore (High Chief) Sor-Lomaak (L)—Commanding.

Woor-Na **Home**—Lightly armed (ten 32 pdrs) heavy transport, specifi-cations as above.

Fristar **Home**—Nominally, if reluctantly Allied Home. Same basic specifications as *Salaama-Na*—as are all seagoing Lemurian Homes—but mounts only ten 32 pdrs.

Aircraft: P-40E Warhawk—Allison V1710, V12, 1,150 hp. Max speed 360 mph, ceiling 29,000 ft. Crew: 1. Armament: Up to 6 x .50 cal Brown-ing machine guns, and up to 1,000-lb bomb. **PB-1B "Nancy"**—"W/G" type, in-line 4 cyl 150 hp. Max speed 110 mph, max weight 1,900 lbs. Crew: 2. Armament: 400-lb bombs. **PB-2 "Buzzard"**—3 x "W/G" type, in-line 4 cyl 150 hp. Max speed 80 mph, max weight 3,000 lbs. Crew: 2, and up to 6 passengers. Armament: 600-lb bombs. **PB-5 "Clipper"**—4 x W/G type, in-line 4 cyl 150 hp. Max speed 90 mph, max weight 4,800 lbs. Crew: 3, and up to 8 passengers. Armament: 1,500-lb bombs. **PB-5B**—As above, but powered by 4 x MB 5 cyl, 254 hp radials. Max speed 125 mph, max weight 6,200 lbs. Crew: 3, and up to 10 passengers. Armament: 2,000-lb bombs. **P-1 Mosquito Hawk** or "Fleashooter"—MB 5 cyl radial 254 hp. Max speed 220 mph, max weight 1,220 lbs. Crew: 1. Armament: 2 x .45 cal "Blitzerbug" machine guns. **P-1B**—As above, but fitted for carrier ops.

Field Artillery—6 pdr on split-trail "galloper" carriage—effective to about 1,500 yds, or 300 yds with canister. **12 pdr** on stock-trail carriage—effective to about 1,800 yds, or 300 yds with canister. **3" mortar**—effective to about 800 yds **4" mortar**—effective to about 1,500 yds.

Primary Small Arms—Sword, spear, crossbow, longbow, grenades, bayonet, smoothbore musket (.60 cal), rifled musket (.50 cal), Allin-Silva breech-loading rifled conversion (.50-80 cal), Allin-Silva breech-loading smoothbore conversion (20 gauge), 1911 Colt and copies (.45 ACP), Blitzerbug SMG (.45 ACP).

Secondary Small Arms—1903 Springfield (.30-06), 1898 Krag-Jorgensen (.30 US), 1918 BAR (.30-06), Thompson SMG (.45 ACP). (A small number of other firearms are available.)

Imperial Ships and Equipment

These fall into a number of categories, and though few share enough specifics to be described as classes, they can be grouped by basic sizes and capabilities. Most do share the fundamental similarity of being powered by steam-driven paddlewheels and a complete suit of sails.

Ships of the Line—About 180'–200' x 52'–58', 1,900–2,200 tons—50–80 x 30, 20 pdrs, 10 pdrs, 8 pdrs. (8 pdrs are more commonly used as field guns by the Empire). Speed, about 8–10 knots, 400–475 officers and enlisted.

Frigates—About 160'–180' x 38'–44', 1,200–1,400 tons. 24–40 x 20–30 pdrs. Speed, about 13–15 knots, 275–350 officers and enlisted. Example: HIMS *Achilles* 160' x 38', 1,300 tons, 26 x 20 pdrs.

Field Artillery—8 pdr on split-trail carriage—effective to about 1,500 yds, or 600 yds with grapeshot.

Primary Small Arms—Sword, smoothbore flintlock musket (.75 cal), bayonet, pistol (Imperial service pistols are of two varieties: cheaply made but robust Field and Sea Service weapons in .62 cal, and privately purchased officer's pistols that may be any caliber from about .40 to the service standard.

Republic Ships and Equipment

SMS *Amerika*—German ocean liner converted to a commerce raider in WWI. 669' x 74', 22,000 tons. Twin screw, 18 knots, 215 officers and enlisted, with space for 2,500 passengers or troops. Armament: 2 x 10.5 cm (4.1") SK L/40, 6 x MG08 (Maxim) machine guns, 8 x 57 mm.

Coastal and harbor defense vessels—specifications unknown. **Aircraft? Field artillery**—specifications unknown. **Primary small arms:** Sword, revolver, breech-loading bolt action, single-shot rifle (11.15 x 60R—.43 Mauser cal). **Secondary small arms:** M-1898 Mauser (8 x 57 mm), Mauser and Luger pistols, mostly in 7.65 cal.

Enemy Warships and Equipment

Grik

ArataAmagi **Class BBs (ironclad battleships)**—800' x 100', 26,000 tons. Twin screw, double-expansion steam, max speed 10 knots. Crew: 1300. Armament: 32 x 100 pdrs, 30 x 3" AA mortars.

Azuma **Class CAs (ironclad cruisers)**—300' x 37', about 3,800 tons. Twin screw, double-expansion steam, sail auxiliary, max speed 12 knots. Crew: 320 Armament: 20 x 40 or 14 x 100 pdrs. 4 x firebomb catapults.

Heavy "Indiaman" Class—multipurpose transport/warships. Three masts, square rig, sail only. 180' x 38' about 1,100 tons (tonnage varies depending largely on armament, which also varies from 0 to 40 guns of various weights and bore diameters). The somewhat crude standard for Grik artillery is 2, 4, 9, 16, 40, 60, and now up to 100 pdrs, although the largest "Indiaman" guns are 40s. These ships have been seen to achieve about 14 knots in favorable winds. Light "Indiamen" (about 900 tons) are apparently no longer being made.

Giorsh—Flagship of the Celestial Realm, now armed with 90 guns, from 16–40 pdrs.

Tatsuta—Kurokawa's double-ended paddle/steam yacht.

Aircraft—Hydrogen-filled rigid dirigibles or zeppelins. 300' x 48', 5 x 2 cyl 80-hp engines, max speed 60 mph. Useful lift 3,600 lbs. Crew: 16. Armament: 6 x 2 pdr swivel guns, bombs.

Field artillery—The standard Grik field piece is a 9 pdr, but 4s and 16s are also used, with effective ranges of 1,200, 800, and 1,600 yds, respectively. Powder is satisfactory, but windage is often excessive, resulting in poor accuracy. Grik "field" firebomb throwers fling 10- and 25-lb bombs, depending on the size, for a range of 200 and 325 yds, respectively.

Primary small arms—Teeth, claws, swords, spears, Japanese-style matchlock (*tanegashima*) muskets (roughly .80 cal).

Holy Dominion

Like Imperial vessels, Dominion warships fall into a number of categories that are difficult to describe as classes, but again, can be grouped by size and capability. Almost all known Dom warships remain dedicated sailors, but their steam-powered transports indicate they have taken steps forward. Despite their generally more primitive design, Dom warships run larger and more heavily armed than their Imperial counterparts. **Ships of the Line**—About 200' x 60', 3,400–3,800 tons. 64–98 x 24 pdrs, 16 pdrs, 9 pdrs. Speed, about 7–10 knots, 470–525 officers and enlisted. **Heavy Frigates (Cruisers)**—About 170' x 50', 1,400–1,600 tons. 34–50 x 24 pdrs, 9 pdrs. Speed, about 14 knots, 290–370 officers and enlisted.

Aircraft—The Doms have no aircraft yet, but employ "dragons," or "Grikbirds" for aerial attack.

Field Artillery—9 pdrs on split-trail carriages—effective to about 1,500 yds, or 600 yds with grapeshot.

Primary small arms—Sword, pike, plug bayonet, flintlock (patilla style) musket (.69 cal). Only officers and cavalry use pistols, which are often quite ornate and of various calibers.